Praise for

MY FUNNY DEMON VALENTINE

"A spicy supernatural good time. With endearing characters and humor baked into a fun and unique love story. I'm so excited for the next one!"

—**Hannah Nicole Maehrer**, #1 *New York Times* bestselling author of *Assistant to the Villain*

"Holy hot grand piano keys! This one hooked me from the first chapter and didn't let go until the very end. Ash was so sweet and lovable but still had the vibe of a man that would bring you the head of their enemies! So perfect, basically. Eva was strong and held her own. Combined, these two make for a deliciously devilish romance."

—**Kimberly Lemming**, *USA Today* bestselling author of *That Time I Got Drunk and Saved a Demon*

BY AURORA ASCHER

The Hell Bent Series
My Demon Romance (novella)
My Funny Demon Valentine
My Demon Hunter
Demon with Benefits
Guardian Demon
Beauty and the Demon
Fallen Demon

Hell Bent

MY FUNNY DEMON VALENTINE

Aurora Ascher

KENSINGTON
PUBLISHING CORP.
kensingtonbooks.com

KENSINGTON BOOKS are published by:

Kensington Publishing Corp.
900 Third Avenue
New York, NY 10022
kensingtonbooks.com

First Kensington Trade Paperback Printing: February 2025

ISBN 978-1-4967-5585-8 (trade paperback)

10 9 8 7 6 5 4 3 2 1

Printed in China

Interior art by INKfluence

Content warnings: sexual content, violence, death, alcohol use, smoking, family secrets

THE BEGINNING
OF A BAD JOKE

Asmodeus, Belial, Mephistopheles, and Raum walked into the smoky nightclub. Not smoky because people were smoking—apparently, that particular indulgence had been outlawed several decades ago—but because a bunch of machines were pumping it out like it was oxygen. To make it *look* like the smoke from cigarettes that had been outlawed.

Stupid. Humans could be so stupid it baffled the mind.

Asmodeus followed his brothers through the crowd toward the bar, ever aware of his surroundings despite the music pounding in his chest and piercing his ears.

That was part of the fun of Earth. Everything was always too much or not enough. A little too hot or too cold, too salty or too sweet, too loud or too quiet. There was always some lack, something that could be changed to make the moment more enjoyable. And it was never-ending—that was the beauty of it.

Belial clapped him on the shoulder with enough force to flatten a human. "Don't think so hard, Ash. You might break something."

Ash raised a brow. "I don't think that's how it works."

"You never know," Meph said over the din. "Humans are fragile. Pretty sure they could make themselves sick by thinking too much."

The youngest of the four of them, Meph had covered every available inch of his skin with tattoos. His entire skull was covered under his short black hair, and the black-ink designs had leaked over onto part of his face. If that wasn't enough, he'd filled that face full of holes—two rings on his bottom lip, one in the center of his nose, studs in one eyebrow, and a whole collection of shit in his ears. It had gotten to the point where his human form looked more demonic than a lot of demons.

"He's not human, idiot," Raum supplied, gold eyes glinting from beneath the hood of his oversized sweatshirt.

Meph punched him in the arm. "Shut it, fucknut."

"You're the fucknut, asshole."

"You're the asshole, fu—"

"Shut up," Bel snapped at the argumentative pair. "We just got here. Can't you wait at least an hour before you turn it into chaos? Look at all the women around you. Find something else to do."

Meph and Raum did look and were quickly distracted. It was the point of this entire trip to the club, after all. For them it was, anyway. Ash's days of boozing and carousing were long over. Now, he was the wallflower who lurked in the back with a scowl on his face.

Meph and Raum disappeared into the crowd on the hunt for carnal pleasures. It wouldn't be difficult—part of their demonic nature was an allure that drew humans to them like moths to a flame. It made it easier to lure them into traps, and now that they weren't bound by the rules, they were free to turn up that charm to the maximum.

Well, his brothers were free. Ash . . . not so much. Ash had no charm. Ash was the antithesis of charm. He tended to blend in—unfortunately, a little too well.

Belial ordered two shots of something and slid one across the bar to him. "So, we're free. We actually did it."

Bel tossed his shot back with a satisfied gasp. The blond-haired, blue-eyed giant was one of the most legendary demons of all time, one of the original angels to fall from Heaven at the start of creation, not that Bel remembered any of that anymore. Even in human form, he was seven feet tall, and his shoulders were at least twice the width of a normal man's. It went without saying he attracted a lot of attention—the opposite of Ash.

"How's it feel?"

Ash sipped his shot like it was water. Because that was what it tasted like. Part of his unique brand of suckiness—tasting and feeling nothing, color blindness, and the best one: partial invisibility. "The same."

"The same? Really?"

He shrugged a shoulder. "I mean, it's all right."

"God, you're dull. No wonder no one else can stand you." Bel grinned.

"The alcohol tastes like water."

His face fell. "The curse didn't change?"

"Nope."

"Damn. I was hoping it would dampen or something after we escaped."

"That's not how it works."

"Maybe it's just the taste thing?"

"It's not. No humans have looked at me."

"Maybe that's because it's dark in here."

As if on cue, a woman approached Belial, wedging herself

between them. "Hey." She craned her head back to flutter her eyelashes at him. "Are you waiting for someone?"

The woman had spoken French—unsurprising, given that Montreal was a bilingual city—but they understood her easily. Demons could speak all languages as well as intuitively adopt the current colloquialisms of wherever they were. It helped them blend in among humanity and made them better manipulators.

Bel's gaze darkened instantly, but he glanced at Ash. "Just talking to my brother."

The woman turned and looked right at him before transferring her gaze back to Bel. "You want to dance?"

Belial was still looking at Ash. He was so tall, he just looked right over her head. "She sees you—"

"They always see me." Ash switched back to English since that was the language they were most used to speaking. "I just don't register in their minds as interesting. I might as well be cardboard. You know this."

It wasn't that he was ugly—he knew he wasn't. It was just the nature of the damn curse.

"But—"

"It's the same, Bel."

"Damn it, I really thought you'd catch a break."

Ash shrugged. He'd known nothing would change. "Go dance with the lady."

"You wanna—"

"No." No, he was not forcing himself on some poor human woman who would be no more attracted to him than she was to her dining room table. "I didn't come here for that."

"You're a lust demon. You—"

"*Was* a lust demon." He'd lost that designation the day he'd been cursed. "Now go."

With a sigh, Belial turned back to the woman, who fluttered her eyelashes again. They melted into the crowd together,

Bel already bending down to whisper something in her ear that made her giggle in a manner that was, frankly, totally unappealing.

Maybe it was a good thing women here weren't interested in Ash, because if all of them were like that, he was pretty sure he'd rather tear his ears off than listen to whatever noises they made during sex.

He leaned against the bar and got busy waiting for what was going to be a long night to pass. He wouldn't begrudge his brothers their fun, nor would he leave the club in case shit went down and they needed his help. Just because they had successfully escaped didn't mean they were in the clear.

Unauthorized Earth visits were expressly forbidden. Demons, with all their lies and manipulations, were always on special orders when they visited the human realm. Demons escaping their duty completely and leaving Hell unsanctioned? So against the rules, it wasn't funny.

And yet, thanks to Belial being one of the most powerful beings in the underworld, the four of them had done just that. And now here Asmodeus stood, on sentry duty in a human nightclub, bored stiff, drinking alcohol that tasted like water and listening to music that made him wish his only properly functioning sense—his hearing—was as dulled as the others.

Just when he'd started losing the fight against his oncoming sour mood, something caught his eye. Up on the stage, a woman walked out carrying a violin. Taking over for the last DJ, she began setting up a keyboard beside the house turntables.

Her hair was wildly curly, falling to her shoulders, the top half tied in a bun on top of her head. Big hoops dangled from her ears, catching the lights in the club like diamonds. Her skin was dark, a similar shade to his brother Raum's.

Her lips were full, and her eyes were big, almost too big for her face, but startlingly lovely. Not the dark shade he would've expected with her complexion, but an unusual light gray that was a striking contrast to her thick lashes. Or at least, they looked gray to Ash since he saw the world in black and white. But he didn't need to see color to know she was beautiful.

And she would look at him like he was as sexy as a dishtowel.

Rolling his eyes, he forced himself to look elsewhere and forget the woman on the stage.

Until her set began.

Her music was still club beats, still pounding bass and electronic drums, but there was a symphonic aspect to it that was entirely unique thanks to the loops she was laying down live with her violin. His eyes were drawn back to the stage and riveted there.

She played like he hadn't seen anyone play in two hundred years, her fingers and bow moving deftly across the strings like it was as natural as breathing. Sure, he'd seen thousands of talented musicians with great technical skill, but with her, there was something more. There was *feeling*. Soul. And the classical influence over the contemporary growling bass tones and artificial drums made an undeniably appealing combination.

He was intrigued. Impressed.

For the hour and a half she played, his night of waiting became an enjoyable concert. It didn't matter that her music was meant for wild dancing; he enjoyed it in his own way. Standing like a statue by the bar, he cast the occasional eye across the club to be sure his brothers weren't in any trouble and soaked up the music like the first heat of the sun in spring after a long winter. Or a tall glass of cool water after a long thirst. Or a pleasant breeze on a hot day. Or—

Damn, he was making similes. It must really be good.

Eventually, her set drew to a close, and he was forced to accept he would once again be on sentry duty sans the entrancing music. That was until Bel approached, arms around two attractive brunettes, closely followed by Raum, his arms around another two women, and Meph, in much the same manner.

"Ash!" Meph called out, grinning broadly. "We brought you a present!"

Ash groaned. "I told you—"

"There are four of us and six of them," Bel said. The women under his arms stared up at him eagerly, utterly oblivious to Ash's existence. "I told them we have another brother, and they're down to share. They won't notice you—"

"And that's exactly my point."

"They won't mind you being there."

"*I'll* mind me being there."

"Lighten up, bro," Raum said. "We're finally free. Have some fun."

How to explain to his brothers that "fun" didn't mean having sex with women who found him as attractive as their old shoes? "No."

Meph stuck out his pierced lower lip. "You're such a buzz-kill. How are we supposed to enjoy ourselves if we know you're not?"

Ah yes, making it all about him—classic Meph.

"Piss off, all of you. I'm not interested."

"But what about—"

"Hey!"

They turned toward the source of the voice, shouting to be heard over the music. It was the woman from the stage, the violinist. And she was looking right at him.

It didn't mean anything. He wasn't actually invisible, just uninteresting.

Looking like they hoped to add another female to the menagerie, Ash's brothers disentangled themselves from their companions and stepped in front of him. It was a well-known fact that if they wanted to bed a woman, introducing her to

Ash was a surefire way to prevent that from happening. Yeah, it sucked, but he'd long since gotten used to it.

"Hey," Raum said.

"What's your name?" Meph asked, offering a seductive grin.

They didn't realize she'd been performing on the stage ten minutes ago—clueless idiots.

"Um, actually, I—" The woman appeared to be trying to see around their broad shoulders to something behind them.

"Are you looking for someone?"

"I wanted to talk to—"

"Maybe we can help you."

"Well, actually—"

"Tell us what you need."

"I wanted to talk to him!" She pushed past the overbearing demons and pointed directly in Ash's face.

He froze. They all froze.

"Him?" said Bel.

"Uh, yeah." She glanced between their incredulous faces. "Is that a problem?"

"Oh, no, it's not a problem at all!" Meph looked delighted.

"Go ahead. He's friendly." Raum pushed her forward.

"Um, right, and does he speak?"

"Yeah," Ash croaked. He was still speechless. The woman was talking to him, looking right at him.

Bel took the hint and steered everyone away, leaving Asmodeus with the violinist.

"Hey," Eva said. Or rather, shouted over Kyle's painfully loud trap beats. God, she hated trap. Why did Kyle always have to follow her set and kill the vibe?

"Hey."

She was glad they'd started the conversation in English

since her French wasn't fluent, but in this case, it wasn't helping her feel any less awkward. "I saw you. From the stage."

The stranger's eyes widened in astonishment. "You did?"

"Yeah. Watching my set."

"You did?"

"Yeah." Why was that so hard for him to believe?

He said nothing more, so she added, "Nobody else was listening. You know, big nightclub, lots of drunk people, not a big surprise. But I saw you watching, and I wanted to say thanks. It's nice to have a real audience occasionally, you know?"

It had taken all the lady balls she had and more to approach this guy, and his disbelief was making it so much harder.

"I loved it," he said, and she relaxed considerably.

"You did?"

"I haven't heard anyone play the violin like that in two hundred years."

"Uh, what?" She laughed.

"I mean . . ." Indigo-blue eyes shifted around. "In a really long time."

"Right. Well, thanks."

"I don't usually like electronic music. I haven't developed an ear for the mechanical sound of it. But yours . . . It was a perfect blend of new and old."

"I— Wow, thanks." He was a bit weird, but he gave great compliments. "A blend of new and old. You know, that's exactly what I'm going for."

"You're achieving it."

"Thank you." She smiled at him.

He smiled back. Holy hell, he was so attractive it burned her retinas.

She wanted to say that appreciation for her one and only attentive audience member was the only reason she'd approached him, but it wasn't. She'd approached him because her one and only attentive audience member also happened to be the most drop-dead gorgeous man she had ever seen. Ever. It was almost surreal. Like she was looking at something that shouldn't exist on Earth.

His skin was lightly tanned, and his hair . . . *Whoa*, his hair. It was jet black and dead straight, and it hung like a silky curtain to his freaking hips, with a few shorter strands falling over his face. A face that was . . . godlike. Perfect, sculpted cheekbones drew the eyes to a mouth that was made for pleasure, and his deep blue eyes were so bright she'd seen them all the way across the club.

She could stare at his face all day. She could compose symphonies about his face. It was incredible, it was—

Embarrassing as hell how she was gawking at him.

"I'm Eva."

"Asmodeus."

She choked. "Asmodeus? That's your actual name?"

He nodded.

"Isn't that like . . . a demon name?"

"It is."

"So your parents named you after a demon? What, were you a really bad child or something?" She laughed weakly, but it died at the blank look on his face.

"You can call me Ash. It's short for Ashmedai, another one of my names."

How many names did he have? "Um, okay, Ash it is."

He smiled a little, and it nearly blinded her. "And you're Eva."

"That's me. Short for Evangeline."

"Evangeline. I like that."

"Thanks. Eva is my artist name too. All caps though, to make it more eye-catching."

"You should get a banner for when you play."

"You're right. That's a great idea."

"Subconscious suggestions work. Repeatedly show someone an image of something, and it will become familiar, whether or not they consciously recognize it. It's a simple way to make humans more impressionable."

Humans? "Uh, yeah. You're right."

Ash shook his head like he couldn't believe he was talking about the power of subconscious suggestion. That made two of them. "Never mind. I don't usually— My brothers are the social ones."

"Those guys you were with that tried to hit on me?"

He winced. "They're going a little crazy since tonight is a bit of a celebration for us."

"A celebration of what?"

"Escaping a bad situation. Starting over. Hopefully," he added, scanning the club suspiciously.

He was definitely weird, but she was oddly charmed by it. And his unspeakable hotness didn't hurt either. "Well, congrats. Why aren't you partying with them?"

"I'm not into their kind of partying, but we have to stick together now that we're on Ear— that we're out. For safety."

"Tight family, then." Except, they couldn't really be his brothers by blood, considering their drastically different appearances. But that was too personal to ask. In fact, she'd been practically drilling the poor guy with questions. He obviously wasn't social, and here she was grilling him on his personal life. *Way to go, Eva. Score one for Team Awkward As Shit.*

"You listen to a lot of music?" she asked, and Team Awkward scored again.

Surprisingly, he shook his head. "I try to, but I don't often get the chance."

"Really? But you obviously know what you're talking about. You summarized my whole style in like, five seconds."

"I like music a lot, but I wasn't allowed to listen before."

"You weren't allowed? Why not?"

"There's no music where I'm from. It was only when I visited Ear— some places that I got to hear it. Now that I'm here I plan to enjoy it more." He shrugged.

Damn, that was sad. No wonder they were celebrating.

"I work at this other club," Eva found herself saying. "A jazz club. If you want, we could meet there sometime. They have a jam night once a week with all the best musicians in the city. I'd love to show it to you."

He was staring at her like she'd sprouted horns. "You would?"

Had he never been asked out before? How was that possible, looking the way he did? In fact, why wasn't every single woman in this club hanging off him like monkeys in a tree full of ripe bananas? His brothers had practically attracted a small army. And though his brothers were all gorgeous in that same surreal, godlike way, in her opinion, Ash was on a whole other level.

"Of course. If you want. No pressure."

"I would like that." He was still staring at her.

"Great." Now was the part where he asked for her number so she didn't have to embarrass herself anymore by doing all the asking herself. Except he said nothing, and she was forced to accept that if she actually wanted to take him out to the club, she'd have to organize it herself. So she took a breath and said, "So, what's your number?"

"My what?"

"Your number? So I can text you and plan when we go to the club?"

"I don't have one."

"You don't have one?" It was her turn to stare.

"I just escaped Hell— I mean, I'm new here. Haven't had a chance to get a phone yet."

"Oh." He'd just escaped what now? "Well, I—"

"Can I have yours?"

He'd asked, thank god. *Dignity preserved.* She recited the digits to him, he repeated them back, and that was that. No writing them down, nothing. He either didn't give a single shit about calling her, or he had an amazing memory. Since she had preserved her dignity, she decided not to ask.

They chatted for over an hour. He bought her a couple drinks, and she bought him a couple drinks. An hour became two. Occasionally one of his brothers would come by and slap him on the back and shout inappropriate things, and Ash would close his eyes as if pained and send them away. They ended up leaning in closer and closer, until they were talking into each other's ears because they were more interested in what the other had to say than Kyle's goddamn trap music.

Except then Eva got all hot and bothered by their proximity, the delicious spicy scent of him, and the way his silky hair brushed her cheek when he leaned in. Her skin burned all over, and she was pretty sure she was actually getting turned on, which was embarrassing. She'd started a slow rocking side to side to relieve the pressure, which was even more embarrassing.

Poor, unsuspecting Ash was asking her all these in-depth questions about her music production and songwriting process, and she was practically humping the bar because she was so hot for him.

The drinks added up, and she began to get tipsy and forget her inhibitions. She caught herself rubbing a strand of his hair between her fingers, quickly dropping her hand when she realized he was staring at her with wide eyes. Then, the innocent hand on his arm was sliding up to feel his bicep, which was so firmly muscular she could have cried. She yanked her hand back when she caught him staring yet again.

He looked at her like he'd never had a woman come on to him before. Even stranger was the fact that not one chick had even glanced at him. She was sitting here talking to the hottest man in the universe and no one else seemed to notice.

Not that she was complaining. More for her. Except she was losing her ability to keep her hands off him. He was too tempting to resist.

"Eva." She wasn't able to actually hear him over the music, but she read the word forming on his lips.

She stared at his perfect face. "God, you're hot."

His eyes widened.

"Shit, I said that out loud, didn't I? No more drinks for me. I'm such a lightweight. Wow, this is embarrassing."

"You're attracted to me?"

"Uh, yeah. Hello. Have you seen your own face?" *Damn it, damn it, damn it.*

"Women aren't usually attracted to me."

"Are you kidding me?" she shouted. Alcohol or no alcohol, that was ridiculous. "You're like, the hottest guy I've ever seen. I'm so freaking attracted to you, I can't keep it in my pants— Oh my god, I can't believe I said that. I'm sorry. I'm definitely shutting up now."

He was staring at her again. "If I kissed you right now, would that be inappropriate?"

"What?"

"Because you're under the influence of alcohol. Isn't it considered wrong for a human male to initiate physical contact with an intoxicated female?"

She stared at him. "You say the weirdest shit, Ash. Human male? What are you, an alien?"

"Demon," he said with a perfectly straight face, and she burst out laughing.

"I get it! Asmodeus. Demon name! Oh my god, that's funny. Well, if you're a demon, you shouldn't care if it's right or wrong, right?"

"Yes, but you're human, and I'm trying to—"

"Honey, I may be a little tipsy, but if you don't kiss me, I'm going to embarrass myself by kissing you first." Damn, she was bold tonight. Or rather, alcohol was in her blood, making her say the stupidest shit.

But she couldn't regret it, because the sexiest man on the planet leaned down and pressed his lips to hers. He kissed her like he was starved. Like he'd never kissed before. But not an awkward, virginal kiss either. His hand landed on the back of her neck, and he pried her lips apart and thrust his tongue inside her mouth like he was invading foreign land and staking his claim forever.

She moaned, way too turned on to be in the middle of a nightclub, and clutched weakly at his shoulders. Tugging her against him, he kissed her until her blood was rushing so fast, there was roaring in her ears.

He dragged his mouth away. "Shit, maybe that was too intense." His eyes were heavy-lidded, burning with intensity.

"Are you kidding?" The rush had cleared the alcohol from her head. "That was amazing. The best."

He smiled a lopsided grin that melted her insides and then leaned back in to kiss her again—

And that was when the gun went off.

2

FLIRTING WITH DISASTER

THE EAR-SPLITTING BANG FILLED THE AIR, OBLITERATING all else. Eva hadn't exactly been around a lot of firing guns in her lifetime, but there was no mistaking that sound. Lord knew she'd seen enough movies to be able to recognize it.

She heard people screaming, herself included. Instinct had her dropping to the floor. Ash was there, shielding her body, but his head was lifted to scan around him. His expression was so intense, it was nearly as frightening as the gunshot.

He leaned down. "You okay?"

"Yeah, I—"

Another shot fired and then another. Kyle's goddamn trap was finally silenced. The emergency lights flickered on. Screaming filled the air.

When the shooting stopped, Ash grabbed her by the arm, hauling her upright. "Let's go."

They tried to run through the sea of panicked bodies, but they weren't getting far.

"Ash!" One of his brothers appeared out of nowhere—the dark-skinned one with the gold-colored eyes. He didn't look afraid. He looked angry.

"Where are Meph and Bel?" Come to think of it, Ash didn't look scared either. In fact, he was almost too calm to be normal.

"Coming. It's here for us, but humans could get hurt if we don't get out of here, and we'll be in even deeper shit than we already are. Leave the girl and let's go."

Ash shook his head. "I'll take her outside first."

His brother opened his mouth to argue, but the gun went off again. With amazing agility, he leapt over the bar to take cover on the other side. Ash remained with Eva.

"What was he saying?" she shouted at him. "Who's here for you?"

"Never mind. We need t—"

The next spurt of gunfire landed a hit, tearing across his back. He went down, blood everywhere. Eva screamed in horror, dropping to her knees, suddenly rendered useless except for her ability to keep screaming and crying and—

He sat up, cursing. "Let's go."

"B-but—"

He scooped her up like she weighed nothing and ran. The next few seconds were so impossible, she must have been hallucinating. With her in his arms, he leapt onto the bar and then up, springing off the side of the wall above the crowd. They landed on another clear surface a good ten feet away, and he sprang off that like a freaking trampoline. The rebounds went on until suddenly they were outside the club, milling through the crowds of people, the night air fresh in her lungs.

"What just happened!" she screamed in his face. "Oh my god, you were shot! What the hell just happened?"

"It's okay. I'm fine."

"You jumped— The wall— I saw— You were shot!"

"Eva, I have to go back inside—"

"What? No! You can't go back in there!"

"I need to help my brothers."

She barely heard his nonsense. "Let me see your back! You were shot!" There was blood smeared all over his face and neck, for god's sake.

But the crazy man shook his head. "I'm fine. Eva, I really have to go. It was nice meeting you. Really, I— Thanks." He flashed the tiniest of smiles and then disappeared.

In the blink of an eye he was gone, leaving Eva standing outside on the pavement amidst the sounds of screaming and sirens, wondering if she was dreaming this whole bizarre night.

She stood there listening to the chaos for a good five minutes before her brain plugged back in and she realized what was happening.

Then it hit her like a ton of bricks.

She'd let Ash whisk her away to safety—in some freak, inexplicable way she would dwell on later when she had time—and then let him go by himself back into the club to find his brothers. What if he got hurt? She was certain he'd been shot in the second spurt of gunfire. She had seen the bullets hit him, seen his blood spray, seen him fall. What if he was already seriously injured?

She had to go back for him.

Charged with purpose, she pushed through the crowds, shoving wide-eyed people this way and that to work her way back toward the club entrance. Flashing police lights lit up the outside of the building, but the cops had only just arrived, so no one was guarding the door yet. She reached it at the right time—the club was empty now save for a few stragglers at the entrance, and once she made it inside, she was free to move around.

She immediately dropped to her hands and knees in case the shooter was still nearby. Crawling behind the bar, she scrambled to the other end and peeked carefully around the structure, searching for Ash or his brothers—

She froze. Her eyes widened, her mouth dropped open—all the usual stuff that happened when someone was faced with something that was, quite frankly, impossible. Something that shouldn't exist and yet was there before her very eyes.

Her first thought was that they were costumes. This was Montreal, after all, and this city was full of funky people. It was one of the reasons she loved it here.

But then, why were people in such elaborate costumes hanging out in a club that had been emptied due to gunfire? Wouldn't they have fled with the rest of the crowds? Unless the gunfire had been staged and was part of some kind of show? But wouldn't they have warned the patrons? And the police were here, so wouldn't they have—

With a shake of her head, she quieted the barrage of unanswerable questions and focused on the spectacle before her, searching for some clue to fit the scene into her accepted reality.

Before her stood five . . . people. If they could be called that. All of them, save for one, were shirtless and had wings. *Wings.*

The most noticeable person was huge, at least seven feet tall, with red skin, curving horns, bat-like wings, and a strangely familiar waterfall of silky black hair. The man beside him had black, feathered wings like a raven, and the biggest one, a blond who was even taller than the red monster, had wings of pure, glorious white. Like an angel.

The fourth man had no wings, and though he was completely covered in tattoos, he was the only one of the bunch who looked normal.

It didn't escape Eva's notice that they looked exactly like the brothers of the man she'd been chatting up at the bar all night—minus the wings, of course—but her brain wasn't ready to make that connection yet.

And then there was the fifth . . . thing. Creature. Whatever the hell she was looking at.

It was short, maybe four feet tall, with slate-gray skin, a hunched spine, and enormous elf-like ears that flared out from its flat, bald skull. Bat wings arched above its head, and its face was adorned with a flattened, piglike snout and a pair of fangs that poked upward from a drastic underbite.

It looked like a pug crossed with Gollum. A pig crossed with a bat. A monkey crossed with Yoda who had bashed its face into a brick wall too many times. It was just ugly in every possible way.

Then, while she was still struggling to make sense of *that*, the red-skinned man turned his head, and she saw his face. It was crimson like the rest of him, and his eyes were completely black, all the way through. No iris, no sclera, just black.

And yet . . . there was no mistaking those graceful features, that long, straight nose, or the hair falling down his bare back, between those impossible leathery wings.

Ash.

Or should she say . . . Asmodeus.

Ash scanned the club briefly to make sure there were no loitering humans. It appeared everyone had fled, and just in time too, because the gargoyle sent after them had shifted shape. And so had he and his brothers—for the purpose of intimidating the gargoyle—though Ash was the only one in his full demon glory. Which, in Meph and Bel's case, was a very good thing.

Meph never shifted because there was a strong likelihood he'd never shift back—a terrifying thought once one got acquainted with the psychopathic terror that was his demon form. And nobody wanted Bel in full demon mode either. Not unless they wanted to burn the building down. Or start the apocalypse.

Even if there were loitering humans, Ash wasn't worried about them being seen. Otherworldly creatures had a natural glamor to disguise them, and, paired with humans' knack for explaining away or conveniently forgetting anything that didn't fit the mold of their preconceived reality, most of the time there were no fears of them seeing something they shouldn't. But it was still good to be careful.

The gargoyle snarled at them. "Time to come home, boys. You're in big trouble, you are. 'Spect there'll be a nice punishment waiting for you when you get back. Something real nasty, I bet. Could be years before they get tired of torturing you."

"Wow, that's doing a great job of convincing us to go back," Meph said.

"You especially," the gargoyle sneered at him. "We both know who still wants his favorite toy back. It'll be just like the good ol' days."

Raum stuck his face in the gargoyle's and stared him down until the creature shrank back, ears flattening against its ugly skull.

"I can't believe it came alone. Stupid thing." Ash's words were casual, but he'd tensed at the maniacal look that flashed in Meph's red eyes. Despite his perpetual dopey grin, Meph was more than a little unstable, thanks in no small part to the shit he'd survived in Hell.

"It's just a messenger," Bel said coldly. "It's a way of showing us how easy we are to find."

"Damn it," was Asmodeus's response.

"What did you expect to happen when we escaped? That they'd just forget about us?"

Meph snorted, successfully banishing his dark side. For now. "Especially you two idiots." He gestured to Bel and Ash. "Like they're going to let their top guys go so easily."

Ash rolled his eyes. He was hardly Hell's "top guy." After his curse, his reputation had taken a serious hit.

Bel yawned. "Can we just kill the thing so we can go home?"

The stupid gargoyle must have known it would be easily overpowered by them, but it had come anyway. That was the bullshit thing about being a demon—no say in their assignments even if they ended in death.

"Haven't got a home yet."

"Back to the hotel, then."

Ash took two long strides, grabbed the gargoyle by the scruff of its ugly neck, and slit its throat with a claw. It bled out in a few seconds—gargoyles had very little blood—and then crumpled to the floor. But its body didn't disintegrate, because it wasn't dead. There were a few precise steps that had to be taken to achieve that.

Ash looked expectantly at Bel. "Finish it."

Bel made a face. "Decapitate it first."

"Do I look like I have a blade on me?"

"I don't have one either."

"Just rip it off like you always do."

"You rip it off. I have to do the next part and it sucks."

Shaking his head, Ash bent over the still form of the gargoyle, flexed his claws, grit his teeth, and got to work. It wasn't exactly a quick job sawing through that thick neck, and when he was done, he had gargoyle blood all over his arms and his hands were cramping.

He dropped the head, straightened, and glared at Belial. "Happy?"

Bel rolled his eyes and raised his right arm. It burst into flame from the elbow down. He held his palm out and launched a steady stream of hellfire at the two pieces of gargoyle. This part was Belial's job because he was the only one of the four of them capable of summoning the flames of Hell at will.

Burning a body to nothing took time. It wasn't like the shit in movies where it ignited and disappeared in seconds. They must have stood there for five minutes while Bel launched pure, concentrated hellfire at it full force until finally, all that remained was a pile of ash.

And ta-da. *Ladies and gentlemen, that's how you kill a demon.*

Bel dropped his arm, flames extinguishing.

"Damn." Meph kicked at the ash pile. "I can't believe the little beast actually found a gun to shoot at us."

"This is America." Raum shrugged. "Anyone can find a gun."

"This isn't America, dumbass. It's Canada. People aren't supposed to have guns in Canada."

"Whatever. They're basically the same."

Meph whistled low. "Don't let the Canadians hear you say that, man. They may be polite, but they've got plenty of pride—"

"Will you shut the fuck up so we can get out of here before we get interrogated as suspects for a goddamn club shooting?" Bel snapped.

Nobody was interested in that, so Ash, Raum, and Bel shifted back to human form. Disappearing their wings, they yanked their shirts over their heads, and then all four of them strode across the club to the back room, searching for another exit away from the crowds.

Halfway there, Ash froze, turning back and checking behind him. Thanks to his curse, his senses sucked, but he could have sworn . . .

He shook his head, telling himself he was imagining things.

They found another emergency exit behind a pile of boxes in the back room. Useless in a real emergency and probably about to earn the nightclub a hefty fine, but it suited their purposes.

Tossing the boxes aside, Ash pushed open the door and slipped into the night, his brothers behind him, leaving the club and the pile of ashes behind.

OPERATION
INVESTIGATION

EVA HAD STAYED COWERING BEHIND THE BAR UNTIL A police officer found her and coaxed her out. After giving a statement she was barely aware of—she *was* aware she said nothing of whatever she'd seen, because what had she seen?—she was allowed to go home.

The cops had told her that, miraculously, besides a few cuts and bruises in the scramble to escape, there had been no casualties or serious injuries in the gunfire. It was as if the shooter had been targeting someone in particular—or four someones, like Ash's brother had said.

Days passed, and Eva didn't stop obsessing over that night. She bartended at Bootleg the next couple nights, barely paying attention to what she was doing until a customer yelled at her for mixing up his drink three times in a row. After getting sent home early, she collapsed on the couch in her apartment, petting her cat absentmindedly. She stared at the wall while images of gorgeous men with wings and horns danced through her head.

She'd always had a sense that she wasn't quite normal. Sometimes it felt like there was something dark inside her, coiled and waiting for the day it would finally break free from its cage. Nothing in her life experience could explain the root of such a feeling, however, and she'd always done her best to ignore it.

But now, she couldn't help but wonder . . . was this it? Was whatever she'd seen the catalyst for finally understanding that inexplicable lack of connection within herself? Or—unfortunately more likely—was the dark thing inside her actually some mental illness causing her to suffer from vivid hallucinations?

Annoyed with her constant obsessing, she scooped Thelonious off her lap, dumped him on the couch, and sat down at the grand piano that was her favorite part of her apartment.

The gas stove in the kitchen had to be from the seventies and the wood floors were all slanted one direction or another, but she'd demanded the lease the moment she'd stepped into the place and seen that piano waiting there. Apparently, it had been brought up decades ago by some determined tenant and no one had ever bothered to move it, which had made Eva a very happy camper indeed.

Her apartment was in an old factory building that had been converted into living spaces with a few businesses on the ground floor. Bare metal pipes snaked across the high ceiling, and the balcony was just a fire escape with a spiral staircase that led to a shabby, graffiti-ridden alley out back.

She'd covered the wall of windows with hanging vines and hung canvases of her art all over the walls. Musical instruments leaned in every corner or hung from mounts, and Thelonious roamed about the funky vintage furniture like he was the king of her castle. The walls were bare brick inside, and the big windows rattled when it was windy. It broke her bank to heat in the winter, but she didn't care. It was worth it for the piano.

Unfortunately, today, even the grand couldn't soothe her troubled thoughts. She stroked the keys lightly and forced herself to play a few chords, but nothing came out. She gave up on the piano and tried the guitar. Then the violin. She even tried the ukulele, for god's sake. Nada.

Sighing, she found her little cannabis stash in the kitchen and rolled a joint. Maybe a mild high would calm her down a bit. She turned on her speakers and cranked up some old-school reggae. Yeah, it was cliché to smoke weed and listen to reggae, but she really needed to chill out, damn it.

Half an hour later, she was sitting on her couch with her sketchbook on her lap, filling up the pages with drawings of bat and raven wings, ugly gargoyles, and some luminescent angel wings too. She'd been sketching with the same fevered obsession for the past two days like she was hoping that if she drew enough of what she'd seen, it would start making sense.

After another half hour of that, Thelonious jumped on her lap, sat directly on top of her sketchbook, and looked at her.

"Hey," she scolded, slumping back against the cushions. "You can't sit there. I was using that."

He blinked. She swore she could *hear* his disdain.

"Yeah, well you try dealing with the amount of confusion going on in my head right now and see if it doesn't drive you to this."

Thelonious flicked his tail.

She sighed. "You're a jerk, but you're right. I need to talk to someone. Enough wallowing." She picked up the sketchbook and cat simultaneously and set them on the sofa when she stood.

It went without saying that as soon as she wasn't interested in the sketchbook anymore, neither was Thelonious, and he leapt down and stalked away. Eva grabbed her phone from the coffee table and did what she should have done the moment she got home from the club two days ago:

She called her mom.

Her parents were not typical parents. They were simultaneously the most awesome and most embarrassing parents to have ever lived. To say they were hippies was an understatement. To look for anything remotely normal about them was an exercise in futility. And yet, Jacqui and Dan were the most stable, dependable people she'd ever met, and she wouldn't have traded them for the world.

The phone rang a few times before her mom answered. "Eva, baby, how are you?" She sounded distracted. "Hold on, let me just grab my robe." She moved the phone from her ear and called out, "Eva's on the phone, honey! I'll be right back!"

"What are you guys doing?"

"Oh, well, you know that photographer friend we made at the art show in Paris last spring? The one doing that nude series called *Real Bodies?*"

"Yes . . ." She was starting to regret asking.

"Well, your dad and I thought we would contribute some—"

"Say no more! I've heard enough. And please do whatever it takes to ensure I never have to view those photos."

"Sure, honey, but they're just bodies. We all have them. It's wrong how our society has taught us to recoil from the sight of our own skin unless we're shaped like an underfed model who has to maintain an unhealthy exercise regime to—"

"Mom, I know."

"Right, sorry. What did you want to talk about?"

"You know that club I DJ at once a month?"

"Of course. How's that going?"

Weird though her parents were, they were also very successful artists. When not traveling around the world, showing their work at major galleries, they lived in a gorgeous ocean-front house on Vancouver Island, off the coast of British Columbia.

Montreal was a long ways away, but Eva had dreamed of being a musician since she was a girl, and in her opinion, there was no better place to be in Canada. After high school, her parents had encouraged her to follow her passions, so she'd moved a few years later. She'd been there seven years now and didn't dream of leaving, though she missed her parents. Luckily, they were free to travel a lot because of their work, and they saw each other at least once a year.

"It's great. But um . . ." Damn, she should have told them about the gunfire incident right after it happened. It wasn't like they would have found out on their own—getting her parents to read the news was like trying to give Thelonious his de-worming medicine. "There was actually a sort-of shooting at it last weekend."

A pause. "A *what*?"

"Yeah."

"A shooting? In Montreal? What is happening! Are you okay? I can't believe this—"

"It wasn't that bad, Mom. Not one was hurt."

"Are you okay?"

"I'm fine. Like I said, no one was hurt. Some idiot just fired a gun in the club "

"Thank god. You should talk to Skye. Or better yet, Maureen's daughter is a great counselor, and she does phone sessions. I could put you in touch—"

"I don't need a counselor. I'm fine, really." *I think.* "That's not why I called. Well, I wanted to tell you about that, but I actually need advice on something else."

"Sure, honey, what is it?" Jacqui sighed. "I can't believe my daughter survived a club shooting. What is this world coming to?"

"Do you . . ." Eva winced. Thank god she'd smoked that joint or she never would've been able to say this out loud. "Do you believe in supernatural stuff? Ghosts, demons, that sort of thing?"

"Oh, sure," Jacqui answered without hesitation. "It's silly to think that what we experience with our senses is the only thing that's out there. As I always say, we don't know what we don't know."

"Right." Eva debated what to say next.

"Why? What happened?"

"I . . . met a guy."

"Really?" Now her mom sounded excited. "Where did you meet him? What's he like?"

"We only met once, and then some weird stuff happened, and now I don't know what to think."

"Oh, is he a vampire? They're very sexy these days. No one thinks they're evil anymore, so don't worry about that. They're just misunderstood, of course."

"I can't believe you sometimes. Vampires?" Eva scoffed and then stopped dead. She was about to ask her mom if she thought it was possible to have red skin and horns. Why wouldn't vampires be real? Oh god, *were* they real?

"Well, you never know. I've seen a lot in my day, and I wouldn't be surprised. You know I once met a real witch?"

"Really," Eva drawled sarcastically, and then she froze again. Were witches real? "What about demons?"

"Everyone knows demons are real."

"They do?"

"Of course. Why? Did you meet one? Are you in danger?"

"I—I don't think so. I think I may have hallucinated one, though. Or a few. I still don't understand what I saw, but it's been driving me nuts for two days and I needed to tell someone."

"You can tell me anything any time. What did you see?"

She took a breath and then blurted out the entire story from start to finish. "Please tell me I'm delusional," she said when she was done. "I need to know I didn't actually see what I think I did."

"Hmm." Jacqui was silent for a while, thinking. It was something Eva loved about her parents. She could tell them anything, no matter how unbelievable, and they would take her seriously. They trusted her and were just open-minded enough not to immediately write her off. Some would say they were *too* open-minded, but it was something Eva had never been more grateful for than she was now.

"You're right," Jacqui finally said. "It's important to figure out whether you hallucinated it or if it actually happened."

"Should I go to a shrink?" Forget that she'd said not five minutes ago that she didn't need one.

"I don't think so. A counselor will assume you imagined it, no matter what. They won't consider the possibility that it was real. No, you need to investigate this for yourself."

"Okay, but how?"

"Did you make plans to see your mystery man again?"

Eva's mouth dropped open. "I just told you I thought I saw him as a giant red monster, murdering an ugly troll thing! Shouldn't I be avoiding him at all costs?"

"You also said you had incredible chemistry, and he was the most attractive man you'd ever met. *And* he carried you out of the bar and used his body to shield you from gunfire."

"Yeah, but that doesn't mean he's not a . . ." She couldn't even say the word. "He said his name was *Asmodeus*, for god's sake!"

"That is interesting. I still think it's important to investigate. You need to figure out what you saw or you're never going to get past this."

Jacqui had a point. Eva hadn't been able to think or concentrate on anything in days, and it was driving her nuts. If she kept up this level of distractedness, she'd be fired from Bootleg, lose her ability to write music, and probably have to take up a career as an artist who could only draw bat wings and gargoyles and sexy men with obscenely long hair. "So what do I do?"

"If he calls you, agree to go out with him, but go somewhere public where you'll be around other people. While you're out, drill him with questions. Ask where he grew up, where his parents are, that sort of thing. Look for holes in his story. You might not need to see the wings again to figure out if you hallucinated them."

"I probably did hallucinate them," Eva said with a sigh. "There's no way it was real."

"Did you take anything that night, honey?"

"Mom!"

"Well, I'm just asking!"

"I didn't take anything. My party days are long over, and I was working anyway. Can't exactly play a set if I'm tripping on acid."

"What about any other pills? Maybe it was a drug reaction. Or food? Did you eat any GMO products?"

"Seriously, Mom?"

"There could be chemicals in processed food that you reacted to."

She did have a point. "I didn't eat or take anything unusual, how's that?"

"All right. Then we'll stick with the investigation plan for now. I want all the details, Eva. You'd better call me first thing after you see him and tell me everything."

"Fine, I will. If he even calls. Chances are high he forgot my number—he didn't even write it down."

"Honey, I'd better go. Your dad is nagging me to get back downstairs and finish the shoot. He says it's cold, and the photos aren't going to be any good if his balls are shriveled u—"

"Mom!"

"Right, sorry. TMI. Call me, okay?"

They hung up, and Eva felt considerably better. Leave it to her mom to come up with a semi-reasonable plan to figure out if she was hallucinating or not. Anyone else would have told her to go straight to a shrink and start popping some heavy medication. Plus, she couldn't help but notice the plan meant she would get to see Ash again, which made her heart race a tiny bit.

If he called. It had been two days, and so far, nothing.

It would be better if he didn't, she told herself. Until she'd met him, her life had been normal. Okay, her parents were artists, and she was a musician who talked to her cat, so she wasn't that normal, but she'd certainly never had any *para*normal experiences.

Which were probably just hallucinations, she reminded herself for the hundredth time.

Strangely, though, she felt a flare of disappointment at the thought. Even if the alternative meant that monsters were real, she supposed she didn't want to believe that life really was as ordinary as it appeared, and that red-skinned demon men only existed in fantasy.

Maybe it was because then she would have to accept that she, too, was as ordinary as she appeared . . . no matter what that little voice inside whispered in her ear.

THERE ARE NO NICE GUYS IN HELL

S HE SAW THROUGH THE CURSE. ARE YOU SURE?"

"I'm sure."

"How? What did she say?" Belial's expression was intense, but it was hard to take him seriously at the moment. He currently stood in front of the stove in their new kitchen wearing an apron, spatula in hand, flipping pancakes. A bottle of pure Quebecois maple syrup and a block of butter waited by the already-cooked stack nearby.

Asmodeus shrugged. "She told me she was attracted to me."

Bel still looked dubious, not that Ash blamed him. He'd felt exactly the same way. "What did she say?"

"She said I was the 'hottest guy'"—he made little finger quotes—"she'd ever seen. She said she was so attracted to me, she 'couldn't keep it in her pants.'"

Bel burst out laughing. The fucker threw his head back and roared with laughter.

Ash cocked a brow, crossing his arms and leaning a shoulder

against the wall, waiting for Bel's little episode to pass. His casual act was all bullshit, though. He was trying to be cool about it, but in truth, he was climbing the walls, dying to get close to Eva again.

A week had passed since they'd met, and he'd spent every second of it waiting for them to get settled enough that it was safe to call her. They'd finished the wards last night. It was time. *Finally.*

"Damn!" Bel wheezed through dying chuckles. "She must really have seen you, then. But how?"

That was the million-dollar question. His brothers could only see him because they weren't attracted to him, thank god. It was only potential sexual partners that looked at him like a piece of old drywall.

Except Eva hadn't. Eva was attracted to him.

Oh, the things he wanted to do to her . . . He'd been up every night for the last week imagining it in detail. It wasn't like he'd been celibate since he'd been cursed—he was a demon, thank you very much—but his sexual partners hadn't exactly been passionate participants. In fact, his sex life was so stark and dissatisfying, he was surprised there wasn't a special corner of Hell reserved for torturing people with his exact circumstance.

Then again, maybe there was. It wasn't like he knew everything that went on in the Nine Rings where the souls of the damned were kept.

"It could be a trap," Bel said. "I hate to go there, but it has to be said."

"I know."

"It's the most logical explanation." Bel flipped a pancake, focused on his breakfast endeavors. There was just something wrong with seeing a guy that enormous hunched over a stove, and yet it was his favorite place to be. "Trick us by sending the gargoyles—make us think that was their first, feeble effort so we let our guard down. But then this sweet little piece of ass creeps in on the side and lures you away."

"Trust me, I've thought of all that."

In the last week, they'd come across two more gargoyles before they'd finally nailed down a place to live and put the wards up, making them untraceable while they were within them. The Sheolic sigils drawn in blood all over the white-washed walls sure looked macabre, but if they kept them hidden, they were worth it.

Their grungy four-bedroom apartment was in a rundown area several blocks from the hipper neighborhoods, so they hadn't had much trouble bribing the landlord to ignore the paperwork.

They had plenty of cash—it was easy to exchange their wealth into Earth currencies at the underworld Blood Market—but they'd chosen to hunker down in this dump instead of choosing a more predictable option. Like, say, the swankiest house they could find with a ten-car garage and swimming pool. No one would believe four demons of the Order of Thrones would settle for such squalid living conditions.

"You admit it could be a trap." Bel flipped another pan-cake. "Are you sure you should call her?"

Asmodeus cocked a brow. How to explain the lengths he was willing to go to have sex with a woman who was actu-ally attracted to him? He decided there was no way to convey his desperation without embarrassing himself. "What do you think?"

Bel scooped a pancake up, tossed it on the plate, and then shot a glance at Ash. He snorted at whatever look he saw there. "Yeah, I get it. I'd probably do the same." He waved the spat-ula. "Go on, get out of here. Be home by midnight or you're grounded."

"What?"

"Kidding, jackass. Been waiting for you to make some mom

joke since you caught me in my apron, but since you didn't, I had to make one myself."

"Well, it was terrible. Almost as terrible as seeing you in that apron."

"Get out of my sight before I spank you with this spatula."

Ash headed down the hall to his bedroom, calling out, "Save me some pancakes."

In truth, he didn't give a shit about pancakes, but he pretended to solely because he wanted to encourage Belial's culinary passions. It was a weird and gross feeling.

"When are you going to learn to cook your own damn meals?" Bel called back. "That's what I want to know."

"You love cooking."

"Not for you, asshole."

Ash snorted, closing the door behind him. That was a load of crap, and they both knew it. Demons didn't need to eat unless they wanted to indulge for enjoyment's sake, and as far as Ash was concerned, there was nothing enjoyable about cooking. If eating meant cooking first, he'd happily go without. Especially because, thanks to his curse, food tasted like nothing. He only ate to appease Belial when he wanted them to eat together like a nice little fucking family.

Ash scooped up his shiny new cell phone from the upside-down milk crate that was his nightstand and flopped on his back onto the rock-hard mattress on the floor that was his bed.

His room was a shithole—their whole flat was. The window was small and ugly, the hardwood flooring needed replacing twenty years ago, and none of the walls were straight. Besides the milk crate and his bed, there was only enough room for a dresser and a small desk jammed into the far corner. At least there was fresh paint on the walls, though they'd gone and ruined that with the wards.

Ignoring his drab surroundings, he searched his memory for

the number he'd been given at the nightclub and typed it into his phone. Then, he hovered his thumb over the green "call" button, feeling indecisive.

Yeah, he wanted to get laid, and he hadn't come close to forgetting the sultry Eva and the way she'd responded to his kiss, but he'd also been killing gargoyles and trying to lay low all week, and he really didn't need any more complications. His idiot brothers were enough.

Meph was unhinged, Raum was a broody motherfucker, and though Bel managed to keep in line most of the time, he had serious anger-management issues that could blow up at the drop of a hat.

Ash seemed to be the only one of his brothers that could talk Bel down from the edge and keep his own emotions in check. That meant he often ended up taking charge, not that he wanted to, and he'd kind of fallen into a pattern of being the reliable, dependable guy who didn't do stupid shit and was always there to bail out his brothers when they inevitably did.

Fuck that, he decided. He wasn't going to be that guy. In Hell, there were no such things as nice guys. Nice guys were dead guys. And Ash wasn't fucking nice. He was just bored and boring because he'd been cursed, and his job sucked, and he was sick to death of doing the same damn thing day after day, year after year, millennium after millennium.

His thumb smacked that call button like an act of defiance to his old, mediocre existence, and he held the phone up to his ear and *dared* Eva not to answer it.

She wasn't going to get away from him again. Not until he'd had his fill of her.

Eva scooped honey from the jar into her mug and stirred diligently while Thelonious wound around her legs, making sure he covered every inch of her pants in cat hair.

"You need to use self-control, Skye. You've got to make him wait."

Her best friend sprawled on the couch across the room and sighed dramatically. "But he was so hot, Eva."

"The jerks always are."

"I thought for sure he'd call, and damn it, he gave me, like, three orgasms first. How could I refuse? It's not my fault I love sex."

She scooped more honey into Skye's cup and stirred that in too. "I don't blame you. Women have needs too. I'm just saying, men are predictable. If you want him to stick around, you've got to make him work for it. If he's in it just to get laid, he'll give up, and you'll be glad you didn't waste your time."

Skye sighed again. "I've never been good at restraint."

Poor Skye was the most impulsive person Eva knew, and she had a sex drive to rival any man's. And she was beautiful too, to top it off, with olive skin and sleek, dark hair.

The problem was, she had terrible taste in men and was also searching for real love. Not a great combination.

"I think you need to learn how to look but not touch," Eva suggested. "Every time you see a guy you like, you go wild. You should try just . . . enjoying him a little, without screwing his brains out on the first date."

"You know what? You're right." Skye jerked upright on the sofa. "I'm swearing off men."

Eva snorted and kept stirring the tea. "Yeah, for how long? Until next week?"

"Shut up! No. For six months."

Eva's brows climbed her forehead. "That'll be a new record for you."

"You don't think I can do it?" Skye got that glint in her eyes that meant she was determined. And when she really made up her mind to do something, she damn well did it. It was one of the things Eva loved about her.

"Six months, no men," she declared. "I will sign a contract in blood if that's what it takes to make you believe me."

"I believe you, but it might be fun to—"

Eva's phone rang, buzzing around on the kitchen counter beside the kettle. Her ringtone was Beethoven's Fifth Symphony because that infamous "dun dun dun *dunnn*" was a pretty accurate representation of how she felt every time she got a phone call. Seriously, who called anyone anymore? It was way too personal.

She glanced at the screen and saw a number she didn't recognize. Even worse.

"Who is it?"

"Dunno."

"Answer it, dummy."

Eva made a face at Skye but answered the call. "Hello?"

"Eva?"

"Who is this?"

"Ash. We met at the club last week."

She froze, dropping the spoon she hadn't realized she was holding. It clattered as it hit the countertop, and her heart pounded. What should she do? Should she hang up? Change her phone number? Flee the country?

She remembered her mom's plan: go out with him, drill him with questions, see if he seemed suspicious. A week had gone by, and she still hadn't decided whether she'd hallucinated or not, nor had she stopped obsessing about it. As the days passed, that night felt more and more surreal, until even her DJ set felt like a dream. Until this moment, she'd started to doubt Ash was even real.

"Are you still there?"

"Uh, hey, yeah, sorry." The palm gripping the phone was suddenly clammy with sweat. Skye was frowning at her from the sofa.

"I wanted to make sure you were okay. I meant to call earlier, but I've been . . . held up."

"Oh, um, I'm fine."

"I'm sorry I had to leave you outside the club like that."

"It's okay. Did you . . ." What, was she going to ask him if he'd turned red, sprouted horns, and decapitated a monster? "Did anything happen?"

"Nothing I haven't dealt with before."

Okay, that was cryptic. But if he really had done those things, he wasn't likely to tell her about it, was he? "Oh, good. Cool."

"I didn't call sooner because I had some shit I needed to sort out. Like I said, I'm new here. We were looking for a safe place to hi— live. But we found one."

"Oh, I'm glad."

"Yeah. Listen, do you still want to show me that jazz club? Now that I'm more settled, I've been thinking I'd like to get out to see some music."

Bat Wings wanted to meet at Bootleg. Slits Throats of Gargoyles wanted to get out to see some music. "Um . . ."

"If you don't want to, it's fine. Maybe you could tell me the name of the bar so I can go by myself."

"You'd just go by yourself?"

"Sure. Or is that abnormal behavior?"

"Uh . . ." Damn, she'd forgotten how weird he was.

She remembered her mom's advice yet again. Bootleg was always packed and everyone there knew her by name from working at the bar and jamming on stage. She would be safe, surrounded by people she trusted. What better place to take Ash for questioning to figure out if she'd lost her mind?

"Let's do it," she decided. "The bar's called Bootleg. The jam is Thursday night. Meet me there at ten."

She hung up a moment later and met Skye's stare. "Um, who was that?"

Eva winced. She wasn't ready to tell Skye about Ash until she figured out whether he was a wet dream come to life or a winged, horned beast man.

"I . . . met a guy last week."

Predictably, Skye's eyes lit up. "Who is he? Where did you—"

"It's still new," she said quickly. "If the date goes well, then I'll tell you all about him. How's that?"

Skye stuck her lower lip out. "Fine."

"Are you working at Bootleg this Thursday?" *Please say no, please say no.*

"No, but now I wish I was. I want to meet him."

It was time for a subject change. Scooping up their mugs, Eva deftly avoided Thelonious and then sank onto the couch beside Skye. She passed her friend her tea, set her own on the end table, and picked up her laptop and headphones from the coffee table.

"Enough about men. I want your opinion on the new track I wrote for my set." She snapped her headphones over Skye's ears and hit play on the track, taking it as a good sign when Skye's eyes closed and her head bobbed.

"This is good!" she yelled, palms pushing the headphones tighter to her head, grinning broadly.

Eva laughed. "No need to shout, but thanks."

"What!"

"I said no need to shout!"

"I can't hear you over the music! It's really good, Eva!"

Eva chuckled and sipped her tea.

ASMODEUS MOZART

THURSDAY NIGHT AT TEN, ASMODEUS CLIMBED OUT THE back of a cab—a laborious method of travel compared to flying, but he had to keep up human appearances now—at the club called Bootleg. The outside wasn't much. A scuffed up black door with a faded sign was complemented by a neon blinking arrow indicating it was upstairs.

He was a little early, so he got busy leaning up against the wall and blending into the shadows. He lit up a cigarette to pass the time.

Demons were impervious to health problems but loved to indulge in human addictions like alcohol and drugs. Ash was a little too "boring" (as his brothers would say) to be a big partier, but he did enjoy smoking.

A minute later, Eva came around the corner at the end of the street, and he ate up the sight of her with hungry eyes. Even in black and white, she was so . . . vibrant. And that wasn't just because she was attracted to him. It was because she was. Even if she'd looked at him like he was as sexy as toilet paper like every other woman did, he'd still have wanted her.

Her wild hair, her short, curvy body, and that ridiculously round ass that he wanted to bite so fucking bad . . . He had to have her. No question.

But first: music.

When she was close enough, he stepped out of the shadows, tossing his cigarette on the pavement and stamping it out with a boot. "Eva."

She stopped in her tracks and stared at him without speaking. For a moment, he could have sworn a flash of straight-up fear crossed her face, but it passed quickly, and he had to wonder if he'd imagined it. "Hey, Ash— Wow."

"What?"

"I forgot you were so— Never mind."

He stepped closer, drawn like a magnet by the heated look she was giving him. Yeah, she definitely saw him all right. "Hey."

"Hi."

The air between them crackled with chemistry. Maybe they could skip the club altogether and get straight to the sex.

"You wanna go inside?"

"Yeah, I do." And he did. Sex could come later. First, he could enjoy some good music.

They pulled open the door and climbed the creaky stairs. Inside was packed body to body, standing room only. The venue wasn't big by any means, and the room was probably way past capacity, but places like this never followed the rules.

Bare lightbulbs dangled from wires over the bustling bar. A few tables lined the sides of the room, but most were empty because everyone preferred to be packed together on the dance floor at the heart of the action.

At the far end, the stage was illuminated by colored lights. A stand-up bass leaned in the corner beside an old upright piano that looked as beat to shit as the rest of the club. The lights reflected off the cymbals of the drum kit, and there was a stack of vintage guitar amps lining the back of the stage. The band was between sets, so only the din of a hundred voices and the thump of the house music filled the air.

"Want a drink?" Eva asked, almost yelling to be heard over the din. Thanks to the crowd, she was pressed right against him. He'd watched her walk up the stairs ahead of him and nearly died. Her ass truly was a masterpiece.

He nodded, so she grabbed his hand and led him through the crowd. At the bar, she chatted with the bartender, introducing him, but of course, the other woman's eyes glazed over the minute she looked at him. Not that he cared. He only had eyes for Eva tonight.

She passed him a beer. "I can pay," he offered.

But she shook her head. "I work here. Free drinks for me. There's a table over by the stage. Let's go."

She grabbed his hand again and led him back through the crowd, stopping occasionally to chat with someone she knew. They had just snagged two seats around the tiny table when the band climbed back on the stage. One of them waved at Eva and she waved back.

"People know you," Ash said in her ear, watching attentively as the musicians fiddled with their gear.

"I'm here a lot. When I'm not working, I'm on stage."

"Are you going to play tonight? You didn't bring your violin."

"I might. But my violin's for classical stuff and my DJ project. When I play jazz, I play . . ." She reached back to pull something out of the bag slung over her shoulder. "Ta-da."

It was a flute. A very scratched and beat-up flute, not in any sort of protective case and evidently well used.

"You play the flute too?" Color him impressed.

"Yeah." She shrugged. "Violin was always my serious instrument. Flute's just on the side. But that makes it more fun sometimes, you know?"

"I want to see you play."

"Then maybe I'll go up later." She smiled at him.

Her lips were lush and indescribably inviting, and his attention zeroed in on them—until he realized they were moving. She was telling him something, and he hadn't heard a word of it.

He dragged his gaze up to her eyes. "What?"

"I said it's cool how much you appreciate music even though you haven't been around it much."

"I've found ways to be over the years." He shrugged. "It's logical, since my hearing is the only sense that functions properly."

"What do you mean?"

Shit. He really hadn't meant to go into that. Bel had lectured him about what not to say around humans since he was so out of practice, specifically warning him not to go into his curse. So, of course, he'd gone and blurted it out immediately.

Eva was waiting for an answer, and he had no choice but to give her one. "I have a . . . condition." He winced at the feeble lie. "I can't see color. Or taste anything. Or feel much."

Her mouth fell open. "Oh my god."

"It's not a big deal."

"You can't see color? Like at all?"

He shook his head. "Only black and white."

"And you can't feel anything either?"

"I don't mind that one. It's handy for ignoring extreme pain."

She looked horrified, and he guessed it was because most humans didn't have cause to ignore extreme pain very often. "Can you smell?"

"No sense of smell either."

Her eyes filled with sympathy. "I didn't know. I'm so sorry."

"It's fine. Trust me, I'm used to it." She still looked upset, and he felt the need to comfort her. "If I'm relaxed, I do feel touch, especially in more sensitive parts of my body." Shit, he was really putting his foot in his mouth here. "But that's why I like music, I guess. Because my hearing is normal."

"But how do you—"

Thankfully, at that moment, the band started up, effectively drowning out Eva's question. They had no choice but to sit back and enjoy the music. And enjoy it he did.

Just as Eva had said, the musicians were fantastic. The lineup played a few tunes, jamming off famous standards or improvised chords, and then some players would swap and a new lineup would form, keeping the energy fresh. They watched together for over an hour, chatting between sets about the music and nothing in particular. Just easy, harmless fun.

Eva seemed oddly curious about him, making him glad he'd had that talk with Bel about what not to say. He wondered if all humans were this inquisitive when they first met—her questions felt like a bloody interrogation at times—but he couldn't say either way. Since being cursed around three thousand years ago, his experience with humans in a social capacity was limited at best, and his experiences with human women even less.

"Where'd you grow up?" Eva asked him.

"Uh, here and there. I traveled a lot."

Her eyes narrowed like she was displeased with his evasiveness, and she switched topics with dizzying abruptness. "What were your parents like?"

He winced. "I never knew them." Or rather, never had them. Demons were created from hellfire by the will of a female demon. Only females could make new demons, but that didn't mean they felt any sort of maternal bond to their creations. Far from it.

"You never knew your parents?" Eva looked sad, which was weird. Why would she care about his parents? "Why not?"

"I, um—" Damn it, Bel hadn't prepared him for what to do if she turned out to have a doctorate in interrogation tactics. "I was raised by my brother." That, at least, was true.

He'd been formed at roughly a human toddler's development and tossed into a horrified Belial's lap. Bel had been an evil motherfucker way back then, and Asmodeus had been just as vile, but somehow, they'd managed to bond in their own disturbed way.

Eva opened her mouth to drill him with further questions, but thankfully, someone waved to her from the stage at that moment.

"I think I'm going up for the next set," Eva said, waving back. "I guess you don't play anything, or I'd tell you to join. I won't be long. Or, if you'd rather I stay—"

"I want to see you play."

"Okay." She smiled. "You should learn an instrument! I bet you'd love it."

"I play the piano," he reluctantly admitted.

Her mouth dropped open. Just seeing it in that little O shape gave him wicked thoughts. "Why didn't you say so?"

Music was a human art. A demon could mimic it, sure— part of their skillset was being able to learn anything they wanted quickly—but it wasn't the same. The mortality of humans combined with their potential for good or evil came through in their creative expression.

Demons were just . . . flat. A demon could be a master pianist, but he would never have the soul of a human player.

Because a demon had no soul. That was what it came down to.

But a demon could still appreciate the human arts, and Ash did. He shrugged at Eva. "Go play your flute for me. I'll be here."

She looked like she wanted to say more, but she turned away and melted into the crowd instead. He watched her climb up on stage, greeting the other musicians, and then the next tune began.

Of course, she stole the show. Her charisma drew gazes, and when she took a solo, a hush fell over the entire club. She was incredible, her fingers delicate on that crummy old flute as the ethereal sounds flew up and down complex scales.

She played a few jams and then returned, and Ash struggled in vain to find the words to commend her performance. She brushed him off and kept peppering him with questions about when he'd learned to play piano until he was forced to explain.

He gave her a glossed-over, "human-safe" version of events. "I lived in Cuba for a few years and made friends with a piano player. I expressed an interest, so he taught me how to play."

The truth was, about fifty years ago, he'd done a solo escape from Hell and hid out in Cuba where he'd met his teacher, pulling the guy out of a fight outside a bar in Havana.

It sounded noble, but it wasn't. He'd killed all four of the men beating on Miguel without a backward glance, and he'd only saved Miguel in the first place because the guys kicking his ass had taunted him into it, and his pride demanded he show them who their daddy was. The friendship and piano lessons had come afterward, purely by chance.

Unfortunately, escaping Hell and killing humans was against the rules, and Ash had been caught a few years later. His first and only human friend was killed in the crossfire.

His emotions about that still confused him. Demons didn't have feelings like humans—they were supposed to be evil and soulless, after all—yet he felt a heaviness in his chest when he thought about Miguel's death, and he had since concluded it must be some form of grief. That he was even capable of that emotion said things about him that weren't good.

"That's amazing!" Eva said. "I've always wanted to study Cuban music. Where's your friend now? Do you still keep in touch?"

"No."

"But why not? You must have been close if he taught you how to play."

"Yeah, I guess so." He winced. Demons were not *close* with people.

"So why don't you keep in touch?"

Damn, she was persistent. The woman had a knack for finding all the weak points in his story.

"He was killed," he finally said.

Her hand flew to her mouth. "Oh my god, I'm so sorry. I keep asking you the worst questions, bringing up stuff that must be hard to talk about."

"It's fine. I don't mind talking with you." And he didn't. Also weird.

Thankfully she didn't ask for more details, instead choosing another topic to drill him on. After another hour or so of drinks and music, their between-set conversation mellowed out from the interrogation into the easy camaraderie he'd felt when they first met.

He found her funny and relatable, and the fact that she was a little bundle of walking sex appeal didn't hurt his enjoyment of her company at all. She talked to him about songwriting, her horny best friend, and her hippie parents, and he actually liked listening to what she said.

The little minx plied him with drinks and conversation until he finally let his guard slip and allowed her to talk him into going on stage. By then, it was one in the morning, and the crowd had thinned substantially. Those remaining were mostly lovers with their heads together, the odd lonely stray collapsed at the bar, and a few groups of over-exuberant partiers staggering about and laughing uproariously at inappropriate moments.

They climbed on the stage together, Ash kicking himself for agreeing to this. He hadn't touched a piano in decades and half wondered if he'd forgotten how to play. That pain in his chest that he thought must be grief was associated with Miguel and, therefore, playing music.

He sat behind the old upright. There were chips in the carved wood and bottle-rim stains all over the top, and a few keys in the lower octaves were missing altogether.

Holding her flute to her lips, Eva looked at him, smiling encouragingly. The silence in the bar suddenly seemed deafening. He took a breath and held his hands over the keys. They trembled slightly, which was embarrassing, so he curled them into fists tight enough that his knuckles cracked. Better.

Stretching them back out over the keys, he tried to think of something to play. He couldn't. Eva was still looking at him. Damn it, this was awkward.

He stopped thinking and slammed his hands down. With distant, detached amazement, he watched himself launch into a wildly improvised montuno with ridiculous chord changes. Somehow, it worked. The Latin-style progression was dissonant as hell, but it worked.

Immediately, he worried he'd gone too fancy and that Eva wouldn't be able to follow by ear, but of course that wasn't the case. She soloed over his chords effortlessly, finding a recurring theme that he quickly picked up on and echoed back to her. He dropped his left hand down an octave to cover the bass while she embellished on that theme, flying up and down the rapidly changing scales with melodic grace.

As their duo picked up energy, he felt a strange lightness in his chest. Like he was flying. Like the rest of the world had melted away. He heard himself laughing—something he hadn't done in years. He was actually fucking laughing. It was exhilarating and addicting, more so than any human drug he'd ever before tried.

Somehow, they finished together in perfect unison. They could have practiced for a month and not nailed a better ending. He stared at Eva and she stared back at him, lowering her flute in slow motion. Distantly, he heard people clapping, but he was only aware of one thing at that moment.

He climbed off the piano bench and staggered off the stage like he was wasted, when in truth, he was mostly just high on whatever thrilling emotion the music had awakened within him. Eva was grinning and staggering like she felt the same way.

The second they stepped off the stage, they were fused at the lips.

He pushed her up against the wall and deepened the kiss. Her arms snaked around his neck, pulling him closer, her flute still clutched in one hand. Their lips parted, tongues winding together. It felt fucking amazing. He didn't try to hide what was going on down below, pushing his hips against hers so she knew exactly what was on his mind.

"Eva, whoa, girl!" someone cheered from behind them.

Ash lifted his head. "We're still in the bar."

Suddenly, he noticed the contrasts of light and dark were exaggerated, different. Something was tingling in his nostrils, making his perception more vivid. Something was way off, and a distant alarm bell started ringing in his head, but he was way too turned on at the moment to care about anything but Eva. His attention lasered in on her, and he was aware of nothing else.

Her chest was rising and falling rapidly, her silvery-gray eyes heavy-lidded. "Oh, yeah."

"I want you."

"Damn," she breathed, eyes closing briefly. "Let's get out of here."

She grabbed his hand and pulled him toward the exit, snagging her coat and bag off the chair on her way past. As they crossed the bar, several female gazes landed on him. One girl's mouth dropped open, another whistled, and another who'd been flirting with another man sat up and stared.

Ash didn't even notice—he was too focused on getting Eva somewhere he could get her naked as soon as possible.

Out on the street, he kissed her again, taking a moment to feel her up. "Where do you live?"

"Two blocks away. We can walk. Let's go!" She grabbed his hand again and practically ran down the street. He was more than happy to follow, watching that perfect, round ass move with her every step. He was *so* going to bite her there.

A FIRST TIME FOR EVERYTHING

EVA'S FAVORITE SCENES IN TV SHOWS WERE ALWAYS THE long-awaited moments when the onscreen couple finally gave into their bursting sexual tension, and it exploded out of them in a clothes-ripping, knocking-over-furniture sex fest.

That was exactly what happened the moment she unlocked the door to her apartment.

Door slamming shut with a stray kick, they stumbled backward into the room, fused at the lips, until she hit something. A wall maybe? But no, it was awkwardly shaped, jabbing into her lower back. She didn't give a damn what it was. She only cared about getting the heavy leather jacket off Ash, dropping it on the floor, and then running her hands all over the most perfect specimen of maleness she'd ever seen.

He picked her up and set her down on whatever it was her back was bumping against—ah, yes, her grand piano. He was tall enough that it was the perfect height for her to wrap her legs around his hips and align their bodies where she desperately wanted them to be.

They started up a heavy grind through their clothes while their tongues engaged in a gold-medal wrestling match. She tugged his T-shirt up his hard stomach until he had to break the kiss to whip it over his head.

"Nice piano," he said before diving back in. "Hard to get a grand . . . upstairs apartment?"

She moaned, tipping her head back while he feasted along her throat, her palms sliding over his bare skin like she couldn't touch all of him fast enough. *So. Many. Muscles.* "I'm lucky. Was here before I moved in. Came with the place— Oh my god, Ash."

He was still grinding his hips against hers, the friction so exquisite she nearly lost it. She could feel the ridge of his hard cock through his pants, and she had never wanted anything more.

"You have a roommate?"

"Cat. Why."

"Wanna fuck you right on this piano."

"Yes. God, yes."

A big hand landed on her chest and pushed her flat on her back against the cool wood. Her own shirt was already off— fancy that. On her back, she got her first proper look at the bare-chested man between her thighs, and her mouth actually went dry.

He was magnificent. Unlike anyone or anything she'd seen before. All that silky black hair spilled over a godlike body that was ribbed with strength, and those luxurious indigo eyes were looking at her like he wanted to eat her for dinner.

She wanted to ask him how he was real, but she was quickly distracted when he stepped back and began pulling her leggings down. He took them and her high-tops and socks off and threw the whole works over his shoulder without a backward glance.

When they were gone, he trailed his mouth up to her inner thighs, stopping to slide her panties off and toss them away too. Watching him do that . . . She was pretty sure she might have come already.

If not, she definitely came within minutes of his mouth dipping between her legs, his tongue expertly working her clit. Her scream probably woke the neighbors.

But he wasn't content with just once. As soon as her body began to relax, he spread her apart with his fingers and feasted once again on her tingling flesh without a shred of mercy. He didn't let up until she orgasmed again, and this scream probably woke the whole building.

This time, he didn't stop when her climax crested, not even when she begged, and miraculously, he pushed her over the edge yet again. The man was a genius.

Gasping for breath, she sat up, pulling him up to kiss her and tasting herself on his lips. Her head spun from pleasure so fast she nearly passed out. Three orgasms in one go? Never before, not even on a marathon with her vibrator.

Ash slid her bra straps down, pushing the cups aside to free her breasts like he had no idea how the clasp on the back worked. Chuckling, she reached back—one pinch and it fell off. He got busy sucking on her nipples. She got busy working his jeans open.

She shoved the intrusive fabric down, and her fingers closed around a cock that was, like the rest of him, too good to be true. Just the smooth, silky feel was nearly enough to send her over the edge again. Long and thick, the satiny head was already slick with pre-cum, and she spread it around with a thumb, fighting a somewhat feral urge to rub it all over her. His responsive moans as she stroked him . . . Unbelievable. Heavenly.

He scooped her up again, her legs winding back around his hips, and then they were traveling. Where? Didn't matter. Just as long as he ended up inside her in the next two minutes.

Her bare ass landed on something cold. The kitchen counter. Slightly lower than the piano—better for penetration. And there he was, pushing at her entrance, the head of his cock stretching her as he just barely pushed inside, making her head spin and her sight blacken and—

"Condom," she gasped, hating herself for saying it but knowing she had to.

"Shit, Bel warned me— I have one." He whipped his wallet out of his back pocket, and, lo and behold, there was the fabled condom. She'd never been happier to see one of those flimsy latex bastards.

Normally, Eva averted her gaze while her sexual partner put on a condom, but this partner was so incredibly sexy that watching him roll on a rubber was nearly as good as foreplay.

But it sure as hell wasn't as good as how it felt when he entered her a second later. He was a little rough, like he *needed* this, would die without it, which was fine with her. There was no easing in gently. He just aligned and thrust, sinking deep in one smooth motion until she thought she'd burst from the fullness.

She cried out and threw her head back, promptly smacking it into the cupboard doors, turning her scream into a curse. The curse turned back into a scream with his second thrust. "Fuck, Ash!"

He picked her up again, fingers digging into her ass hard enough to bruise, and they were traveling once more. They hit a wall. He pressed her into it, fucking her against the drywall like his life depended on it. She threw her head back again, smacking it on the wall of course, and clutched him desperately, lost to the wildness of the moment.

"Bed. Where's your bedroom."

But she couldn't speak. He was hitting her in just the right spot, and she started to come *again*. He moaned as her inner muscles convulsed around him, and they slid down to the ground like his legs couldn't hold them anymore.

He fucked her on the floor, her body contorted in an awkward, half-bent position because there wasn't room to lie sideways in the hallway. It didn't matter. She soon discovered if she lifted one leg, she could brace it against the opposite wall and meet his thrusts with her own.

He liked that, moaning some more, and his hand landed on the wall above her head. Then things got really serious. He was tensioned between the wall and floor, and she was pushing against the other wall with her leg, their bodies braced for maximum thrust action.

And that was exactly what happened—hard, hot, heavy pounding with sweat dripping and hair plastered to faces and necks. It was glorious. Heavenly. She felt like she was flying. She forgot she was anything besides the white lights of pleasure bursting behind her tightly shut eyelids.

Ash's whole body tightened as he climaxed. She felt his cock swell and flex inside of her, and a deep, sexy groan escaped him that made Eva's eyes roll back in her head.

A moment later, he collapsed on top of her like he was boneless. The breath whooshed out of her lungs, and she lay flattened to the floor beneath him, her head spinning, complete satiation rushing through her veins.

That was when she remembered the bat wings.

And the long, black claws cutting off the creature's head.

Her eyes flew open, and she stared at the ceiling. "Meet him at the club, ask him questions": that was the plan. Not "get him back to her place ASAP and fuck his brains out."

But damn. That was the best sex she'd ever had, hands down. She'd never felt that kind of desperate, explosive chemistry with another person before, and right now, basking in the afterglow, it was impossible to regret anything about tonight.

Ash's glorious hair was spread all over her chest, his face buried in her neck. Slowly, he lifted his head. Their gazes met. His midnight-blue eyes seemed to glow, and there was a warmth in them she hadn't seen before.

Duh. Of course there was.

She'd just given him the orgasm of a lifetime. And that wasn't some grandiose statement—she knew it was true because she felt the same way. Looking into those eyes and seeing that connection, the strange, dark memories faded away again. At least for a little while.

"That was amazing." She lifted a shaky hand and smoothed some of the hair off his neck. "Incredible. The best."

He smiled. A real smile, a naked smile. One that warmed her heart. "Evangeline."

"Asmodeus." She chuckled at his ridiculous name.

"I never did find your bed."

"I've never had sex on the floor in a hallway before."

His smile turned wicked. "There's a first time for everything."

"Take me to bed, you crazy man. First door on the left, behind you."

He lifted her and stood up like she weighed nothing—every curvy woman's dream—and then he took her to bed and ravished her until the sun rose.

Sometime the next morning, Eva sat bolt upright in bed, clutching the sheet around her naked body. Beside her, the man who'd spent all night inside her in every possible position still slept soundly.

He was on his side, arms flung out in front of him where they'd been wrapped around her. His hair was spread over the bed behind him, a few long strands winding down his chest between his arms. The sheets bunched around his naked hips, and his skin looked darker through the curtains' shade, currently blocking the rays of morning sunlight.

She stared at him with a combination of horror and amazement. Horror, because what the hell had she been thinking? Had she gotten too wasted last night and lost control of herself? But no, she couldn't pretend that was the case. She'd barely been tipsy on the walk home.

The truth was, their off-the-charts chemistry and his indescribable hotness had swept her off her feet, and she'd been more than happy to ignore the memories of the beast burning to ash after having its head chopped off. By claws. That grew out of Ash's fingers.

Was she ever going to stop thinking about that night? Was she going to push away what seemed like the perfect man because of what was probably just a hallucination, brought on by shock from the shooting in the club?

But it didn't feel like a hallucination. It felt real. But wasn't that what all hallucinating people said?

And what about that whispering voice, telling her she was on the verge of discovering why she felt like she didn't know herself?

Why did she feel like she didn't know herself anyway? She wasn't that complicated a person, but she'd always felt oddly vacant, and it made no damn sense. All the soul searching in the world couldn't give her the answers she sought.

Would she ever make sense of that? Was it a byproduct of the hallucinations or the cause of them?

She may have been sidetracked from her recon last night, but it wasn't too late to look for clues.

Leaning in, she inspected Ash's hands as closely as she could without touching him, looking for signs of claws. A little voice in her head screamed that she was being completely irrational, but she ignored it. The memories were too real.

Unfortunately, or fortunately, his hands were perfectly normal. The only abnormal thing about them was how incredibly sexy they were. The veins on the backs were clearly defined, and his fingers were long and graceful. He had the hands of an artist. The hands of a man who could give her multiple orgasms.

She'd never realized she could be so attracted to a man's hands, for god's sake. But of course, with him, she was. She was pretty sure she'd be attracted to his ear.

Slipping out of bed, she skirted around the side to look at his back. His hair was in the way, so she gently brushed it aside. He gave a soft moan and stirred slightly, and Eva's heart instantly melted. She stared at him with hearts in her eyes for a moment until she kicked herself back into focus.

His back was free of any sign that enormous wings might be anchored beside his spine. It was just a normal, human, muscular, sexy back that she wanted to lick and bite every inch of.

Fighting the urge, she tiptoed down the hall until she found where Ash had shed his pants after their first bout of lovemaking and pulled out his wallet. There was no ID, no indications of identity at all. Just a fat wad of cash. Suspicious, certainly, but nothing that said red skin or horns.

She found his phone in his other pocket. It had no passcode and was even less interesting than the contents of his wallet. No apps, emails, or pictures, and only three contacts: Bel, Meph, Raum. Were those his brothers? He'd never actually told her their names. What kind of name was *Meph* though? *Mefff.* Weird.

Guilty conscience alive and humming, she jumped about a foot in the air when the phone rang in her hand at that moment. The call display said "Bel." She froze, wondering if she should shove it back in his pocket and pretend she hadn't been near it.

"Eva?" came a sexy, sleepy voice from the bedroom.

"Your phone's ringing. Want me to bring it?" There. No lying involved.

"Sure."

She went back to the bedroom where Ash was sitting up,

dragging a hand through that gorgeous mane, and passed him the phone. Answering it, he climbed out of bed and strolled shamelessly naked across the bedroom.

"What do you want, Bel?"

"Where are you?"

Asmodeus found his discarded pants and donned them before wandering over to the grand piano, a smile curving his lips when he remembered eating Eva out on top of it last night. He sat on the bench and pressed middle C with his free hand, the clear note ringing through the quiet apartment. "Where do you think?"

"Did you get laid?"

"Yeah."

"Congratulations."

He rolled his eyes. "I can't believe you just said that."

"Well, hell, it's been a while. I feel like I should get you a trophy or something."

"Do that and I'll shove it up your ass." He played a minor-major-seventh chord for ominous emphasis.

Bel chuckled. "Look, you should probably get back here. Meph ran into another gargoyle last night when he was out."

That was the fourth one this week. "And?"

"And there could be more."

"I'm not coming back for that. You can kill a gargo—" He cleared his throat. "Deal with it yourself."

"I already did, and I got fucking blood stains on my favorite pants for my trouble."

"If you dealt with it, then what's the problem? Besides your fancy pants."

"There could be more."

"So call me if more show up."

"Damn it, Asmodeus, this is serious. I don't like how easy it is for them to find us. We should be staying behind the wards as much as possible."

Gargoyles weren't trackers. They didn't have the brains, nor did they possess any unique powers to aid them. They were just strong and stupid, and there was an abundance of them, so they were used for everything. "It's probably a coincidence that they're here."

"Or they're following orders."

Ash climbed up a chromatic scale with his thumb and forefinger. "Whose orders?"

"You know who."

His hand curled into a first. "There's no way they'd send him this early on in the game."

"Yes, they would. I'm a goddamn King of Hell."

He had a point.

"Look," Bel said, "if the Hunter's involved, he could have already tracked you to the human's house. You should leave now."

"I'm not leaving."

"You're a stubborn jackass."

"And you're a neurotic, overbearing bastard."

"*Ass*-modeus."

His eye roll was epic. "Never heard that one before, *Bel*-ligerent."

Bel snorted. "All right, fine. Stay with your human for now, but I'm calling you if anything happens. Anything at all, and you get your ass right the fuck back home, got it?"

It was annoying when Bel tried to give him orders, but Ash played along for the sake of their dysfunctional little family. "Life or death, Belial. Don't call me unless it's life or death."

CHIVALRY ISN'T DEAD

SMODEUS HUNG UP THE PHONE AND SAW EVA STAND-
ing in the hall wrapped in a sheet, staring at him with
a crease between her brows. "Was that your brother?
Do you need to go home?"

"No. He just likes to nag me."

"His name is Belial?"

"Yep."

"Isn't that another demon name?"

"It is." He wasn't giving her more than that.

They probably should have chosen fake names, but demons
playing by the rules always used them on Earth, and everything
about their escape from Hell had been about breaking those
rules. Even if it was kinda, sorta stupid.

"What is with your family? What are your other brothers'
names?"

Again, he should probably lie, but he didn't feel like it.
"Meph and Raum."

"What's Meph short for?"

"Mephistopheles."

"Oh my god."

"That's why he goes by Meph."

"Don't you mind being named after demons? Why don't you change your names?"

"We're not named *aft*—" He stopped himself from going any further with that and shrugged. "It's who we are. We don't mind it."

Though it was annoying how they'd developed a rep over the ages. Every paranormal TV show these days had a demon called Asmodeus. They even had their own Wikipedia pages.

Eva was looking at him like she wasn't satisfied with his answers, and he suddenly wondered if she knew more than she was letting on. She was smart as a whip, and who knew what had slipped out of his mouth before he'd endured Bel's counseling session on what not to say in front of her.

Then he looked at her again and stopped thinking about all that. She was naked except for a bedsheet, the white fabric contrasting appealingly with her dark skin. Her wild curls were piled in a messy bun on top of her head, and her full lips were just begging to be kissed. He hadn't had nearly enough of her to satisfy him yet.

"Come here," he growled.

She hesitated. She still looked suspicious of him, which was weird considering he'd screwed her brains out last night and she hadn't seemed to mind then. From what he knew about humans, they didn't often have sex with people they didn't trust.

Ash stood. He knew Eva was attracted to him—a bloody miracle—and he wasn't above using it against her to get what he wanted. Sure enough, he watched her gaze travel down his body.

He'd thrown on his pants when Bel called but left them unzipped, and he was shirtless and commando. His hair was a tangled mess, but he didn't think Eva cared. Modern females seemed to be more open-minded about long-haired males, not that it had ever mattered to him. Thanks to his curse, his hair was the least of his concerns when it came to finding bed mates. But even if he could get laid on the regular, he wouldn't have cut it for anyone.

He waited for Eva to obey his directive, not appreciating that she hadn't listened to him. Last night she sure had. Whether he was telling her to turn around, bend over, spread her legs, whatever, she'd done what he said, no questions asked. Now, she was shifting on her feet looking like she wanted to flee, and he didn't like it.

"Evangeline," he warned, and she actually flinched a little bit. What the hell? Had he accidentally said too much on the phone?

He walked toward her, and her eyes slid up and down his body again. When he reached her, he stopped close enough that he was invading her personal space, but not so close that they touched. He looked down, and she looked up so their gazes met.

"Do you want some coffee?" she blurted. "I'm a bit of a coffee snob, and I can't function without my latte in the morning."

So she wanted to play the evasive game, did she? He'd let her. For now. "Sure, I'll have coffee." It would just taste like water.

"Great." Her smile looked forced, and she stepped back. "There's a cafe downstairs. I'll go grab some and get pastries for breakfast."

He studied her, trying to see if she was up to something. "You want me to come?"

"No, that's fine. It's right downstairs. Stay here and play my piano."

He dug his wallet out of his back pocket and tossed it at her. "Buy whatever."

"Oh, that's okay, you don't have to—"

"Eva."

"What?"

"Chivalry may be dead, but I'm not that big a bastard. Let me buy your breakfast."

Her chuckle seemed to sneak out of her against her will.

"Fine. You have a point."

She disappeared into the bedroom to get dressed, to his consternation. He'd wanted more sex, not damn pastries. But Eva was human and needed to eat. Sex could come after. He wasn't leaving without it.

She came out in a bulky sweater and leggings and slipped on her high-tops, carefully avoiding his gaze. "I'll be right back. Make yourself at home."

He leaned against the piano, trying to figure out why she was so jumpy. "Do you want me to leave?"

She finally looked at him. "What? No."

He didn't believe her. "I'm not one to linger, Eva. Say the word and I'm gone."

For the first time, her gaze softened. "I want you to stay, I swear. I don't do this very often, and I guess I'm being awkward."

He felt the need to reassure her, though he wasn't sure why. "I don't do this often either."

"Really?"

"Really." And when he did, he left so fast, the female hadn't even caught her breath before he'd finished dressing and evacuated the premises. Demon females were likely to claw his face off if he stayed, and human women were likely to start crying when they realized how desperate they had to be to have sex with someone they found as sexy as potting soil. And what little pride Ash managed to retain throughout those miserable encounters dictated he get out of there fast to avoid subjecting himself to that.

"Can I be honest?" Eva asked.

"Sure. I want you to be."

"I just . . . find that hard to believe. I mean, look at you. You're not exactly average looking." Her gaze darted away again, but this time from shyness instead of suspicion. He preferred that.

And he damn well enjoyed the compliment. Fuck if he didn't deserve it after all this time. He knew he wasn't actually ugly or boring, but it still felt good to get a little validation now and then. He smiled.

"Let's just say, I'm not a people person. I tend to keep to myself." It was all true. Since he'd been cursed, all his wily lust demon ways had been replaced by an increasing broodiness that annoyed him but was his only refuge from feeling shitty and embarrassed in public settings.

Eva finally smiled at him. "Well, I'm glad you went out with me last night. You're an incredible musician, and you shouldn't hide it. I'm taking you back to Bootleg next week, and you're going to jam with all my friends, and they're going to love you."

He winced. "I don't know about that."

"I have a week to talk you into it. Now don't go anywhere because I'm just running downstairs to get our food, and I really do want you to stay. Promise you'll be here when I get back?"

"I'll be here."

She slipped out the door and was gone. He sat down at the piano again and was about to play when movement from the kitchen caught his eye. Looking over, he saw a little gray cat watching him. He'd forgotten Eva said she had a pet.

For the most part, cats hated demons. The little bastards had good instincts and knew they were in the presence of something wicked. The creature arched its back, its fur standing on end. It hissed at him, baring tiny fangs.

Asmodeus allowed his own fangs to grow nice and long and

his hands to morph into claws. He flexed them and hissed right back. The cat jumped about a foot in the air and then took a few crab-like side steps, making that god-awful wailing sound only a cat could make as it slunk away to Eva's bedroom.

Ash smiled, pleased with his victory.

Then he turned back to the piano and, for the first time in decades, played for no other reason than because he wanted to. Even last night hadn't counted because he never would have done it if Eva hadn't coerced him into it, not that he regretted it.

But right now was *his* choice. No one was there to listen. He played because there was a piano in front of him, and because playing made him feel that euphoric emotion that was the furthest thing from demonic but felt too good to care.

Eva really was going to the cafe to get them some breakfast, and she really hadn't wanted Ash to leave, but she also had a hidden agenda:

Phone Mom. Part two.

The second she was in the elevator, she dialed, waiting for her mom to pick up.

She did, yawning. "Eva, honey, it's too early."

"It's eleven thirty."

"Eight thirty in my time zone. You know how early that is?"

"It's not that early."

"It's early." A deep male voice rumbled in the background. "Your dad says he's sleeping and to leave him alone." Jacqui moved the phone from her mouth. "It's your daughter, Dan. Be nice." The rumbling sounded again. She put the phone back. "He says hi and that he loves you, but he's still sleeping."

"I need to talk to you. I don't have long."

"Hold on, I'll get up." She murmured some words of endearment to Dan, and then there was rustling as she threw on a robe, followed by the sound of a door closing. "Okay, I'm up. Putting on coffee so I can stay that way. What's going on?"

"Well, you remember mystery man?"

"Did he call?" She instantly sounded alert.

"Yep."

"And? Tell me everything!"

Eva told her about what happened at Bootleg.

"He's a musician? Oh honey, he sounds perfect!"

"Yeah, I was pretty blown away. Like . . . really blown away."

There was a pause. "You slept with him, didn't you?"

"Um . . ."

Jacqui burst out laughing. "You were supposed to be finding out whether you hallucinated a supernatural fight scene!"

"I know, Mom, but I— He— Damn it, you have no idea how hot he is."

"I really want to. Send me a pic? What's his Instagram? I'll check him out."

"He doesn't have Instagram."

"Who doesn't have Instagram?"

"*He* doesn't! That's what I'm trying to tell you. He—"

"Was he good in bed?"

"This is so weird to talk about with you."

Jacqui scoffed. "Whatever. Tell me."

"Yes, he was amazing. The best I've ever had."

"Wow."

"Yeah, but I'm trying to tell you, he didn't exactly pass my investigation."

"What, is he underequipped? That's not necessarily a deal breaker. Before your father, I had a lover who was smaller than average, but let me tell you, he knew how to wield the thing like—"

"Ew, Mom! And no, he was not underequipped. Definitely not. The opposite."

"So what's the problem?"

"I asked him a lot of questions about his life, and his answers were really evasive. And I went through his wallet, and he had no ID. I also checked his phone, and his only contacts are his three brothers. And get this, they all have demon names too! There's Belial, Raum, and Meph, which is short for Mephis-something."

"That's odd. But if he is actually . . . *supernatural*, why would he tell you names that would make you suspicious?"

"I don't know, but he didn't seem to care that I found it weird."

The sound of the coffeepot gurgling came over the line as Eva's elevator dinged, and she climbed out, heading down the hall toward the street.

"Do you feel safe with him?"

She stepped into the morning sunshine. The spring air had a bit of a bite to it, but she was too happy to see the sun after months of winter to care about being cold. "If I was in danger, I would've had some kind of feeling, right?"

"Not necessarily. Some people are very good at hiding their darkness."

"Hmm." She walked toward the cafe, which was only about five steps from the door to her apartment. "It's just, I'm really into him, and he's an incredible musician, and it seems stupid to throw that away because I had a hallucination."

"Maybe I should consult your dad. He's the one that knows about the occult stuff."

When he wasn't making modern art with her mom, Dan was obsessed with occult studies and witchcraft. What could she say? Her parents were eccentric. She'd long since accepted it.

Eva leaned against the glass beside the cafe entrance and

crossed her feet at the ankles. "Yeah, maybe it's not a bad idea. You could ask him about their names."

"If someone's heard of it, your dad will know about it."

"Dad's so weird." Eva laughed fondly. "Both of you are. How did I end up with such weird parents?"

"Good karma, obviously. Now, get back to your mysterious lover. But first, I have one last suggestion for you."

"Hit me."

"If you really like this guy and see it becoming more serious, you should consider telling him what you saw."

"What? No way. If I really did hallucinate it, he'll think I'm a nutjob!"

"As someone who has been married for twenty-seven years, let me give you some advice. If you want a real relationship, it has to be built on trust. If the foundation is weak, the structure will fall. If he cares about you, he'll accept it if you hallucinate things occasionally. And if you really did see something, maybe he'll tell you what you saw. Maybe there's a logical explanation. Maybe he's into role-play."

"Mom."

"I'm just saying, if you like the guy, consider talking to him. You don't want to start a relationship on such a distrustful footing. You went through his wallet and phone, for heaven's sake."

"I had to!"

"I know that, but you can see how that doesn't exactly scream 'healthy boundaries.'"

"Yeah, I can. All right, I'll think about it."

Eva said goodbye a minute later and headed into the cafe. She opened Ash's wallet and fingered the wad of cash. She might have found it strange that he had nothing in there, but the fact that he'd handed her the thing and told her to spend his money said he wasn't concerned about her knowing.

How could someone be suspicious if they didn't try to hide

it? Wasn't that the very nature of being suspicious? God, her head hurt.

"Can I help you?" The guy behind the counter smiled expectantly.

She rubbed her head and tried to focus on the pastry display.

8

SEXCAPADES AND
PASTRIES

E VA STOPPED IN THE HALL OUTSIDE HER APARTMENT.
The hairs on the back of her neck rose at the music
coming through the door. As she listened, she recog-
nized the chords and melody Ash was outlining between
tasteful embellishments.

"My Funny Valentine"—the classic jazz ballad. The way he
was playing it reminded her of the Chet Baker version. It was
heartrending. Soulful. Melancholic. It made her want to laugh
and weep and make love all at the same time.

She wanted to hear better. Coffees and pastry bag balanced
in one hand, she opened the door as quietly as she could, intent
on not disturbing him. The piano was angled away from the
door, and she managed to slip in unnoticed.

Ash was hunched over the keys like a regular brooding
Beethoven, still shirtless, his sleek black hair falling down his
back. She sighed in appreciation.

How was he real? He had to be too good to be true because

otherwise he would have been snatched up by some smart woman a decade ago.

The dreamy music continued to serenade her, reaching deep inside and wrapping its sorrowful melody around her heart until tears pricked at her eyes.

She tried to be quiet as she kicked off her shoes, but apparently, he hadn't been kidding about his hearing being good because he instantly stopped playing and spun around on the bench, spine ramrod straight. The air felt hollow without the music.

He relaxed as soon as he saw her, but she hadn't missed the dangerous glint in his eye for that split second, and honestly, it scared her. Something told her he was not the kind of guy who liked being snuck up on, or ever allowed it to happen, for that matter.

"I'm back," she said to cover the empty silence. "Sorry if I startled you, but I didn't want you to stop. I love that song. That was so beautiful."

He shrugged, climbing off the bench and coming over to take the coffee and pastries from her. "I was just messing around."

"That's some pretty epic messing around." She wanted to ask him if his "messing around" always made people want to cry but decided against it. Instead, she said, "Do it again? I'd love to try and play along on my violin."

He'd already lifted one of the coffees halfway to his mouth, but his eyes lit up at that, and he set it back down without taking a sip. "Okay."

She had to grin. The guy really loved music.

Too good to be true, that stupid little negative voice warned.

Shut up, she told it. She wasn't missing out on this for the world.

Half an hour later, they had jammed the hell out of "My Funny Valentine," and the music came to its natural conclusion.

Ash put his hands in his lap, and she lowered her violin, and they stared at each other in silence.

Her heart felt achy from the music and yet was racing at the undeniable fact that she had incredible musical and physical chemistry with a man for the first time in her life. Yeah, the circumstances were questionable, but she'd never felt connected to someone this way before. She was powerless to resist.

He seemed to get her line of thinking because he rose from the bench and crowded her up against the side of the piano. Their gazes met.

"Eva." It came out like a growl.

"Ash." Hers came out like a sigh.

A mischievous glint suddenly entered those midnight-blue eyes. "I never did fuck you on the piano last night."

Her entire female reproductive system lit up like a carnival parade. Like she had a freaking "Turn me on!" button on her forehead for a ride that only he could operate.

She took two steps, practically tossed her violin onto the couch, and then turned and sprinted into her bedroom where she had a condom stash in the nightstand. She grabbed one, raced back into the living room, and threw it at him. His bewildered expression vanished as he caught it, and then he looked like he might laugh, but she didn't give him a chance because she threw herself at him next.

He caught her, bent down, and crushed their mouths together. And then it was like they hadn't already had sex ten times, because suddenly they were desperate to get closer. She ripped her clothes off and panted while she watched him shove his jeans down and kick them away, and then their naked bodies were pressed together, and their tongues were back to more wrestling antics. Ash's big hands encircled her butt cheeks and gripped them hard enough to lift her off her feet.

"Your ass is so fucking fine," he growled against her lips.

She could only moan as he ground his hard-on against her

while she dangled in the air from his grip on her behind. She went to wrap her legs around his hips, but he stopped her.

He set her on her feet, gripped her hips, and spun her around.

Her eyes widened as he lifted her again and then laid her on her stomach on top of the piano. Her legs hung over the edge, not quite reaching the ground. She dangled helplessly with her ass in the air, completely at his mercy.

He spanked her. She yelped at the sting and felt another flood of wetness between her thighs in response.

Whoa. Apparently, she was into spanking, though she hadn't known it until right then. He pried her legs apart with a firm grip, thumbs on her inner thighs, so close to where she was desperate for his touch.

Splayed out on the piano, her palms pressing into the cold wood, she peeked over her shoulder and watched him hunch down as if he was going to eat her out. She moaned in anticipation, but he surprised her again.

He bit her ass.

He actually *bit* her right on the ass. And she freaking loved it. Hell, she nearly came just from seeing his white teeth digging into her ass cheek. Who knew she was such a dirty girl?

She no longer wanted him to eat her out. She wanted fucking. Hard, fast fucking.

"Please!" And no, she wasn't above begging for it.

He straightened, and there was a moment of painful anticipation while he put on the condom. The cold air on her bare ass made her feel exposed and somehow even more turned on. And then, lord have mercy, his thick cock was nudging at her entrance, and she nearly cried from gratitude at the feel of him filling her.

And fill her he did. He stretched her wide, but it was just the right amount, just what she needed, and yet not enough because he wasn't moving, damn it—

He got the memo on that, and his hips punched forward as he bottomed out inside her. He withdrew and then pushed deep again. He fucked her hard, pounding into her while she was sprawled across the top of the piano, screaming like a banshee and loving every second of it.

He reached over her, palms landing on top of hers, holding her hands down. His legs spread inside hers, prying hers wide open.

She couldn't move an inch. She was totally and completely dominated by him, powerless to do anything but feel as he filled her up and fucked her into oblivion.

She screamed as she reached her peak, and next thing she knew, Ash was coming too, and she nearly climaxed again at the feel of all his strength channeling into her at his moment of total release.

They stayed sprawled on the piano for at least five minutes without talking. She couldn't find words, or even form thoughts, to describe what had just happened. Her mind was blank, her body humming with endorphins.

"Holy shit," was the first thing that came out of her, and by his satisfied chuckle, she could tell he agreed.

He straightened, pulled out, and walked to the kitchen to throw out the condom. She watched him, still draped wantonly over the piano, not caring at all. He looked over from behind the island and smiled at the sight of her. Lifting his hands, he mimicked the shape of a camera and snapped an imaginary picture. "Perfect."

They ended up sitting on the floor by the windows, eating pastries, drinking coffee, and listening to Oscar Peterson—naked.

Eva had always been a bit self-conscious—she was one of those short and thick types, with a booty that needed special big-assed-woman pants to fit in—but Ash made her feel delicate and feminine. He looked at her the way she looked at chocolate cake, which had to be a good thing.

It was a simple moment. Neither of them spoke much, content to listen to Oscar's sultry piano melodies, and the silence was comfortable. She felt so relaxed and connected to him, more than she'd ever felt with another person.

I really hope this isn't one-sided.

Hallucinations or not, it wouldn't take much for her to fall for him. And she was pretty sure it *had* been a hallucination. She'd found nothing unusual about him besides his mysterious past, and it wasn't unreasonable to assume she'd imagined what she'd seen, resulting from the severe stress of the gunfire. It was what any therapist would say, as her mother had pointed out.

As for her mom's opinion, well, Jacqui was always looking for magic where there was just everyday, black-and-white normalcy. It made her a great artist, but Eva knew she shouldn't take anything she said too literally.

She'd just dusted off the last bite of croissant when a phone rang. It wasn't Beethoven's Fifth, so it wasn't hers.

With a groan, Ash climbed to his feet, and she watched his sexy ass move as he crossed the room to grab his pants and pull his phone out of the pocket. "Yeah?"

God, his hair. What man had hair like that? When he stood straight, it brushed those biteable ass cheeks. All that shiny black against his lighter skin tone . . . He was a freaking work of art.

"Fuck you. I'm not doing shit for you."

She snorted. He was obviously talking to his brother.

"I'm not—" He made a frustrated growl. "I told you not to call me unless it was life or death. This isn't life or death and therefore is not my probl— Bel. Shut the fu— Bel!" He jerked the phone away from his ear with a wince, and she could hear his brother's shouting from where she sat. "Shit."

He hung up, glanced apologetically at her, and then dialed another number. "It's me. Bel is having a rage attack. You need to get back to the apartment before he burns it down."

Eva blinked.

"I don't give a shit where you are. Damn it, Raum, don't even thi—"

Ash looked at the phone and growled. "Motherfucker hung up on me." He dialed a new number. "Meph. Bel is raging out and Raum's being a dickhead. You need to get home now. I don't care that you're at the gym." Ash tipped his head back and closed his eyes. "Fine, I'll come. Fuck you. See you soon, asshole."

He hung up, looked at Eva as if just remembering she was there, and winced. "My brothers are fu— uh, really annoying."

She laughed. "I don't care about your potty mouth, but damn, you'd better never let my grandmother hear you talking like that."

"It's not my fault. I'm surrounded by bad influences." His smile faded. "I have to go."

"I guessed by that interesting conversation."

He shook his head. "My brothers can't do shit without me there holding their hands. With the way they're acting, you'd think this was their first trip to Ear—" He cleared his throat. "Uh, away from home."

Had he been about to say *Earth?* She briefly entertained her alien theory again and then discarded it. Nah. That was crazy. "It's okay. I know how it is with the family stuff. Mine can be a handful too sometimes. They annoy you but you love them, right?"

"Love?"

"Uh, yeah."

His mouth twisted like he'd tasted something foul. He may have been better at sex than any man alive, but he was still really freaking weird.

Oh, well. A girl couldn't have it all.

A few minutes later, they were dressed and approaching what was sure to be an awkward goodbye by the door. After donning his jacket, Ash bent to lace up his boots, hair falling over his face like a curtain. She stared at him, trying to think of something to say and coming up blank.

He straightened and swept his hair back. "Thanks for last night, Eva."

She panicked inwardly. *He's never going to call. He's going to walk out that door, and I'm never going to see him again.* She wanted to beg him to stay, but she was a strong fucking woman, damn it.

She squared her jaw and waited for the inevitable brush off. "No problem."

He searched her gaze. *Here we go. He's going to give me some bullshit excuse about how he's busy and doesn't have time for a relationship.*

"I want to see you again."

She blinked.

"Is that . . ." He winced. "Is it abnormal to say that? I don't know how to do this shit, and Bel told me I should leave without making promises to make you think I wasn't interested."

She couldn't help it. She burst out laughing. "Your brother is a huge dick."

He snorted. "Yeah. He is."

"And to answer your question, no. It's not 'abnormal.' Actually, I'm glad you said it because if you didn't, I was going to stew about how much of a dick *you* were until you called me." Damn it, that sounded a little desperate.

"You want me to call you?"

"Uh, yeah." She tried to play it cool. "You were inside me like, an hour ago. A girl usually hopes for a phone call after that."

His gaze darkened. "I want to be inside you again."

Her lady parts did that clenching thing again. "I want that too."

"Fuck. I'll call you."

"Yeah. Do that."

He shook his head, and his I-want-sex look vanished. She mourned its loss. "I have to warn you, though. I'm not—" His gaze shifted away. "My life's not exactly stable right now. If I don't call, it's not because I don't want to. But I will if I can."

"I'm a big girl. You don't have to make any promises." She talked a big game, but her heart sank a little.

"I'm glad we met, Eva."

"Me too."

The corner of his mouth curved, and then he pulled open the door and was gone.

Alone, she spun around and faced her empty apartment, feeling bereft and lonely and then annoyed because it was way too soon for those kinds of feelings. For *any* kinds of feelings, for that matter.

The apartment seemed too quiet, though, and she suddenly realized she hadn't seen Thelonious once all day. He was probably hiding under her bed, which was odd because normally he liked new people. She was convinced he showered them with affection in an attempt to make her jealous.

Her phone rang—dun dun dun *dunnn*—and she ran to grab it off the kitchen counter, glad for the distraction. She grinned when she saw Skye's name.

"What is this I hear about you leaving Bootleg with a hot guy last night?" her friend shouted before Eva could get a word out.

She thought of her advice to Skye—*If you want him to stick around, you've got to make him work for it*—and burst out laughing.

Talk about hypocritical. She hadn't come close to following her own lofty advice. And now here she was in her best friend's shoes, wondering if the guy was ever going to call her again.

Karma was a bitch.

9

WALKING ON EGGSHELLS

ROUGHLY FIVE THOUSAND KILOMETERS AWAY, IN A beautiful oceanfront house nestled between old-growth cedars, Jacqueline Gregory stretched her feet out on the sofa and watched her shirtless husband trudge past her to the kitchen, rubbing sleep from his eyes.

She smiled to herself. She was a lucky woman. Twenty-seven years of marriage and she still found her partner sexy. And how could she not? Dan was a handsome man who kept himself in peak physical condition. And besides his sweet tooth, he'd always been a health nut, which meant he'd aged remarkably well. So well, in fact, that she sometimes wondered if he'd aged at all.

"What did Eva want?" he asked, pouring coffee into a mug.

Jacqui took a sip of her own coffee and looked out the tall A-frame window. She never got tired of the view. The cedar branches and fern leaves textured the foreground while the gray ocean tossed in the distance. Mossy rocks covered the beachfront. It was raining today, but then, this was the West Coast. It was always raining.

"She met a guy," Jacqui said.

Dan peeked around the corner of the pantry. "She what?" She chuckled. This was why Eva had called her mom for advice, not her dad. "She needed some womanly advice."

"I hope you told her to send him packing."

"I didn't! I told her to be strong, set healthy boundaries, and drill him with questions about his past."

Dan ducked back around the pantry, and she heard the sound of him scooping copious amounts of sugar into his coffee. She made a face. How he could stomach that waste-of-perfectly-good-coffee swill would forever be a mystery to her. She liked hers black and strong.

"Who is this guy?" Dan grumbled, diligently stirring, the spoon clinking against the mug. "What's his number? I'll give him a call and drill him with questions myself."

"That's not happening. Eva is a grown woman." Twenty-seven years old she was now, but of course, Dan would see her as his baby forever.

Jacqui had only been twenty when she'd given birth to Eva, and though it had been one of the most stressful periods of her life, she gave thanks every day for her family and was grateful things had turned out the way they had. She'd gotten a loving husband and an amazing daughter out of it, and she'd somehow still managed to make it as an artist.

"I trust her judgment and know she can make good decisions about who she spends time with. She seems really into this guy, and she's smart enough to decide for herself if he's good for her."

Dan sighed, coming around the kitchen with his mug of swill in hand. "I just worry about her and how far away she is. I miss her."

"I know, hon. I miss her too."

He smiled as he sank onto the sofa next to her. "She's passionate, our girl. She had to go off and chase her dreams."

Leaning against the arm of the sofa, Jacqui lifted her legs and put her feet in her husband's lap. He curled his free hand around her ankle, and they sat with the ease of a couple who'd been together for years.

"He's a musician," she told her husband, smiling.

Dan grunted, unimpressed.

"She said he was an amazing pianist."

He grunted again. "He could be Mozart reincarnated, and he wouldn't be good enough for her."

Jacqui laughed. "He could be a real live heavenly angel and you'd say he wasn't good enough for her."

"That's true," Dan replied in all seriousness.

She laughed again. "You're such a caveman."

He grinned, setting his coffee on the table beside him. "Then you're my cavewoman." She knew that look in his eye and quickly set her coffee down too, just in time for him to pounce. He loomed over her, still grinning, pinning her into the sofa and looking far too pleased with himself. She rolled her eyes at him but couldn't fight her smile.

"Make me a fire while I go out to catch something for us to eat," her Neanderthal grunted.

Jacqui's eyes lit up as sudden inspiration struck. "We should do a series themed on modern relationship parallels to primitive ones! Oh, that's good! We could have scenes of a present-day couple alongside our cave couple and draw comparisons between their expected societal roles." She seized his strong shoulders in a tight grip and pretended to shake him, not that she could. "I'm a genius!"

Dan grinned. "It's a great idea, hon." He climbed off her and leaned back into the cushions. "Draw out some sketches and we can talk more about it later. I've got to work on that damned vulture. The head fell off again. I'm this close to scrapping the whole thing."

"Oh no." But she laughed. That silly scrap-metal statue had become Dan's nemesis of late.

Jacqui thought of her conversation with Eva again and wondered how best to go about asking what needed to be asked. She loved her husband, but he was a bit overprotective at times, and she didn't want Eva to feel stifled. She decided to pick and choose what to tell Dan about her daughter's interesting challenges of late.

"Have you done any of your occult stuff lately?" she asked, taking a sip of coffee to hide the spark of interest she knew flared in her eyes.

"Not really. I was working on that project about witchcraft in the Middle Ages, but it's so depressing that I started to wonder why I was bothering."

"I thought we were going to make a piece about it. Correlations to modern feminism and all that."

"We are. But like I said, it's depressing."

"Do you ever . . ." She sipped her coffee again. "Have you ever studied demonology?"

"Sure, why?"

"I heard these four demon names recently, and I thought they were interesting. I wondered what the background was on them, since I was considering using them in my writing."

While visual art was her true passion, she had a bit of a side gig as a fantasy writer. She hated lying to her husband about why she wanted to know about the names, but she wanted to give Eva time to figure things out for herself before she got Dan involved.

"What names?" Dan asked, sipping his sugary coffee. His other arm was flung out along the back of the sofa, and she took a moment to admire him.

While Dan had no living family, Jacqui's was extensive, and her parents were very old-fashioned. She still remembered the looks on their faces when she'd brought home her blond-haired, silver-eyed husband-to-be for the first time. To this day, she shuddered to think what would've happened if they'd found out she was already pregnant. But they'd grown to love Dan, especially after Eva was born. Who wouldn't love a man who gave them such a perfect granddaughter?

She tried to remember the names Eva had told her. "Asmo-something."

"Asmodeus?" Dan snorted.

"Yeah, that's it. What's funny?"

"I'm just surprised that you haven't heard that name before. Asmodeus is legendary. There's a royal ranking system for demons called the Order of Thrones, and Asmodeus is a Prince of Hell. That means he's of the second-highest level and one of the most powerful demons in the underworld. I think he was a King at some point, but I'm not certain. He was once the most renowned lust demon of all time, but in recent times, he's faded into obscurity."

"Really?" *Interesting.* It lent credibility to the hallucination theory. The odds of a legendary, powerful demon being interested in jamming with Eva seemed slim.

"And what were the others?" Dan asked.

"Belial?"

Dan nearly spit out his coffee.

"What?"

"Belial isn't just a demon, hon. He's, like, *the* demon. It's basically another name for Satan."

"So not a minor legend, then."

"No. He's a King of Hell, and one of the original angels that fell from Heaven at the start of creation. It's said that the only other who rivals his power is Lucifer himself."

"What about Mephis— Meph—"

"Mephistopheles?"

"Yeah, that."

"He's a famous one as well, though he's more elusive, since he's not mentioned in most grimoires, and he doesn't have a rank in the Order. He's originally known from the Faust legend, which is one of the original tales about a man who makes a deal with the devil."

"Interesting. And what about Raum?"

"Also powerful. An Earl of Hell, I believe, who can take the form of a crow." Dan looked at her. "When did you get it in your head to study demonology?"

She shrugged. "I just thought they had cool names."

"I suppose so. But all four of them are very well known. Unless you want to write about demons, I'd suggest picking something different or you're going to have to explain the correlation." He eyed her sidelong. "Where'd you come up with those four in particular?"

"Oh, I must have read them somewhere. I'm not sure."

She winced, hating lying to him. But she was more convinced than ever that Eva had suffered from a stress-induced hallucination. She would have been more suspicious if Dan had told her those four names were random, little-known demons, or if he'd never heard of them at all. The idea that four legendary demons had teamed up and gone to a nightclub was pushing it.

Likely, they just had very strange parents who had picked awful names for their sons—which wasn't a big stretch of the imagination considering Asmodeus had told Eva he was raised by his brother. She decided there was no point in worrying Dan about it for now.

She also decided that if her daughter was suffering from stress-induced hallucinations, it might be a good idea to get her some help. She would talk to Eva some more and see if she couldn't convince her to at least speak to a therapist.

Dan stood suddenly, draining the rest of his mug. "Any more questions for me, babe?"

"Nope, that's it for now. Where are you off to in such a hurry?" Normally their rainy day activities included at least an hour of cuddling and coffee drinking before they did anything productive. It was one of her favorite parts about being self-employed—making time to be with her family.

Dan was already in the kitchen, topping up his blasphemous sugary coffee. "I'm going out to the studio to try and conquer that damned vulture once and for all."

When they had first bought the property, they'd converted the old barn next to the house into a workshop. The main room was shared for collaborative projects, and they each had a personal, closed office as well. They had an unwritten rule never to disturb each other's private spaces, which Jacqui appreciated for those times she needed a little solitude.

"I'll make breakfast and bring you some."

"You're an angel."

"Love you!" she called out as the door shut.

She chuckled, sipping her coffee. He'd sure taken off fast. He hadn't even taken the time to grab a shirt, and she'd bet her house he'd gone out in bare feet. Luckily, she knew he had a few sweaters discarded around the studio to wear if he got cold.

Dan had been putting off that silly vulture sculpture for weeks and now suddenly he was all fired up about finishing it. She smiled fondly and shook her head. Her husband was a bit of an enigma at times, but she loved him all the more for it.

Ash flung open the door to their shitty apartment, bracing himself for a confrontation. When he'd hung up the phone, Belial had been lost to a full-blown rage attack. If one was concerned about the preservation of one's life, Bel in a fit of temper was not something one should stick around to see.

So of course, Ash had left Eva's house with all due haste to rush home for the show.

But it wasn't like he had a choice. He hadn't been kidding when he told Raum and Meph to keep Bel from burning the building down. Because he would.

Except, when he stepped inside, he found Bel in the kitchen with his apron on, cooking. Behind him, Meph was sitting at the table, still wearing his workout gear. It was a harmless scene, and yet the tension in the air was so tangible, it crackled like electricity.

Belial looked up. "Asmodeus. Pleased you could join us." His voice was flat. Calm.

Ash blinked. This was not what he'd expected. "What—?"

Meph caught his eye and shook his head rapidly.

Ash looked back at Bel and studied him closer, and then he saw it. Bel was calm, all right. *Too* calm.

Damn. This was almost worse than if he'd been fully raging. This eerie eye-of-the-storm calm was liable to blow at the drop of a hat, and when it did, it would be scary. Humans would not survive it.

Ash caught Meph's eye again and nodded to indicate he got the message. He looked around. "Where's Ra—"

Meph shook his head frantically again.

Bel turned, lowering the spoon. "I don't know, Asmodeus." His tone could freeze an active volcano. "Where *is* our brother Raum?"

Meph winced in the background.

"I don't know." Perhaps a subject change was in order. "So, uh . . . whatcha cooking?" Ash propped a hip up against the kitchen counter and tried to act cool.

"Risotto."

"Looks good."

Bel's hand clenched around the wooden spoon he held. His nostrils flared like an angry bull about to charge. "It will be good. Everything I cook is delicious because I'm a fucking fantastic chef, and if you don't agree with that you can get the *fuck* out of my kitchen before I gut you with this spoon."

Ash held up his hands. "Nope, no arguments here."

Damn it, he had no clue what had set Belial off and, thus, no idea how to fix it. He decided his best course of action was to retreat and try again later.

"I'm going to go take a shower." He spoke like he was talking to a feral animal—slowly and clearly. "I'll be in the bathroom. Not going anywhere else."

Bel's clenched jaw flexed and a vein in his temple bulged, but he said nothing, so Ash slowly backed away, one step at a time. He caught Meph's eye and jerked his chin toward the bathroom.

Once there, he turned on the shower at full blast. He only had to wait a minute for Meph to slip in behind him and shut the door.

"What the fuck is going on?" Ash hissed, careful to speak quietly so the sound of the running water disguised their voices from Belial.

"He's fucking livid, man." Meph shook his head. "I had to dump a full bucket of water on him after you called, and let me tell you, he was not happy about it. He didn't ignite again after that, but he's a powder keg about to blow."

"Why? What set him off?"

Meph dragged his hands through his hair. Of all his brothers, Meph was the only one who would pass for Ash's blood relation if they defined the word "brother" by human terms. Though he kept his hair short, it was the same midnight color, and their skin was roughly the same shade as well. Except on Meph, that skin was so completely covered in tattoos, it might as well have been solid black. He was bulkier in muscle mass than Asmodeus, but shorter in height. They were demons— they were all naturally attractive and fit—but both Meph and Raum were obsessed with working out.

"It's the Hunter," Meph said. "He's onto us."

"I don't believe that. There's no way they'd send him yet."

"Well, you'd better learn to believe it fast because it's true. Bel got word from one of his Hell groupies."

Though Belial had never given any indication he wanted to rule Hell, he'd never lost the support of a bunch of whack-jobs that worshiped the ground he walked on and wanted him to take down Lucifer—the last thing Belial wanted to do.

Bel's days as a purely depraved, violently evil bastard were long over, and these days, he was as confused about who he was as Ash was. As all of them were. It was why they'd decided to escape.

"Shit." Ash dragged a hand down his face. "What did they say?"

"I don't know." Meph leaned against the door and crossed his arms, T-shirt straining at the seams around his shoulders. "Bel went homicidal right after he got the message, and I wasn't going to try talking to him like that. I was too busy disabling the fucking smoke alarms, dumping buckets of water all over the fucking house, and cleaning them up afterward like a fucking maid. Fuck."

"What a mess," Ash agreed.

Meph grinned suddenly. "You smell like sex."

Ash remembered a time when his nose had been sensitive enough to pick up such subtle odors. Ah, the joys of being a demon with properly functioning senses. "Yeah, well, I had a lot of it, so it makes sense."

He couldn't help it. He grinned back.

The meathead punched him in the arm. Hard. "About time, bro."

Ash rolled his eyes. "Yeah."

"You deserve it. Who gives a fuck what the female thinks after."

He realized that unless Bel had told him, Meph didn't know

that Eva could see through his curse. He opened his mouth to tell him but shut it again. Strangely, he didn't feel like talking about Eva with anyone. He figured it was probably because it had been so long since he'd had enjoyable sex, he wanted to avoid the inevitable cross-examination he was going to get when he told his brothers about it.

Meph was still grinning that lopsided smile. "I never understood why you don't just blindfold them. Or do them from behind. No face, just ass. Problem solved."

Ash mentally reaffirmed his decision not to talk about Eva. "Maybe I have higher standards than you. Now get out of here because I actually want to shower before all the hot water's gone."

"What are we going to do about the Hunter?"

"I don't know, but we can start by getting Raum back here."

"I'll call him again. He slunk out somewhere last night and probably got lucky so he's taking his time coming back. Like someone else I know, hey, champ?" Meph punched his shoulder again. "How's it feel to do the walk of shame?"

"It feels like I want to shower without my annoying brother in the room with me."

"Spoilsport."

"Get out of here and find Raum."

"What do we do if Bel loses it again?"

"Same thing as before. Throw water on him. Walk on eggshells."

"I get seriously sick of his shit sometimes."

"At least we're not in Hell. It could be so much worse."

They exchanged knowing looks, remembering how bad Belial's rage attacks could get when his powers weren't dampened as they were on Earth.

"Ain't that the truth," Meph said.

10

HEAD HUNTER

MAYBE THEIR LUCK WAS TURNING, BECAUSE WHEN ASH got out of the shower, Raum had returned, and the worst of Belial's rage seemed to have passed. Ash found everyone in the dining room, eating risotto. Food always had a way of chilling Belial out—a damned miracle.

He remembered the days before Bel had cooking as an outlet for his infamous temper. Nothing and no one could stop it from blowing or calm the storm until it had reached its natural conclusion. It had made him a legend in Hell. He had fan clubs and groupies and even an underworld pub named after him.

But now, he had food. And thanks to food, their apartment building had not burned down. It was a good day.

Ash took the fourth chair and watched his brothers digging in. Raum, the jackass, just shoveled it down and gave no explanations for where he'd been. He sprawled in his chair, the hood of his oversized sweatshirt over his head, the scowl on his face daring them to challenge him.

"You want some?" Bel asked Ash. He was back to his usual self, and no one was going to say a word about it. That was always how they rolled—they'd figured out long ago that if they mentioned the rage, they were flirting with another disaster.

"I'm good."

Flames sparked in Bel's eyes.

"Sure, I'll have some," Ash quickly amended.

"Great." Belial rose to his towering height and went to the kitchen. He returned with a bowl for Ash, and they ate in silence. Bel never expected him to make any comments on the taste of the food—they all knew he didn't taste a thing—but he still expected him to eat.

Belial was weird. He'd stopped questioning it long ago.

"The Hunter is tracking us," Bel said when they had all finished eating. He dropped his spoon in his empty bowl and leaned back in his chair. His size made it look like a seat for toddlers, and the wood creaked ominously under his weight.

"I heard," Ash said cautiously. Bel appeared calm, but he'd been wrong before and the stakes were high. "We're safe in the wards here, though."

"Yes. But not outside the wards."

"Which means we can't leave the apartment," he finished with a sigh, and Bel nodded.

"That's so lame," Meph complained. "I'll go crazy in here."

Bel crossed his arms. "It's either that or get caught."

No one replied because no one wanted that outcome.

"We can't just stay here indefinitely," Ash felt the need to say. "We need a plan."

"I think we should leave Montreal," Bel said. "Half a dozen gargoyles already found us. There's a chance the Hunter knows we're here."

Ash immediately balked at that idea. He wasn't sure why, but he knew he was going to fight with everything he had to stay. It probably had something to do with the decadent little Eva whom he was in no way done indulging in.

"We killed all the gargoyles," he said. "They never got a chance to report."

"We killed the ones we saw. There could have been more we didn't."

"That would imply they were able to spy on us without us knowing. They're not that smart."

Bel frowned. "It's a risk, Asmodeus. I know you like it here, but you have to admit that."

"Yeah, but so is leaving when we've got a safely warded apartment to hide in."

There was a tense pause.

"Fine," Bel finally said. "We'll stay for now. But we need to figure out some further protection so we can go outside. I didn't escape Hell to get trapped in this shithole apartment for all time."

"What we really need is to get our hands on some Nephilim blood," Meph said, putting to words what everyone was already thinking.

Raum scoffed, fidgeting with the end of his spoon where it rested in the empty bowl. "Good luck with that."

"The last time I heard of a readily available source was a century ago," Ash agreed.

"It's still available if you know where to look," Belial said.

"If anyone can get it, it's you, big brother." Meph grinned, and Bel cocked a brow.

"Even if I can get it, it won't be cheap."

"We should be able to afford it, right?" Meph linked his hands behind his head and rocked back on two chair legs. "I mean, we're not broke by any means, though we're sure as hell living like it."

"Sure, we could probably afford it for a while, but what happens when we're out of money and the blood wears off? We're right back where we started."

"We have to take it one step at a time," Ash said. "Right

now, we need a way to leave the apartment safely. Once we figure that out, we can find a more permanent solution." He smiled wickedly. "Maybe we could catch a live Nephilim to keep as a pet."

They all chuckled.

"Can you imagine?" Meph sighed. "Our very own source to use at our leisure? We could go anywhere, do anything. We'd be free."

Bel stood suddenly. "I'll get in touch with my contact now. Don't disturb me unless you want to die." He passed through the kitchen, stooping under the doorframe and heading down the hall. "You can clean the dishes since I fucking cooked!" he called before his bedroom door slammed.

"I did it last time," Meph whined.

"No, you didn't," Raum shot back. "I did."

Ash rolled his eyes. "Neither of you dumbasses did it, because *I* did." He always did the goddamn dishes, and he was the one who couldn't even taste the food. "And I'm not doing it this time, so unless you want Bel to lose his shit again, you can do it together."

Meph and Raum groaned simultaneously.

"I'm going to crash." Ash skirted around the table, grabbing his jacket from the hook by the front door on his way past.

He slammed his bedroom door in a similar fashion to Belial and flopped onto his back on his bed. Pulling out his phone and the little Bluetooth speaker Eva had lent him from his jacket pocket, he connected them and cranked up some Herbie Hancock on the music app she'd downloaded.

He smiled, remembering the horrified look on her face when he'd told her he didn't have a speaker or any way to listen to music. She'd spent half an hour teaching him how to use the damn app, but now, as he listened to Herbie shredding a solo on "Chameleon" in that classic crunchy synth tone, he had to admit it was worth the effort.

Stretching out on the bed, he put his hands behind his head and closed his eyes. It was getting late, the sun had set, and he was tired from lack of sleep the night before. But he didn't drift off.

Instead, he thought about Eva.

He thought about the sex because *duh*. But he also thought about playing music with her. At the club, and then again at her apartment, when she'd caught him playing freely because he thought no one was listening.

She'd picked up her violin and joined in like she'd been there all along, and he'd experienced that feeling like he was flying again. It was fucking enjoyable. There was no denying it.

His eyes popped open, and he grabbed his phone from beside him and punched in her number. Then he stopped, thumb hovering over the call button.

His brother had given him a bunch of bullshit advice on how to make sure he got laid. Compliment her a bit, but not too much. Look interested, but not too much. Make her work for his attention. A bunch of real dickhead moves that, unfortunately, were highly effective for the average modern woman. It was a sad state of affairs out there in the world.

But it was different with Eva. He'd thrown all that advice out the window with her. And yeah, he'd been desperate to get inside her, but strangely, it hadn't been the only thing on his mind. He just . . . enjoyed her company.

And now he wanted to call her. Why? He couldn't see her. He couldn't leave the damn apartment. But he still wanted to talk to her. To hear her voice. Make her laugh.

He cringed. He sounded like a sap.

But that didn't stop him. After putting Herbie on pause and disconnecting the speaker, he hit that call button as decisively as he had before, and he didn't let himself think too deeply about it.

He was a demon. He didn't think too deeply about anything.

It rang a few times, and he was just about to give up when Eva answered. "Ash?"

"Hey."

She hesitated. He mentally kicked himself. Maybe he shouldn't have called after all.

"Hey. I—" She cleared her throat. "I didn't expect to hear from you so soon."

"I know." He dragged his free hand down his face, feeling like an idiot. "You know what, never mind. It's probably not a good time. I'll just—"

"No! No, it's a great time. I'm glad you called."

"Yeah?"

"Yeah. My friend Skye is coming over in a bit, so I have some time to kill until then."

"Oh. Cool." What else should he say? "What did you get up to today?"

"Just . . . dealing with my brothers. Raum fucked off somewhere, which set off Bel, and then I had to calm everybody down. Usual shit."

Eva laughed. "I want to meet your brothers."

"No, you don't."

"I mean, I saw them briefly in the club that night, but I was a little distracted."

"They're tools."

She laughed again. "They're your family. You love them. They're probably awesome."

Ash frowned. What was with her and the whole love thing? Demons couldn't *love*, and the way she kept suggesting he loved his brothers was creepy and, frankly, offensive.

"I guess," he grunted.

"You're funny, Ash. My mom told me I should drill you with questions about your past and try to figure you out."

"You told your mom about me?"

Eva seemed to hesitate. "Is that weird? Maybe I shouldn't have told you that."

"I don't know if it's weird. I don't have a mom."

"I'm sorry."

"For what?"

"That you don't have a mom."

"Why?"

She hesitated again. "Because it's sad. I love my mom. We're really close, and she's always there for me. It's sad to think that you never had that kind of support growing up."

"Oh. Uh." He shifted uncomfortably. "I'm fine. Where I'm from there wasn't really— We didn't exactly have—" Fuck, what was he trying to say here? *In the fiery pits of Hell, there was no place in my dark and somber existence for the nurturing love of a matriarch.* Yeah, that would go over well.

"I had Belial," he said lamely.

"You guys must be close."

"He's a tool."

Eva burst out laughing. "I really want to meet your brothers."

"What did you tell your mom about me?" Ash asked to change the subject.

"I told her I went out with a super hot guy last night. Who was an amazing piano player."

His face felt hot, which was odd. Maybe he should open the window. "Oh."

She chuckled. "Too bold?"

"I don't know."

"You're funny," she said again.

Asmodeus had been called many things throughout his

endless existence as a creature of darkness, but "funny" wasn't one of them.

"My mom thinks I need therapy," Eva blurted. "Oh my god, that's way TMI. Just forget I said that."

"Why?"

"No, seriously—"

"Tell me."

She sighed. "After that shooting at the club. I thought I handled it okay, but I guess I didn't."

Ash frowned. He'd heard of humans having adverse psychological reactions to traumatic stimuli, but he hadn't considered that she'd find what had happened at that nightclub traumatic. No one had died. There hadn't been a single decapitation.

Well, besides that gargoyle, but Eva didn't know that.

"What happened?" he asked.

"I . . . I think I hallucinated some weird shit."

"Oh."

"I shouldn't have told you that," Eva said quickly. "It's just, my mom gave me this huge lecture on how I should be honest because that's the way to build a strong foundation for a relationship— Not saying we have a relationship or anything! Wow, I'm really putting my foot in it here. But she said that since you were there, you might relate to what I'm going through, but really, please forget I said anything—"

"It's okay. I don't know if I can help though. I didn't hallucinate anything."

She laughed weakly. "I figured you didn't. You seem like a pretty unshakeable guy."

"I've seen a lot."

"Yeah?"

"Yeah." No way was he elaborating on that. "So, what did you hallucinate?"

"You're going to think I'm crazy."

"Probably."

"Then I'm definitely not telling you!"

"Crazy is good, Eva. I like crazy." Shit, he really sounded like a sap.

"Yeah?" But her tone had softened, so it was worth it.

"Yeah. So, tell me."

"Don't judge me, okay?"

"Spit it out."

"Fine. Here goes nothing. Remember how you carried me outside?"

"Yeah."

"Well, I could have sworn I saw you get shot first. Like a bunch of times. I even remember seeing blood all over you."

He winced. He had been shot a bunch of times. And there had been blood all over him. But thanks to his curse, he hadn't felt a thing, so he'd been able to ignore it easily. And he wasn't about to explain to Eva that he could get shot a bunch of times in the back and keep running. Then she'd know for sure he wasn't human.

Really, the worst part had been when Meph had picked the bullets out of his back later that night. He'd talked the whole time, and it was annoying as hell.

"Oh. Uh, that's weird," Ash said lamely. "Pretty sure I'd know if I'd been shot."

"Yeah." She snorted. "I doubt you'd have just kept running either."

"Probably not." But now his head was spinning as he tried to recall what had happened. The gargoyle-in-human-form had opened fire on him, so he'd scooped Eva up and gotten the hell out of dodge. He remembered leaping off the bar and walls to clear the crowds of scrambling humans.

Shit. She thought she had hallucinated all that, and he wasn't about to tell her otherwise. Oh well. Humans loved going to therapy. Eva would probably benefit from it some-how. She'd be fine.

"You know," Eva said, "I feel better talking to you about it. I think my mom was right. It's putting my fears to rest."

"That's good."

"Yeah, I mean, can you believe I thought I saw you with giant bat wings?"

Ash jerked upright on the bed.

"I was convinced for days that I'd seen you with wings. And red skin. And big horns. Who *does* that?" She laughed.

His hand clenched around the phone. "What else did you see?" He tried to keep his tone even.

"It was so bizarre. You were a giant, and you had these humongous black wings and so did your brothers. No, except the blond one had angel wings! And then there was an ugly monster thing, like a gargoyle, and you cut its head right off before your brother magically lit it on fire! Cold-blooded murder by beheading and mystical flame. Right before my eyes." She chuckled. "I think I must have passed out from shock and had a really vivid dream."

Asmodeus stared at the wall with his mouth open.

How in the hell had she seen any of that? There should have been no way. Glamor prevented humans from glimpsing the supernatural world. In a high-stress situation or after repeated exposure, yes, it was sometimes possible for them to catch glimpses of something they shouldn't, but not like this.

Maybe Eva would have seen a flash of claws, or a shadow cast by wings on the floor, or the flickering apparition of the gargoyle in her peripherals, but no way should she have been able to witness the entire scene clear as day. No way. There was only one explanation:

Eva had the Sight.

How in the fuck did she have the Sight? What *was* she?

She doesn't know, he realized, and he managed to relax infinitesimally. There was no way she knew what he was, or she'd never have spent five minutes in his presence without trying to perform an exorcism or stab him with a consecrated blade.

So, somehow, she had the Sight without knowing she had it, though it seemed impossible that she wouldn't have seen something in the past and figured out what was happening by now. Supernatural creatures were everywhere.

Perhaps she'd been born with it, he hypothesized, but because she hadn't developed it, her Sight hadn't been triggered until she'd seen something big—like, say, four greater demons and a gargoyle facing off. Maybe she was the descendant of a blood-born witch. That was a reasonable explanation.

Was that why she could see through his curse?

The thought struck him like a lightning bolt to the brain, and his eyes got wide. If so, the implications were enormous. Maybe he could seek out other witch descendants for bed partners from now on and actually enjoy sex again.

The thought was strangely unappealing, which was odd considering the three thousand years he'd spent obsessed with it. But . . . he'd already enjoyed sex again. Sex with Eva. And he wasn't feeling any particular desire for anyone else as long as he could have her.

"Ash? Are you there?"

Shit, this meant he was going to have to be extremely careful around her from now on. *If* he saw her again. He really shouldn't. It was asking for trouble.

If she saw anything else, she would likely refute the conclusion she'd drawn about having hallucinations and question if it was real again. And if that happened, he'd probably have to kill her because she could start blabbing to everyone that she'd met the great Asmodeus, and that would make it a lot easier for the Hunter to find him.

Yeah, so they probably ought to have used fake names like other demons who came to Earth, but whatever. *Sorry, not sorry.*

If all that happened and he had to kill her, he'd be in even bigger shit than he already was for escaping *and* killing an unsanctioned human. Not to mention, he liked Eva and killing her wasn't exactly at the top of the list of things he wanted to do to her. So he should definitely stay away from her.

But the sex, a little voice whispered. *The sex is so good.*

His eyes closed involuntarily just recalling the feeling of sinking into her hot, tight body while she moaned his name, watching him with so much desire in those deep gray eyes.

Fuck no, he wasn't giving that up yet. No way.

"Ash, hellooo?" Eva sighed. "Look, I'm sorry if I freaked you out. My mom told me I should tell you, and I guess I got a little carried away, but—"

"I'm here," he said, shaking his head to get back in the game. "I was thinking."

"About how you wish you'd never met Miss Crazy Pants?"

"No. Just wondering if you're descended from a witch."

"A what?"

"A witch."

"A *witch*?"

"Yeah. You know, maybe it wasn't a random hallucination. Maybe you had a vision."

"A vision? Because I'm descended from a witch?"

"You never know." He wanted Eva to look into her ancestry and figure out why she had the Sight, since it might provide him with some answers about his curse. If someone else in her family was a descendant, he could appear to them and see if they saw through the curse too.

But he wasn't about to tell Eva what she'd seen was real either. This way, he'd planted the idea in her head and made her inquisitive without giving too much away.

"Oh my god, you're as crazy as I am."

"Probably more," Ash agreed, smiling despite himself. Something about Eva made him feel . . . Fuck, he didn't know.

Good. He just felt good. And that was as far as he was going into it. "Ask your mother if you're descended from blood-born witches. You never know."

She laughed. "I never expected you to say that in a million years."

"I'm full of surprises." Still smiling, he lay back down on his bed and hooked his free hand behind his head.

"That you are."

"I keep thinking about fucking you on the piano," he blurted.

She paused. "Me too." Her voice softened, and he instantly got hard. "I don't think I'll ever be able to look at my piano again without thinking about it."

"I want to do it again."

"Damn. Me too."

His thoughts went down the gutter with record speed. "Only this time, I want to sit you on the keys and fuck you while you wrap your legs around me. I wanna hear that sexy ass smash all the notes every time I pound into you."

"Oh my god," she whispered.

His hips rolled involuntarily on the bed at the images springing up in his head, and he decided to go with it. "And when that's done, I'm gonna turn you around again and bend you back over. But this time I'll lift up your foot and put it right on the keys and fuck you nice and hard from behind. I'll hold your leg up so you can't move even though you're going to try to struggle when I hit you so deep. It'll feel so fucking good when you come all over me."

"Oh damn. I'm so turned on now." Eva's heavy breaths fuzzed out the phone speaker.

"Me too."

"My turn."

"For what?"

"To tell you my piano fantasies."

"Fuck, yes. Tell me."

"I want to shove your sexy ass up against the keys, and then I'm going to lick and bite my way down your naked body."

His eyes fell shut. Shit, he couldn't take it. He ripped open his pants, shoved them down, and fisted his cock. "Keep going, Eva."

"And then I'm going to get on my knees."

"Fuck." His strokes got harder.

"And then I'm going to lick you from balls to tip like a popsicle. Mm, you'll taste so good."

His eyes rolled back into his head. He stroked harder. "You're going to make me come if you keep talking like that."

"Are you . . . ?"

"Yes. Keep going."

"Oh my god. Me too. I thought I was being a pervert."

"No. Don't stop, Eva."

"Okay. I'm going to lick my lips and get them nice and wet, and then I'll suck you into my mouth so deep you hit the back of my throat. And then I'll swallow and take you even deeper."

He groaned. He was close already. "Then what?"

"And then I'm going to slide out nice and slow, looking into your eyes the whole time. Damn, I'm close to coming right now just from picturing your big cock in my mouth."

He shuddered.

"You'll taste so good when you come, and I'll drink it all down, and lick off every last drop—"

"Oh fuck, I'm coming." He groaned loud as he came all over his hand and his pants and even his damn shirt.

There was silence in the aftermath, the both of them breathing hard. "Did you come?" he managed to ask, his voice hoarse.

"Yeah."

He pictured her sitting there, talking to him with her hand

in her pants, pleasuring herself. "Damn, Eva, you're so damn sexy."

"When can we enact that fantasy?"

"Soon. I have to stay here for a few days and sort some shit out, but as soon as I can get away, I'm there. I want you to do every single thing you just described to me. That was so hot." He looked down at the mess all over him and groaned. "Except I'm covered in cum now."

"Too bad I'm not there to lick it off you."

"*Eva.*" She was too much. Not enough. Just right. Fucking perfect.

"You're bad, Ash. I can't believe I just had phone sex with you—"

"You did *what?*" someone shouted over the line.

"Oh my god!" There was a lot of rustling and some frantic female voices that he couldn't make out. A moment later, Eva picked up the phone again. "Skye is here. Oh my god, she just walked right in and heard me say that!"

"It's a good thing she didn't arrive any earlier."

"Yeah, no kidding." She chuckled. "Okay, I have to go. Call me tomorrow?"

"Yeah." He wanted to, too. He didn't care if that made him lame or whatever his brothers would call it. He wanted to hear her sultry voice. "I have to go take another shower now. Have fun with your friend."

"Be nice to your brothers."

"Don't count on it."

She chuckled softly. "Okay . . . bye."

"Bye."

Neither of them hung up.

She giggled. It was a soft, feminine sound. It was . . . cute. "Okay, I'm hanging up now. I'm not doing this with you. We're both adults. We can hang up the phone."

"Okay, Eva. Go for it."

"Bye, Ash. Call me when you can."

She hung up on him. He liked that she was decisive. He liked that she didn't try to force a commitment out of him about when he'd see her next. He liked that she'd made him come so hard he saw stars just from talking about sucking him off. She hadn't even touched him, and he'd gone to heaven.

Well, as close as a demon could get, at least.

He couldn't wait to get outside the apartment again.

11

SACRIFICES MUST BE MADE

B ELIAL SAT IN HIS ROOM TAKING CALMING BREATHS. *In, out, in, out. Inner peace. Calm.*
Except none of that meditation shit worked on him because he was a demon. Demons didn't have human souls that they could connect with through meditation and yoga. Thus, all his deep breathing and visualizing did shit all. Actually, it was often detrimental because it frustrated the hell out of him that he couldn't control his fucking temper.

Well, he could control it a *bit*. There'd been a time where the snap of a twig would've set him off. He'd explode, decimating anything and everything in his path like a freaking atom bomb. He was a lot better now, especially since he'd learned how to cook, but he still knew he was a basket case. His brothers knew it too, always tiptoeing around him, careful not to set him off.

The lack of control pissed him off. Angry at himself, he was thus prone to more fits of temper. The vicious cycle continued, on and on throughout the ages.

And now look where he'd ended up. From one of the most feared demons in Hell to a fugitive, questioning his purpose and existence, his mighty powers dampened while he was on the mortal plane.

Here on Earth, he was nothing special. He had a reputation, sure, but that wasn't going to save his or his brothers' asses if Hell caught them. Despite his issues, his brothers looked to him for protection, and he was damn well going to make sure they got it.

That meant summoning the last person in any of the worlds he wanted to speak to.

Bel grabbed all the dirty laundry off the floor and threw it on his bed to clear a spot for the summoning sigil, sketching out the complex design in chalk on the hardwood.

Under normal circumstances, demons couldn't summon other demons. The one advantage clawless, fleshy humanity had over their underworld neighbors was their ability to summon and bind them to their will with Temporal magic. Thankfully, a true summoning was a near-impossible feat for the average human, and it rarely occurred.

Demons used Sheolic magic, however, and it served their own purposes. Wards could be drawn around territories to (mostly) keep out intruders, hellgates could be used for travel, requests could be made for meetings, and more. But the only instance when a demon could be summoned by another against their will was if that demon was bound as part of a bargain.

Such was the case with Bel's summoning today.

After completing the sigil, he lounged on his bed with his back against the wall and waited for his visitor to appear. There was a whole lot of dramatic smoke and gusting wind— thankfully, all sealed within the confines of the sigil—and then *she* appeared.

She rarely disguised her demonic characteristics, and now

was no exception. One of the most legendary demons of all time, she saw no reason not to flaunt her true nature. In Hell and on Earth, she was worshiped and adored, a symbol of seduction.

She was a succubus, one of the Queens of Hell, a sadistic bitch, and . . . Bel's sort-of ex. If the deranged affair they'd once had could be called a relationship. It probably couldn't, but he had no idea how else to define their on-gain, off-again bouts of indulgence and aggression.

"Naiamah," he grumbled, already regretting this.

"Well, hello, Belial. What an unexpected surprise." She grinned from ear to ear, revealing a mouth full of razor-sharp teeth. Not just a pair of cute little vampire fangs, nope. Every single tooth was a pointed weapon that he knew from experience she wouldn't hesitate to use. A pair of wicked horns curled back alongside her skull, and her hair was a shimmering curtain that fell to her waist.

She was clad only in a small strip of leather that hung down the front of her body, secured at her hips with chains fastened to a similar-sized strip down her back. The material flared slightly at her breasts, just enough to cover her nipples, and hung from more chains over her shoulders. Her pale skin was decorated with black tattoos of disturbing images—men being beheaded, monsters disemboweling humans, the usual shit—and she wore a delicate headdress of still more silver chains over her sleek, midnight hair.

She was a raging bitch, and Belial hated her with a burning passion. She was also indescribably hot, and unfortunately for Bel, his dick didn't care whether he hated her or not. It just wanted to fuck her. And it often got its wish.

He had this terrible habit of screwing her every time he saw her, despite the fact that as soon as he was finished, he wanted to punch himself. He always told her he hated her and never wanted to see her again afterward, but she didn't care. In fact, rejecting her had the opposite effect. Naiamah, being a psychopath, adored it and kept coming back for more.

She wasn't desperate by any means—she had harems of demons back in Hell begging to serve her, and entire cults of male human worshipers on Earth who had these nasty masturbation rituals to summon her that she probably reveled in—but she was an attention whore, and she got off on watching his self-loathing increase every time he touched her.

She loved the idea that he couldn't resist her sexual allure despite his apparent disgust. She thought it gave her power over him, and damn if she wasn't right.

The truth was, Naiamah hated him as much as he hated her, and her primary objective in all their interactions was to make him suffer. She was punishing him for something he'd done over a thousand years ago, and for the control he still had over her to this day.

The worst thing was . . . a part of him knew he deserved it. A part of him felt guilty. A part of him might have even wanted to suffer a little.

Naiamah sauntered to the edge of the sigil and cocked a hip. She knew all his weaknesses and how to perfectly exploit them. She knew how to stand so her breasts almost spilled out of her dress, and she knew how to pucker her lips and toss her hair to get a reaction out of him.

And it was working already if the state of his cock was anything to go by. The damn thing betrayed him every time he saw her.

"It's been a while, Belial." Her voice was sultry and soft. Like fingernails on a chalkboard. "You're looking tense. Why don't you come into the circle, and I'll help you relax." She glanced down at his lap and licked her lips. "You know as well as I do that I'm the only one who can soothe your wrath."

In the past, the only thing that had helped him get a hold

on his temper was sex. But not some nice, vanilla human sex. No, he needed some real kinky shit, and Naiamah was always happy to deliver.

But he had cooking now. He loved cooking. He was going to make a six-course meal after this, fit for a King of Hell, if it meant he didn't touch her.

He planned the meal out in his head to distract himself. *For the amuse-bouche, we'll do an herb-infused cream cheese spread on a slice of toasted crostini, garnished with parsley. The soup will be a creamy lobster bisque with a slice of fresh sourdough and aged cheddar on the side. The appetizer will be fried ravioli with—*

"I hope you didn't summon me here just to stare at me," Naiamah drawled. "Though I am flattered by the attention."

"I need Nephilim blood," Bel said, getting straight to the point. The sooner he got this over with, the sooner he could start cooking.

Naiamah blinked. "You're that desperate already? I thought you'd last at least a few months before it came to this."

Belial scowled. "Mishetsumephtai is onto us."

He wasn't worried about Naiamah betraying him. He didn't trust her as far as he could throw her—which would actually be pretty far considering how strong he was and how much he hated her, so maybe that wasn't the best analogy—but she couldn't sell him out even if she wanted to.

Naiamah had needed his help long ago, and he'd trapped her into his service with an open-ended contract that was valid to this day. The Queen of Hell owed him one thousand favors, of any nature, collectable at any time. It had been one of the finest and most ruthless bargains he'd ever struck, but he would have released her from it ages ago if she wasn't so useful. He hated her that much.

Unfortunately, she was too well connected and influential to let go. She had eyes and ears everywhere, and her servants were loyal to the point of groveling. Bel needed her, and he couldn't deny it.

"The Hunter has been sent already?" She scoffed. "Impossible."

"Not impossible. Got word from one of my legions that he's been dispatched."

Naiamah's lips pursed. Lips that were made to be wrapped around a cock. Lips that had been wrapped around his many a time and drove him to distraction just by being in his presence. He could still see the obscene stretch of her mouth as she fought to work her jaw around him, and it sent a pulse of heat down his spine. *Damn her.*

"You trust this source?" she asked.

Bel rolled his eyes. "The informant was from one of my legions that's been plotting to get me back on the throne for forever. I keep telling them to give it up, but they never do. They're dumbasses, but they're loyal, and they have way too much to lose if I'm caught."

"Maybe you *should* plot to take over the throne." Naiamah's eyes lit up. "Lucifer is a useless twat, and everyone knows your power rivals his."

"I'm not interested."

"No, the great and legendary King Belial, whose name is synonymous with evil itself, would rather hide in human form on Earth." She gave him a reproachful look. "How the mighty have fallen."

He shrugged. Once upon a time, he would have roared a mighty roar that shook the foundations of the underworld with his rage at such an insult. Now, he was just wondering what sauce he should use with the ravioli.

Ash had been smart to plot their escape from Hell. None of them belonged there anymore, and it was only a matter of time before they were found out. Running had been the only option.

"So can you get the blood or not?" he asked.

Naiamah looked disappointed that she couldn't get a rise out of him. Maybe the mighty had fallen, but he was glad he had better control now. "Probably. I think Naberius has some, and he owes me a favor."

"I thought his Nephilim was killed a hundred years ago."

"It was, but not before he harvested a lot of blood from it. He's been using it sparingly, selling it for a fortune. I'd hazard to guess there's not much left now. It's going to cost you."

"I can pay."

"It's a temporary solution."

"I know."

"You won't be able to hide forever."

"I'll think of something."

"It's never been done, Belial. Every demon that has ever escaped Hell has been caught in the end. Whether by Heaven or Hell, they're caught."

"Those demons weren't me or Asmodeus."

Naiamah cocked a brow. "Remember Eligos? Even he, the legendary Duke, was found and destroyed mere months after he went rogue."

Bel winced inwardly at the reminder, but still, he refused to doubt himself. "I'm a King, not a Duke. If I get my hands on Mishetsumephtai, he won't survive it."

Naiamah looked unconvinced, but he didn't care. He didn't have the luxury of caring. It was do or die. Or worse than die, considering he wasn't exactly sure what would happen to him anymore if he was destroyed.

Ash was convinced they were no longer one hundred percent demon, which meant the rules didn't apply. Bel didn't like the sound of that at all.

Naiamah cocked her other hip. "I'll ask around, but you know it's going to cost you a favor. You have so few left. Are you sure it's wise?"

"I still have a hundred."

"Ninety-nine," she corrected with a lifted brow.

He stared blandly back at her, but he mentally cursed. She knew how valuable her services were. Over the ages he'd blown through her favors until he'd become reliant on having her assistance available whenever he needed it.

It was another reason why he hated her. He despised being reliant on anyone or anything, and between that and the sex, Naiamah had far too much power over him.

"Of course," she drawled, "I might be persuaded to offer my help in exchange for a favor of my own."

"We're not fucking," he snapped. "I told you, we're done."

Naiamah threw back her head and laughed. "And yet you always come crawling back for more, precious."

That she spoke like Gollum did not make him feel any better.

"No one can satisfy you like I can. No one has what you need. And really, it's a small price to pay for my services."

"I have money to pay for the blood," he growled.

"Oh, the blood will certainly cost you money, in both Hell and Earth currencies, I'm sure. But you have to pay for my retrieval services. I'm offering a compromise so you can hold on to that one-hundredth favor for another time."

"It's not happening."

Naiamah turned around, revealing an ass too perfect for words. Thick and full, the flesh jiggled slightly when she moved, and his mouth went dry. More blood rushed to his cock, and he dropped a hand over it so she didn't see him make a tent out of his fucking pants.

"Most males offer *me* favors to get a piece of this," she purred. "And I refuse them."

She spread her legs a little, braced her hands on her thighs, and then twerked that masterpiece at him like a girl at a nightclub. The tiny strip of leather barely covered her slit. A breeze could lift it and he'd see everything.

He groaned, dropping his head back until it thumped against the wall.

"You know you want me," she said over one shoulder, rolling her hips in a circle now.

"Fuck you."

"That's what I'm asking for, precious."

That was the problem with this damned succubus. She always wanted it, but it left him drained and feeling like shit afterward. He despised letting Naiamah feed off him, but he'd done it enough that she was obsessed with the taste of his energy now. As a fallen angel and one of the oldest, most powerful demons in existence, his essence probably gave her an unparalleled high.

And she was right, in a way—asking him to bang her in exchange for her retrieval services was far from the worst form of payment, especially if it meant keeping one of his precious favors. But he hated going back on his word, and he'd sworn to himself he'd never touch her again.

Amazing the powers females had. Whether a lowly human or a legendary succubus, every male in existence was only one conniving woman away from becoming a self-loathing piece of shit.

"Come on, Belial," she cooed. "No one fills me up like you do. No one tastes as good as you. All that power and rage." She moaned like she was going to come from thinking about it.

He groaned again. "Go fuck Lucifer if you want power."

"Lucifer has a pencil dick."

He had to laugh. Lucifer was the most powerful demon in Hell. Even if he did have a pencil dick, he could have done something to fix the problem. But Naiamah had always hated him with a burning passion and wouldn't go near him.

She rose and faced Bel again, crossing her arms over her chest, which only served to push her breasts together. He wanted to slide his cock between them and come all over her chest.

Fuck.

"Give me what I want, and I'll track down your Nephilim blood," she said, the light of victory already shining in her eyes. "Your precious brothers will be safe. Think what will happen if they're caught, Belial. They'll be tortured and destroyed. You have to protect them, and to do that, you need to keep your favors."

Bel closed his eyes. He'd probably be willing to risk it if he was just worrying about himself, but he had his brothers to think about too.

She knew exactly what buttons to push to manipulate him. He was changing, becoming something less and less demonic, and he shouldn't have been able to care about his brothers the way he did. But he did care, and Naiamah knew it, and she wasn't above using it to get what she wanted.

Worse, he wanted to give it to her. He wanted it so fucking bad.

He couldn't seek the sources for the Nephilim blood himself either. Naiamah was bound by their old bargain not to betray him, and besides his legions—who weren't powerful or connected enough to be able to get what he needed—there wasn't anyone else in Hell with that kind of reliability. It was her or no one.

"Fine," he said, sighing with resignation while his cock jerked with excitement. "But I'm binding you to this with a contract. We fuck, I get the blood."

A triumphant smile split her perfect face. "Fine. But the blood will cost you, and I'm not paying. I'm only finding you a source."

"Fine."

"Let me out of the sigil, and we'll play on your bed. You said your apartment is warded. No one will find me."

"No. We fuck in the circle. I don't trust you not to try to escape."

Her lip curled. "As if I'd want to linger any longer than I have to on your precious Earth. Humans are dirty little things, and I hate having them near me. No, it's only you and your brothers who actually *want* to be here, though for the life of me I can't fathom why."

Like Naiamah, most demons of the Order of Thrones were uninterested in the human realm, where their powers were muted and they were forced to abide by strict rules. In Hell, they could rule their territories as they preferred and revel in the blood and chaos.

Kings and Queens of Hell were responsible for authorizing visits and rarely had cause to go to Earth themselves. They sent others on special missions to coerce humans susceptible to evil, the goal always being to thwart the opposing efforts of their angelic nemeses.

It was boring as, well, Hell.

What was the point in all that good-versus-evil bullshit? Why bother at all? Why not live their lives doing what they enjoyed and leave others to do the same?

That was all Belial wanted. And, being a King of Hell himself, it had been relatively simple for him to secure himself and his brothers their one-way ticket to freedom. The hard part was making sure they stayed free. Sacrifices would have to be made.

Starting with the recanting of his vow not to touch Naiamah again.

It shouldn't have mattered to him. Demons weren't supposed to be capable of keeping that kind of vow in the first place. He was so messed up, and this shit was too complicated to dwell on. He'd need a PhD in psychology to even begin to understand the wars that were being waged inside his head.

Which he could actually get if he got the damned Nephilim

blood and then found a way to permanently secure his and his brothers' freedom on Earth.

Belial climbed off the bed and rose to his full height. "Turn around. Don't look at me or I'll gouge your eyes out. Don't touch me or I'll rip your arms off."

Naiamah moaned like his threats were as good as foreplay, and she immediately complied.

He closed his eyes and took a breath, skin already crawling with self-hatred, though his blood pumped with arousal. Thank fuck he'd put a sound-sealing sigil on the door so his brothers wouldn't hear what he was doing.

Oh, the things I do for this family.

12

SOMETHING SMELLS FISHY

ROUGHLY FIVE THOUSAND KILOMETERS AWAY ON Vancouver Island, in the private office of his art studio, Dan Gregory cursed a blue streak. Cursing some more, he grabbed the eraser and wiped the series of complex chalk sigils off the blackboard and then slammed the decaying grimoire shut. A cloud of dust blew out from the pages.

It had been a week since Jacqui had sprung those four names on him out of the blue, and he'd been performing tracking sigils with dogged determination every spare moment since.

The results were clear. They didn't make a lick of sense, but they were clear.

It only gave him more questions. Where had Jacqui gotten those names? His beautiful wife had told him she "must have read them somewhere." She was lying. It was too great a coincidence that she would hear those four names in particular, and then he would get these bizarre results. Not that Jacqui knew the real reason he'd hurried out to the studio that day, or any of the secrets he'd kept from her throughout their lives together.

She'd lied to him last week, but he'd been lying to her for twenty-seven years.

He hadn't, however, made up any of what he'd told Jacqui about those four demons that day. He'd just downplayed it a bit. What he hadn't told his wife was that this wasn't the first time he'd heard mention of these four demons together, though he didn't understand why.

Demons didn't have friends. They were demons. But some connection existed between them, and his wife had somehow pulled their four names out of a hat.

And coincidentally, all four of them were missing from Hell.

The tracking sigils were clear. A successful result would tell him what realm the demons were currently in and, if he added a few extra details to the designs, tell him where precisely in those realms they were. They were no ordinary sigils and they'd come from no ordinary grimoire. They were ancient and powerful and unknown to all save for a secret sect of protectors that had been guarding Earth from demonic influences since the dawn of time.

Dan was certain the demons weren't in Hell. That much was clear. There could be no doubt that Belial, Asmodeus, Mephistopheles, and Raum were all loose on Earth at this very moment. If that wasn't frightening enough, Dan had been completely unsuccessful at pinning down *where* on Earth they were.

The only conclusion he could draw was that the demons were hiding behind wards or, god forbid, had somehow found a new source of Nephilim blood—a possibility that scared the hell out of him. But it made no damn sense.

Why would a King of Hell come to Earth and then hide?

He was a King of Hell. If he came to Earth, he came to make himself known. What would he have to hide from?

Dan didn't know, but after a week of getting the same inconclusive results, he realized that he needed answers. He had a bad feeling, and it was getting worse with every passing day. If Jacqui hadn't asked him herself about those four names, he'd have been happy to let it go. He was retired, after all. He wasn't supposed to concern himself with this anymore.

But she had, and she'd clearly lied about why she wanted to know. At the very least, he needed to make sure she wasn't somehow involved in something she shouldn't be. He had to make sure she hadn't inadvertently put herself in danger.

It was time to talk to her, though he was hoping he could get the information he needed without giving himself away.

He remembered what Jacqui had told him of the advice she'd given Eva. *If you want a real relationship, it has to be built on trust. If the foundation is weak, the structure will fall.* It made him feel sick to his stomach.

He'd been lying to his wife from the day they'd met. With every passing year, it grew harder to keep doing it, but it never stopped being impossible for him to tell her the truth. Now he feared his chance for honesty had long passed.

If she ever found out, she would never forgive him.

The following Thursday, Eva hid behind a corner in an alley and tried to gather her nerves. She'd been talking to Ash on the phone every night, but she hadn't seen him in a week. And now, he was going to be waiting for her outside Bootleg, and her heart was racing.

She had it bad, it was undeniable.

But how could she not? She'd never had more chemistry with another person. Conversation flowed so naturally between them. Sometimes they talked for hours without noticing how much time had passed. He was a great listener, and he seemed to be interested in all the same things she was.

All week, they'd talked about music and shared their influences. They'd had more phone sex. She'd told him about her artist parents, and he'd told her about his out-of-control brothers. And she'd finally convinced him to meet her at Bootleg again tonight.

Apparently, he'd been working with his brothers on something important, though he'd been vague on what it was, and they had been successful after a week of hard work. Ash had admitted he wanted a night out, and she'd convinced him to come jam.

Unfortunately for him, he'd called a few hours ago and told her that when he'd explained to his brothers where he was going, they had all insisted on coming along. He'd sounded pissed, but Eva was kind of excited. She wanted to meet them properly. She'd certainly heard enough about them to be curious.

So here she was with her back against the brick wall, knowing that when she stepped around the corner, Ash and his brothers would be waiting outside the club. She was nervous. She couldn't help it. She'd never been this hung up on a guy before, and though she told herself it was too early for it to be serious, she couldn't help fantasizing about what kind of future they could build together.

Heart fluttering, she psyched herself up for the big reveal and peeked around the corner. There they were. Four brothers hanging outside the club entrance. She watched them, thankful they hadn't seen her yet.

Ash took her breath away even though he was smoking a cigarette. He leaned against the brick wall, boots crossed at the ankles, gorgeous hair spilling all over his leather-clad shoulders. Good god, it shouldn't have been possible for a man to be that attractive.

She stared at his brothers next, and her eyes bugged. Where the hell had these guys come from? She couldn't wait to see Skye's expression when they came upstairs.

The huge, tall one who must be Belial looked like a Greek god come to life. He was built like a football player and the size of a small mountain. He had to be seven feet tall and towered over everyone, even Ash. Clad in a white T-shirt and jeans, his short, platinum-blond hair fell onto his forehead with that perfect, messy look like he'd just rolled out of bed.

Beside him stood the other black-haired brother, Meph. It was hard to notice anything about him except the tattoos. They covered every available inch of his body, spilling over onto the left side of his face, and he had piercings in his lip, the center of his nose, his ears, and one eyebrow. It certainly gave him an intimidating appearance, yet despite that, he had a big lopsided grin plastered across his face that was strangely endearing.

He was the shortest of the four but made up for it by being a freaking bodybuilder. His arms went beyond jacked into legend territory. She could see the veins bulging and individual tendons of muscles from there. He wore baggy workout sweats and Nike high-tops—definitely a gym rat.

And his favorite gym buddy was probably the fourth brother, Raum. He had dark skin and hair trimmed to the scalp. A thin line of facial hair traced his upper lip and chin, and he was as obscenely jacked as Meph. His eyes were a brilliant and unusual gold, bright enough to notice from a distance. She'd never known eyes could be that color. The somewhat broody look on his face told Eva he wasn't one to smile often.

Compared to them, Ash almost looked normal, she thought with an inward chuckle. Unfortunately, her stalker routine hadn't calmed her nerves. If anything, it was worse. She wanted Ash's brothers to like her. He'd said over and over that they were jerks, but they were obviously still important to him.

She told herself to woman up. She knew she looked hot. She'd put on her favorite gold cowl-neck top and a pair of hoop earrings to match. Her curls were piled in a messy bun on top of her head. Black leggings and scuffed-up Dr. Martens completed the look. She was pretty sure Ash wasn't going to give a damn about her clothes anyway. If he was thinking anything like she was, he'd only be concerned with how soon he could get her out of them.

She took a breath and stepped confidently around the corner, striding toward the brothers as if she hadn't been lurking in the alley like a creep. They all stopped what they were doing and stared at her. Ash had frozen with his cigarette halfway to his lips, and she could see his eyes darken into that hungry look she'd been missing all week.

She stopped beside him and smiled. Her lady parts were clenching just from the sight of him, which was embarrassing because his brothers were all grinning at her like they knew exactly what she was thinking. She did her best to ignore them and looked at Ash. "Hey."

"Hey."

When he smiled, it was breathtaking. He held her gaze, and the rest of the world fell away. A bomb could have gone off and she wouldn't have noticed.

Damn, she was falling fast, and it was terrifying. She wanted to say all this cringey stuff like *I missed you* and *I thought about you all week*, but she held her tongue.

"Well, hello," said another voice, reminding her they weren't alone. "I'm Meph."

He stuck out a tattooed hand—even his palm was covered—and when she shook it, he bowed low and kissed the back of her hand, which looked odd coming from a guy who looked like he was on his way to a gang meet.

"It's an honor to meet the mysterious woman who's

interested in poor old Asmodeus here." He straightened, released her hand, and eyed her suspiciously. "Tell me, why did you seek out the ugliest, most boring man in all the world? Self-torture, perhaps? A healthy dose of guilt means you don't believe you're worthy of having a sexual partner you're actually attracted to?"

Eva's mouth dropped open.

"Meph, shut the fuck up," Belial growled.

Ash looked like he wanted to stab the lit end of his cigarette into Meph's eye. She wouldn't have blamed him if he did. Hell, she might have helped hold him still.

She planted her hands on her hips and got good and pissed. Ash had warned her his brothers were tools. *Guess I should have believed him.*

"First of all, it's none of your damn business who I want to sleep with or why, asshole. And secondly, Ash is ten times hotter than you could ever dream of being, so I suggest you look in the mirror before you go calling him boring and ugly."

It wasn't completely true. Meph was undeniably gorgeous if one wasn't put off by all the ink and piercings, but he needed to be taken down a notch, and she was full of righteous indignation on Ash's behalf.

"Oh, snap," Raum said.

"Meph, she can see him," Belial said.

See him? What the hell was he on about? And had she thought Ash was weird? Because he had nothing on his brothers.

Meph's retort died before he got a chance to begin it. He looked up at Belial. "Wait, what?"

"She can see through his . . . you know."

See through his what?

Meph stared at Eva with his mouth open. Raum stepped beside him and did the same. She felt like a bug under a microscope. "But how?"

"I don't know," Ash said through gritted teeth, "but can we not talk about this right now?"

"Are you a closet lesbian?" Meph asked.

Eva sputtered indignantly. "Excuse me?"

"It's a valid question! The only people who see Asmodeus are people who aren't attracted to him sexually."

"What the hell are you guys smoking?" she snapped. "*See* him? He's standing right there! And no, I'm not a lesbian, not that it's any of your damned business!"

"Are you sure?"

"Yes! Trust me, I'm sure."

"How can you be certain? Have you—"

"Yes, okay? In high school. I experimented. It was fun, but not for me. I like men. I like dicks." She huffed. "Unfortunately for me."

All four of them were grinning at her now.

She threw up her arms in disgust and glared at Ash's brothers. "You guys think so little of your own brother that you assume I'm a freaking lesbian rather than consider that I'm actually attracted to him? What the hell's wrong with you?"

Belial dragged his fingers through his pale hair. "It's not like that."

"It's the opposite," Meph agreed quickly. "We think very highly of Asmodeus. We know he's real hot stuff, right Ash?"

"Shut the fuck up," Ash said, dragging hard on his cigarette.

"We're just making sure you want him for the right reasons, that's all."

"He's sensitive," Raum agreed, his teasing words belying the perma-scowl on his face. "We don't want you to hurt his feelings."

"I will kill you all slowly and painfully," Ash growled.

Some of Eva's anger dissipated. They were just looking out for their brother, though they had a messed up way of showing it. "You guys remind me of my dad," she said, rolling her eyes. "He used to drill all my dates with questions until they cracked under the pressure."

"Hear that, Ash?" Meph punched Ash in the arm, earning him another glare. "Think of us as your dads."

Ash recoiled. "No."

"Too far," Belial agreed. He shook his head and looked down at Eva. Way down, because he was so tall. He had one of those super masculine faces, with a jaw that could cut steel and a long, straight nose. His eyes were bluer than the sky on a clear day, and she'd never seen such light-blond hair. Skye was going to die when she saw him.

"Let's start again." He stuck out a palm. "Bel."

Eva shook it. His huge hand swallowed hers completely. "Eva."

She tried not to cower under his direct stare. There was something incredibly intimidating about him, more than just his size and attractiveness. Tension vibrated from him even though he looked relaxed, and she got the sense making this man angry would be a fatal mistake.

He released her hand and gestured to the other two brothers. "Birdbrain there is Meph, and that idiot is Raum. Just ignore everything they say. I do."

"Nice to meet you," she said.

Meph was back to grinning again. She hadn't noticed before but his irises were red. *Red.* How the hell was that possible?

"Let's go inside," Ash said, tossing his cigarette onto the curb. She winced. She'd been raised to respect the environment and couldn't stand littering.

"Did you know a cigarette filter can take up to ten years to disintegrate?" she asked sweetly.

Meph laughed loudly.

Ash looked at the butt and then back at her with a blank expression. She sighed. They'd have to work on that later.

"Never mind." She grabbed his hand. "Let's go play some music."

Upstairs was, as usual, packed. Standing room only, back to front, as it always was on Thursday nights. It was going to be an effort just to make it to the bar.

"You guys want drinks?" she shouted, and the brothers nodded at her as if she was asking them if they, too, breathed oxygen. Keeping hold of Ash's hand, she led the strange siblings through the throng of tightly packed bodies toward the bar.

Her guests were already attracting stares, especially Bel, who loomed over every single person in the club. She had never seen a guy so big before. Most people as tall as him had the whole willowy thing going on, but not Belial. He was as broad as he was high. The guy was a walking Everest.

And judging by the expression on Skye's face as they approached the bar, he was making an impression on her too.

"Hey!" Eva called to her friend from across the counter.

Skye had frozen halfway through polishing a glass. "*Who* is that?" she whispered like she was being blessed with a heavenly visitation.

Eva was more excited to show off her own date. "Skye, meet Ash."

She turned to the man still holding her hand. Their eyes met, and her stomach flipped at the instant connection. Man, their chemistry was off the charts.

"Ash, this is my best friend, Skye. She's the one I told you about."

He nodded at Skye but said nothing. She could tell he wasn't used to socializing much, and didn't blame him for being shy, considering the circumstances. The bar was packed and loud and not the best place for making new friends.

Eva looked back at Skye, waiting for her friend's inevitable reaction to witnessing firsthand the level of sexiness that was currently holding her hand.

Except . . . Skye's gaze traveled right over him like he wasn't even there. "Yeah, hi," she said blandly.

Eva blinked. After she'd told Skye about Ash, her friend had been almost more excited than Eva was to meet him, so why was she acting like this?

"This is the guy I told you about," Eva said, giving her friend a pointed look.

Skye frowned and glanced disinterestedly back at Ash. "Him?" She seemed confused.

Eva frowned. First his brothers had implied she couldn't be attracted to him, and now Skye was glazing over when she looked at him. Skye loved gawking at hot guys. This was so unlike her, it was like Eva wasn't talking to her best friend. Was this some kind of mean joke?

She glanced over at Bel, Meph, and Raum, who had already found a group of women to flirt with. They hadn't been near the bar yet. There was no way they could have orchestrated this.

She looked back at Ash to see if he looked hurt or pissed, but he seemed fine. "What's wrong?" he asked, reading her confused expression.

"Skye is being weird. She was so excited to meet you, and I don't know what's gotten into her." Maybe it was embarrassing to admit she'd been talking him up to her friend, but she felt bad, damn it.

"Don't worry about it. Let's get a drink and a table. I want to sit where we did last week so we can see the stage."

She glanced over the crowd and saw their spot was open. "You go hold the seats. I'll get us drinks."

He bent suddenly, planting a kiss on her lips that had her wanting to abandon their jamming plans and take him straight back to her place. When he pulled back, she could tell by the look in his eyes that he was having the same thoughts.

The only reason she held off was because she wanted to encourage him to play music. He was so talented, and she wanted him to overcome his reluctance to play in front of others. "Go get that table. I'll meet you there."

He nodded and released her, melting into the crowd. She watched him go, frowning as she noticed how nobody seemed to be aware of him. A few guys in the crowd stepped back warily, but not one female head turned.

Look at him! she wanted to scream at all of them. *Are you all freaking blind?*

She stepped up to the bar, waved Skye back over, and ordered two beers. "What is up with you?" she snapped at her best friend while she filled the drinks from the tap. "You were dying to meet Ash all week, and you barely looked at him."

"Forget him, who are *they?*" She was gawking at his brothers again.

"His brothers," Eva growled.

"His brothers?" Skye's mouth dropped open. "Girl, why the hell are you dating him when his brothers look like that?"

Eva's mouth dropped open too. "Are you freaking kidding me? You did not just say that!"

"The tall one is what I fantasize about at night with my vibrator! I have never seen a man that size before. I didn't know guys could actually look like that!"

"They're all players," Eva snapped, pissed at Skye for reasons she couldn't properly identify. "They're all the kind of assholes who will sleep with you and never call again. The reason you swore off guys, remember?"

"I don't even care," Skye said, still drooling over the sight of Bel's broad back. "He can never call me again all he wants if it means I get a taste of that."

"Ugh." Eva snatched up their drinks. "I'm going to find Ash."

"Tell his brother to come talk to me!"

Eva grumbled as she wound her way through the crowd and found her date sitting at their table. She passed him his drink, and they sipped them in silence while she tried to shake off her irrational anger.

"Eva, don't worry about it," Ash said, accurately reading her mood. "I get it all the time."

"How? I mean, I'm not blind. I know you're not ugly or boring. Why did your brothers think that?"

He shifted on his seat. "I guess I kind of . . . blend in."

"You don't *blend* in!" How could anyone ever say that about him?

"I really don't care, Eva. Trust me, I'm used to it. I came here to play music with you. You spent all week talking me into it, remember?"

"You're right, I'm sorry. I don't know why I'm making such a big deal out of this. I don't even know what I'm making a big deal *of*." Catching sight of the guitarist on stage, Tim, who was in charge of the rotating lineup, she took a final gulp of her drink and stood. "Let's see if I can get us up to jam for the next set."

A few minutes later, she returned to the table, grabbed her flute from her bag, and yanked Ash up by the hand. "Come on, we're up!"

They went together onto the stage, poor Ash looking like he'd rather be anywhere else. The other people in the band were friends of Eva's and welcomed him with friendly handshakes. She had vouched for him as a musician, so they had no concerns about letting him come up.

The band members were mostly Francophone, and she experienced a moment of amazement when Ash switched to flawless French to communicate. He'd said he wasn't from here, so she'd assumed he didn't speak French at all. How had he learned to speak so fluently? And where *was* he from, anyway? She realized now that she'd never actually gotten a straight answer when she'd asked last time.

A moment later, however, she quickly forgot all that when Tim started the jam, firing off a few tasty chords on his guitar before the rest of the band joined in.

Unsurprisingly, Ash was amazing. He knew just what to add to complement the other players, accentuating his parts when it was his turn and never overshadowing anyone else in the band. The others made room for him to take a solo, and with some hesitancy, he did, and of course, it blew her mind. It blew everyone's mind, judging by the reaction of the crowd.

Eva's anger was quickly replaced with satisfaction. The crowd was riveted, watching his every move, cheering at all the right times. He wasn't boring or invisible to them anymore. And the band loved him too. They jammed together on another two tracks before it was time to switch the lineup.

As Eva climbed off stage, she overheard Tim asking Ash if he wanted to stay up for the next jam as well. He started to decline, but she could tell by the glint in his eye he was riding the high from the music and would keep his butt glued to that piano bench all night if he could.

She raced back up on stage and jumped between him and Tim, effectively cutting him off. "He'd love to stay up for as long as you want him," she interrupted, grinning at Ash when he glared at her.

"What about you?" he asked, melting her heart a little bit.

"Eva, stay up too if you want," Tim offered.

"No, that's okay." She smiled at Ash. "This is your time to shine, baby. Knock 'em dead."

She wanted him to get comfortable with the others without

her there. It was all part of her little scheme to loosen him up and build his musical confidence.

Before he could protest, she darted back off the stage, waving at him from the audience. He shot her a look, but she could tell he was secretly dying to keep playing.

"My work here is done," she said proudly to herself, and then she weaved her way back through the crowd to find Skye.

That was when shit got weird.

Eva hadn't reached the bar yet when Skye started waving frantically at her. "Oh my god, *who* is that piano player?" she exclaimed when Eva reached her.

Eva frowned. "That's Ash. I introduced you earlier, remember?"

Skye laughed. "Yeah right, I'm pretty sure I'd remember if you had introduced me to him. Eva, that guy is a freakin' god. Look at that hair!"

"I know that! You were the one who didn't notice him before!"

"What? You've gotta lock that one down tight, girl."

"Skye, what is going on with you? I literally introduced you an hour ago, and you barely looked at him!"

"Eva, hon, that was *not* the same guy you introduced me to. Pretty sure I'd remember if I'd met him before."

"You *have* met him!"

Skye scoffed, and Eva kept staring at her, beyond confused. A tingly feeling went down her spine, and she spun around to look at Ash up on the stage. She scanned the crowd, gauging their reactions.

It was night and day from before. There was no mistaking it. There was a noticeably strong female presence right up front beside the piano, and they were all craning to get a better look at him. Ash was talking to the others in the band and didn't seem to notice. Eva scanned the crowd and looked for his brothers. Her confusion deepened.

They weren't flirting and messing around anymore. They were standing in a circle, talking suspiciously to each other, looking as confused as she was as they watched Ash on the stage.

Something was going on. Something not normal. Images of bat wings and headless gargoyles flashed through her mind, but that didn't make sense. What could her hallucinations possibly have to do with . . . whatever this was?

FEELING OFF-COLOR

ASMODEUS STAYED UP FOR THREE MORE JAMS. HE couldn't help it. The guitar player and band leader, Tim, kept asking him to stay, and he couldn't refuse. He was having way too much fun. He felt bad for ditching Eva, but she was the one who'd encouraged him to stay up. He hoped she didn't mind.

Finally, after the third set was finished, he called it quits. He needed a drink, and he wanted to find Eva. All the built-up exhilaration from playing music was making him feel high, and he wanted to release into her. Physically. With sex. Lots of sex.

He stood, already looking forward to executing that plan, thinking that Earth was a weird, mostly shitty place, but that there was absolutely no comparison to the good experiences. He'd existed for countless ages in Hell and never felt close to as good as he did now just from jamming with some strangers for a couple hours. Strangers who were all smiling and clapping him on the back as he left the stage.

He made a mental note to thank Eva for encouraging him to come out tonight, since Bel had finally gotten his hands on that Nephilim blood and he'd been looking for the perfect way to celebrate.

He didn't notice anything unusual until he stepped off the stage.

As soon as his foot landed on the floor, a woman approached him. She smiled. Looked him right in the eye. Her hair was brown, her eyes blue. Not black or gray, but brown and blue.

He froze in his tracks.

"Hey." She smiled and twirled a lock of hair around her fingers. There was no mistaking the look in her eyes. "That was amazing."

"Uh—" he croaked, wondering if he'd been knocked unconscious and was having a vivid dream. Smells of beer and bodies and stuffy air assailed him. *Smells.*

"I'm here every week, and I don't think I've seen you before. Are you new here?"

"Yeah." Surely this wasn't really happening.

"I'm Carly."

"Ash."

"That's a cool name."

"Yeah." He scanned the bar, looking for his brothers or Eva, suddenly feeling totally out of his element. Everywhere he looked, he saw colors. There was blue and red and yellow and orange and purple and green and— "If you'll excuse me, I'm looking for someone."

"Oh, sure." She looked disappointed. "See you around?"

"Yeah." He didn't look back as he stepped around her. His heart was beating strangely fast, and it felt uncomfortable.

Another female immediately approached. This one had dark brown skin and a curly black afro. Her shirt was red. She smelled like floral perfume. "Hey, you really made an impression up there!"

This can't be happening. This is not happening. I'm dreaming. "Uh, thanks."

"Where are you from? I've never seen you around before. A lot of us are regulars and you get to know people."

"I'm from . . . somewhere else." He looked over her head, desperate to escape though he didn't understand why. This had been his dream for millennia. Not one but *two* women were hitting on him. Subtly, with class, but he could tell by the look in their eyes that they were interested.

But even stranger, he didn't return that interest in the slightest. He was panicking. It was weird and pathetic, but he wanted nothing more than to get the fuck out of there. He wanted Belial to come up and clear the crowd with his hulky frame so he could escape like a scared little rabbit.

Asmodeus, Prince of Hell, former Prince of Lust, wanted to flee a crowd of human females because they were attracted to him.

If his ass was dragged back to Hell right then, he would surely have found it frozen over.

Another woman approached, wedging herself in front of the girl he was already talking to. "Hey, I'm Mina. You are so talented!" This one was more direct, her gaze openly lustful. Her hair was honey-blond, her eyes brown. He was even more desperate to escape.

He scanned the grounds and finally saw Belial, towering over the people by the bar. His brother was already staring at him, blue eyes wide, looking as confused as Ash felt. Meph and Raum were probably nearby.

"I *love* your hair," Mina gushed. "Can I touch it?" She reached out and grabbed a handful without waiting for permission.

Ash recoiled, which was such a freaking lame reaction to having someone hit on him, but he couldn't help it. It was instinctual. He just didn't want her touching his hair.

"Oh my god, your hair is totally gorgeous," yet another girl cooed. "How long have you been growing it?"

His heart was racing, his breaths shallow and fast. Why the fuck was he reacting like this?

"You really impressed me up there!" another new woman said, fighting her way to the front of the stampede.

He stopped paying attention to the women and tried to catch Belial's eye again, but when he looked back to where he'd been, he saw no sign of his brother. *Fuck.*

Another woman was touching his hair against his will, and he fought the urge to snap or growl or hiss at her. Or better yet, shift into his demon form and roar at all of them until they pissed themselves from fright and left him the fuck alone.

He didn't care if his curse was somehow defective and he wasn't invisible for the first time in as long as he could remember. He didn't want these women.

He just wanted Eva.

She appeared then as if summoned by the realization that he truly wasn't interested in any other female except her. It stunned him. Nearly knocked him on his ass.

His curse was malfunctioning, and all these women wanted him. He could have them, too, probably all at once. That was what his brothers would do. They would turn up their irresistible demon charm and whip them into a sexual frenzy that resulted in the orgy of all orgies. A dozen women all fawning over him, desperate to fuck him.

He'd been the Prince of Lust, for fuck's sake. He'd been a legend. Insatiable.

But he didn't want any of that right now. He didn't want anyone but Eva.

"Hey," she said, fighting her way to his side. Her messy bun of curls was black, her skin a rich brown, complemented by the sparkly gold of her tank top and hoop earrings, a sharp contrast against her light gray eyes. He was oddly glad that her eyes were still gray when the rest of the world was in color. "I was wondering where you were."

He didn't try to hide his relief at seeing her. He did, however, prevent himself from falling at her feet in gratitude for saving him. She accurately interpreted his expression and came right up to him. Winding her arms around his neck, she pressed their bodies tight together and kissed him right in front of all the other women.

He instantly calmed. He stopped with the weak-ass anxiety attack, and his mood backflipped from "freaking out" to "ready to get freaky." He fought the urge to rub against her.

When she pulled back, those sultry gray eyes told him she wouldn't have minded if he did.

"We keep doing this," she said, grinning.

"Doing what?"

"Getting hot and heavy after we jam."

His gaze darkened. "I want you."

"You also look like you want to get away from all these thirsty people." Eva glanced at the retreating women melting back into the crowd.

He didn't know what to say to that. He didn't know what the hell was going on, and he was almost more weirded out by how quickly he'd calmed when Eva showed up.

"They can't have you," she purred, "because you're mine."

He fought the urge to grab her ass and failed. And once he grabbed it, he chastised himself for fighting it in the first place. Such an ass should never *not* be grabbed.

"You want to get out of here?" she asked, a smile curving those luscious lips.

"Yeah, I do."

"Thank god because I've been dying to get you back to my place. I want to make love to you nice and slow, all night long."

He laughed. "Why do I feel like our roles have reversed all of a sudden?"

She fluttered her lashes. "What's the matter, baby? Not used to seeing a woman in her power?" She gestured up and down her curvy little body, encouraging his gaze to land on the cleavage showing between the loose fabric of her shirt. "Can you handle all this?"

"Oh, I can handle it. I'll show you how I *handle* you as soon as we get out of here."

"Yep, we're going. Right now."

She grabbed his hand and pulled him through the crowd, but they ran into Belial. *Bit late, asshole.* Ash would feel embarrassed at how poorly he'd handled the horny women later. He wasn't worried about forgetting that particular shame because he'd bet all the gold he had that Meph was never going to get tired of making fun of him for it.

"What the fuck is going on?" Bel hissed. He was trying to keep his voice down so Eva didn't overhear, but Ash knew she was listening close to every word. "The women—"

"I have no idea. But I'm leaving with Eva."

Belial glanced at her and then back at Ash. "You want her?"

"Yeah."

"*Just* her?"

"Yes, asshole." He lowered his voice and hissed, "She's also standing right there so try not to be such a dick."

"Look around you. There's—"

"I know, okay? I don't know what's going on but I'm leaving with Eva. We'll talk tomorrow."

Belial nodded and clapped him on the shoulder with a big hand. "You're a rock star, baby bro."

"Not your baby bro," Asmodeus growled. His ego was never going to recover from this night.

Bel grinned. "I never knew you were such a good musician. Why don't you ever play?"

"What, like I was going to take up piano lessons in Hell? That'd go over well."

Bel arched a brow, and he realized his slipup. *Shit.*

"I'm leaving. See you tomorrow." He turned and fled with Eva before he made things any worse.

Ash planned all sorts of fast, frantic fucking scenarios in his head as he and Eva walked back to her place, but when the time came, the mood was . . . different.

She closed the door to her apartment, and they went into her bedroom without saying a word. He watched hungrily as she stripped out of her clothes just like that. She didn't offer him a drink first, didn't try to chat him up. She just got naked.

She left the sexy hoop earrings on but yanked the tie out of her wild hair, sending all those out-of-control curls spilling over her shoulders. She let him stare for a moment and then said, "Your turn."

Fair was fair, so he ripped his shirt over his head and kicked off his pants, and then tackled her down to the bed. Their naked bodies intertwining, they made out like high school kids who'd just discovered how, with tongues and saliva and all the messy stuff.

"God, I missed you," Eva said. "Is that abnormal behavior?" She chuckled, but he didn't get the joke.

"I don't know, but I feel the same way." Was that him speaking, admitting such mushy crap? He didn't recognize himself anymore. He didn't care right now. He'd thought about her all week, and now she was here.

"Good." She reached between their naked bodies and got a good grip on his cock. He groaned into her mouth, hips rolling.

A lesser man would have been scared of her, he thought, but he was no lesser man. No wonder he didn't want those women at the club. Nothing compared to her.

"I had all these plans of kinky shit I wanted to do to you," he growled as she stroked him, "but right now I just want to feel you."

"Works for me." Releasing him, she scooted across the bed from beneath him, rolling onto her stomach to reach the nightstand. She reached forward and tugged open the drawer, fishing around inside. He hoped it was for a condom, but he was too distracted by the ass in his face to notice anything else. He got a good grip on said ass and then flexed his fingers, loving the way it overfilled his hand. So full and delicious.

He bit her there again. Right on the cheek, nice and hard.

She moaned, which made it even better. Shifting onto his elbows, he spread her cheeks with his palms, ducked his head, and licked right up the center of her, from front to back. The very back. He wasn't shy about it.

Her hips jerked, and she moaned some more. A second later, a condom hit him in the face. "Put that on and get inside me."

He didn't need to be told twice. He donned that latex fucker with lightning speed and crawled over top of her. Using his knees to force her legs apart, he reached back and hefted her hips up, leaning forward and pressing his cock against her entrance. She was soaking wet and ready for him, but she still squeezed him like a fist as he eased inside her.

"Fuck, you're so tight." He pushed in a little more and saw stars.

She spread her legs wider and stuck her ass higher up, her back arching deeply. "More."

"Demanding." He gave her more. Every inch he slid in further was another inch closer to paradise.

And then he was all the way inside her, her body welcoming him like she was made for him. Bracing himself by his hands, he started a slow and steady rocking pace, flexing his ass and tilting his hips to sink deeper. Her eager cries spurred him on.

Something suddenly shifted inside him on a visceral level. He had the urge to turn them to their sides, so he went with it. Wrapping his bottom arm around her so his bicep was her pillow, he lifted her leg up with his other arm and spread her wide open so he could fuck her as deep as possible. Their bodies aligned from top to bottom, her back pressed against his chest.

Her moans were so soft and sweet, it made him feel this crushing sensation in his chest. And when she tipped her head back, he trailed kisses along her throat and jaw. Asmodeus didn't trail kisses on throats and jaws. And yet, for her, he did. He was pretty sure he'd do fucking anything for her.

Eva turned her head some more, so he kissed her lips. She tasted amazing. She felt even better. He wanted to drown in it. He continued to fuck her nice and slow, all the while thinking he'd never felt anything as incredible as this. He could stay in this moment forever.

He collared his hand around her throat, but not to choke her. Just to hold her against him in a way that told her she was his. Because she *was* his. Right now, she fucking belonged to him, and he would rip the heads off and the guts out of anyone who said otherwise.

Her inner muscles fluttered around his cock like the world's best massage, and he knew she was close, so he released her leg and slid his fingers between the folds of her pussy, rubbing her tight little clit with just the right amount of pressure. She moaned against his lips and was coming a moment later, and *damn*, the clenching of her muscles around him felt way too good.

He fucked her faster, working his hips so he bottomed out with every hard thrust, and then the little minx reached down, lifted her leg again, and got a vice grip on his balls.

It was the last thing he'd expected after all the touchy-feely shit, and it sent him flying over the edge. He moaned louder than he usually did as the climax smashed into him like a two-by-four to the brain.

His hips kept rolling as he finished coming like they were loath to accept the sex was over. *We'll go again soon*, he promised them. It wasn't even one o'clock in the morning yet, and he had plans to keep her up all night.

Eva reached back to thread her hand through his hair, and they kissed lazily. "That was so good," she purred, and he wanted to beat his chest like a gorilla. "You feel so good, Ash. I don't want you to pull out."

He didn't either. "I have to throw this thing away, but I'll be right back."

"Mm." Her eyes were closed. She looked so relaxed and trusting, lying there in his arms. It made his chest ache and his stomach feel light and fluttery.

Fuck, she was so beautiful. Soft and warm and indescribably inviting, yet fierce and fiery when she needed to be. She was incredible, and he was completely entranced. He fought the urge to crush her against his chest, suddenly afraid someone might try to take her away from him.

Promising himself he would find her if they did, he shook his head at his bizarre thoughts and then pulled out and climbed off the bed. He hit the bathroom to toss the condom and then heard the sound of Beethoven's Fifth symphony coming from the kitchen. "Eva, what—?"

"That's my phone. Hold on, I'll get it."

He came out of the bathroom just as she walked by, and she gave him a long look up and down his naked body. He lounged against the doorframe and checked her out right back, unable to suppress his satisfied grin. He suddenly hoped he'd left a bite mark on her ass.

"Meet me back in bed," she said. "I'm not finished with you yet."

He cocked a brow. "Demanding."

"You know it." Grinning back at him, she walked past to the kitchen.

His smile broadened when he saw her ass. There *was* a bite mark. He was going to add a matching one to the other cheek.

Eva fished the phone out of her bag and groaned when she saw the caller ID. It was one o'clock in the morning. Why was her *dad* calling her? Well, it was only ten where he was, but still. He knew about the time difference.

She muted the ringer and let it go through to voicemail. She loved her dad, but she was not talking to him when she had a naked man in her bed. Just no.

Except it immediately rang again. And then she noticed her notifications. She had ten missed texts from him too, all saying, "CALL ME RIGHT NOW." He'd even used periods. That meant it was really serious.

She groaned again and answered the call. "Dad, it's one o'clock here. What if I was sleeping?"

"I know you don't go to sleep that early. You're a musician."

"Still, now isn't a good time. Can I call you in the morning?"

"Your mom told me about the guy you've been seeing. I had to interrogate her to get her to admit where she got those four names from, but she finally caved. I wish you'd told me."

She blinked, speechless. That was what this was about? She couldn't believe he was calling her at one in the morning to ream her out over a guy.

"Look, honey, I need you to promise me you won't see him or any of his brothers again."

"Yeah, that's not happening."

"Eva, this is serious. You're in danger."

"Why? Because he has a funny name? Or because I had a stress-induced hallucination and you think I need therapy?"

"What? A hallucination of what?"

Oh. Apparently, Jacqui hadn't told him everything after all. She smiled into the dark kitchen. *Way to go, Mom.* "Nothing. Look, can we talk about this tomorrow? It's late and Ash—" She broke off. *Let's not tell Dad that demon-name guy is in my bed right now, shall we?*

But he put it together. "Is he with you right now?" He sounded panicky. "Answer me, Eva. Are you with him right now?"

"Dad, what is with you? Look, I get being protective, but this is going too far. I'm a grown-ass woman, and it's not really your choice who I date. I appreciate your concern, I really do, but now is not the time for this conversation."

"Where are you? Honey, this is important. Please tell me where you are."

She frowned. He sounded really worried. Scared, even, which was so unlike her fierce daddio it wasn't funny. "I'm home, and I'm fine."

"Is he there with you?"

"I'm not answering that! Dad, this is too much. I'm hanging up—"

"I'm coming to you right now. I won't be long. Promise me you won't go anywhere."

"Uh, last I checked it's a five-hour flight, so, sorry, but you can't exactly promise that. Look, Dad, love you lots, but I'm going to hang up the phone now, and we can talk in the morning. Goodnight."

She hung up the phone, put it on silent, and then tossed it back in her bag. She shook her head. Her dad was taking over-protectiveness to an unhealthy degree, and it was embarrassing that Ash had overheard all that. She'd been telling him all week how awesome her parents were, and her dad had gone and blown it, big time.

"Sorry about that," she called out, knowing Ash would hear from the bedroom. "My dad's crazy." She turned to the sink, grabbing the glass she kept beside it and filling it from the tap. "I don't know why he's acting like that."

She heard footsteps creaking the old wood floors as Ash walked up behind her. "He's normally really cool," she said, lowering her voice since she sensed him standing right there. "We actually get along, so I don't know why he—"

A sudden icy sensation trailed down her spine, and she stiffened. Somehow, she just knew.

It wasn't Ash standing behind her.

Suddenly, she was terrified to turn around. And yet she knew she had to.

Slowly, she twisted on her bare feet, lifted her head, and forced herself to look.

She saw the dark shape of a massively tall being, mostly silhouetted by the big wall of windows behind him.

Even in the darkness, there was no mistaking the outline of a pair of enormous wings. Spread wide, arcing above his towering form. Nor was there any missing the set of glowing yellow eyes. No iris or sclera, just yellow all the way across, with vertical slits for pupils.

It opened its mouth. Every tooth was a fang. There were two rows, top and bottom, one after the next of razor-sharp, lethal saw blades made for tearing into flesh like it was butter.

Eva opened her mouth too. And screamed.

LA BELLE ET LA BÊTE

BELIAL HUNCHED ON A FLIMSY BARSTOOL THAT THREAT-ened to collapse under his weight, lost in his thoughts. Currently, the band was between sets, and old-school hip-hop beats were thumping from the speakers while people took the chance to mingle and refill their drinks. That meant bodies were pushing up against him from all sides, invading his personal space and threatening to make his temper snap.

He tried to ignore it, still reeling about what he'd witnessed before Ash had fled. The curse had malfunctioned. Somehow. It had something to do with the music, but he didn't understand how.

Ash had been bound by the angel Raphael after a big-time transgression, and it wasn't like the heavenly prick had stuck around to explain the mechanics of it afterward. The only thing Bel could think of was that since Asmodeus was a demon, and music wasn't exactly a demonic pursuit, something had happened while he was playing to counteract the binding.

They needed to experiment further, figure out what triggered the reversal, because Bel was certain tonight's malfunction was only a temporary reprieve. Most likely, whatever had caused the curse to lift would fade after a short period of time and Ash would be back to his invisible, colorless existence.

They had a month until the dose of Nephilim blood Naiamah found wore off, and Bel planned to spend every spare second that he wasn't searching for more blood—or a more permanent solution—investigating this new loophole in Asmodeus's curse.

He was excited for his brother. He was also stressed as hell because he knew everyone was going to look to him as the provider of all the fucking answers. Answers he didn't have.

Someone stumbled into him with enough force to jar him slightly to one side, and his temper flared. His hands flexed around the bar counter enough to dent the solid wood, and the burn in his eyes told him there were flames flickering in them. He squeezed them shut, taking deep breaths. *In, and out. Inner peace. Inner fucking p—*

Another person bumped him, and he snapped.

He lurched to his feet, stool screeching against the scratched wood floor, spun around, and seized the offending human by his throat. The man took one look at Bel's eyes and tried to scream, except he couldn't because Bel was cutting off his air supply.

The human's friends caught on to what was happening quickly enough, and pretty soon there was a whole lot of "Whoa, whoa, whoa!" and "Calm down, man!" and general commotion. It all faded into a dull roaring at the back of Belial's skull while he wrestled with the urge to burst into flames and send the whole place straight to Hell.

"Let the human go, brother," Raum growled. The shifty bastard had just appeared from nowhere.

Belial's fingers flexed. The humans around him continued to shout and panic, but his rage drowned it out like a river rushing in his ears.

"Just open your fingers and let him go," Raum said, that deep voice the only sound to penetrate the din. "Think about it. You don't want to make a scene here or Ash won't be able to come back and play music."

Asmodeus. The curse. His brothers. With a monumental expulsion of will, Belial forced his fingers to unclench and released the human.

"Yo, what the fuck, man?" someone was saying, trying to step up and get in Bel's face.

The human he'd just let go of stumbled back and then grabbed his friend's arm and shook his head with a panicked expression. The poor bastard had looked into Bel's demon eyes and knew better than to fuck with him. After having his life spared, he likely wanted nothing more than to get out of there.

He had good survival instincts, then.

"S-s-sorry 'bout that," he croaked at Belial without meeting his gaze, and then he dragged his friends back into the crowd.

The remaining bystanders eyed Bel warily, their murmurs lost under the thump of the house music, but eventually, the crowd shifted, and the vibe returned to normal.

"You need to get your shit together," Raum said as Bel swung his head around to pin him with a glare. "If you can't keep yourself from murdering people when we go out, you should stay home."

Belial grunted, turning and sitting his ass back on that goddamn barstool. "People were bumping into me. I didn't like it."

"Then don't come to a packed bar, idiot." Raum glanced around. "Shit, and now I lost Meph. Thanks a lot, dipshit."

Bel glanced over his shoulder to see if he could spot his loose cannon of a brother anywhere and saw nothing but a sea of human faces.

Raum shot him a glare. "I'll go find him. Just . . . stay here. And don't kill anyone." He slipped into the crowd, shaking his head.

Mumbling a curse, Bel spun back around and planted his elbows on the bar, dragging his fingers through his hair and trying to force his mind back to thoughts of Ash's curse and not violence. Raum was right—if he couldn't keep his shit together, he needed to stay home.

"Hey, can I get you a drink?"

The female voice snagged his attention, and he lifted his head to meet the gaze of a human woman standing on the other side of the counter. Her smile was innocent, but her eyes were full of invitation.

Belial lifted a brow. Sweet little thing like her? He'd chew her up, spit her out, and use her bones to pick his teeth after.

Tempting.

"I'm good," he grunted.

He was already having enough trouble getting thoughts of Naiamah's perfect, twerking ass out of his head, and the last thing he needed was to lessen his control with more alcohol. The drink he'd had earlier certainly hadn't helped keep his temper at bay.

"Are you Ash's brother?"

He frowned. "You know him?"

"He's dating my best friend, Eva. She introduced us earlier."

"Oh. Yeah, he's my brother." *Say something flirty if you want to bed her, asshole.*

A million sleazy pickup lines ran through his head, but he didn't have the energy to verbalize them. Instead, he felt this empty feeling in his chest like there was nothing but a vacant pit between his ribs and spine.

"I'm Skye." She reached a hand across the bar, and he shook it.

"Bel."

"*Belle* as in French for beautiful?"

He snorted. "No. Bel as in Belial."

She smiled. "That's a nice name."

His brow lifted. *Go google that shit and see if you still think it's nice, sweetheart.*

"It wouldn't be bad if it meant beautiful, you know." Skye leaned toward him, bracing her forearms on the countertop, offering a fantastic view down the front of her shirt.

"I'm not sure I agree."

She smiled. "It would suit you."

He managed a smirk. The female was smooth. "Are you making a pass at me, Skye?"

"If I was, would you object?"

He tilted his head, considering. He wondered how far he could take things with an innocent little human like this before she ran screaming.

Except then she suddenly straightened and blew out a breath. "I'm sorry. I'm totally leading you on right now and that's not fair."

He had to laugh. "Are you concerned for my virtue? Because I assure you, I have none."

"No, it's just . . ." She winced slightly and blurted, "I swore off guys for six months."

"Really. Why?"

"Because I have no self-control. I love sex. I just . . . love men—and you are, like, the king of sexy men, by the way—but I'm looking for more. And I know that if I'm ever going to find something serious, I need to break this bad habit first, you know?"

He blinked. "I have no idea what you're talking about."

She laughed. "I'm not surprised. I'll put it this way. Have you ever made a promise to yourself not to do something, and then you went and did it anyway, and you felt disgusted with yourself after? And then you promised it again, and broke it again, and kept doing it over and over until finally, you feel like you don't respect yourself anymore?"

Belial stared at her. "I do know that feeling." He'd practically invented that fucking feeling. It was like she'd read his mind.

"Well, I've given it a lot of thought, and I realized that the only way I'm ever going to respect myself is if I stop giving in. I have to put my foot down. I have to strengthen my willpower." Bel leaned way over the counter. He felt like he'd stumbled upon a pot of gold at the end of a rainbow. "So what do you do? How do you strengthen your willpower?"

"Easy. You use it. You refuse to bend. All those promises you keep making to yourself? You keep them. You say no. It doesn't matter what the circumstances are, the answer's always no."

Belial nodded slowly, considering this.

"So, for me," Skye continued, "that means when I say 'no sex for six months,' I literally can't have sex for six months. No exceptions. Even if the sexiest man alive walks into the bar and sits right there on that stool"—she pointed right at Belial and raised a brow—"I still say no. Why? Because I made myself a promise, and there are no take-backs."

"So how do you keep yourself from breaking it? Do you sign a blood— a contract?"

"No, I just choose to keep the promise. Then, I have to avoid temptation and stay away from situations that might tempt me to break it. That's going to be the hardest part for me, but I'm determined."

"I should do this," Belial mused, thinking, yet again, of Naiamah's perfect ass. Only this time, he was reflecting on the aftermath, when he felt strung out and disgusted with himself.

How many times had he sworn to never touch her again? And how many times had he caved and done just that? He hated her, she hated him, and he hated himself too every time he gave her what she wanted.

Bloody hell, he was her whore, wasn't he? Naiamah had made him her whore. He'd never thought of it that way before, but now that he had, he couldn't deny it. He fought down yet another surge of his infamous rage.

He was Belial, King of Hell. Rivaled only by Lucifer himself. He was no one's fucking whore.

Suddenly full of determination, he slammed his fists onto the bar. Skye jumped about a foot into the air and nearly dropped the glass she was polishing. Unfortunately, he used a little too much force, and the solid wood dented under his fists. He flattened his palms over the holes so she wouldn't notice.

"I will do this," he told the startled human. "No women for six months."

No Naiamah for six months, specifically. He'd use up all one hundred of his remaining favors to keep that promise if he had to, because he wasn't touching her.

He supposed he didn't have to swear off all women, but Skye had inspired him. He wanted a fresh start. He wanted to cleanse his palate, as it were.

Since the dawn of time and his infamous fall from Heaven, so long ago he didn't remember it anymore, he didn't think he'd ever gone six months without sex. Ever. So, was he totally delusional for agreeing to this now? Probably. Was it going to be the hardest thing he'd ever done? Likely.

Did he have any clue how he was going to keep his anger under control? None at all. Sex had always been the easiest outlet for pent-up energy that could easily morph into rage and hellfire. He supposed he'd be looking forward to a lot of buckets of water to the face, and he inwardly groaned.

Skye grinned. "I'm excited for you! Since we're both doing it, let's shake on our promise."

She held out a hand, and he clasped it, her palm swallowed by his.

"Repeat after me," she said. "I solemnly swear that I will not touch anyone in a sexual way for six months."

Bel repeated the vow. It wasn't a binding promise. There was no magical weight behind it. And moreover, he was a demon. He was supposed to swear things and then do the opposite. Except this time, he didn't want to.

Skye smiled up at him. "I'm excited for this now, when before I was dreading it. Thank you."

He nodded, dropping her hand and climbing off the barstool. Standing at his full height, he searched over the heads of the crowd until he spotted Meph and Raum.

"What are you going to do for the next six months?" Skye asked.

Keep my brothers out of Hell. Figure out what's going on with Ash's curse. Try not to murder any humans. Get rid of Mishetsumephtai. Try not to burn down the apartment. Stay the fuck away from Naiamah.

"Cooking. I love to cook."

Her eyes widened. "You actually— You're—" She shook her head roughly. "Wow."

"You?"

"I'm in school. I'm going to focus on that."

He nodded. "Good luck." *And stay away from monsters.*

"Good luck with your cooking."

Bel said goodbye to the surprisingly insightful human and shoved through the crowd without a care for who he knocked over. Grabbing his brothers by the ears, he dragged them out of the bar, feeling like something monumental had just occurred. It was dumb. All he'd done was make a verbal promise, and vows that weren't contractually binding meant nothing to demons.

But somehow, this vow meant something to him. This had been the point of coming to Earth in the first place, the reason he'd been willing to risk everything to escape.

He wanted a fresh start. A new beginning.

Meph whined and Raum punched him repeatedly, but he refused to release them until they were on the street.

"What the fuck was that for!"

"We're going home," Belial announced, and then he turned and headed down the street without waiting for them to follow.

"Human," the creature hissed at Eva, and she screamed some more.

Ash was there in a heartbeat. One moment he wasn't, and the next, he was standing in front of her, blocking her view of the monster. To a certain extent. The thing was huge and towered over both of them, especially with those enormous black wings. She could see its yellow eyes over the top of Ash's head, and its long, whip-like tail snapping restlessly from side to side.

"Asmodeus. Your human has the Sight." Its voice was deep and rumbling, and Eva had to fight back another scream.

"How did you find me?" Ash asked.

"Your Nephilim blood was wasted—I scented you here a week ago. All I had to do was wait for your return."

Ash cursed. Brain firing off a whole lot of *What the fuck?*, Eva slowly reached down to the cutlery drawer beside her. Sliding it silently open, she felt around inside until her fingers clasped around a big carving knife.

No, she had never stabbed anyone before. No, she didn't have any epic self-defense skills—she was a musician, for god's sake. And yes, she probably had no hope of fighting off the monster if it decided to attack her, but she wasn't exactly thinking clearly at the moment.

"It is time to return to Hell, Asmodeus. You can't hide forever."

Hell? Was he serious? Images of bat wings and gargoyles flashed through her mind, and she realized that yes, he might very well be serious.

"I'm not going back."

"You have no choice. It's against the rules."

"I haven't done anything. Why can't I just be left alone?"

"It's against the rules," the monster repeated.

"I don't give a flying fuck about the rules."

"We are demons. Following the rules is our role in creation."

Oh god. *Demons.* They were demons! No, wait. That was ridiculous. Completely insane. But it would explain the bat wings and those freaky yellow eyes. There was a loud buzzing ricocheting around Eva's skull, and it made it damn near impossible to think straight.

I could be hallucinating again. But this feels way too real.

"Is that why you destroyed Eligos?" Ash said coldly. "Because he wasn't fulfilling his 'role in creation'?"

The demon-monster fell silent, his tail waving back and forth with increased agitation. *His,* because once she got over her initial shock at his appearance, it became obvious he was male. He wore only a pair of black leather pants, and his upper body was built with lean muscle.

"You will come now," he finally hissed. Like a snake.

"No."

"It would be a shame if any harm came to your pretty human."

A low growl rumbled in Ash's chest, and he stepped backward, closer to her. Eva's hand tightened around the knife. It suddenly crossed her mind that they were both still naked, but it was the least of her worries at the moment.

"You can't hurt her, Mist. It's against the rules." Ash's tone was mocking.

The creature bared his teeth in a horrifying, sharklike grimace. "I was given dispensation to do whatever is necessary to return you to Hell alive. It is understood that there might be collateral damage."

"If you lay a claw on her, I will destroy you. You know as well as I do that I don't make idle threats."

Mist's head cocked to one side in a feral way, shifting his mane of shoulder-length black hair. "You have formed an attachment with this female. You actually care about her wellbeing." He appeared perplexed. "I do not understand this phenomenon."

His head jerked back up to center, and he hissed between his saw-blade teeth. "You're lucky it was I who found you. Come with me now, and your failings will remain a secret. If anyone else learned of this, you would find yourself in worse trouble than you're already in."

Ash's growl was starting to sound less and less human.

"Careful or you'll scare your human," the monster said. "Or does she already know what you are and accept you?"

"Leave her out of this."

"You are the one that involved her. If you really cared for her, you would have left her alone."

Ash was still growling, his hands curled into fists, his stance spread like he was ready to spring into battle at any second. Eva just stood there naked as a jaybird, knees trembling, clutching that knife with a white-knuckled grip.

"I don't want to fight you, Mist."

"I have my orders, and I must fulfill them."

"You could choose to disobey them like I did. You could be free."

"That is not an option for me."

"Why not? Why are you so loyal to Paimon? What does she have on you?"

Mist growled and tensed to attack, and then several things happened.

First, giant wings exploded out of Ash's back—the very same wings Eva had seen back at the nightclub. Similar to the monster, they were black and leathery and had fine, fingerlike bones separating them into jagged sections, and a large, curved talon at the top.

Not a hallucination.

Then, Ash started to . . . grow. He got bigger and bigger until he was nearly as large as the other monster. And then his skin turned red. Bright, crimson red. Foot-long black claws grew out of his hands. Huge, black horns extended from the sides of his head, curving along his skull and then swooping upward to sharp points. Just like she'd seen at the club.

Oh god, Ash really was a demon.

Eva screamed.

Ash lunged.

And the other demon . . . dissolved into smoke.

He reformed in front of Eva, but Ash must have predicted this because he attacked again from behind. The two demons collided in a whirlwind of movement, far too fast to be detectable to human eyes. Flashes of red skin and black wings passed before her amidst animalistic growls and grunts.

The other demon dissolved again, and reformed behind Ash, and then there was a great crash as Ash was thrown—literally *thrown*—across the room. He hit the brick wall hard enough to kill a man and crumpled to the floor.

Eva screamed yet again as Mist reformed right in front of her. He was reaching for her, about to grab her. Up close, she realized his skin was a dark, ashy-gray color, almost black, and patterned with strange designs around his neck, forearms and chest. He was seconds from grabbing her—

Huge, red Ash attacked again from the side, and the tornado of fury spun around the kitchen, drowning out Eva's continued screams. It traveled across the room, ramming into the fridge, the walls, the piano, the sofa—

There was an enormous *crash!* as they smashed into the wall of windows, shattering the glass. The two battling demons went right through and disappeared into the night.

Silence.

Eva ran to the window, choking on horror and shock and

the bile rising up her throat, arriving in time to see an elegant swoop of black wings. Ash landed on his feet on the ground below. His wings folded against his back, and before her very eyes, he shrank. His skin returned to his original color, his hands became human hands, his horns retreated into his skull and disappeared.

There was no sign of the other demon.

Staring at Ash's tiny form from three floors up, human except for the wings folded against his back, her denial finally slipped away. Everything she'd seen in that club had really happened. Everything she had just witnessed here had really occurred. The amount of sheer terror coursing through her veins assured her that this was no hallucination.

This shit was one hundred percent real.

Knees shaking, Eva almost collapsed. Almost. But knowing the danger wasn't over, she fought back the urge to fall apart. As she watched, Ash spread his wings again. He crouched and leapt, and with a great pump of the leathery appendages, launched into the air. Several more pumps of the powerful wings sent him higher, and Eva realized he was coming back to the apartment.

She backed away from the window, torn between wanting to flee in terror, stab him with the kitchen knife, and throw herself into his arms. Instead, she grabbed the blanket off the couch and wrapped it around her naked body just as Ash returned.

With impossible grace, he tucked his wings against his back, shot through the jagged hole in the glass, and flared them back out. He landed crouched on one knee, one hand braced forward for balance. Straightening to his full, naked height, he looked at her cowering by the wall and winced.

"So . . . that happened." He rubbed the back of his neck.

Eva stared at him, clutching the blanket closed with one hand and that stupid kitchen knife with the other.

Ash flexed the wings, folded them back against his body, and they . . . disappeared. *How in the hell is that possible? How is any of this shit possible?*

"Are you okay?"

She nodded mutely.

"He didn't hurt you at all? I have no sense of smell, so I can't tell if you're bleeding or not."

"I'm f-fine." Her voice came out as a hoarse croak.

He nodded. "We need to get dressed and get out of here. Your apartment isn't safe anymore."

"What about the m-monster?"

"He's gone for now. I got him pretty good with my claws, and he needs time to heal. But he'll be back. You need to come with me, Eva. It's not safe here."

"You're b-bleeding."

Ash looked down at himself. There was a sizable gash down his side, along his obliques, and another smaller wound in his shoulder, near his throat. The side wound was far worse. The skin was flayed open and there was a significant amount of blood running down his hip and leg.

If he'd been a normal man, he'd probably have been unconscious already, and she would've been screaming and calling an ambulance, but nothing about this situation was normal.

"Damn." Ash shrugged and looked back at her. "We need to go."

"I— I don't know."

"I won't hurt you."

"You're a— a—" She couldn't get the word out.

His gaze was so intense, it felt like he was boring a hole into her head. "Say it. I know you know."

"D-demon."

"Nailed it."

"You could be lying to me about all of this. Demons lie."

"Yes, they do. But I'm not. Unfortunately, there isn't time to prove that to you. You're just going to have to trust me."

Trust a demon. Wasn't that the number one thing you weren't supposed to do?

Ash sighed, gaze landing on the knife still in her trembling hand. "Look, I don't blame you if you're scared of me now. It means you're smart. But think about it—who do you trust more, me or Mist? If you stay here, Mist will be back for you. He knows you're with me, so you've become a target."

Eva did think about it. She wasn't ready to believe a single word out of Ash's mouth at this point, but she had to admit that between the two creatures fighting in her house, if she had to trust one, she'd pick him in a heartbeat.

Her gaze traveled to the gaping hole in her window, and her breathing hitched. Somehow, that stupid hole in the glass felt more real than anything else. "My apartment . . . I can't just leave it like this."

"You can call someone to come fix the window, but we have to go."

"My c-cat." Her protests were nonsensical, but she was just trying her best not to fall apart.

Ash looked impatient. "We can't bring your damn cat."

"I'm not leaving him." It was the strongest her voice had sounded so far.

"Fuck." Ash scrubbed his face with his hands, and it was such a humanlike gesture that she could almost forget he'd been a red-skinned, horned giant five minutes ago. He looked up. "Do you have a car?"

She nodded.

"Fine. We'll take your car, and you can bring the cat. But I'm driving, and we have to go now." He didn't wait for her response but went back into the bedroom where she assumed he was getting dressed.

Eva stood there, wrapped in the blanket, staring blankly ahead. She felt numb. In shock, probably. Definitely.

"Eva, come on," Ash called from the bedroom.

She was crazy for going anywhere with a man who'd admitted to being a demon. She ought to run out the door right now and not stop until she'd reached another province. No, another country. No, fuck it, she'd buy a flight to another continent and hide there for the rest of her life.

But that wasn't an option, was it? That monster was coming back for her, and he could probably find her anywhere in the world. Ash was right: she'd rather trust him than Mist any day.

And then there was that little whisper inside her that had suddenly gotten louder. It was telling her she was close to something vital, close to uprooting the dissociation that had plagued her her entire life. It told her she needed to keep pushing, to dig deeper, and despite her fear, she wanted to listen.

She wasn't losing her mind, she hadn't hallucinated, and the world wasn't as ordinary as it seemed. Surely that meant there was more to her existence as well? Surely that meant she could find a way to feel whole?

She forced her feet to work and managed to walk in a daze into the bedroom, dropping her useless weapon on the kitchen counter as she went past. She reached her room just as Ash came out. He was wearing pants but had his T-shirt pressed against the wound in his side to stem the bleeding.

Somewhere in her bewildered brain, she remarked that he still looked like her sexy, not-quite-a-boyfriend-yet boyfriend, but she couldn't reconcile that image with everything she'd just seen. She wasn't ready to bridge that gap yet.

He reached for her as she approached, and she recoiled. He winced and dropped his hand. "Grab a change of clothes. I'm not sure when we'll be back. I'll find your cat, but I'm not touching the little bastard. You want him, you carry him out."

"D-don't hurt him."

Ash scowled. "I'm more concerned about *him* hurting me. Cats hate me."

"W-why?"

He gave her a dry look. "Because they have good goddamn instincts. Now, hurry up. I'll be waiting."

15

SPEED DEMON

ASMODEUS—THAT REALLY WAS HIS NAME BECAUSE HE really was a demon—drove her car like a bat out of hell. Oh god, he *was* a bat out of hell.

Eva's head felt like it was going to burst, but she was too busy holding onto the dash and passenger door for dear life. Thelonious howled from his pet carrier in the back seat. Ash had been right—her cat really didn't like him.

While Ash phoned his brothers and told them to meet him at their home—he hadn't explained what happened because he said Belial would flip a lid—Eva had gotten dressed and thrown as many clothes as she could into her backpack. Thankfully, she'd had the presence of mind to pack a tooth-brush and the detangling products for her hair.

Her phone and charger had been next, and she'd already fired off a text to her landlord asking for his help fixing the window, though it was far too late to expect a response now. For obvious reasons, she'd lied and said a piece of furniture had fallen through the glass instead of two battling demons. How the hell she was going to afford the repair if insurance didn't cover it, she had no idea, but she was taking things one step at a time.

Right now, that meant surviving this death-defying car ride. "You should've let me drive!"

She braced her legs against the floor as Ash flew around a corner amidst a barrage of honking. Thelonious hissed from the back. Thank god it was two o'clock in the morning because if Ash had tried driving like this during the day, he would have caused a pileup at every intersection.

"You don't know where we're going, and there wasn't time to explain." He was perfectly calm. He might as well have been reading the newspaper, not weaving in and out of traffic like they were in a high-speed car chase.

The wound in his side was still bleeding steadily, but he needed two hands to drive so his T-shirt was discarded on his lap rather than being used as a compress. He was looking a little pale, but he'd said he was fine, so she took him at his word.

"If you crash my car, you're buying me a new one!" If he could. Did demons have money? How did they learn how to drive? How did they learn to play piano, for that matter, or any of the stuff Ash could do?

"Deal."

God, this night could not get any worse. Or weirder. "You really are a demon."

"Yep."

"But . . . how? And why are you here?"

He shot her a look, which took his eyes off the road for longer than she would've liked considering he was in the process of running several red lights. "You heard my conversation with Mist. I'm here because I went rogue. And as for how . . . I'm not really sure how to answer that. I am what I am. I didn't choose it any more than you chose to be a human."

Eva shook her head, overwhelmed. In shock. Freaking the hell out and totally numb at the same time.

"I spent the last two weeks convincing myself I hallucinated what I saw at the nightclub." She scoffed bitterly. "What was I supposed to think? It's not every day you see guys with wings and an angel and whatever that hideous troll thing was that you murdered."

Ash had the nerve to laugh, the asshole. "You didn't hallucinate. Well, unless you count the angel thing. Trust me, Belial is no angel."

"Is he even your real brother? Can demons have brothers?"

"We're brothers. We made a blood pact."

"What does that even mean!" She tried not to scream at him.

Ash jerked the wheel hard and went around the corner on two wheels. Her grip on the door was white-knuckled. "We formed a bond. We agreed never to betray each other. We'd seen how humans remain loyal to their families, and we decided we liked the concept and wanted to become brothers."

"You can't just *become* someone's brother."

He shrugged. "Brothers are brothers because they share blood, right?"

"Well, kind of, but—"

"We made a blood pact. We shared blood. Now we're brothers."

He said it so matter-of-factly, as if that was all there was to it. She couldn't bring herself to burst his bubble and tell him that there was more to family than mixing up a blood cocktail, so she changed the subject. "Why did you escape Hell in the first place?"

"Because I was sick of playing meaningless games, following pointless rules, and fighting over shit that doesn't matter. I was sick of being Lucifer's bitch."

He whipped the car around another corner with more force than necessary, giving her a hint of the rage behind his words. Thelonious made a god-awful howling sound from the backseat, and Eva wondered if cleaning up cat vomit was going to be the cherry on top of this horrible night.

"Lucifer as in . . . Satan? The devil?"

"Satan is more of a concept. The evil force in the world. Lucifer is a fallen angel who rules Hell."

"And what are you?"

"Told you. A demon. We're created to serve the evil force. Bringers of darkness, treachery, all that fun stuff."

Oh, dear god. Should she start praying? Because that did not sound like the sort of creature she wanted to trust behind the wheel of her car. "So if you're an evil demon, why would you want to escape Hell? Wouldn't you like doing whatever it is demons do? I still don't get it."

Ash swerved onto the wrong side of the road to dodge a slow-moving vehicle. "I have a theory."

"What?"

He jerked the car back into his lane. "Demons are conscious. We're not humans, and we don't have souls. But we're aware. So we have some kind of conscious life force animating us."

He didn't have a soul? That was so messed up on so many levels, she couldn't try to count them.

"Conscious beings evolve. That's how the universe works. You're born, you fuck shit up, you learn your lesson, you evolve. It doesn't matter whether you're a human, animal, or even a plant. You evolve, grow, or you decay and dissolve. So why not demons?"

"You think demons evolve. What's your point?"

He slowed marginally at a stop sign and then gunned it through the intersection without stopping. "I'm old. Really old. I'm so old, I don't remember how old I am. And I've done a lot of really bad shit. Please don't ask me to tell you, because I really don't want to. But just trust me when I say it was bad."

Great. That wasn't making her any more inclined to trust him driving her car.

A demand for him to pull over and let her flee was on the tip of her tongue, but another part of her was dying to hear more. How could she not be? She was sitting beside a real, live demon who was now giving her some kind of theology lesson. It was morbidly fascinating.

"A few thousand years ago, I was bound by Raphael after really fucking up."

"You were what? By who? And did you say a few *thousand?*"

He ignored the questions. "It was then things started to change for me. It was a slow process, and it was only in the last few hundred years I really felt different."

"I don't get it. You think you evolved? How?"

Ash actually stopped at the next red light. "I don't know. But I do know I don't belong in Hell anymore. I can feel it. My brothers too—they're in the same boat as me. I knew that if we stayed there any longer, we were going to get found out and probably destroyed. Bel's powerful, but even he couldn't save our asses if everyone turned against us. Our only choice was to escape and try to hide on Earth. I made the colossally stupid mistake of thinking we'd have more time before Mist came after us, however, and now I'm paying the price. Or rather, *you're* paying the price."

He cast her another sideways glance, hands tightening on the steering wheel. "For what it's worth, I'm sorry. I never intended for you to get involved in this."

That was nice and all—an apology from a demon was probably a rare thing—but it didn't change her current, unbelievably messed up predicament.

In the meantime, she had a million more questions. "Who is Mist exactly? And who is Raphael, and how did he bind you? And what did you do that made him bind you? What is a binding? And why do they want you back in Hell so bad? And did you say they would destroy you? Destroy as in, kill you? Can demons die?"

Ash dragged a hand through his hair. She hated that she was still aware of how gorgeous that hair was. "That's a lot of questions, Eva."

"Then you'd better get started answering them."

"Where do I begin?"

"Start with Mist."

"All right." The light turned green, and he slammed on the gas. The car swung around a sharp corner, no turn signal. "Mist is Hell's best tracker. We call him the Hunter. His senses are heightened, even on Earth where our powers are dampened, and he's a master of stealth. I'm sure you noticed his whole dissolve-into-mist trick."

"Is that why he's called Mist? Because he can become . . . mist?"

"Yeah, and because his full name is Mishetsumephtai. Mist is a nickname. Or Mishetsu."

"Oh."

Ash accelerated. They were pushing seventy kilometers an hour on a residential, one-way street. *God help me.* "Yeah. When someone reneges on a bargain, or a demon or a soul escapes Hell, Mist gets sent after them. But only in the most severe cases."

"What happens if you get caught?"

"We'll get the fuck tortured out of us and potentially be executed."

Jesus. "What happens when you execute a demon? Can you even die?"

"This is getting really complicated, Eva. Are you sure you—"

"Answer the question."

"Fine." He made an illegal right turn on a red light. Again, no turn signal. She was starting to wonder if he knew they existed.

"Like I said, demons aren't like humans, since we don't have souls. When humans die, they go to Heaven or Hell. If they're good, they chill in Heaven for a while until they get bored, and then they reincarnate on Earth and do it all again. If they're not good, they get sent to Hell and, well, bad shit happens. It's supposed to make them improve, though I've never really seen how torturing someone will make them a better person." He shrugged. "But that's not my problem."

"Wait, reincarnation is real?"

"For humans it is. For demons, not so much. When a lesser demon is destroyed, they just dissolve. Their consciousness merges with the consciousness that upholds the universe. They're just gone. But greater demons, the more powerful demons—and this goes back to my theory—I think they start to develop some kind of soul. When they're destroyed, I believe that 'soul' gets trapped in a special area of Hell, since there's no way Heaven would take them. I don't know where, and I have no idea what happens to them. But they still exist." He visibly shuddered. "To me, that's worse than dissolution. I'd rather vanish from existence than end up trapped somewhere in Hell I could never escape."

"But you think that would happen to you if you were killed. Because you evolved."

"Yeah." The tightening around the edges of his mouth betrayed how much he didn't like the sound of that.

"Who is Raphael?"

"An angel."

Eva stared at him. "An *angel*. Angels are real too, then. Okay."

"Yeah, and they're self-righteous pricks." He floored it through a yellow light and shot her a glance. "You're doing great, by the way. Most people would hyperventilate the second I flashed these." He stuck out his hand, and in the blink of an eye, those deadly claws shot out of his fingertips.

She screamed and jerked back. "What the hell!"

The claws disappeared, his hand landing back on the steering wheel just in time to whip around a corner. During another red light. "See? You're taking this well."

"Damn it, Ash! You're going to give me a heart attack!"

"No, I'm not. Which proves my point."

She glared furiously at the side of his perfect head. "Tell me about the angel."

His mouth twisted. "It wasn't one of my finer moments. I don't like telling this story."

"Tell me, damn it."

"A few thousand years ago, I was sent to this crappy village full of shitty humans. Killing, raping each other. Bunch of assholes going straight to Hell. But there were a few decent ones. In particular, this one chick, Sarah, was pure of heart, and she was the one I was sent after. I was still the Prince of Lust back then, so naturally, my job was to tempt her, try to corrupt her, you know."

"Why?"

"Because it's part of the never-ending war between Heaven and Hell. We want to make more evil humans so we can claim their souls for Hell, and Heaven wants the opposite. Supposedly, there has to be opposing dark-light forces on Earth to balance everything, but then, Heaven always takes credit for everything anyway, and I've long since given up trying to understand."

"So what happened to Sarah?" Her hand flew to her mouth. "Oh god, don't tell me you killed her."

"I didn't kill *her*."

Eva winced. "I still don't like the sound of that."

"Sarah was the most beautiful woman in the village, and she was considered even more so because of her innocence and purity." He scoffed. "Gross, if you ask me. Innocence is not beautiful in itself. Anyway, she had suitors lining up outside her door. Seven of them—well, eight if you count me."

"You?"

"That was my job: to go undercover in Sarah's life and try to corrupt her. And I succeeded too. Innocent, *pure* Sarah took a shine to me, and we started, um . . . fooling around a bit. If you catch my drift."

Eva made a face. "*That's* gross."

He shrugged. "I was just doing my job. Poor Sarah didn't know I had no intention of sticking around long enough to marry her, and she told the rest of her suitors she had chosen me. The entitled pricks didn't like that in the least, especially since my fake human identity was an orphaned farmhand without a penny to his name."

"That poor girl," Eva thought, imagining some innocent woman falling helplessly in love with a demon who tempted her into sex before marriage. Talk about your rude wake-up calls.

As for herself, well, she absolutely refused to feel jealous of something that happened a few thousand years ago with a *demon*, for heaven's sake.

"She was better off, if you ask me," Ash continued. "She didn't have a clue about anything when we met. She didn't even know a woman could orgasm, which is just sad." He cleared his throat. "Anyway. So Sarah's suitors got jealous and decided to take matters into their own hands. They rallied the town and came after me one night—you know, the classic 'angry villagers with pitchforks and torches' thing. I guess they suspected me of being a demon. Or maybe they just couldn't imagine a situation where a woman would pick a poor man over their rich, fat asses. Either way, they came for violence. So . . ." He glanced sidelong at her. "I killed them all."

She blinked. "Um, what?"

"I killed them all," he repeated.

"You killed *seven* people?"

He winced. "Seven people . . . plus the rest of the villagers with them."

She slapped a hand to her mouth. "Oh my god." She'd expected he'd killed people—he was a demon after all, and he'd already said he'd done a lot of really bad shit. But hearing him admit to mass murder was a wake-up call as to what he really was.

"Why? Couldn't you have just . . . injured them?"

He shrugged. "I got carried away, you know."

"No, I don't know!" She was sitting in the car with a murderer. A demon murderer. "You have wings—you could have flown away!"

"In hindsight, that would have been the better option."

"Jesus Christ."

"He hadn't been born yet, thankfully."

Eva rubbed her eyes.

"So, after that many unsanctioned human deaths, Heaven got pissed off and sent Raphael. He bound me and booted my ass back to Hell. Sarah eventually married, hopefully to a guy who knew how to give her an orgasm, but I doubt it. Those were pretty dark times."

Eva continued rubbing her eyes.

"But my corruption worked a little too well on her. When she found out what I was, she didn't want to admit what she'd done, so she made up a bunch of lies about how I tried to corrupt her and failed, and how she begged Raphael for his help to save her after I ruthlessly murdered her suitors. Worse, her version of events got recorded in the Book of Tobit, which is still around today, and it makes me look like an asshole."

Dropping her hands back in her lap, Eva squeezed her eyes shut and struggled to process all that. The car swung around another corner sharp enough to make her stomach heave, and her eyes snapped open again. It was either that or puke. "What do you mean, Raphael *bound* you?"

"He dragged me out to the desert and put a curse on me. Demons are all about the senses. He took mine away."

"That's why you can't see color?"

He nodded as he ran another stop sign. "There was one more side effect of the curse," he said, "which is why I lost my title. Raphael made me sort of invisible."

"You look pretty visible to me."

"I know, it's a miracle. I have no idea why."

"I'm confused."

"Part of the curse is that members of the opposite sex, or anyone who might be attracted to me as a potential sexual partner, don't see me. I mean, I'm there. You can meet me, even have a whole conversation with me, but I come across as completely uninteresting. As attractive as plain cardboard. As dull as a rock." His mouth twisted. "It's the perfect torture for a lust demon."

"Oh my god." Eva's thoughts raced. She remembered his brothers' bizarre comments outside the bar. Ash's bewilderment the first night they met, his utter confusion when she admitted she was attracted to him. Skye's weird dismissal of him when they'd first been introduced.

But that only dredged up a thousand more questions. "But what about that crowd of women at the bar? You weren't invisible to them."

He glanced at her. "I don't know what happened tonight. Nothing like that has ever happened to me before in three thousand years. I have no idea why. But the curse is back now, so maybe it doesn't matter."

Okay, this was confusing. "I'm not sure this curse is very effective. I mean, *I* saw you right from the start. I picked you out of the crowd from all the way across that nightclub during my set. And I'm not a lesbian, despite what your brother thinks."

He smirked. "I know you're not. And I have no idea why you can see me. You're an anomaly, all right. You also have the Sight—you can see the supernatural without any special training. That could be part of it."

She remembered when she'd told him about her "hallucinations" and grit her teeth. The bastard had gone along with her erroneous assumption. Then again, she could see why he'd be reluctant to tell her he was an actual demon from Hell. No way she'd have taken him home again tonight. *Asshole.*

"You told me I was descended from *witches* and was having a *vision*, dickface," she spat. "I get wanting to keep the truth from me, but did you have to feed me such a crock of shit?"

"It's not a crock of shit. Well, minus the having a vision thing. But you being a witch is a very possible explanation for why you have the Sight."

Eva blinked. Blinked again. "Witches are real too? Oh my god. This is too much. I don't understand any of this." She hunched forward and put her face in her hands but dropped them quickly back into her lap because it made her feel carsick with his terrible driving.

"I'm pretty confused myself."

She sat up straight again and glared at the side of his head. "So, that's what this was all about, then? You finally met someone after thousands of years who was attracted to you, so you wanted to get laid."

"Yeah." He turned another corner, finally slowing down as they entered another neighborhood.

It surprised her how much that hurt. But he was a freaking demon, after all. What did she expect him to say?

And hold on a hot sec, was she really sad that a *demon* didn't have feelings for her? She ought to be jumping for joy. The last thing she wanted was a demon that was capable of murdering an entire village because he "got carried away" declaring his undying love for her.

Were demons even capable of love? Probably not. In fact, had Ash said he *did* have feelings for her, he'd likely have been lying. His blunt address was probably the most honest answer he could have given. It should have comforted her that he was truthful and that she didn't have to worry about some sort of twisted attachment on his end.

It should have. But it didn't.

But then, he frowned. "But also, I really did like your music that night at the club. It soothed me. And I like jamming with you. And I like being around you. Your company is . . . enjoyable." He looked confused about that.

Wow. She was overcome by the heartfelt sentiment. *Not.*

"Wait, how did you learn to play piano if you're a demon?"

"I told you. Miguel taught me before he was killed. Demons can assimilate any human skill relatively quickly, but we can never be real artists. We can only mimic what humans can do. We have no soul, and so any expressions of creativity are equally soulless. That's why I don't really consider myself a musician."

"But you said you think that demons could evolve into something with some version of a soul."

He shrugged. "It's still not the same as a human soul. All humans have the potential for divinity, and it comes out in their art. Demons are just . . . demons."

She didn't buy it. Lying asshole or not, as far as she was concerned, he was a damn good musician and there wasn't a single "soulless" thing about it.

But that conversation would have to wait—Ash finally turned her car into a potholed parking lot beside a crummy apartment building. He'd driven them across town to one of the most run-down neighborhoods in the city. Laundry hung from balconies with junk piled in the corners, and she could hear the dull roar of heavy metal music coming from one of the basement units even at this ungodly hour.

"You live here? You couldn't afford anywhere nicer?"

He cocked a brow. "I could afford nicer. But we picked this place because no one would expect us to, so it makes a good hiding spot."

He pulled into a parking spot next to a rusted out sedan and switched off the car. "Come on, my brothers will be waiting inside."

Wondering if she'd fallen that night at the club, hit her head and ended up in a coma, and this was all a dream, Eva climbed out of the car. Thelonious's hiss as she pulled him and her bag out of the back suggested otherwise. In what coma-induced fantasy did one get stuck carrying around their severely pissed cat in a pet carrier? Maybe in a nightmare, she supposed. *Maybe I've died and gone to Hell.*

"Give me your bag," Ash said, reaching for it. "You take the cat." She handed him her backpack, and he locked her car. She followed him toward the dumpy building, noticing he appeared to be swaying on his feet. He really didn't look good.

"Are you sure you're okay?"

"What? Oh, yeah, fine."

"I can take my bag if you need."

"It's fine." They reached the door, which had a broken lock and was stuck ajar, and Ash held it open for her.

Was it normal for demons to hold doors for people, or was it a sign of his "evolution"? Or maybe demons were always polite and charming as a way to lure humans into their traps?

Ugh. She decided she was done with speculating for the night. It was way too late for earth-shattering revelations. No more questions until she'd had at least six hours of sleep.

16

ALL THE RAGE

ASH LED EVA UP TO HIS THIRD-FLOOR APARTMENT, wondering why it was so hard for him to climb stairs right now. Maybe he'd been injured worse in the fight with Mist than he thought. Made sense—the T-shirt still pressed against the wound in his side was steadily soaking through with blood.

Oh well. He couldn't die from blood loss, and thanks to his curse, he could take the pain. That was the one and only benefit of Raphael's fuckery.

He hauled his exhausted ass all the way up to the third floor and unlocked the door to his place, pushing it open and gesturing for Eva to go inside. He could feel her eyes taking in their apartment, and he took a breath. *Wait for it, wait for it—*

"Oh my god, what is that!"

"It's a ward," he said, closing and locking the door behind him. There was another one drawn on the inside of the door.

"Is that—"

"Blood."

"Whose—?"

"Ours."

"But—"

"Ash?" It was Belial's voice.

"Yeah."

Bel stepped around the corner from the kitchen, caught sight of Eva, and immediately, flames danced in his eyes. *Shit.* Then he glanced down at Ash's bare torso—wound in his shoulder, T-shirt balled against his side, blood smeared all over him—and those eyes got wide. "What happened to you?"

"Mist happened."

Belial blanched. "Mist?"

Ash nodded. "You might want to put your cat in my room," he told Eva. "He's going to hate Bel more than he hates me."

The cat responded to this by hissing.

Eva was too busy eyeing Belial warily to respond. Some innate, intuitive sense was probably telling her she was close to something deadly, and it was right. Bel looked pissed, and it wouldn't take much for him to go off.

"What happened with Mishetsu?" he growled. Flames flickered in his eyes. "And why did you bring a human here?"

Meph and Raum appeared from the dining room behind him, moving slowly and staying quiet. Everyone was walking on eggshells.

"The *human* is standing right here," Eva grumbled.

"She knows," Ash tried to explain, but Bel wasn't having it.

"This isn't the fucking time, Asmodeus. I get you're attached to her, but if Mishetsu actually found you, the last thing we need is—"

"She knows."

"Shut up. If Mishetsu caught you with her, he could have tracked you back to her place, and—"

"He already did. He already has. She already knows."

"And if she ends up involved, we—" Bel blinked. "She knows what?"

"If you're talking about the creepy, gray demon trying to take Ash back to Hell," Eva said, "then yes, I know."

Ash groaned and closed his eyes. *Here we go.*

Bel stared at them.

"Mist already found us," Ash explained, waiting for the other shoe to drop. "He attacked me in Eva's apartment, and we took a dive out of a third-story window. Wings got involved. She saw the whole thing."

"Oh, shit," said Meph.

"Are you fucking kidding me?" Bel's eyes were almost completely covered in flame now, and his big chest was heaving. They were so fucked.

"Oh, but that was only confirmation of what I already knew." Eva sounded oddly like she was enjoying this.

Ash shot her a furious look over his shoulder, and she glared right back at him. Evidently, this was some kind of punishment for lying to her and putting her in danger. He supposed he deserved it.

The air around Belial began to waver with heat. "What?"

"She saw everything that first night at that club." He had no choice but to explain this all now, thanks to Little Miss Stubborn. "She saw us kill the gargoyle."

"I snuck back inside," Eva explained, "and saw your fancy angel wings, and I saw you guys murder that ugly troll thing."

"That's not possible." A few sparks shot off into the air around Belial's head. Shit, the bastard was about to ignite. Eva took a step back warily, finally starting to understand what sort of bear she was poking.

"She has the Sight," Ash said, shooting a quick glance at Raum, who had crept quietly to stand beside the kitchen sink. He jerked his chin to tell him to get ready to defuse the situation.

"And you didn't think to tell me that, Asmodeus?" There were actual smoke tendrils coming off Bel now. "You didn't once think it *might* be a fucking good idea to share that important fucking information with me? Did it never *once* cross your mind that it might not be smart to hang around *a fucking human that has the fucking Sight?*"

"Easy, bro."

"*Don't tell me to take it easy!*" Bel spun and punched the wall. His fist went right through the drywall.

"Great," said Meph with a sigh. "There goes our security deposit."

"You need to chill, Bel. There's a human here, and we need to talk about Mist."

Belial had grown a bit. His head was inches from the roof now. "*You* led Mishetsu right to us. This is supposed to be our safe place, and *you* fucked it up!"

"I didn't—"

"ASMODEUS, I'M GOING TO KILL YOU."

His voice boomed around the room, preternaturally loud. Everybody slammed their palms over their ears, cringing. The sound of Eva's cat howling from inside the carrier filled the air.

And then the shit really hit the fan.

Those sparks crackling in the air around Belial suddenly ignited, and the huge bastard burst into flames. Giant feathery wings exploded out of his back, shredding his T-shirt in the process. And since he was heading into full rage mode, those white wings burned with hellfire too.

Belial grew even larger until his head hit the roof, his biceps the width of tree trunks and his fists like clubs. His eyes filled completely with flames, and his blond hair miraculously grew until it swirled around his head and shoulders, part of the vortex of flame and smoke and sheer fucking terror.

Ash sighed. He'd seen Belial fly into rages ten thousand times, but Eva hadn't, and if the scream that tore out of her throat was any indication, she was terrified.

She cowered behind him and gripped his arm with a clammy hand, and he felt kind of nauseous knowing she was scared, which wasn't a pleasant sensation.

That she sought protection from him after everything that had happened tonight sent another weird feeling bouncing around his gut. Heavy and fluttery at the same time. He didn't understand any of that, but he did know it made him want to give her what she sought.

Belial was advancing on him now, flames surrounding him. The air pressure spiked like they'd taken a dive deep underwater, and a phantom wind gusted through the apartment. The cat was still yowling. All the lights were flickering.

Normally, Ash would fight it out with Bel a bit, let the poor guy blow off some steam. He always got a few burns for his trouble, but he never felt the pain, and he healed quickly enough.

But now wasn't time for fighting. He wanted Eva to feel safe. There was no using reason to talk Bel down once he'd fallen this far off his rocker, so that left only one option.

"Raum," Ash said quietly, as the enormous, raging demon advanced on him with murderous intent. "Get the jug."

Raum didn't respond, but he heard the tap running and knew his request was being fulfilled. Without looking away from Belial, he stretched out a hand as Raum crept up behind Belial, reached around, and placed the jug in it.

Ash took it and threw it in Belial's face. "Snap out of it!"

Instead, dead silence fell. Even the cat went quiet.

The flames around Bel's head extinguished from the water. Of course, this was hellfire and could easily be reignited, but the water sometimes worked as the necessary distraction.

Or, it made him *killing* mad.

But this time, they got lucky.

Bel squeezed his eyes shut and shook his head roughly, spraying droplets of water everywhere from his suddenly flowing locks. The rest of his body extinguished, and his white wings folded against his back and disappeared. He shrank substantially, though standing at seven feet tall in human form, he would never not be a giant.

Unfortunately for Bel, once his hair grew in a rage attack, he had to cut it to make it short again. The pale locks now hung past his broad shoulders to his chest, dating him back a few thousand years. He went from looking like a football player to a gladiator. It was a little bit hilarious.

Belial finally opened his eyes—blue again—and glared daggers at Asmodeus. "I *will* kill you."

"Sorry, bro, but now isn't the time for a temper tantrum."

Belial kept up the cold stare, but it was somehow less effective with his wet hair dripping all over his shoulders. Sighing, he ripped the tattered remains of his T-shirt over his head and chucked them on the floor. "I just bought this fucking shirt. And I have to get another fucking haircut now, damn it."

"Third one this month," Raum said from behind him.

"I will kill you all," Bel grumbled, shaking his sopping wet head.

"You need therapy, bro," Meph said.

"Big time," Raum agreed.

"Fuck you both. And fuck you, Asmodeus, for bringing a fucking human into our apartment!" He glanced at Eva who was still hiding behind Ash. "No offense."

Eva made a sort of choking sound in response.

Ash passed the empty jug back to Raum, who set it on the kitchen counter.

"What happened with Mishetsu?" Bel rolled his eyes at Ash's wary look. "You can tell me now. I won't lose it again."

"Can't promise you'll feel the same once I tell you," Ash grumbled.

"That bad, huh?"

He dragged a hand through his hair. Or tried to—it was a tangled mess from the fight, and his fingers got stuck halfway over his skull, so he gave up and yanked them out. His other hand was still pressing his T-shirt into his wounded side. The fabric felt pretty wet now, but he ignored it.

"He said he was able to pick up my scent at Eva's place from the first time I was there, and then he just waited around until I came back."

"Fuck." Belial ran his hands down his face. "It's too easy. We should have left the city like I said."

"He was bound to find us eventually," Raum said, now leaning against the counter. "He's called the Hunter for a reason. What I want to know is why you let him get away, Ash."

"He escaped." Ash replied, shooting him a glare. He'd like to see Raum try to catch a demon that could turn into mist. "But I injured him pretty badly in the fight, and it'll take him time to heal. We have at least a few hours to come up with a game plan before we have to worry about him coming back."

"We have to be out of this city before then," Bel said, "because when he does, it'll be with the whole cavalry."

Everyone groaned. Except Eva, of course. Ash shot another glance over his shoulder. She stood there with those spooked eyes and stared at them like she was seeing ghosts. If only she was looking at something so harmless. He felt another twinge in his gut.

The Eva he knew was fierce and vibrant. She wasn't scared and meek, and he didn't like seeing her that way now. And his inability to change it was frustrating as hell. It made him want to grab her by the shoulders and shake her until she became the old Eva again, but something told him that wasn't the right way to go about it.

"But we just got here," Meph complained. "I don't wanna leave."

"You also don't *wanna* go back to Hell, dumbass," Bel snapped.

"Okay, so we go," Raum said. Looked like he was being the reasonable one tonight. "Where?"

"Someone needs to be on the other end to draw the gate sigil," Ash pointed out. His vision swam a little bit, the odd black spot dancing here and there. He was tired as hell all of a sudden.

"We don't necessarily have to travel by gate," Meph said. "We've still got Nephilim blood fresh in our systems. Mist won't be able to find us anywhere."

"Eva has to come with us," Ash said. "And Mist knows her scent. Which means all the Nephilim blood in the world doesn't mean shit. We have to go somewhere he won't think to look for us or we'll be right back to where we started, and we have to travel by gate or he'll be able to track us." He hated to leave Montreal, but he couldn't deny they had to go. Bel was right—when Mist came back, he wouldn't come alone.

"Fuck, Asmodeus!" Belial's arm jerked like he wanted to punch the wall again.

"W-wait." Eva's tiny, frail voice interjected. Nothing about Eva could ever be described as tiny or frail, and yet, that was what it was. "Go with you where? What are sigils? And what is Nephilim blood?"

Everyone was glaring at Asmodeus suddenly. "I thought you said she knew everything."

He glared right back. "Not *everything*. There wasn't exactly a lot of time for talking. I just told her the basics."

Belial blew out a sigh so huge it threatened to take the building down. "There isn't time for a goddamn history lesson. We need to figure out where the hell we're going."

"We have at least a few hours," he reminded Bel. "Like I said, I injured Mist pretty badly. And if we're going to be dragging Eva around with us, she needs to know."

"Tell me," Eva said, finally stepping out from around him. Her voice sounded a little stronger, and it made the fist squeezing his gut unclench slightly. "And you can all stop talking about me like I'm not here, thank you very much. I'm in shock, not incompetent. What is Nephilim blood, and what are sigils?"

Belial looked at her. "I'll give you the abbreviated explanation, so pay attention."

She nodded quickly.

"There are three types of magic in creation: Temporal magic, Sheolic magic, and Empyrean magic. Witchcraft or any magic performed by humans on Earth is Temporal magic. Demons use Sheolic magic, and angels use Empyrean magic. Each type has its own rules and methods of practice. With me so far?"

"Magic is real. Got it." She swallowed.

"Most magic is done with sigils, which are symbols of power for a variety of purposes. There are wards, gates, keys, seals, whatever. Demons can travel through sigils called hellgates. To use them on Earth, we draw the sigil where we are, and then someone else draws it where we want to go. We step inside, and boom, we're there."

"So, those creepy symbols on the walls everywhere are sigils?"

"Yeah, but those are wards, not gates."

Her eyes darted around the room like she was struggling to assimilate everything. She was starting to get that same wild-eyed look she'd had when Ash had flown in through the broken window. He feared she could only learn so many new things in one night before she snapped, and he decided he'd better keep an eye on her.

Strangely, though, he was finding it hard to keep his eyes anywhere. They kept drooping and sliding in and out of focus. The T-shirt still pressed against his ribs was now fully soaked through with his blood, so maybe it had something to do with that.

"So demons can travel through hellgates," Eva said, "but can humans?"

They exchanged glances.

"There are ways," Ash said weakly, blinking hard to keep his head in the game. He was hoping to avoid explaining that one for now because she wasn't going to like what he had to say.

"Okay." Thankfully, she let it go. "And what about Nephilim?"

Belial clenched his jaw. "That's a long story, and there isn't time right—"

"I'll tell you the short version," Meph interrupted with a grin.

Belial and Raum groaned.

"What? She needs to know." Meph's smile was slightly evil. "I promise to make it quick."

SUCKS TO BE A NEPHILIM

"ONCE UPON A TIME," MEPH BEGAN, "THERE WERE A bunch of stuck-up angels protecting Earth, floating around with their thumbs up their asses. Then, a few of them got a little too interested in humans, if you know what I mean, so they got the boot from Heaven because sex is bad for sanctimonious douchebags."

"They became fallen angels and did the nasty with the humans, and all was right in the world. Except they still felt the need to fulfill some boring heavenly mission, so they took it upon themselves to be protectors of humanity from the evil forces of Hell plotting to corrupt their innocent souls. The angels were called Grigori, Earth's heavenly Watchers."

Bel growled in annoyance. "This is the dumbest fucking thing I've ever heard."

Ash was inclined to agree.

"Shhh, bro." Meph held up a finger. "I'm not finished. Eventually, the Grigori knocked up their humans, and lo! A race of human-angel hybrids was born, called the Nephilim. The Nephilim had special blood, and demons, being the weird, perverted fuckers we are, discovered that if they drank that blood, they would become untraceable, among other cool things. So if a demon wanted to, say, escape Hell, all he had to do was take a hit of blood, and *ta-da*. He'd be invisible."

Eva looked part overwhelmed, part revolted. "So you guys just found one of these Nephilim and drank its blood?"

"It's not that simple," Belial cut in. "Nephilim are ceaselessly hunted by both Hell and Heaven. Hell, because demons want to use them for their abilities. Heaven, because angels don't want demons to have the blood, and consider human-angel hybrids an abomination. If a demon gets its hands on a Nephilim, they're looking at a life in captivity, being kept alive solely as a blood source. If an angel finds one, they kill that sucker faster than you can say, 'Have mercy.' Which they don't."

"Sounds like it sucks to be one of these Nephilim guys," Eva said.

"It sucks a lot," Meph agreed.

"Okay." Eva took a deep breath. "I think I'm nearing the point of information overload. No one talk for a second while I put this together. You guys drank the blood of some poor creature, and now you're untraceable. Or something."

They nodded.

"You can travel through gate thingies, and wherever you end up, Mist won't be able to track you. But the catch is that somebody on the other end has to draw the same sigil in order for us to be able to travel through it, which means we have to find someone we trust."

"Bang on the money," Meph said, grinning. "You're smart for a human."

"You're dumb for a demon," Raum shot back.

"Hey, that was unwarranted."

"Look, while all this sounds very scary, I can't just leave Montreal indefinitely." Eva was starting to sound more like herself again, which was such a relief to Asmodeus that he felt light-headed. Or maybe that was from blood loss. Yeah, that was more likely.

"I have a job, and I have to pay rent and get the window in my apartment fixed. And I have a gig in two weeks."

Had he thought he felt relieved? With those words, that fist around his gut clenched nice and tight again and the feeling evaporated. It was his fault Eva's life was being upended. That kind of thing had never mattered to him before, but suddenly, it did.

He wanted to promise her he'd keep her safe and disembowel anyone who touched her, but he was using up all his focus staying upright and keeping his eyes open. His heart pounded in his temples, and he was so damn *tired*. The tile floor at his feet was starting to look really cushy.

"It's either come with us or let the Hunter get you," Meph pointed out bluntly.

"So what, you guys can never return here?" Eva's voice rose like she was starting to panic again. "And what about me? Am I going to be in danger for the rest of my life?"

Ash tried to drag a hand through his tangled hair again, but his arm felt heavy, and when he lifted it, his head spun. He gave up on that and focused on speaking. "All of us want to find a permanent solution, but we're more concerned about immediate survival at the moment. There's no point worrying about the future right now."

She looked at him and took a breath. "Fine. But I'm beyond pissed at you for dragging me into this. Before you came along, I was a clueless human living my life with no knowledge of any of this. And I never would've had to have that knowledge if you had left me alone in the first place."

His fingers clenched around his bloody T-shirt, sending a

fresh trickle of liquid down his side. Hearing her say that made him feel more uncomfortable shit. This emotion settled like a lead weight in his chest and made his skin crawl. For once, he could actually name this feeling because he'd experienced it before.

Guilt.

The last time he'd felt it had been when Miguel was killed. Now, he felt it for upending Eva's life. Mist had said it best: *If you really cared for her, you would have left her alone.*

"Don't blame Ash, sugar," Meph said, flashing his customary devilish grin. "You're the first woman to be into him in thousands of years. What would you expect him to do? He's a lust demon, after all."

"*Was* a lust demon," Ash grumbled. How many times did he need to make that goddamn clarification? "And don't call her that."

Eva threw up her hands. "Oh, well, that's totally fine, then! Of course I understand. He's completely forgiven now."

"Really?"

"No, Meph," Raum drawled. "That's called sarcasm."

"I know what sarcasm is."

"Can we get back to the fucking point?" Bel snapped. Flames flickered in his eyes, and everyone snapped to attention. They were not risking another blown-fuse Belial. "I'm the oldest and most powerful, and I say all five of us are leaving this city. If you don't like it, too bad."

"No one's objecting, bro." Meph held his tattooed palms up. "But we need somewhere to go."

Unfortunately, no one had an answer for that.

"Fuck." Ash dragged his free hand down his face. He was having the damnedest time focusing on the conversation.

"You okay, Ash?" Meph asked, studying him. "You're looking pretty pale."

"I'm fine. Just tired."

"He's right," Bel said suddenly. "You look like shit."

"I'm fine," he growled, suddenly impatient to escape the scrutinizing gazes of his brothers. Unfortunately, as he turned to step around Eva into the hall, he got really light-headed and staggered into the wall.

He would have gone down if Bel hadn't been there to catch him. "What the fuck?"

Ash straightened and tried to jerk out of his hold. "I'm fine."

"How much blood did you lose?"

"I said I'm fine." He tried again to fight off Bel's grip on his arms.

"You don't look fine. Move your hand and let me see the wound."

"I'm fi—" Except as soon as Bel finally let go of him, he staggered again.

Bel caught him and jerked his chin at Raum. "Move his hand so I can see the wound. I'll hold his arms."

"Fuck you!" Ash protested, struggling in Bel's iron grip, but he was weak from blood loss and couldn't break free. Raum came over and yanked his hand back from the wound, still clutching the blood-soaked T-shirt. Blood immediately leaked over from the gaping wound.

To make matters worse, his hand had tightened around the shirt when he was forced to move it, and he ended up accidentally wringing it out. A steady stream of blood dripped from the shirt into a nice little pool at his feet.

Eva gasped. Her cat hissed again, just because.

Belial cursed a blue streak. "Turn on the stove and get a knife. We have to cauterize this."

Raum rushed to obey while Bel shot a glare at Eva, eyes flickering with flames. "You didn't notice how badly he was wounded?"

"This isn't her fault," Meph said, uncharacteristically

reasonably. Ash would have said the same, but he was suddenly using up all his concentration on not passing out.

Eva flinched. "He said he was fine."

"He can't feel pain," Bel snapped. "He'll always say he's fine."

"Leave her out of this." Ash's voice came out slurred. "I said I'm fine."

"Shut up. Raum, get that blade heated up."

"Already on it."

Eva gasped from somewhere. "You're not actually going to—"

"You're a fucking idiot, Asmodeus," Belial snapped. "Bleeding all over yourself and not telling anyone or doing anything about it."

"Fuck you," he mumbled. "Go ahead and rage out and make this about yourself like you always do, asshole."

"Maybe if you didn't excel at pissing me off, I wouldn't have to!"

"Heyyy now, let's not fight," Meph interjected.

"Shut the fuck up, Meph!" they both said simultaneously.

"You never know when to quit, do you?" Belial bellowed in Ash's face. "Always sulking around with the weight of the world on your shoulders, blaming everything on me!"

Ash mustered strength from somewhere and said, "I'm not the one who can't carry on a conversation without bursting into fucking flames!"

"You should have told me you were bleeding out, damn it!"

"I'm not bleeding out!"

"Yes, you are!"

"Told you . . . I'm fine . . ." The room was spinning.

"Shit—"

"He's passing out!"

"Bel, you dickhead, I'm sure you can see how shouting at him really helped!"

"Oh my god!" Eva screamed. The cat was howling again.

Ash rolled his eyes. He was so sick of the goddamn drama. Oh, no, actually his eyes were rolling back into his head because he was about to pass out. When the blackness came, he welcomed it. Maybe when he woke up, he'd find that none of this shitty night had happened, and things would go back to how they were before.

He would show up at Eva's and they'd play some music together and then fuck nice and slow, and then they'd wake up together in the morning and eat tasteless pastries naked by the window in the sunlight. Yeah, that sounded nice.

He held on to that little fantasy as the blackness claimed him.

"Fuck, he's out cold," Belial said, catching Ash as he sagged. "Raum, get over here and seal this wound. He's bleeding everywhere, the idiot."

"Blade's not hot enough yet." Raum was holding the tip of a short dagger into the gas flame of the stove, and it was starting to glow red.

"Here." Meph handed Belial a dishtowel, which he took and pressed into Ash's side to stem the flow of blood. Ash's bloody T-shirt had fallen to the floor with a wet slap when he lost consciousness.

Despite herself, Eva's eyes filled with tears. She felt awful. Ash had been bleeding a lot the entire drive home and then throughout the entire conversation, and she'd ignored him. She'd been so mad at him for lying about what he was, and since she'd discovered he wasn't human, she'd believed him when he said he was fine.

"I thought he was okay," she said. "He said he was." She set Thelonious's cage down and hovered behind a still-shirtless Bel as he scooped up Ash like he weighed nothing.

Bel carried him to the other room and dumped him unceremoniously on the couch. All Ash's gorgeous black hair was tangled, some of it stuck to the dried blood on his shoulder wound, which had closed, thankfully. Her heart ached looking at him, though she kept telling it to shut up because she was still furious with him for lying to her and being an evil demon from Hell.

"He will be." Crouched beside Ash and keeping pressure on his wound, Bel looked over at Eva wringing her hands and sighed. "I shouldn't have shouted at you. He's a stubborn prick and wouldn't have told anyone he was bleeding out. It's not your fault."

"Is he really bleeding out?" She really didn't like the sound of that.

"He's fine. We can't die this way. He'll just feel a little . . . parched for a while. We could feed him some blood, but I don't have an easy source unless you're volunteering. It has to be human blood."

Eva choked. "*Feed* him . . . ? Blood?" Surely he didn't mean what she thought—

"Annnd that's enough chit chat." Meph jumped between her and Bel from out of nowhere. "Eva, you want to keep some pressure on that wound? Thanks, doll." Without waiting for her to comply, he grabbed Bel by the arm and dragged him back to the kitchen.

Eva hastened to Ash's side, pressing the dishcloth against the wound, and heard furious whispering coming from the other room. They were trying to keep their voices down, but she picked it up anyway.

"Don't you think she has enough to deal with tonight without you trying to feed her blood to Ash?"

"Well, I don't know! I thought she liked him. He'd heal faster with it, so I thought I'd at least ask."

"All you're going to do is freak her out and make her *not* like him. Poor bastard deserves a break after three thousand years of misery."

"Fine." Bel sighed. "He's an idiot for not saying something."

"You're an idiot for shouting at him."

"Fuck you."

"Fuck you too. Go deal with the human. And put on a damn shirt so you don't scare her. You look like a berserker with Ash's blood all over you."

"Shut up. And *you* deal with the human. I have to figure out where the fuck we're going to go now that Ash is unconscious."

"We can't go anywhere."

"We don't have a choice!"

"We can't leave the wards, and we can't use a gate until he wakes up."

"Damn it, Meph!"

"How is this my fault?

"Because it's always your fault, jackass."

While Meph and Belial argued, Raum suddenly rushed into the living room carrying the now red-hot knife. He bent down beside Ash, brushing Eva's arm aside and pulling off the dish towel, holding the knife out—

"Wait!"

Raum glanced at Eva, who was suddenly seized with horror. "Can't. The blade will cool."

"If I give him my blood, will he heal?"

His face softened. "He really won't feel a thing, Eva."

"But—"

A hideous sizzling sound filled the air, followed by the sound of melting flesh. Eva gagged and stumbled back, sickened by the sound and smell and the sympathy she felt for the unconscious demon on the couch.

In that moment, with him lying unconscious, his skin pale from blood loss, it was hard to hate him for what he was. He just looked like Ash to her. The guy she'd thought she was falling in love with.

A moment later, Raum stood and lowered the blade to his

side. "He'll be fine. His wounds will heal in a few hours, and he'll wake up with a bit of a hangover from the blood loss, that's all."

Eva stared at Ash's still form, unable to keep from staring at the hideous burn mark on his side. He had gotten injured protecting her from Mist. He'd attacked him to keep her safe.

Suddenly filled with resolve, she looked back at Raum. "I'll give him some of my blood."

Raum shook his head. "We don't have needles or medical shit. We'd have to do it the old-fashioned way, and Ash would kill me if he found out."

"We won't tell him, then."

"He's really going to be fine—"

She held out her arm. "Do it or I will."

Why was she so adamant about this? She was too exhausted to think about much of anything, and she didn't have the energy to question her motivations. She just knew she didn't like that grayish tint to Ash's skin.

Raum must have read the determination on her face. "All right. I like you, human." He smiled suddenly, and she realized she hadn't seen him do it before. While Meph seemed to be the joker of the family, Raum was darker and broodier. Something in his golden eyes told her there was a reason for that.

But of course there was. He was a *demon*.

"It's going to freak you out," Raum said.

"Why? I mean, besides the obvious fact that he's drinking my blood."

He cocked a brow. "Come here and I'll show you."

With only a little hesitation, Eva did as he bade, and they crouched besides Ash's still form. He really did look pale, and her resolve strengthened.

"Give me your hand," Raum said, setting the knife down on the floor.

Eva put her palm out. He curled his much bigger hand

around it, holding out her index finger. With his free hand, Raum reached forward and parted Ash's lips.

"See his canines? They look sharp, don't they." He gave her a look.

"No . . ." Her eyes widened. "He's not a—"

"No. But they're created with demon blood, and since Ash is the real deal, he's got the hardware."

"Wait, vampires—?"

But her thoughts scattered quickly as Raum pressed the tip of Eva's finger into Ash's canine. Somehow, the tooth was sharp enough to draw blood, and as soon as she touched it, both canines elongated.

Eva gasped and jerked back. "Oh my god."

"Not exactly." Raum looked at her. "Still offering?"

She stared at those intimidating teeth and considered saying no. Then she thought, *What the hell.* She'd already seen him turn into a seven-foot-tall, red-skinned monster with horns. What were some measly vampire fangs after that?

She looked into Raum's gold eyes and nodded.

"Okay." He gently grasped her wrist in one hand and her forearm in the other. "Unconscious or not, he's going to bite your wrist when I put it in front of him. It's instinct. Fair warning, it's going to hurt. Ready?"

She nodded, so nervous she felt sick.

Raum lowered her arm over Ash's mouth. Just as Raum warned, he struck like a freaking cobra, jerking forward and stabbing those sharp teeth right into her arm. She gasped at the pain, her eyes watering.

Ow. There was nothing romantic or sexy about this. Screw all those vampire kinks because this fucking *hurt!*

One of Ash's hands jerked up and grabbed her wrist, holding it to his mouth so she couldn't escape, and he growled deep in his chest. The sound was kind of sexy. Ugh, she was messed up. He was drinking her blood, for god's sake.

"Okay, that's enough," Raum said. "He doesn't need much." In one fluid motion, he ripped Ash's fingers off her arm and disengaged his fangs from her wrist, shoving Ash back when he instinctively lunged for her again.

Raum held him down with two hands. "Enough."

Ash growled like a feral animal while Eva sat on her ass on the floor, looking between him and the twin puncture wounds on her arm. "Holy shit."

She'd let a demon drink her blood. She was doomed for sure.

"Holy shit is right. Look how fast he's healing." Raum glanced at Eva with a frown. "You must have some pretty potent blood."

Eva sat up onto her knees to watch Ash's horribly burned wound healing before her eyes. Within minutes, it had faded to a scar. She looked at his face, amazed to see the color coming back to his cheeks. He exhaled deeply and relaxed into the couch cushions.

Raum stood. "Let's put a bandage on your arm."

She glanced at her wrist. The fang wound pulsed a little blood when she stopped putting pressure on it, but already seemed to be slowing. Damn, those teeth were sharp. She couldn't stop staring at Ash.

"He'll be fine," Raum said.

She finally dragged her eyes away and climbed wearily to her feet.

She followed Raum down the hallway, past the silently staring Belial and Meph, apparent witnesses to that entire spectacle. On her way past, she scooped up Thelonious's cage, feeling sorry for her poor claustrophobic cat.

In the bathroom, Raum opened a medicine cabinet with cracked glass and pulled out two Band-Aids. He motioned for her to hold out her arm and, with exquisite care, put them over the wounds.

"There." He tossed the garbage and turned back to her. "Good as new."

"Thank you."

He shrugged. "We can't go anywhere by gate until Ash wakes up, so you should get some rest."

"Won't the Hunter come looking for us?"

"As long as we stay behind the wards, he won't be able to find us. We're fine here for a bit."

"Where are we going to go?" She was trying to follow Ash's advice and take things one step at a time, but it was hard not to panic about her uncertain future.

With another shrug, Raum turned and dug through the cupboards behind them. "You want a shower? Here's a towel." He tossed a terry cloth bundle at her. "You can sleep in Ash's bed. You'll probably want to borrow some clothes to sleep in. Follow me."

He pushed past her into the hall, and she followed obediently, more curious to watch the demon playing gracious host than anything.

In Ash's room, he pulled a black T-shirt out of the dresser and threw it on the bed. "There." He turned to leave, but his gaze caught on Thelonious's carrier, still in her hand. "That your cat?"

"Yeah."

Raum's bright gold eyes lit up. "I like cats."

Oh god, please don't tell me he eats cats or something.

"Can I see him?"

Eva hesitated. "Ash told me cats hate demons."

"Except for me. They like me."

"All right." Hoping she wouldn't regret this, she bent and opened the pet carrier.

Thelonious shot out like a rocket, and she expected him to go straight into the closet. But instead, he leapt . . . right into Raum's outstretched arms. The demon stroked her cat lovingly, the little fur ball dwarfed by his big arms. To Eva's amazement, Thelonious curled right up, purring louder than she'd ever heard him before.

"He really likes you." He didn't even like *her* that much, damn it.

"Can I keep him with me?" Raum asked, blinking at her with puppy-dog eyes.

"Sure."

He smiled, and she blinked in amazement. It wasn't fair to human men that he and his brothers were that gorgeous.

Raum left, and Eva was alone in Ash's room. She stood there staring at the wall for at least a minute without moving and then glanced at the clock and recoiled. Almost four in the morning. No wonder she felt like she was viewing the world through a big glass bubble over her head.

Scooping up the T-shirt from the bed, she trudged down the hall in a daze, deciding that no matter how exhausted she was, she wasn't passing up a shower. And it was worth it—the hot water felt amazing cascading over her stiff muscles, and it seemed to wash away any residual terror and panic clinging to her.

By the time she stumbled back to Ash's room, she felt almost normal. She could almost pretend she wasn't sleeping in a house with four demons because her life was in danger. Imagine that.

Curling up in the blankets, she inhaled the scent permeating the sheets and her borrowed clothes. It was a delicious, spicy man-smell that made her toes curl.

She was fast asleep the next instant.

18

COOL AS A CUCUMBER

E VA WOKE UP AT EIGHT O'CLOCK. SHE HADN'T HAD close to enough sleep, yet she felt strangely well rested. Her first thoughts were anxious, however. Why hadn't anyone woken her up? Why hadn't they left yet? Wasn't anyone concerned about the Hunter coming after them?

Sitting up in bed, she clenched her fingers around the blankets and stared at the unfamiliar space. She told herself that the demons knew what they were doing, and if there was cause for concern, they would have woken her.

Then again, maybe not. She really hoped they'd come up with a plan by now, but something told her that was too much to ask.

Ash's room was bare except for a dresser, a desk, and an upside-down milk crate that served as a nightstand. The speaker she'd lent him sat on top of the dresser, and there were a few items of black clothing discarded on the floor. The sheets were gray. One pillow.

A good night's sleep was supposed to make everything better, and she could feel the truth in that. Yes, all of this still seemed impossible, but she wasn't on the verge of a panic attack anymore, and the things that had felt so insurmountable last night were a little less daunting now.

Leaning over, she reached out and hauled her backpack into her lap, pulling her phone out of the front pocket. When the screen lit up, she swore loudly.

It had to be a record-setting number of missed calls. Most were from her dad, and a few were from her mom. She opened her texts and saw another gazillion unread messages there, and then cursed again when she remembered that she'd put her phone on silent last night before Mist showed up. Her dad's call had been an unpleasant interruption after that amazing sex with Ash, and she'd slapped that sucker on silent so she'd never have to put the words "dad" and "sex" together in a sentence again.

Frowning, she suddenly recalled the subject of her dad's call. At the time, he'd seemed irrational, but now it seemed eerily coincidental that he'd called and told her she was in danger right before Mist had shown up. But what would her *dad* know about any of this?

She needed to get up and make sure the demons had a proper game plan, but she couldn't ignore her dad's urgent messages, so she called him back.

"Nice one, Dad," she grumbled when it went through to voicemail. All those missed calls, and he wasn't even there when she finally got back to him.

She called her mom next. The phone rang only a few times before Jacqui picked up.

"Eva, honey! I've been trying to reach you all night."

"Yeah, I left my phone on silent. Sorry about that."

"Are you okay?"

"Um." She didn't know where to begin.

"What happened?"

"Well . . . a lot."

"Honey, I need to tell you something."

"Yeah, Mom. Me too." She decided there was no way she was going through all this madness without telling her mom. "It's about Ash."

"Oh, good, because I wanted to tell you something about him too."

"Last night, I— Wait, what do you want to tell me?"

"This is going to sound crazy."

"Trust me, it won't be as crazy as what I've seen."

"Remember what you saw at that club shooting? Well, I'm not sure you hallucinated after all."

"What? Why?"

"I think your boyfriend . . . I really don't want to scare you, but I think your boyfriend might actually be— He might not—"

"Be human?"

Jacqui choked.

"He might not be human because he's a demon?"

"How did you—?"

"How do *I* know?" Eva barked a bitter laugh. "Well, have I got a story for you! But first, how do *you* know?"

"It's your dad."

She squeezed her eyes shut. "Of course it is."

"Last night, he came bursting into the room while I was reading and asked me where I heard the names of your boyfriend and his brothers. I tried to hold out for your sake, but I eventually cracked under pressure and told him. I didn't mention what you saw at the club because I knew he'd really freak, but he still freaked quite a bit anyway. He said he was going out to his studio, and then he never came back. I went into his office to look for him even though we usually don't disturb each other's private work spaces. But I was knocking at the door, and he wasn't answering, so I had to check and see—"

"And then what happened?"

"I found a book. I think it's called a grimoire? In your dad's office."

Eva blinked. A *grimoire* in her dad's office? Okay. Not at all what she was expecting to hear.

"It was written in Latin, I think, interspersed with some other language I didn't recognize, and there were these symbols. Very complicated symbols, with circles and keys and squiggles, all intersecting."

Oh god, that sounded a lot like the sigils Belial had described. What on earth was her dad doing with that? Was he trying to summon demons? *Please god, don't let him be that stupid.*

"Inside the grimoire there were these loose-leaf sketches," Jacqui continued. "Done recently, in your dad's handwriting. They were the same symbol drawings, but very complex, more so than the others in the book. I was able to decipher the writing at the top of one of the drawings, and the same again interwoven into the design."

"And?" Eva was gripping the phone so hard it nearly shot right out of her hand. "What did it say?"

"Honey . . . it said Asmodeus."

Oh, shit.

"And there were three more papers underneath. Belial, Raum, Mephis— Mephistof— Mephi—"

"Just call him Meph," she blurted.

"Meph. But honey, I think your dad is trying to . . ."—her voice dropped to a whisper—"summon *demons*."

Eva paused. Waited for more.

And then realized she wasn't going to get it.

"That's it? Just the sight of a fancy book and you're convinced demons are real?" She barked another laugh. "Do you know how crazy that sounds? Totally, completely—"

She stopped suddenly, rubbing her eyes until she saw stars.

"You're right," she finally said. "They are real."

There was a pause.

"Eva, I want you to start at the beginning and tell me everything."

"Mom? Hello? Are you still there or did your head explode the way mine's been threatening to?"

"I'm here," Jacqui said quietly.

Eva shifted on Ash's bed, adjusting the pillow supporting her back where she leaned against the wall. "So . . . you don't think I'm completely nutty?"

"Oh, I've always thought you were nutty, hon."

"Mom."

She sighed. "You know I believe you. It's just . . . a lot to take in."

"Trust me, I know." Eva had spent the last ten minutes telling her mom everything. And by everything, she meant *everything*.

"I wish you hadn't gotten tangled up in this," Jacqui said. "I don't like knowing you're in danger."

"I don't like it either. I'm freaking out, and I have no idea what to do."

"And I'm sorry about your boyfriend. It's never fun to find out your trust in someone you care about was ill founded. I'm sorry you had to have your heart broken."

"Yeah."

Her mom hesitated. "You have broken up with him, right?"

Had she? "It's not like we've really had time for that conversation yet."

"But you're going to, right?"

"I dunno," she snapped, suddenly annoyed. "I've been a little too busy worrying about whether I'm going to survive the next ten minutes to spend time thinking about how to dump my demon boyfriend!"

"Okay, okay, I just want to make sure you're okay, that's all. I want you to make the right decisions."

Eva sighed. "I know, I'm sorry. This is all a bit much for me. I mean, I don't even know what to believe about demons, because nothing any of these guys do seems very *demonic* to me. I mean, they're all kind of assholes, sure, but they take care of each other."

"You said they escaped from Hell because they didn't feel like they belonged there anymore. Maybe they have evolved, like Asmodeus said. Still, I don't think it's smart to get involved with him at such an unstable time in his life."

Eva snorted. She made it sound like Ash was changing careers or moving to a new city. Then again, he kind of was.

"And then there's the age difference to consider. He's astronomically older than you."

"I know."

"That's a little weird, isn't it?"

She winced. "Yeah, I never really thought of it that way. He's kind of immature in some ways, though. I think it's because he's just figuring out how to be a normal, functioning person and not evil and conniving, or whatever demons are."

Jacqui snorted. "That's not exactly a ringing endorsement."

"I know."

"And then there's the obvious lifespan difference. I don't see how you could ever be seriously involved with someone who is immortal."

"Immortal . . . ?"

"If he's as old as you say he is, that means he's immortal. He's never going to age. Even if he turned out to be the perfect man for you, twenty years down the line, there are going to be some serious challenges springing up in your relationship. Imagine if you married him, and then a few years later, people started asking if you were his mother. Then, his grandmother."

A sickening feeling twisted up Eva's stomach, but she brushed it off with a laugh. "God, Mom, I think it's a little early to be thinking that far ahead."

"I know, but you have to admit it's a consideration. How

can you start a serious relationship with someone when you know it can't last forever?"

"I haven't— I don't—" She shook her head. "I never said I wasn't breaking up with him. I just said I hadn't had time to think about it. I mean, obviously I have to—"

The bedroom door burst open with a bang, the handle smacking the far wall. Belial ducked under the frame and entered the bedroom without waiting for an invitation.

"Good morning, Eva."

His hair was still miraculously long, and the platinum-blond strands hung past his wide shoulders to his broad chest. Combined with those sky-blue eyes, he really did look more like an angel than a devil. After last night's little outburst, however, there was no way Eva would ever make the mistake of forgetting what he was.

And then there was the smile on his face. It was malevolent and slightly terrifying: the furthest thing from friendly.

She stared at his imposing form, half wanting to shout at him for barging into the bedroom, half wanting to crawl into the closet and hide.

"I couldn't help but overhear the entire conversation with your mother," he said.

"Oh. Shit."

Ash had told her demons had heightened senses, but she'd forgotten. How much had they heard? Probably everything. Oh god, had Ash woken up and heard her talking about breaking up with him?

"Asmodeus is on the balcony," Bel said, answering her unspoken question. "So you'll have to dump him in person later." He glared at her a little, and she winced.

"Who are you talking to?" Jacqui asked into the phone.

"Belial," Eva replied.

"If you'd allow me to speak to your mother," Bel said, "I think I've figured out where we can go."

She frowned. "Where—?" And then it dawned on her. "No way. I don't want her involved in any of this."

"It's the perfect solution. No one would suspect we would visit a human's mother. And, even better, it's a place we've never been before."

"I don't want her in danger."

"Honey, let me talk to him," Jacqui said, obviously overhearing the exchange.

Bel held out a hand for the phone. "She wants to talk to me."

Damn, he really could hear everything. "I really don't think—"

"Let me talk to him!" Jacqui said louder.

Bel wiggled his fingers.

"No!" Eva was quickly losing control of the situation. "She's *my* mother, and I don't want her involv—"

Faster than eyes could track, Belial crossed the room, ripped the phone from her hand, and held it to his own ear.

"Good morning, ma'am," he said, smirking in triumph at Eva.

"You asshole!" she snapped. "Give that back!"

"Yes, my name is Belial, and yes, I really am a demon."

Eva scrambled out of bed and tried to snatch her phone back, only to realize she wore nothing but Ash's oversized T-shirt and her underwear. The shirt was large enough that it fell to mid-thigh, but it rode up precariously when she reached up and tried to snatch her phone back from Bel's grip.

Unfortunately, he was too damned tall, and she couldn't reach it even standing on her tiptoes and jumping. And he was fast, too. He twisted out of her reach every time she got close, until she was dancing all around the room—one hand awkwardly pulling the bottom of the T-shirt down to keep herself covered—while he remained cool as a cucumber.

"I can assure you we mean your daughter no harm." His voice was smooth as silk. "In fact, we seek to protect her at all costs. You see, my brother Asmodeus is quite taken with her. She's the first human to pay him any interest in three thousand years, and he's become attached."

Belial started describing how hellgates worked while Eva continued her fruitless battle to regain possession of the phone. He was oozing charm, putting on his best show for her mother, and she could tell Jacqui was eating it right up.

"Of course I would walk you through the process of drawing the sigil," Bel said smoothly. "And I will take care of activating it, so that's all you'll have to do. Once we arrive, I'll put wards up around your house to ensure Eva's continued safety."

There was a pause while Jacqui replied in which Bel grinned smugly at Eva.

"Excellent. If you would give me one moment, Mrs. Gregory."

He held the phone away from his ear and looked down at Eva. The urge to wither under his piercing blue stare was hard to fight, and she found herself shrinking back a little.

Gritting her teeth, she fought her wariness and tried to grab the phone again, but he held it aloft. His hand touched the ceiling without his arm being fully straight. There was no way she could reach it.

"I made you some breakfast, Eva. It's waiting on the kitchen counter, so help yourself. I'll return your phone as soon as I've finished talking to your mother."

"Damn it, Belial, this isn't funny! Give it back—"

"I beg your pardon, Mrs. Gregory— Yes, it would be my pleasure to call you Jacqui." He turned and strode out of the bedroom without a backward glance. "I did make her breakfast. She is my guest, after all." The door closed firmly behind him.

"Manipulative bastard!" Eva hissed under her breath.

GUILT TRIP

AFTER A QUICK DETOUR TO THE BATHROOM, EVA
pulled on a pair of leggings and then tiptoed into the
kitchen, nervous about facing the other demons. She
couldn't believe they'd heard her entire conversation with her
mom. She hadn't exactly held anything back.

She was still pissed at Belial for commandeering her phone
and involving Jacqui, but try as she might, she couldn't think
of a better escape plan, and she was starting to get panicky
about leaving. If Ash could heal from his wounds in just a few
hours, then surely Mist could too?

The demons' lack of concern about their situation was
both comforting and unnerving, and her trust in them wasn't
exactly high. Having her mom's input would be helpful, she
decided. She promised herself they would stay with her parents only long enough for them to come up with a better
plan.

As Belial promised, there was a plate of food waiting for
her by the stove, and she stared at it in amazement. The omelet
was full of vegetables, garnished with parsley, and served with

toast and cheese slices. It was a simple meal, but the presentation told her there was nothing simple about the quality or ingredients.

She carried the plate into the dining room and froze when she found Meph and Raum already there, staring at her. Raum was sitting at the far end, Thelonious purring in his lap. The furry little traitor had his head tipped back, eyes shut in bliss while Raum scratched his chin with two hands.

"'Sup," Meph said.

She took the vacant chair at the end of the table opposite Raum. There was a chair open beside Meph too, but she just wasn't comfortable sitting that close to him. With all the tattoos and those freaky red eyes, he was intimidating as hell, and that was before she'd found out he was a demon.

She forced herself not to think about that and started eating. As soon as the first bite melted in her mouth, her eyes fell shut. "This is amazing."

"Bel likes to cook," Meph said.

"He's good at it."

Raum transferred his intense gold eyes back to the cat in his lap, dark brow furrowing in concentration as he continued diligently scratching Thelonious's chin.

She watched her purring cat in amazement. He'd always been friendly, but not that friendly. "I think my cat likes you more than me," she said, scowling a little.

"Raum has a thing with animals." Meph smirked. "You should see him with the crows in the park."

Raum glared at him and shrugged at Eva.

Awkward silence fell again. While she ate, she studied the two brothers and they studied her too, though everyone tried to be discreet about it.

Meph sipped a cup of coffee, tattooed hands wrapped around the mug. He was definitely scary, but he was almost always smiling. Raum, on the other hand, exuded a dark

intensity that was all coiled strength waiting to strike. He reminded her of a panther stalking through the bushes.

"Where's Ash?" she asked after swallowing her last bite.

"On the deck sulking and chain smoking," Meph said.
"Bastard stole my headphones too."

"Is he okay?"

"Oh yeah. All healed up. Your magical blood did wonders."

"Too bad it couldn't heal his personality," Raum added,
and the brothers snickered.

"Does he remember . . . ?" She trailed off, unable to actually say *drinking my blood* out loud.

Raum shook his head.

Meph said, "And we're not about to remind him either."

"Works for me. Did he eat?" Why did she care?

"Ash doesn't eat much."

"Why not?"

"We don't have to eat to survive, but demons love indul-
gences, so we choose to because it's fun. But Ash doesn't taste
anything, so he doesn't get any enjoyment out of it. He only
eats when Bel makes him."

"Oh." Poor Ash.

Eva finished her breakfast and went into the kitchen to
wash her plate just as Belial appeared, holding her cell phone.
He took one look at her standing by the sink and smiled.

"Hey, assholes, look at this. Eva's washing dishes. You
should come here and take notes. Or better yet, help her."

"I hate dishes," Meph complained. "I like to kick back after
eating. That takes all the fun out of it."

"You know what really takes the fun out of it? Me punching you in the stomach."

Eva couldn't stifle her grin. The crazy brothers were growing on her.

"Here's your phone." Bel set it on the counter and then
crossed his bulky arms. "Your mom seems cool."

She dropped the dishcloth and turned to glare up at him, pretending she wasn't still severely intimidated in his presence. She summoned all her courage for her next words. "She is cool. And if anything happens to her because of this, I will study witchcraft for as long as it takes to learn how to trap you and force you to experience burning agony for the rest of all time. Is that clear?"

Belial nodded encouragingly. "Very creative and descriptive. I like it."

"I'm threatening you. You're supposed to be cowed, not impressed."

He patted the top of her head like she was a toddler and went into the other room to speak to Meph and Raum. "We're going to meet Eva's mother, and we need to leave now. One of you go get Asmodeus and tell him the plan."

"You go," Raum said.

"No way," Meph replied. "I already went out there, and he tried to stab me with a lit cigarette."

"He shouldn't be outside at all," Bel grumbled. "He knows the wards don't extend onto the deck."

"I tried to tell him that, but he wasn't exactly in a listening mood," Meph said.

Bel sighed. "He's extra moody today."

Raum dropped his voice to a whisper. "Give him a break. His human's going to dump him."

Eva winced. She may have underestimated their hearing, but she was pretty sure they underestimated hers as well. She continued washing dishes as quietly as she could, straining to hear.

"He'll be fine," Bel whispered, "we just have to get him to play music and figure out how to make the curse lift. Women will swarm him again, and he can go back to being the Prince of Lust if he wants."

"You're sure that's how it happened?" Meph asked.

"It's the only explanation that makes sense."

Eva stared at the soapy dishwater, recalling the events of that night. Was that why those women had approached and Skye had suddenly noticed him? Because playing music somehow counteracted the curse?

"You're forgetting something important," Meph whispered. "He had a crowd of women after him, but he didn't want any of them. He just wanted *her*."

Belial scoffed. "This is so like him, the idiot. Always wanting what he can't have. The last time he got involved with a single human female, he decimated a whole village and got saddled with this fucking curse."

Eva gritted her teeth. They made it sound like Ash was stupid for wanting to spend time with a person he shared common interests with, and she didn't like it. And, though she didn't condone his actions in the least, blaming him for what had happened to get him cursed didn't seem fair either. She'd bet money his brothers had done worse in their lifetimes.

Drying her hands on a dishtowel, she marched into the dining room, silencing their whispered conversation. "Ash is on the balcony?"

They all nodded.

"I'll go tell him the plan."

She turned to go, heading toward the patio door in the living room.

"Neither of you should be outside," Bel said. "The wards—"

"I'll just be a couple minutes, and then we're leaving the province altogether, right? It'll be fine."

"Just make it quick. Oh, and Eva?"

"What?"

Something flashed in his eyes. "Ask Ash to tell you how a human can travel through a gate."

She frowned. "How?"

"Just ask him."

She found Ash sitting on a plastic deck chair in the sun, dark sunglasses over his eyes, Meph's headphones on his ears, smoking like a tree. The ashtray beside him was piled full of butts. At least she knew the cigarettes didn't affect his health now, but it was still super gross.

He was wearing a pair of sweats and a black tank top that looked sexy clinging to his muscular upper body. Still wet from a recent shower, his hair hung over the back of the chair like a black waterfall, almost brushing the ground.

Eva sat on the other flimsy chair beside him, and he glanced over, pulling the headphones off his ears and then looping them around his neck under his hair. She could just make out the sound of a sultry trumpet solo coming through.

Actually, the melody sounded familiar. "Is that . . . ?"

"Miles."

Of course he was listening to Miles Davis. Because it wasn't enough that he was the most perfect male specimen she'd ever seen. He had to have impeccable taste in music to go along with it.

He smokes. And he's a demon. Right. Not so perfect.

"Nice," she said lamely. When he said nothing, she blurted, "I told my mom everything, and Belial stole my phone and asked her to draw the other sigil thingy. So we're going there."

Ash just looked at her, giving no indication he was even listening.

She kept talking to fill the silence. "It's all ready now, and we should get going. I mean, no one else seems to be in a rush, but I thought we were worried about Mist finding us, and I don't see why we're not taking this more seriously. It's making me nervous, honestly. So, I came out here to tell you we're leaving."

He nodded and took a drag of his cigarette. "All right."

"Are you feeling—"

"I'm fine."

Okay, then. She fell silent and focused on her hands fidgeting in her lap. Miles wound his way around the notes of a sultry scale from the headphones around Ash's neck.

"You told your mom everything?" he asked eventually.

"Yeah."

"What did you say about me?"

She shrugged. "I told her how we met and what I saw at the nightclub, and how we connected through music. And I told her how I thought we had something special, but then I learned who you were and how this was only about sex for you, and yeah."

"Oh." He looked away at the admittedly terrible view.

They were facing another equally ugly, gray apartment building with water stains on the brick under all the window sills. On the balcony opposite them, a man wearing a stained undershirt was scratching his armpit.

Eva frowned at Ash. He looked dejected, sad even, but she couldn't be sure. She didn't trust any of her assumptions about him since learning what he was. "You're the one who said that, Ash."

"Yeah." But he didn't sound all that sure of himself.

What was she doing, talking about this with him? She didn't want to date a demon, right?

He could shapeshift into a creature from nightmares . . . but he was still Ash. Try as she might to forget everything she'd learned about him while they were getting to know each other, she couldn't. She'd been blown away by how compatible they were, how many similar interests they share, and how easy it was to talk to him.

It was somehow easier to keep pretending the red-skinned monster was a figment of her imagination than to forget all that.

In her head, she kept hearing his laugh when they talked for hours on the phone, seeing his eyes light up when they played music, and worse, remembering the way he moaned when he came inside her. Or how he looked naked. Or how amazing it felt when they'd had sex on top of her piano. Or how—

Okay. So she was still wildly attracted to him. Demon or not, he was still the hottest man, creature, person, *thing* she had ever seen.

So where did that leave her? Was she deranged? Deeply disturbed? Shouldn't knowing what he was kill any desire she felt for him?

"I'm having these . . . feelings," Ash said suddenly, and she glanced at him in surprise.

He looked about as relaxed as a man sitting on a cactus. His muscles vibrated with restless tension, and a grimace twisted his features. All the while, Miles kept up his soulful trumpeting from the headphones.

"Um, what feelings?"

"I don't know." He shrugged and dragged hard on his cigarette. "I don't know feelings."

"Right." God, he was weird. Guess she knew why now, though.

His eyes narrowed. "Like, when you were scared, I kinda felt like puking. And I had this urge to make sure you weren't scared anymore."

"Oh." Okay, gross. But also kind of sweet.

"And when you told me you couldn't leave your life here, I had this kind of achy feeling." He rubbed his chest. "It hurt. Which is strange because I can't feel pain." He frowned. "I didn't like it. And I also felt guilt. That feeling I know."

Damn, her heart hurt now too. It was sad and a little sweet, but mostly just sad. Poor Ash had no idea how to identify his own emotions. It made her want to cry for him. It made her want to hug him.

She remembered his theory about demons evolving. Was it possible he had evolved to the point where he was genuinely experiencing human emotions, and he couldn't understand them because he had no past experience with them?

If that was true, it brought up a thousand more questions. In her understanding of demons—which, granted, was very little—they were supposedly the antithesis of positive emotions, the pinnacle of those being love.

But if Ash was having these humanlike emotions, did that mean he was capable of experiencing love? He might have no clue what it was if he felt it, but it might be there all the same. It would explain so much about him. His relationship with his brothers, his passion for music . . .

Was it possible he could learn to love *her*? Did she want him to?

Ash puffed hard on his cigarette. He was inhaling that toxic, formaldehyde-laced poison like it was the air he needed to breathe.

"I feel . . . attached to you. Like I am to my brothers, but different. More." He scowled, keeping his gaze locked straight ahead. "It's uncomfortable, and my chest aches all the time, and I fucking hate it."

She couldn't help it. She smiled. It was the sweetest, most incompetent way she'd ever had someone tell her they cared.

"Ash . . ." What was she going to tell him?

"We should go," he grumbled, taking another drag of his cigarette. The thing had burned into a pencil-shaped point, he was smoking it so hard.

She couldn't help it. She reached forward and ripped it out of his hand and crushed it in the ashtray.

"What the hell?" He glared at her, and she was immediately transfixed by those midnight-blue eyes.

"Smoking is gross."

"I like it."

"It smells nasty."

"I can't smell."

"It's addicting."

"I don't care."

"It's bad for the environment."

"I don't care about the environment."

"You should care! The more you damage the Earth, the less enjoyable it will be for you to live here in the future when all the resources are used up, the air is polluted, there's garbage in the rivers, and all the forests have been cut down!"

She suddenly realized she was shouting and shut up. Then she realized their argument had nothing to do with smoking or the environment and was really about something else altogether.

Still glaring, he crossed his arms, making his biceps bulge. *That hair. Those eyes* . . .

She wanted him. It didn't matter if that made her a demon consort, devil worshiper, or in need of serious therapy. She still wanted him. And she wasn't sure what to do with that information.

"You're right," she said suddenly, not ready to think about it yet. "We should go."

She might still want him, but it didn't change the fact that he'd blatantly told her he was only interested in her for sex. His emotions might say otherwise, but she told herself that he needed to learn how to understand them before she would consider anything more.

She stood. He stood too. They stared at each other for a moment, and then he gestured toward the door. "After you."

Right, then. She turned and slid the heavy glass door open, slipping back inside. She was too aware of Ash coming in behind her. Too aware, because it felt like she had turned her back on a fire. She could feel heat on her neck and a sort of tingling that made her want to spin around and look again. To stare into the fire in fascination and never look away.

Mishetsumephtai the Hunter ghosted up the side of the concrete building and reformed on the roof. As soon as he took physical form, the sizable hole in his throat began gushing blood, but he ignored it. He was used to suffering.

The persistent hum of multiple air conditioning units filled the air, and the noxious fumes of scented laundry gusted from numerous vents, causing his sensitive nose to wrinkle. What was it about the human world that fascinated others of his kind? Parts of it were hardly an improvement from Hell.

And what was it about human females that made them willingly submit? Humans were soft and seemingly harmless, and yet this was not the first time Mist had witnessed a powerful demon fight his nature to cater to a female's wellbeing. Nor was it the first time he had witnessed a female's apparent acceptance of a demon's true form.

Asmodeus was unaware Mist had been eavesdropping when he had admitted his "feelings," and Mist felt quite sure he wouldn't have spoken of them had he known. That a Prince of Hell was capable of "feelings" was . . . unsettling.

It was true Asmodeus had severely wounded Mist during their fight, but vapor could not bleed, and it had been simple enough to remain in his nonphysical form while he followed the car to this secondary location. Which also appeared to be the hiding place of Belial, Raum, and Mephistopheles. And, though wards prevented him from entering the apartment, thanks to the conversation he'd just overheard, he now knew exactly where they were going.

Mission accomplished.

It was time to return to Hell and report, since reinforcements would be required in order to force Belial's compliance.

And yet . . . Mist hesitated. Again.

Indeed he had faltered in his duty once before. He had broken the rules. The remembrance caused his heart to thump and his tail to flick nervously. Rule breakers were punished. The consequences were never worth the infraction.

So why did he persist in this rebellion?

Why did he protect those that owed him nothing? Why was he sitting upon this roof, holding his ruined throat together while his blood spilled over his fingers, pondering Asmodeus's relationship with a human instead of reporting his whereabouts to Paimon? And why was the Duke of Hell Eligos still safely ensconced in his oceanfront hideout with his human lover? Mist had proclaimed him destroyed rather than revealing his location, and he still wasn't sure why.

The last time he had checked on Eligos and Natalie, he'd found them sharing a meal upon a blanket at the top of the cliffs, Natalie's small frame intertwined with Eligos's hulking, monstrous one.

It was bizarre. It was *wrong*. A violation of so many rules it was impossible to count. And yet, Mist could not erase the gnawing hunger and emptiness that consumed him when he pictured himself in their shoes.

Was he experiencing "feelings" of his own? Which ones? Longing? Jealousy?

Pondering this was an exercise in futility, however. Such freedom was not an option for him. There was no escaping his fate, and he had long since given up hoping otherwise. There was only so much disappointment a mind could take before it lost its will to live.

The smart thing to do would be to return to Paimon's lair now and report the location of Asmodeus and his so-called brothers. It was too late to admit to his lie about the true fate of Eligos, but he could still save himself from repeating his mistakes.

Mist rose to his full height and stretched his wings. He crouched and then sprang, pumping them hard to gain altitude until he was among the low-hanging clouds. There, he dissolved his physical form until his essence mingled freely with the mist.

He reformed again above Evangeline Gregory's apartment, folded his wings against his body, and shot like an arrow straight through the hole in her window.

Landing neatly, he surveyed the wreckage of the flat, once again questioning his motives. He couldn't for the life of him explain why he had returned or why he was *still* hesitating. But he couldn't make himself leave either.

The sight of an upturned plant caught his eye. The soil spilled upon the hardwood was mildly disturbing to his somewhat compulsive nature, and he decided he would right it. It was he who had upended it in the first place, after all.

But when he stepped forward to complete the task, he hit an invisible wall of pure, concentrated energy, the antithesis to everything he was. White light flared, blinding him, and he was thrown backward to land in a heap.

Shock coursing through him, he climbed to his feet. It was only then that he noticed the design inscribed upon the floor around him.

He was, in fact, standing in the middle of a powerful binding sigil.

20

Bonus Chapter

IGNORANCE ISN'T BLISS

WHEN EVA STEPPED INSIDE, SHE WAS GREETED BY THE sight of Belial leaning against the wall in all his looming intensity. His arms were crossed, and his jaw was set. She got the sense his patience was running thin, and she really didn't want to find out what happened when it finally ran out.

Then again, she could guess. The sight of him bursting into flames was probably going to give her nightmares for a while.

"You're ready to go, then?" he said. "The hellgate's ready."

"I just need to grab my stuff," Eva replied quickly. "And put my cat in his carrier." She shot a look at Raum, who was still seated at the dining table beside Meph, Thelonious in his lap. "Just give me five minutes."

"Fine," he growled. "Just hurry up."

She nodded and scurried away, eager to escape his intensity.

"Chill out," she heard Ash say to Bel before she slipped

back into his room. She paused in the doorway to listen. "Don't scare her."

Eva bristled slightly. It was true she was a little nervous, but she didn't need Ash fighting her battles, and she didn't want him making her look weak to his brothers. The last thing she wanted was for Belial to know she was afraid of him.

"I'm not," Bel said defensively. "I've been perfectly nice."

"You wouldn't know *nice* if it hit you in the face with a shovel."

"Funny, because hitting you in the face with a shovel is exactly what I'm going to do if you don't get your shit together in the next five fucking minutes so we can leave."

Ash mumbled a parting insult, and then she heard him stalking down the hall toward her. She hurried into the room, looking for something to do with her hands so it wasn't obvious she'd been eavesdropping.

She settled on making the bed, which took all of ten seconds. When she straightened again and spun around, Ash was standing behind her. He'd closed the door, and for some reason, that made her heart race.

Which was stupid. They'd been alone on the balcony two minutes ago. She'd had sex with the man multiple times. He'd kissed and touched and licked every inch of her body.

She did not need to be thinking about that right now.

They stared at each other, a beat of silence passing.

He broke the connection first, stalking over to the dresser and setting the headphones he'd been using atop it. The speaker she'd lent him was beside them. He suddenly tugged his tank top over his head, giving her a view of his muscled back, long hair spilling over it. Her mouth went dry.

"What are you doing?" she croaked.

"Just gonna change my shirt before we go." He balled the old shirt up, tossed it onto a pile of black fabric in the corner, and then pulled open the dresser drawer and started digging through it.

She stood there and stared at his back, watching the play of tiny muscles as he moved. Mesmerized.

With a mental smack, she dragged her eyes away, trying to remember what the hell she was doing here. *Getting my stuff so we can go.* Right. Stuff. She had stuff. She'd brought a backpack full of haphazardly packed clothing, yet she was still wearing Ash's T-shirt.

Whatever. It was comfy and smelled good, and she didn't feel like changing.

She grabbed her bag from the floor and stuffed yesterday's outfit into it. When she straightened, she found Ash watching her, a fresh T-shirt in his hands that he had yet to put on.

Their eyes met and held yet again. She cursed him for drawing her into those indigo depths. She cursed him for being so damned attractive. Her gaze wandered down his bare torso against her will.

And then she realized the skin was perfectly smooth and unblemished. Even the scar she'd seen yesterday was gone.

"You're really healed," she said, remembering the sickening smell of burning flesh as Raum had cauterized the wound. She hadn't doubted his brother's word, but it was still a shock to see with her own eyes.

Ash looked down at himself, sending his hair swooping forward. He brushed a hand over where the wound had been. "Yeah. Usually I'd have a scar for a few days." He frowned. "I don't know why it healed so fast."

Because I fed you my blood, probably. But she wasn't telling him that.

"I'm glad you're okay." Her voice was slightly breathless, and she winced.

He looked back at her. "Thanks. I—" He swallowed. "You too."

"I wasn't hurt."

"You were scared." He glanced away. "I don't like it when you're scared."

Damn it, he was not cute. "I wasn't that scared," she said, suddenly remembering his earlier words to Belial. "And you don't need to protect me from your brother either."

He frowned.

"I'm not scared of Belial." *Lie.* She totally was.

Understanding dawned. "Bel is a dick. I was just reminding him to watch his step around you."

"I can handle him." Actually, she highly doubted that was true, but she was putting on a brave face, and "fake it till you make it" was still the best advice she'd ever heard.

"Eva." His eyes were suddenly beseeching. "I—"

"Did you get the speaker to work?" she interrupted, gaze landing on the device on the dresser. She wasn't ready to hear anything more about feelings right now. Demons weren't the only ones capable of being overwhelmed by emotions. She still wasn't ready to let go of her anger and sense of betrayal, but it was hard to stay mad when he looked at her with those big sad eyes.

His head turned to look at the speaker. "Yeah. I figured it out the first time I called you. The night we first— Yeah."

She coughed lightly and pretended not to feel the wave of heat that washed over her at the memories of his moans distorting her phone speaker. She'd never thought she'd be into phone sex, but damn, it was extremely hot with him. "What did you listen to?" she asked to distract herself.

"Herbie."

She chuckled. "Herbie Hancock, Miles Davis, Oscar Peterson . . . You really like the old-school guys, huh."

"To be fair, the last time I was on Earth, they weren't old school."

She blinked. Damn, that was too weird. But then that

would mean . . . "You haven't heard any new music since when? The seventies? Eighties?"

"Eighties, I guess?"

"Oh my god," she breathed, and she couldn't help it. Her eyes lit up with the possibilities. "Old school is brilliant, but you need to listen to some current innovators. Shit, I have so much music to show you!"

His eyes lit up too. "Yes, please."

"Some of my favorite modern jazz artists are piano players. I know a few with a style that reminds me of yours. Honestly, Ash, it's amazing you've got such a unique style without having any current influences. You're going to die when you hear—"

"Are you two fucking ready yet?" Belial's voice boomed from down the hall.

Eva smiled sheepishly, realizing they'd been distracted. Ash smiled too. *That smile.* He was so damn pretty, she could stare at him for hours and not get bored.

"Later," he said. "Show me later."

She nodded. "You're going to love my parents' house. They have a sweet music room with a grand piano. It's way nicer than mine."

His eyes lit up again at that.

"We can jam 'My Funny Valentine' again."

"I'd like that," he said eagerly. Adorably.

Stupid, Eva. He's a demon, remember? A demon jazz pianist. She snorted a laugh at the absurdity of it all, and he frowned.

"What?"

"Nothing. You're just . . . an anomaly. Or an enigma, I don't know. Maybe both."

He looked more confused, if anything.

"I mean, a demon musician? That sounds crazy to say out loud."

He shrugged and looked away, and was he . . . blushing? She couldn't tell, but his expression seemed shuttered and he was avoiding her eyes. "Demons can't be musicians," he said.

"That's a stupid statement," she replied. "You're a musician. And a demon. Ergo, a demon musician."

"Yeah, but like I said before, demons don't have souls, so they can't—"

"And that's bullshit. I've seen you play. You're incredible. I don't care who or what you are. That's a fact."

He looked intently back at her, and yet a-fucking-gain, she found herself caught in the trap of his gaze.

He stepped closer, and she was suddenly painfully aware of the fact that he wasn't wearing a shirt, and that he was still just as stupidly gorgeous as always, and she still hadn't developed any method of resisting him.

If he'd been charming, flirtatious, she'd have been able to brush him off, but it was his awkward vulnerability that robbed her of all her defenses.

He seemed so confused by her sometimes that she knew he was being completely open with his emotions. He didn't understand them well enough to hide them, and damn her, but she found it endearing.

He reached up, fingering a curl that lay over her cheek. When he brushed it back, tucking it behind her ear, a shiver raced down her spine. The curl sprang free again, so he tucked it a second time.

"You're so pretty," he said, gaze wandering all over her face. "I could look at you forever."

Her cheeks heated with a blush. "Ash . . ."

"I noticed you from across the club, even before I knew you could see through my curse. You looked so vibrant. You drew me in and I couldn't look away. I'd never seen anyone like you. I'd never heard anyone play like you."

Her heart fluttered dangerously. The curl sprang free from

behind her ear again, and when he lifted his hand to tuck it once more, she couldn't help it. She turned her face into his touch.

He cupped her cheek and then dragged his thumb over her lower lip. A small breath escaped her.

He repeated the soft stroke, and something low in her belly clenched. He stooped and tilted his head. There was only a small gap between their mouths now. She wanted him to kiss her so badly.

"Show me," she whispered before he could.

He blinked in question.

"Your other form. Show me."

If she was going to do this again, she wasn't going to be in denial. She wasn't going to pretend he was something he wasn't.

Right now, his enormous, red-skinned form lived in her hazy memory like a nightmare. She still couldn't quite reconcile the man in front of her with that form, and she knew she needed to if she was going to give into . . . whatever was happening between them. She still wasn't ready to define it.

"Eva . . ."

"I want to see."

He hesitated, searching her gaze. She couldn't give him the assurance he probably sought. She couldn't guarantee that she wouldn't flinch away from him in fear. In fact, she probably would. A part of her wanted a chilling reminder of what he was because she *wanted* it to scare her away.

There were so many reasons not to get involved with him, so many reasons it was a terrible idea to start a doomed relationship with a supernatural being from Hell that was destined to spend the rest of his immortal life on the run. Maybe seeing that terrifying, red-skinned form again would be the wake-up call that she needed.

And maybe Ash understood that, because his expression

changed. That open, earnest, slightly hungry look shifted to one of acceptance with a hint of sadness. She loved how easily she could read him. She probably understood what he was feeling better than he did.

But then . . . she watched as the black of his pupils bled out until it filled both of his eyes. And he wasn't quite so harmless anymore.

In fact, he was frightening. Deadly. She sucked in a breath at the sight of that void-like blackness staring down at her.

And then she gasped again when a sharp, black claw curved out from the thumb still pressed against her lower lip. He started to drop his hand, but she caught his wrist and lifted it to study.

His hands were still those gorgeous piano-player hands. Long fingered and elegant, with strong veins on the backs. But the claws that curved from the tips of his fingers were decidedly impractical for playing an instrument and definitely made more for ripping out someone's throat.

The artist was gone; this was the demon. The killer. The thought sent a chill through her.

As if to emphasize her point, she watched as the hand she held in her grasp suddenly morphed to a deep, blood red. Startled, she dropped it and looked up, back into his face, only to find the change to his skin had taken over his whole body.

Her breath caught, and her heart started to pound. She was truly staring at a supernatural being that shouldn't exist. But he did exist, and the proof was right before her eyes.

He wasn't human.

He wasn't fucking human.

Yes, she'd seen Ash fight the Hunter, and she'd seen Belial burst into flames. Yes, Ash and his brothers had told her about the supernatural world, about angels and demons and Nephilim and Watchers and demon hunters and ancient battles.

But here and now was when the last shred of her denial and disbelief finally fell away.

She waited for the fear and panic to hit.

It didn't.

All of this was really fucking real and it was happening to her, and it was happening right now. And she would never be the same again. The entire course of her life had altered, and she didn't know what that meant yet.

But she did know she didn't want to go back.

That empty feeling, that sense of longing, that confused, baseless searching . . . Maybe this was where it had always been leading. Maybe she'd had an intuitive sense that this was real all along, and that was why she'd always felt like some part of her was missing.

She didn't believe ignorance was bliss. Ignorance was ignorance, and she would much rather know and face hard facts than live in the dark.

Ash was still missing his wings, she realized. And his horns. And his height. He'd been enormous before: as tall as Belial. She was glad he held off on the remaining changes, however. She wasn't sure she could handle everything at once.

"Eva," he said softly. His voice hadn't changed, but she remembered it being deeper when he was bigger, which made sense. "Say something."

She took a breath.

And then she whispered, "Kiss me," before she lost her nerve.

He didn't need to be told twice. He bent his head and took her mouth with such possessive intensity that she melted against him without a second thought.

He backed her up a few steps. Their lips parted. His tongue snaked between them, and she let out a breathless moan as it swept against hers. She reached up and threaded her fingers into his silky hair, bunching it up in her hands. Strong arms enveloped her, and he pulled her firmly against his body. His hard, muscular, *familiar* body.

God, she hadn't realized until this moment that she'd missed him. She'd been mourning the loss of him after finding out what he was, and yet, he was still right here. Kissing her just like he had before, when she'd been falling hard and fast and telling herself it was too early to start envisioning a future with him.

But he was still the same Ash. Red skin or not, he was still—

His claws pricked against the skin of her back as he dug his fingers into her, and her mind blanked.

Okay, so he wasn't completely the same. But she was finding it harder and harder to care, and her resolve to stay away from him was slipping, and—

"I told you to hurry the fuck up!" Belial boomed from outside the door, and just like that, the spell was broken.

They broke apart, both of them breathing heavily. Her hand flew to her chest, clutching at her racing heart.

The black bled from Ash's eyes and his skin returned to a warm tan, and suddenly, he looked human again. But he wasn't, and she would never think of him as such again.

Everything was different now, and she had to decide what she was going to do about it.

"We'd better go," he said, giving her one last heated look before turning away. He looked like he wanted to devour her, and she wanted him to.

It was a good thing Bel had interrupted him. Not just because their lives were in danger and they needed to run away, though that was a fairly valid reason. But because Ash needed to sort out his feelings for her before she let things go further between them.

Until he could admit that he wanted her for reasons beyond her ability to see through his curse, she couldn't give him more. She had too much self-respect for that.

They needed to have a conversation, she decided. A real heart-to-heart. Ash was going to hate it, and she smirked to herself at the thought.

But not now. Now, they had to go.

Ash tugged the T-shirt still in his hand over his head and then went to the closet and grabbed a jacket and donned it, pulling his long hair out from under the collar.

"You need me to carry anything?" he asked.

"I— Um. No. I've got it." She picked up her bag and swung it over her shoulder.

Their gazes met again, and she could tell he wanted to say more, but he didn't. He turned away and opened the door, and the two of them stepped back into the hallway.

Meph, Raum, and Belial were waiting in the living room. There were flames sparking in Belial's eyes again, and she immediately tensed.

"You said five minutes, not five fucking hours," he growled.

"Shut up, Bel."

"Did you tell her?"

Ash frowned. "Tell her what?"

"About the gate."

"What about it?"

Oops. "Belial told me to ask you how a human can travel through a gate," Eva explained.

"You didn't even ask?" Bel asked her.

"I forgot."

"And you couldn't tell her yourself when it came up?" Ash rolled his eyes. "Asshole."

"Why?" She narrowed her eyes, looking between the two demons. "How does it work?"

"You're not going to like it," Ash said warily.

"Just tell me." She raised a brow. "You already told me a bunch of stuff I didn't like. What's one more thing?"

His mouth twisted, but he obliged her. "Hellgates are

Sheolic magic, which means only demons can use them. But if a human ingests demon blood, they temporarily take on some demonic abilities, which means they *can* travel by gate."

Eva's mouth dropped open. "You're not telling me I have to . . . drink your blood?"

His expression said it all.

She looked at Belial. He nodded. She looked over at Meph and Raum. They shrugged simultaneously, which would have been funny under any other circumstance.

Horror filled her. "No way!" she exclaimed. "That's disgusting and so freaking wrong on so many levels." She jabbed a finger at Ash. "There is no way you'll convince me to drink your blood, so go on and give up that idea right now because it is *never* happening!"

ALL GATES LEAD
TO HELL

EVA DRANK THE DEMON BLOOD.

She actually opened her mouth and swallowed a mouthful of blood that had come from Ash's veins after he made a sizable cut in his arm right in front of her. And then, of course, she immediately sprayed it everywhere and gagged so hard she almost threw up her breakfast.

At least she didn't have to worry about diseases—apparently, demons were immune to everything. *Yay.*

They'd repeated the process. Three more times.

Only her guilt about Ash having to cut himself again when the wound started healing motivated her to keep it down the final time. It was the most disgusting thing she'd ever done.

Strangely, however, the moment she swallowed back the last wave of nausea, a strange sense of satisfaction filled her. Deep inside, the whispers went silent as something shifted on a fundamental level. That questioning, longing, and emptiness went silent, as if it had finally found the answers it sought in a mouthful of iron-tasting hemoglobin straight from a demon's vein.

Which made no sense whatsoever.

When she shook off the effects and straightened her spine, she felt taller. More powerful. In control and connected to herself for the first time in as long as she could remember.

Damn, she thought, rubbing her temples to clear the bizarre thoughts, *apparently demon blood is potent stuff*. She supposed she could handle a mild high as long as she didn't turn into a vampire.

After sufficiently recovering, she grabbed her backpack, coaxed Thelonious back into his carrier—apparently, cats were more demonic than anyone realized, because they could travel through hellgates with no problems—and then followed everyone into Bel's bedroom, where an intricate design was drawn on the floor.

"Ready?" Bel asked, and they nodded. "Doors are locked?" More nods. "Dishes done?" Nods. "Windows clo—"

Meph shoved him hard. Bel stumbled into the circle and disappeared.

"Oh my god," Eva breathed, staring at the empty space. "He's gone."

"Gates are cool like that." Meph grinned and stepped into the sigil. He, too, disappeared.

"Oh my god," she said again. It didn't seem any less miraculous the second time around.

Raum went next, carrying Thelonious in the carrier, and then she was alone with Asmodeus. Since it was her first time, they would travel together. She hoped it would be her last time too; she wasn't keen on a repeat of the blood-drinking experience.

Just thinking the word "blood" had her stomach churning. Drinking blood was not sexy. This experience had cured her of any illusions she may have had about that. *No sparkly vampires for me, thanks*.

"Ready?" Ash asked, and she nodded.

He held out his hand.

She hesitated, staring at his open palm and intuitively sensing this signified something more than just stepping into the sigil with him. This was one of those point-of-no-return moments.

Fuck it, she thought, *it's too late to go back now.* She remembered her earlier conviction that ignorance wasn't bliss and she wouldn't return to how she'd been before learning all this even if she could.

And then she put her hand in his.

They stepped into the gate together, and the world turned into a vortex, her stomach dropping out the bottom of her.

Blackness. Swirling, swooshing blackness surrounded her as they plummeted through the abyss. And then time froze, and everything went red. Red and black.

The air felt too cold and too hot at the same time. It smelled like a mixture of hot tar and burning plastic. A lightning storm thundered across the red sky. Blackened, thorny vines crept across the ground. Dead, gnarled trees speckled the landscape. In the distance, she could see mountains, rocky and barren. She felt cold, yet her skin was sweating, her blood boiling.

And then, like a hook behind her navel was yanked with sudden force, she was shooting through the void again, this time up instead of down. She never loosened her tight grip on Ash's hand, and it was only his steady presence that kept her from screaming.

A moment later, they landed hard.

Finally letting go of Ash, she went flying back and would have fallen had his arms not locked around her, pulling her against his chest.

Looking up, she shook her head to dislodge the mass of curls in her eyes and saw the face of the man holding her. His hair was windswept, draped around his shoulders like the softest silk, his dark blue eyes full of concern and so beautiful she lost her breath. His lips, his cheekbones, his brooding dark brows . . . He was a living, breathing work of art.

"You okay?" he asked.

"What *was* that place?" Images of the horrible, red-and-black wasteland sent shivers through her.

"Hell."

Dear god. She certainly hadn't imagined Hell would be a picnic, but that . . . She understood their motivation to escape in a whole new way.

"All gates lead to Hell," Ash explained, helping her regain her balance. "Even using them on Earth, you have to make a stop there along the way."

"Oh."

"You were scared." He frowned. "I should have warned you first."

"It's okay—"

"Eva!"

It was her mom's voice. She jerked around, Ash releasing her, just in time to see Jacqui come bursting into the big barn studio.

Eva raced out of the sigil and threw her arms around her mom, glad to be home.

"Come in, come in," Jacqueline Gregory said, waving them into the house through a glass patio door.

She was the spitting image of her daughter, though her skin was several shades darker, her eyes brown instead of Eva's pale gray, and instead of Eva's wild curls, her hair had been tamed into thin dreadlocks, currently twisted in a knot on top of her head.

"How was your trip? Is that weird to say? I'm not sure how this works exactly." She wrung her hands. "Have you eaten? I could whip something up. Oh, leave your bags by the door, and you can let Thelonious out. We'll sort out the sleeping arrangements later. Come in and make yourselves at home."

"Don't touch anything," Ash hissed at Meph as he looked around the house.

There was art everywhere—paintings on the walls, sculptures on the shelves made of metal, stone, and clay. You name it, Meph could break it. Ash had seen it happen.

They stepped into the living room, and all four of them stood transfixed by the view for a moment. It had been a long time since any of them had the opportunity to experience nature, and Jacqui's house was right in the middle of it. A tall, A-frame window opened onto an ocean view—choppy waves tossed on a rocky shore covered with dark moss and seaweed—and the house was sheltered by tall cedars on either side.

Meph, of course, went right ahead and touched everything anyway. He dropped his bag at the door per Jacqui's instruction, wandered straight into the expansive living room, and picked up and examined all the art on the shelves.

"Meph—" Ash hissed, just waiting for disaster to strike.

Jacqui appeared behind him with Eva in tow.

"Meph, damn it, put that back—"

"Oh, no, that's all right." Jacqui smiled. "Go ahead and touch anything you like. Art is meant to be experienced with the senses."

Meph spun around with a delicate clay sculpture of a dragon in hand. "This is cool." He grinned and held it aloft.

Raum, Ash and Bel all winced.

"Thank you," Jacqui said brightly.

"Meph," Bel growled, "if you don't put that down right now, I will fu—" He glanced at Eva's mom. "I will . . ." He trailed off, apparently unable to complete a threat without the word "fuck" in it.

"Be angry," Raum finished for him.

Meph returned the dragon to the shelf, and they breathed a collective sigh of relief.

"Right," Eva cut in. "Guys, meet my mom, Jacqui. Mom, this is Ash, Bel, Meph, and Raum."

Poor Jacqui seemed a little shell-shocked. "Wow— Sorry if I'm a little— I can honestly say I never expected to have visitors of your— Well, what you are—"

"Demons?" Meph said, that stupid-ass grin never leaving his face.

"It's not offensive to call you that?" Jacqui asked, still wringing her hands. "I don't want to say the wrong thing."

Raum shrugged, stroking the little gray cat that had jumped back into his arms. "We are what we are."

"Being offended is for humans," Meph agreed.

For some reason, Jacqui appeared charmed by the idiot. "You know, that's probably true." Then she looked at Ash, and her expression turned calculating. "So this is the mysterious man who has captivated my daughter."

He shrugged weakly.

Her eyes narrowed. "Hmm."

"He probably looks boring and ugly to you," Meph piped up, "but that's only because he's cursed."

It took all Ash's self-control not to punch him in the face. "Meph—"

"He's actually a handsome devil." Meph chuckled at his own joke. "Before he was cursed, he was actually the Prince of Lu—"

"Shut up," Raum hissed in a low voice. "You don't tell your girlfriend's mom you were the Prince of Lust."

Jacqui was still studying Asmodeus intently. He'd been interrogated by Lucifer himself and never felt this fucking uncomfortable. "He doesn't look boring or ugly to me," she said. "Actually, he's quite striking. Definitely not invisible."

Everyone stared at her.

"But that's impossible," Belial said. "His curse makes it so that any potential sexual partner is completely uninterested—"

"Bel, stop," Ash groaned. God, he was worse than Meph.

"Well, that explains it right there," Jacqui said. "I would have to be the world's worst mother to look at my daughter's boyfriend as a potential sexual partner."

Ash put a hand over his face and wished to disappear.

"Oh my god," Eva said. "I can't believe we're having this conversation."

"Eva, darling, he's very handsome, and I can't wait to hear you play music together, but you can rest assured I have no designs on him. I am, after all, a married woman—"

"Mom! Seriously!"

She smiled at Ash when he lifted his head. "It's nice to meet you. Thank you for keeping my daughter safe."

He mumbled a response, but it didn't sound like words.

"He's shy," Meph stated, still grinning. "After three thousand years of being invisible, he lost all his people skills."

"Pretty sure he has better people skills than you, jackass," Bel shot back. "Do you ever shut up?"

Meph sneered at Belial.

Jacqui smiled at Meph and quickly changed the subject. "I love your tattoos. I'm fascinated by the concept of using the body as a canvas. If I were a braver woman, I might have explored it myself."

Meph blinked. "Uh . . . thanks." It appeared that for the first time ever, he'd been shocked into silence.

"Can I ask you what inspired you to cover your whole body?"

Eva pressed her fingers to her forehead. "Mom—"

"Bel told me it's an outlet for my self-destructive tendencies," Meph said, having no filter on what was or wasn't appropriate to say. "He said I channel my need to harm myself into getting tattoos instead of doing stupid shit that will one day get me killed."

"That's not quite how I said it," Bel grumbled.

"I'm pretty sure that's exactly what you said."

"I think that's beautiful," Jacqui said. "We all carry a certain amount of darkness inside us. Art in any form is a safe way of expressing and releasing it. There's no need to feel shame about it."

Meph nodded. "It helps me. When my skin is full, I think I'll peel it off and start over again."

Jacqui's mouth dropped open.

"Meph, shut the fuck up," Raum hissed.

He glanced around. "What?"

There was an awkward silence.

Then, Jacqui clapped her hands. "Who's hungry?"

Dan Gregory stood in the wreckage of his daughter's apartment and surveyed with cold disinterest the demon writhing in pain within the sigil at his feet. He felt no sympathy, considering he'd had to sweep aside shards of glass and debris to clear space to draw the design. He'd picked up only three energetic trails here—his daughter, Asmodeus, and this fucking demon.

Mishetsumephtai, Hell's notorious Hunter, thrashed wildly as Dan twisted the end of his sword in the creature's back. The binding sigil prevented him from turning into mist, and without it, it would've been impossible for Dan to catch this powerful demon on his own. Even then, he'd gotten lucky. He'd set the trap, and it had been pure chance that Mishetsumephtai had walked into it.

"Where is she?" Dan growled, twisting the sword again.

The gray-skinned demon's leathery wings were draped limply over him, his claws digging into the hardwood from the agony. It was no regular weapon that Dan had stabbed into his back. He was quite certain the Hunter would have barely blinked had it been. No, Dan was armed with the only type of weapon really capable of killing a demon.

Unfortunately, he couldn't kill this one. Mishetsumephtai was on sanctioned duty from Hell, sent to locate four rogue demons. It was against the rules to destroy a demon on an authorized Earth mission, as long as that demon continued to follow the rules during its foray.

Asmodeus, Belial, Mephistopheles, and Raum, however, were fair game.

They were not sanctioned to be on Earth. They were not following the rules. And though it seemed Hell was trying to retrieve them without destroying them—at least for now—they knew very well what Heaven's response would be were they to get their hands on the rogues.

Dan didn't give a shit about the rules anymore, really. He had retired years ago when he'd met his wife and hadn't planned on getting involved again.

That was until Eva had gotten dragged into this somehow.

He fought the urge to shout with frustration. *How* had she gotten involved? He'd done everything, taken every precaution, to keep her safe from this world, and yet she'd ended up with a Prince of Hell in her apartment. And their energies were commingled, particularly in the bedroom, which was enough to send Dan into a full-blown rage if he thought too hard about it.

"Where is she!" he shouted at Mishetsumephtai, digging the consecrated sword into his spine a little deeper.

"I'll never tell you," the crazy demon hissed, laughing between cries of pain as Empyrean light cascaded over his writhing form.

"Why are you loyal to Asmodeus?" Dan spat. "He betrayed you. He escaped from Hell."

"I have no loyalty to anyone other than my mistress, and I would kill her in a second if I could."

Dan rolled his eyes. *Demons*. It was amazing they managed to get anything done when they were so busy stabbing each other in the backs.

"Asmodeus broke the rules," Dan said. "He must be punished. You of all people should respect that."

The Hunter's unbending adherence to the laws followed by demons and angels on Earth was well known, and considering he was usually here collecting rogues and rule breakers, he was one of the few demons Heaven held in relative esteem.

Turning his head, Mishetsumephtai grinned, showcasing a mouth full of pointed teeth. "I am learning how to be a rebel."

Great. So much for "unbending adherence." Biting back his frustrated growl, Dan yanked his sword out of the demon's back. "Why are you protecting him?"

Mishetsumephtai rolled away, crumpled wings folding under his enormous ash-gray body. "I want what he has." He blinked his eerie yellow eyes slowly as if the confession was as much a revelation to him as it was to Dan.

"What does he have?"

"Freedom. A human pet."

Dan roared at hearing his daughter being referred to as a "pet" and stabbed the goddamned demon yet again.

"I'll let you destroy me before I give up Asmodeus and end his fun," the Hunter hissed through the agony.

"You're here to take him back to Hell!" Dan shouted, unable to believe he could be facing off yet another defector. What was going on down there? Was the underworld facing some kind of uprising? "*You* are here to end his fun!"

"I've been watching him." The demon's spine arched as another wave of white light cascaded over him. "He doesn't know. He thinks he's safe from me, but I know exactly where he is."

Dan jerked the sword. "Tell me!"

"I'll never tell." He laughed maniacally and said in a sing-song voice, "I'll never tell, I'll never tell!"

Dan's cell phone began to vibrate in his pocket.

Growling in frustration, he struck the demon upside the head with the flat side of his sword. He collapsed unconscious.

Dan yanked the phone out, hoping it would be Eva. He'd called her over and over last night without her answering, and they'd been playing phone tag ever since.

But it was Jacqui's number on the screen.

He grimaced. He had no clue how he was going to explain any of this to his wife, but when the time came, he knew it was going to be ugly. His heart ached at the thought of losing her, but it was an all too likely outcome. And he would deserve it, too.

He couldn't ignore her calls any longer, though he wanted to. She deserved better. "Hey, honey."

"Dan! I've been calling you all morning!"

"I know." He winced. He should have picked up sooner, but he'd been futilely trying to delay the inevitable.

"Where are you?"

"I'm, um . . ." He looked around Eva's apartment. "It's a long story. Hon, have you heard from Eva?"

"Yes! That's why I've been calling you all morning."

"You have?"

"Yes! She's here now."

He blinked. "She's . . . with you?" But her energy was all over the apartment, and it was recent. There was no way she would have had time to fly home between then and now. "But how?"

"She brought her four demon friends, and they traveled through a hellgate."

Dan stopped breathing.

His heart stopped beating.

Actually, he was pretty sure the Earth stopped turning and

everything froze in stasis for a moment, allowing him a second to come to terms with what he'd just heard.

It didn't help.

"She *what?*"

"Yes, so whatever you're doing, come home now and meet Eva's friends. I think you'll love them. Belial is a darling. He helped me make lunch, and he's an amazing chef! And Meph has incredible body art from head to toe. I've never seen anything like it. Raum is a tougher nut to crack. I've been trying to get him to open up, but no luck so far. And of course there's Eva's new boyfriend. He's not at all what I expected. I've been keeping my eye on him, and let me tell you, I'm not sure he's all that bad—"

"Jacqui, I'm coming home right now. Take Eva and lock yourselves in my office in the studio. There are wards above the door to keep out intruders, but you need to activate them. You will need to prick the tip of your finger and press a droplet of blood into the center of the—"

"I *knew* it! I knew you knew about all this! What were you doing with that big spell book in your office?"

Dan fought down a surge of panic. He'd been in such a rush to make sure Eva was safe last night that he'd accidentally left the grimoire in his office.

He'd wanted more time to figure out how he was going to explain everything to Jacqui, but it looked like that was no longer an option.

He'd never wished more than he did right then that he was more of a skilled teleporter because he'd have already shown up back home. As it was, he needed time and silence to concentrate.

"Listen to me," he said, trying to keep his tone even when he really felt like screaming. "I will explain everything. I promise. But right now, I need you to get away from the demons. Take Eva and get into my office. Activate the ward."

"There's no cause for concern, Dan. Eva told me why they escaped Hell, and I think I understand. They're definitely a little roguish, but I don't see evil in them. I think they're just looking for a second chance."

"Jacqui, they're *demons*. They trick people. That's what they do. You're not safe."

"How do you know about all this? Why didn't you tell me?"

"There isn't time to explain. Just take Eva and—"

"You know what? I'm going to need more than that. Eva has been honest with me, and so have her demons, and it seems you have not. I'm finding myself less inclined to listen to someone who has obviously been lying about something important for . . . how long, Dan? How long have you known about this and not told me?"

Dan winced. If he told her the answer to that, she would flip out. No, that was going to be one of the last things he explained. "Jacqui, honey, I need you to trust me."

"Sorry, but I have to go." Her voice was flat. She never shouted, but she didn't have to. He could tell by that tone alone she was pissed. "Belial is washing the dishes by himself, and I'd like to help. I'll see you when you get home. Love you."

She hung up on him.

He called her back. She ignored it.

"Damn it!"

A sense of being watched had his gaze returning to the demon trapped on the floor. Mishetsumephtai was regaining consciousness, blinking groggily. "You've broken a lot of rules yourself, haven't you, Watcher?"

Dan stared at him. There was no surprise in those yellow eyes. How much did he know? Did he suspect what Dan's relationship to Eva was?

If so, then, against the rules or not, Hell's Hunter had to die.

He scowled at the bloody, trapped demon. "I'll deal with you later." Once he made sure Eva was safe, he would find out what Mishetsumephtai knew and deal with him accordingly.

He needed a plan, and he needed to be smart about it. One Dan against four greater demons was not great odds. His best bet, he decided, was to lay traps like he'd done for the Hunter. They would have to be extremely powerful to hold Belial, and they would have to be well hidden to avoid detection by demons that had thousands of years of practice avoiding them.

He struck Mishetsumephtai with the blunt side of his sword again because he needed the quiet to concentrate. When the demon crumpled, Dan closed his eyes and focused, gathering his power.

A moment later, he vanished into thin air amidst swirling winds.

As he disappeared, the last remaining gust teased the chalk line at the edge of the sigil containing the unconscious demon, smudging it slightly.

DIVINE INTERVENTION

JACQUI HUNG UP THE PHONE, MORE DISTURBED THAN she cared to admit. Why was Dan involved in this? And how big of a secret had he been keeping from her? She had a strong suspicion she wasn't going to like the answers to any of those questions.

She slid open the patio door and stepped back inside, closing it behind her. Eva had warned her the demons had heightened senses, and she hadn't wanted them to overhear, so she'd made sure to walk a distance away from the house before calling Dan.

Back inside, she could hear Meph and Raum bickering about something in the living room, the muffled conversation featuring an array of creative profanity. Belial washed dishes in the kitchen, and there was muffled music coming from the den, not quite buried beneath the sound of clinking porcelain.

The music was what really caught her attention.

She stopped, hand still wrapped around the door handle, and listened closer. Sultry piano chords were complemented by the ethereal tones of Eva's violin as she outlined the mournful melody of "My Funny Valentine."

Jacqui wandered into the kitchen in a daze, needing to share the moment with someone. That was the beauty of art at its finest—it was always better when there was another who understood your wonder.

Belial glanced up from the sink when she entered.

"That's your brother? He's . . . They're . . ." She actually had to wipe a tear from her eye. "They play together so beautifully. Like they were made to."

Bel nodded and went back to scrubbing. He had a face like an angel, but there was a hardness to those features that made him intimidating and difficult to read. Not to mention, he had to be seven feet tall, and it was hard to see his face at all from that height.

"We found out recently that music makes Ash's curse lift," he said. "The effect seems to be temporary, but I'm daring to hope he can find a way to lift it permanently if he keeps experimenting. It's never been a possibility before now."

She grabbed a dish towel and took over drying and putting away. "How did it happen?"

"Eva and Asmodeus played together at Eva's jazz club. Afterward, he got attacked by women. They swarmed him like wasps on shit."

She had to laugh at the analogy. "What did he do?"

"After three thousand years of being invisible, he panicked." Belial snorted. "Eva came to his rescue and dragged him out of there."

"He wasn't tempted by the women?"

"Nope." Belial shook his head. "He's always been a bit weird, but that was taking it to a whole new level."

Well, that was interesting. "Why do you think the curse lifted?"

"Something to do with the music. Ash always said he wasn't a real musician because he's a demon, and I think it ties into that."

Jacqui scoffed. "He sounds like a real musician to me."

"I know. But he thinks music comes from humans' souls, and since demons don't have souls, whatever art he creates is just a mockery of the real thing."

Jacqui paused while drying a plate and considered this. "There may be some truth to that, but I think he's missing an important point. In fact"—she lowered the plate and looked up at Belial—"I think all of you are."

The imposing demon tilted his head as he met her gaze. It would be oh so easy to wither under that piercing stare, and she was glad there was no malice in it. "What point?"

"You escaped from Hell because you didn't feel you belonged there anymore. Eva told me about Asmodeus's whole 'theory of demonic evolution,' and well, I think it's true. While you may not be humans with human souls, I don't believe you're entirely demonic either. I think you may be something in between. And if you look at things from that perspective, it makes perfect sense why Ash's curse would lift when he plays music."

Without breaking eye contact, Belial passed her another plate to dry. "Why?"

"If music is an expression of divinity, then every time Asmodeus plays, he's becoming a little more divine and a little less demonic. The curse was on his demonic self, so it won't affect this newer, more human side of him."

Belial stared at her without speaking for so long, she finally caved and looked away. But it didn't help. It felt like his eyes were burning a hole in the side of her head as she focused on drying her next plate. She hoped she hadn't angered him by suggesting Ash wasn't demonic, but she wasn't going to take back what she'd said.

Something in her pressed the importance of connecting with these beings, even one as ancient and formidable as Belial. If there was truly such a thing as demons that could evolve, then helping them along that process seemed like a necessary service to the world.

"That makes sense," Belial finally said, and she breathed a silent sigh of relief. He shrugged enormous shoulders. "Too bad it wears off eventually. Ash said that after a few hours, he was back to normal."

Jacqui smiled, setting the dried plate on top of the stack in the cupboard. "Then I guess he'll have to keep playing music regularly, won't he? I bet that if he keeps fostering this new side of himself, the curse will eventually go away forever."

Belial's mouth lifted in one corner, and the dimple that appeared in his cheek nearly knocked her flat. "You're right."

Underneath that aura of danger, there was a powerful charisma to him that was profoundly compelling. And he was, of course, devastatingly handsome. All the demons were. Eva had warned her about his short temper and the resulting chaos, however, so she remained wary.

That half-smile suddenly became a full-fledged grin, upping his devastating handsomeness to an eight-point-oh on the Richter scale. "You know, I've been searching for ways to break Asmodeus's curse for millennia, and you've gone and solved it in one go. What's more, he's obsessed with music. And you're telling me all he has to do is keep playing."

"It's probably the same with your love of cooking. Cooking is an art form, a passion for creation. It's an expression of divinity."

Just as suddenly as it had arrived, the smile disappeared, and his face hardened once again into an impenetrable mask. "My problems are a little too complicated to be solved by cooking."

"Nonsense. I happen to believe art is, in one way or another, a solution for everything. In fact, my husband and I use that concept behind all our . . ." She trailed off, her whole conversation with Dan coming back in a rush.

Belial glanced at her as the sink drained with a gurgle. "What?"

She sighed. "My husband has been hiding something from me. Eva must have told you about that book I found in his studio, and he's been acting very strange."

"I may have overheard something about it over the phone, but Eva didn't tell me about a book."

"I think it's a grimoire. It was full of symbols like the one I had to draw to get you here."

His eyes widened and suddenly, he was radiating intensity. "What's he doing with a grimoire?"

"That's just it. I have no idea." She sighed, hanging the dish towel off the stove handle. "We've been married for twenty-seven years, and he's never given any indication he knew about all this supernatural stuff, and yet he obviously does."

"What's in the grimoire?"

"I don't know, since I can't read Latin anymore, but I found four pages he had drawn himself that very clearly had your names on them."

Belial's stare intensified until actual flames flickered in his eyes, causing her to recoil. She could have sworn the temperature in the room dropped several degrees.

"He has a sigil with *my* name on it?"

She nodded warily.

Meph and Raum appeared in the kitchen.

"There's no way it's your seal," Meph said. "And if it was, it's not like he'd be able to use it."

Bel looked at Jacqui. "Could you show us this grimoire?"

She hesitated. "What kind of seal are you talking about?"

"Every demon has their own unique seal that can be used to summon and bind them," Meph explained. "For greater demons, it's extremely difficult to do, and most of the time the summoner makes a mistake and ends up dead."

"But occasionally, they get it right," Raum added.

"And when they do, the demon is bound to the summoner. He has no choice but to obey. And the more powerful the demon, the more chaos the summoner can make him unleash. And good ol' Bel here"—Meph slapped his brother on the back—"is one scary motherfucker."

Bel shot him a dark look but said to Jacqui, "If someone were to bind me, the destruction I could cause would be apocalyptic."

"It could literally start the apocalypse," Meph supplied.

"You erased all records of that seal thousands of years ago," Raum grumbled. "There's no way Eva's dad has it."

Jacqui stared at them, horrified by the implications. "Well, we should probably make sure, just in case. Follow me."

The four of them headed outside toward the studio, Raum depositing Thelonious on a chair on their way past. No one considered disturbing Eva and Asmodeus.

The way it always did when they played together, Eva and Ash's music came to its natural conclusion and ended perfectly—as if they'd spent hours practicing when, of course, it was a total fluke.

They were so in sync when they played, it was like she could read his mind. She'd never experienced anything like it. "My Funny Valentine" was her new favorite song and playing it with him felt like speaking their own secret language, communicating in a way that only they understood.

She set the violin down on top of the grand piano and stared at Ash, who stared back at her. He was a master musician, a passionate lover, a mystery she was dying to solve. She was transfixed. Fascinated.

In love with him.

Damn it.

"The curse lifted again." Ash studied his hands like he'd

never seen them before and then closed his eyes and inhaled deeply. "It smells so good here. The briny ocean. The cedars." His eyes opened and fixed on her. "You."

"Me?" Her heart started racing.

He stood and came toward her. "You're so fucking beautiful." His eyes roamed up and down her body like he was trying to consume her with his gaze. "Your brown skin, your black hair, your light gray eyes." He stepped closer, and her heart beat faster. "There are flecks of blue in them. I didn't notice before." He inhaled again. "Fuck, you smell good."

Oh god, he was turning her on.

No, no, no, she had to fight this. She wasn't giving in until he opened up to her. "You do realize that if every time you play music your curse lifts, you can have sex with a thousand different women who find you attractive, right?"

That was the metaphorical equivalent to a bucket of ice water on her libido.

He shrugged. "Yeah." He barely seemed to be paying attention to the conversation, too busy scanning up and down her body, and damn it, that libido sprang right back to life like a weed that wouldn't die.

"So . . ." She tried to glare at him. "You don't need me anymore. You can have all the women you want. So you can stop with this whole 'pretending you're into me' thing."

His eyes flashed to her face. "What?"

"You can stop pretending I'm special to you!" she snapped, the hurt from before finally rearing its ugly head again. "You can stop pretending there's anything more between us. You can go sleep with all the women in the world and forget all about me." Damn it, that sounded petty.

"I don't want to sleep with all the women in the world." His eyes narrowed.

She threw her hands up. "Well, just a select few then, I don't know!"

He frowned. "Why are you acting like this?"

His cluelessness was cute before, but now it was pissing her off. "Hm, maybe because you blatantly admitted to using me for sex, and since I'm not a goddamned automaton, hearing that shit hurt more than a little!" She accidentally shouted the last part.

"I already told you it was more than that. I told you about my . . . feelings." He grimaced at the word.

"That's not enough, Ash. I'm interested in you for more than just sex, and if you don't feel the same way about me, then I need to protect myself and end this now."

23

FACE THE MUSIC

I DON'T WANT TO END IT," ASH GROWLED, AND SHE couldn't help but be charmed by his fierceness.

"Me neither," Eva replied, her tone gentling despite her best efforts to remain pissed, "but I need more than that from you. Don't you get it?"

"No." And the look on his face said he really didn't.

She sighed. Was she really going to do this? Bare her heart and soul only to get potentially trampled over? But he genuinely wasn't going to understand if she wasn't blunt about it, and honestly, she preferred the up-front method anyway even if it hurt worse in the moment. At least when it was over, she would know she'd given it everything she had.

"Look, you say you're . . . attached to me in some way. Well, I feel attached to you too." God, that was such an unhealthy way of putting it, but she figured attachment was probably the only form of caring he was familiar with.

He frowned. "You do?"

"Yes. I still have feelings for you even after learning you're an actual demon from Hell." She blew out a breath. "I should probably be trying to thwart your attempts to lure me onto the path of wickedness or whatever."

"Don't say that." His mouth twisted. "It makes my stomach feel weird again."

She grit her teeth to keep from softening. *He is not cute. He is not cute.* "But there's more to being in a relationship than attachment. At least, I need more."

"You want a relationship?"

"Uh, yeah, what did you think we've been doing?"

"I dunno." And once again, the look on his face said he really didn't.

God help her. Literally, she needed help from the big guy. *Dear God, please help me, because I'm about to have the relationship talk with a demon because I have genuine feelings for him. Amen, or whatever you're supposed to say. Sorry if that was offensive.*

She took a breath and launched into it. "When people care about each other, they make a commitment. Generally, it's exclusive. It means no sex with other people, no flirting, nothing. You're honest, and you tell each other secrets. You become friends, but you also build something deeper than friendship that hopefully turns into love."

Ash grimaced at the word love.

Yeah, thought that might happen. "There's no guarantee that will happen, but both people go into it hoping for that outcome." She took a breath. "When I met you, that was what I wanted. It's what I still want."

"Love . . . ?"

He could barely get the word out. Damn it, this was hopeless. What had she expected to happen?

"Yes. Love. What we have is really new, but before the whole demon thing came up, I was hoping that was where we were heading. Now, I don't know, but I can't keep doing this unless you're willing to admit you want the same thing. Dating a demon is already crazy enough, but letting a demon use me and break my heart—no freaking way."

"I . . . don't want that."

"Neither do I." She blew out a tired laugh. "Trust me, it sucks."

He scowled suddenly. "You've experienced this before?"

"In high school. I got crushed by this guy I was into for years. He blew me off in front of all our friends, and I was devastated. I don't think I've ever felt so embarrassed."

"I'll kill him," Ash growled, hands curling into fists. "Tell me where he lives."

"No, Ash, that's not the point of the story. The point is that the way you've been acting is doing the same thing."

"I don't want that," he said again.

"So, then tell me what you *do* want," she pressed, while a big part of her was shaking her head and preparing for disappointment. "Tell me it's not just about sex to you. Tell me I mean more to you than that."

His lip curled. "Emotions are for humans."

She crossed her arms, trying to act tough. "Yeah, well, I'm a human, so you're going to have to deal with it. And if you don't have emotions, then you obviously don't care whether we're in a relationship or not."

"Maybe I don't want a relationship."

Okay, that one hurt. *Don't let it show.* "Then it's over."

He scowled. "No."

"Yes."

"No."

"Yes!" she snapped. "I can't do this unless you're willing to talk about your feelings. It's all or nothing, baby."

He crossed his arms and glared at her. "That's not fair."

"It's perfectly fair. You lied to me about everything from the start, and while I understand why considering how messed up the truth is, it's not exactly a good foundation for a relationship. If you don't want this to be over, then you're going to have to convince me your intentions are good."

"I already told you my feelings." His eyes narrowed to angry slits. "I want you enough that I'm not interested in anyone else. I could have other women, and I don't care. What more do you want me to say?"

"That's a start, but there's more to a relationship than just sexual attraction."

He rolled his eyes. "I don't see why."

"Because it's not fulfilling or healthy otherwise! I refuse to date a guy who can't think of one other thing he likes about me besides sex."

"Fine. I can't believe you're making me do this." He heaved a sigh and dragged his fingers through that gorgeous hair. "I like your music. You play better than anyone I've heard in centuries. There's a . . . light in you that comes out in everything you do, and I'm obsessed with it. You make people care about you because you care about them first. You know you're beautiful, but you still have humility. You're confident but not conceited. You aren't afraid to be vulnerable. You say exactly what's on your mind without fear of how others will react, yet you're never callous.

"I've never enjoyed my existence more than the time I've spent with you. I have never felt more alive than when I'm inside you. If I could go back in time and reverse the curse Raphael put on me, I wouldn't do it because it would mean I wouldn't get to meet you. All the bullshit I've endured for the last three thousand fucking years was worth it for the time I've spent with you." He grimaced. "Is that good enough? Can I stop now?"

Eva stared at him with her mouth slightly open. It was the most beautiful thing anyone had ever said to her.

Ash threw up his hands, misinterpreting her blank look. "That's all I've got, Eva. I'm not a human and I never will be, nor do I want to be. I can't change what I am, and I've spent the last three thousand years hating my existence, and I'm sick of it. From now on, I'm going to do things I enjoy, and I'm done catering to others' demands, whether it's Heaven or Hell or even you—"

She pressed a finger to his lips. "Shh."

Yes, she had just shushed a Prince of Hell. And by the look on his face, he wasn't happy about it. But this was important.

She stepped closer, tilting her head way up to look at him. "I'm not expecting you to say it any time soon, or understand it right away . . ." She took a breath, throwing caution to the wind. "But if you've actually never enjoyed your life more than when you're with me, that sounds like love."

He growled and looked away.

"And guess what? I feel the same way. It's why I'm so adamant about making you admit this to me."

His gaze snapped back to hers. "You do?"

She nodded. "I've never felt this way about anyone before. I feel so connected to you, it scares me sometimes. When you're with me, I feel complete, and when you're not, I want you back by my side."

His eyes flared. "That's how I feel. Tell me more."

She had to smile. "Honey, that's what love is. Don't you understand? This"—she gestured between their bodies, though only inches separated them—"has the potential to become love, if we're not already there. Those uncomfortable feelings you have are because love makes you vulnerable, and it's scary. I want us to be loyal and stand by each other's sides."

"I want that too."

Her heart went from breaking to overflowing. "So you *do* want a relationship, then?"

This time, he nodded slowly like he was finally grasping her explanation and deeming it acceptable.

"You want to commit? You want to be a team? A *monogamous* team?"

"Eva, I spent three thousand years feeling numb. After enough time, I stopped longing for my old life and started wishing for a new one. I've had centuries to clarify what I was looking for, so when I say I want you, I mean it."

Her heart melted. It liquified into a puddle of mushy goo that spilled at his feet. "I want you too. More than anything."

Screw the fact that he was a demon, and that she was a human who would age and get wrinkly while he would be beautiful forever, and the fact that he had hordes of demons trying to drag his ass back to Hell. They would deal with all that later.

He lifted a hand and stroked her cheek. "So you liked my feelings? I passed your test, and you won't leave now?"

"I'm not leaving." Eva reached up to the hand at her cheek and wove their fingers together. "It was so sweet what you said, and I loved all of it. And you know I feel the exact same way. Thank you for telling me."

"Good. I'm . . . happy."

"Me too."

"I like seeing you in color. You're just as bright as I knew you'd be." He lifted the hand not clasped with hers and traced his finger along her eyebrow with deep focus, murmuring, "I like that your eyes are still gray though. They looked exactly the same the first night I ever saw you. The world was black and white, but you still looked colorful to me."

Her heart felt like it would burst, and she smiled up at him. He said the sweetest things sometimes without realizing it, and she loved him all the more for it.

Yes, love. She was in love with a demon. *So sue me.*

And maybe it would take Ash a while to admit to feeling actual *love* himself, but she knew he felt the same about her in his own way.

"Want to see my bedroom?" she blurted, grinning mischievously. She was suddenly in the mood to demonstrate her affection.

His lips curved. "Do I need to answer that?"

"Nope." She grabbed his hand again. "Come on."

He opened his mouth to reply and then froze. His smile dropped, his body became rigid with tension.

"Wh—?"

He jerked to the side and ducked just in time to dodge a huge sword swinging through the air, aiming right where his neck had been seconds before.

Eva screamed.

"Through here," Jacqui said nervously, ignoring the part of her that wanted to run screaming from the demon beside her. Since telling Belial about that grimoire, the tension had been pouring off him in waves, and her instincts were screaming *DANGER.*

She fought them with logic—he was angry about the book and the risk it presented, not at her. He was learning to fight his urges and control his temper. He was trying his best, and he really did seem like a nice guy. Remembering their earlier friendly conversation helped her calm down a little more.

"Meph, what did I tell you about touching shit?" Raum hissed.

Jacqui looked back and had to smile. Meph had picked up the vulture's head from Dan's sculpture and was holding it up to the neck as if trying to work out how to attach it.

"If you can figure out a way to make that head stay on, be my guest. Dan's been trying for ages, and no matter what he does, it keeps falling off. He's ready to scrap the whole project." The vulture was huge, nearly six feet tall, and constructed out of scraps of metal from old machinery.

Meph studied the head in his hands and then looked up at Jacqui with a grin. "Cool."

Belial looked skyward. "Meph—"

"It's okay," Jacqui said. "I really don't mind. I'm not kidding about Dan being ready to throw it away, and I like that he's interested."

"All right, but don't be surprised if he breaks stuff. Because he will break stuff."

"I'll take the risk. The artist in me can't stand to discourage someone showing interest in creativity."

Raum cocked his head and blinked his gold eyes. "You're an interesting human."

"Thanks?"

She chuckled, wondering how any of them got by without giving away the fact that they weren't human themselves. It seemed to her they would stand out like sore thumbs, making comments like that.

"Follow me, you two, and I'll show you that book."

She ushered Raum and Belial into Dan's office while Meph played with the vulture, pointing them to the grimoire on the desk. Dan's office was a mess—one of the reasons they liked to have their own private workspaces. Jacqui couldn't concentrate amidst clutter, while Dan always got stressed when she moved anything, claiming it disrupted his creative flow.

"Oh, shit," Raum breathed as soon as he saw the old book.

Belial bent over the grimoire and carefully flipped through the worn pages. Raum hovered beside him while Jacqui watched from across the desk.

Belial flipped to the bookmarked page, and they all stared at it.

"Fuck," he said.

"Well, at least it's not your summoning seal," Raum muttered, fingering Dan's hand drawn sketches. "These are just modified tracking sigils."

"Not sure this is any better."

Jacqui's heart pounded. That didn't sound good.

Belial closed the book suddenly, studying its cover.

"That ain't no regular grimoire." Raum shook his head, and they regarded it warily, as if at any moment, it might leap out and grab them.

Belial's head snapped up and he focused on Jacqui. She flinched at the flames flickering in his eyes. "Where did you find this?"

"Here."

"You've never seen it before?"

"No. I rarely enter Dan's office, but the few times I have, I've never seen anything like this."

"You have no idea what your husband is?"

"*What* he is?" She frowned. "You make it sound like— What is he?"

The demons exchanged glances.

"He can't be." Raum rubbed the back of his neck. "If he was, then you know what that would make Eva. They were banned from making more ages ago."

"Unless she's not his daughter by blood," Belial suggested.

"He might have found the grimoire by accident. It doesn't prove—"

"There's no way they would have let this fall into human hands."

"Yeah, but don't you think it's a bit of a stretch—"

"Is Eva adopted?" Belial asked Jacqui all of a sudden.

"What? No, of course not."

"Were you ever unfaithful to your husband?"

Her mouth dropped open. "No! Why would you— That's not—"

"He can't be," Raum interjected. "We would have sensed by now if Eva was Nephilim."

"If Eva was what?" Jacqui asked, starting to really freak out now.

"But it would explain how she could see through Asmodeus's

curse from the beginning," Belial said. "Her angel blood would give her that ability."

"Her *what?*" Jacqui nearly shouted. "What the hell are you talking about?"

"This grimoire . . ." Bel pointed at the book. "Was made by angels."

24

FADE TO BLACK

EVA CAUGHT A GLIMPSE OF WHITE WINGS AS THE ATtacker struck again before Ash had time to recover.

Time froze in a tableau of horror as the blade swept across his chest, and white light cascaded over his body like lightning. He roared as it swung again, Eva screaming all the while.

When he moved to dodge the strike, she caught sight of his attacker, and the scream dried right up in her throat.

It was her father.

Her dad had feathered wings and was wielding a broadsword, raising it above his head and swinging it down toward Ash's neck. And Ash was throwing his body to the side, which was rapidly getting larger and redder, but he wasn't moving fast enough.

Another scream erupting from her throat, Eva threw herself at him without thinking. Colliding with Ash, she knocked him to the ground, his body now fully in demon form beneath her, his blood staining her clothes.

He grabbed her and rolled them at the last possible second

as her dad's blade sliced into his back, spraying more blood. There hadn't been time for him to pull back his strike.

If Ash hadn't rolled her, her dad could have killed her.

Dan seemed to realize this, because a hoarse shout burst from his throat, and he stumbled backward, eyes wide with horror. Eva quickly turned her attention back to Ash.

He was huge now, around seven feet tall, his skin back to that vivid crimson. His shirt hung off him in tatters, torn by the sword strikes and the wings that had erupted from his back. Black horns parted strands of his silky hair, curving along his skull and swooping up to sharp points. His leathery wings were draped protectively over her, and his claws dug into the hardwood.

Their gazes met and locked briefly. At least, she thought they did—his eyes were solid black again, and it was hard to tell where he was looking.

Then his head jerked back, and he growled in an animalistic way at her dad who was approaching again with the sword held high.

"Dad, no!" she shouted.

Ash crawled off her and climbed gracefully to his feet. He raised his claws to his neck and tore the remains of his shirt from his body. Blood poured from his wounds, and she saw his breath coming in sharp pants against the pain he wasn't accustomed to feeling, thanks to his curse lifting. How the hell was he still standing?

"Grigori," Ash snarled.

Okay, that was weird, considering her last name was Gregory, not Grigori, and why he thought that mattered right n—

It sank into her shock-confused head. The wings. The sword.

DUH flashed in her mind's eye like a blinking neon sign.

"You want me?" Dan's voice was low, attention fixed on

Ash, sword raised as he slowly backed across the room toward the exit. "Then come and get me."

Ash growled in that feral way again, but remained where he was, his body angled protectively in front of Eva.

Dan frowned like he was surprised Ash wasn't taking the bait, but his smile returned. "I'm on my way to kill your friends. Think I'll start with Mephistopheles, since he's the youngest—"

That got him going. Ash roared and launched across the room at Dan amidst Eva's cries for them to stop. She didn't know if she was shouting at her idiot dad for provoking Ash, or if she was shouting at Ash to please not attack her dad even if he was being an idiot.

Dan darted out of the den into the living room, moving miraculously fast, and Ash chased after him just as rapidly despite his wounds. Eva raced behind them, still screaming futilely at everyone to stop fighting. In the few seconds it took her to cross the room, she heard Ash's enraged roar fill the air.

It was earsplitting, and Eva stumbled through the doorway with her palms over her ears. She skidded to a halt, and her mouth dropped open.

Ash was standing on a sigil drawn onto the floor, looking none too pleased about it. He was roaring like an enraged dragon and swiping his claws at her dad, who was swinging his sword, trying to stab it into the circle.

Somehow, Eva pieced together that her dad must have lured Ash out of the den so he would cross into the sigil he'd somehow drawn without either of them noticing his presence. And now Ash was trapped, and her dad was trying to kill him.

"Dad, no!" she shouted yet again, running across the room to intervene. Where was her mom and Ash's brothers? Why hadn't they come to help?

"Eva, get out of here!" Holding her back with one arm,

Dan didn't even glance at her. He continued trying to stab her boyfriend while he was injured and trapped. Ash gave as good as he got, swatting away the sword with those deadly claws and ducking out of reach.

"Stop, damn it!" She yanked on her dad's arm with all her strength, trying to throw him off his game and distract him from trying to kill Ash.

For a moment, she thought she'd succeeded. He lowered his sword, stepped back, and she breathed a sigh of relief. Then he spun, grabbed the hand on his arm, and slapped something cold and metal onto her wrist. She froze, staring at the metal blankly for a second, and then it dawned on her.

Her dad had just handcuffed her!

Ash figured it out too because he did the whole dragon-roar-of-fury thing again.

"What the fuck!" Eva shrieked in her dad's face, struggling madly as he scooped her into his arms. He crossed the room and deposited her at the base of the staircase.

"Honey, I'm so sorry about this," he said, and then the motherfucker cuffed the other side of the handcuffs to the wrought-iron banister.

Eva stared in utter astonishment, unable to believe her own father had handcuffed her to a staircase so he could continue trying to murder her boyfriend.

"What are you doing?" she bellowed at the top of her lungs. "What the hell is wrong with you!" A roaring filled her ears, a dark wrath springing to life at the center of her being.

"I'm so sorry, honey. I'll be right back, I promise." His eyes were full of regret.

She was way too pissed off to care. Especially as he turned to Ash and said, "I'm going to go deal with your friends, Asmodeus, and then I'll be back for you."

And then he turned and ran out of the house amidst Eva's furious screams and Ash's rageful roars.

༼ ♥ ༽

Jacqui stared at Belial. "Angels?"

"Well, fallen angels, to be precise."

"They're called Grigori," Raum supplied. "Or Watchers."

"Horny angels," Meph called out from the other room, which made no sense whatsoever.

"I'm sorry," Jacqui said, "I'm really not following."

"Grigori are fallen angels who came to Earth to get involved in the drama and mate with humans." Belial straightened from the grimoire that lay open on the desk in front of him, lip curling in distaste. "They consider themselves protectors of humanity."

"Okay, so these Grigori wrote that book? But how does that prove anything about Dan?"

"Only a Grigori would be in possession of it or have the knowledge to draw these tracking sigils. If your husband has it, that means he's a Grigori."

"Dan?" A hysterical laugh burst out of her. "My husband is a lot of things, but an angel isn't one of them."

"Technically, he's fallen," Belial said, but that didn't make it any less ridiculous.

"And if he's a Grigori," Raum added, "that means your daughter is a Nephilim."

"Which means we have a serious fucking problem."

"What is a Nephilim?" Jacqui screeched. "What is wrong with my daughter?"

"Nephilim are the kids of the horny angels, and they're hunted for their magical blood," Meph called out from the other room again.

"Look, we don't have time to talk about this," Belial interjected. "Your husband was trying to track us. We need to get Asmodeus and get out of here now."

"But what if Eva's a Nephilim?" Raum asked him.

"Then we help her out by the getting the fuck out of here even faster before I'm forced to kill her dad."

Jacqui choked.

"Ash won't like that," Raum said.

"Asmodeus will do whatever keeps her safe."

"What is a Nephilim?" Jacqui asked again, barely following at this point.

"There's no time to explain now," Belial said, already moving toward the door. "But you can ask your husband. If he really is a Grigori, he'll have all the answers you seek. If he's not, then you have no need to know anyway."

Bel left Dan's office and crossed the open studio space, Raum and Jacqui following behind.

"Check it!" Meph exclaimed as they approached, stepping back from the vulture statue with a grin. He flung a tattooed arm toward the sculpture.

Jacqui's mouth fell open.

The vulture's head was attached flawlessly. He'd even put a slight angle in its position, so it appeared to be tilting its head inquisitively. It brought a lifelike poise to the sculpture that it hadn't had before.

"Amazing!" Despite everything, she couldn't help but be impressed. "How did you do it?"

He shrugged. "I used these scrap thingies and some of this wire."

"It's beautiful."

Meph ducked his head and shuffled a foot like he wasn't used to hearing praise, and her heart melted. A sudden tenderness filled her, and she was struck with the urge to serve him meals and tuck him into bed at night. He just looked like he needed a mother's love, and she wanted to give it to him. The last thing she needed was to adopt a demon, but she couldn't help it.

Her phone rang in her pocket, snapping her back to the present. "It's Dan."

"Ask him about the grimoire," Belial said.

She accepted the call and held it up to her ear. "Dan?"

"Honey, I need you to come outside."

"Where are you?"

"Come outside first and then we'll talk." His voice was low, and he was speaking slowly. It was the kind of voice people used to address someone who had a really big spider on their back.

Jacqui was really getting sick of all his vague mysteriousness. "Dan, what is going on? Where are you? And why do you have a grimoire made by fallen angels in your office?"

"Come outside, and we'll talk. I promise I'll tell you everything. Just come quickly."

"I'll be right there," she said and then hung up. It was obvious the three demons watching her had overheard. "I'm going to go find out what he wants," she told them.

"Careful," Raum warned. "It could be a trap."

She scoffed. "He's still my husband. I'm not afraid of him."

She headed toward the exit but stopped when she noticed the demons following her and arched a brow. "I'm pretty sure I can talk to my own husband without backup."

"He's up to something," Bel said with narrowed eyes.

"If he really is one of these Grigori, I don't want you to fight with him. I may be angry at him, but he's still my husband. It would be better if you waited here." She wasn't about to forget Belial's offhand comment about killing him anytime soon, that was for sure. Though she was still having a hard time believing he was some sort of fallen angel warrior.

Hard time? Scratch that. She thought it was ridiculous. But her demon guests were genuinely concerned, and she respected their feelings, so she played along.

"I'll be right back." With a smile at her guests, she stepped outside the studio into the sunlight—

And was immediately seized around the middle by Dan's strong arms and dragged a good ten feet away from the building. How the hell had he moved so fast?

"Jacqui, thank *god.*" He clutched her tightly, pressing his face against her neck like they'd been apart for ages.

That was nice and all, but she was too confused to enjoy the hug at the moment. She struggled in his hold, but his arms remained locked around her.

"Dan, let me go. What's going on? Where were you? Why aren't you wearing a shirt? Is that a *sword*? And why do you have that grimoire?"

"I can't explain now, but I will." And then he transferred his grip, securing her against his side with his left arm like she was a sack of rice, which only made her madder.

"Let me go!" she snapped, struggling in his grip, a sense of alarm rising quickly within. A small part of her marveled at his strength. He'd always been strong, but she hadn't realized he was *this* strong. He held her with one arm like she weighed as much as a feather pillow.

"I'm really sorry, honey, but I can't let you go back in there." There was genuine remorse in his voice, but Jacqui didn't care about that right now. All she knew was that her husband was freaking her out and pissing her off, and she did not like being restrained like a recalcitrant child.

She struggled harder. "Let me go!"

"Heyyy," came Meph's voice. "Why don't you release the nice lady, and we can have a chat like adults, yeah?"

She jerked around in Dan's grip to see the tattooed demon standing in the doorway of the studio. It was then she noticed the big symbol painted on the front wall beside the door.

The other side of the double doors was thrown open and Belial and Raum came to stand beside Meph. Flames flickered in Belial's eyes, and he looked furious, but he remained rooted to the threshold, as if he could go no further.

"Demons," Dan said, still restraining Jacqui's wiggling form. "Prepare to die."

Meph scoffed, crossing his arms and leaning a shoulder against the doorframe. "Yeah, no thanks."

The attitude was mostly just a cover up for anxiety. The Watcher asshole had warded the building, only this time the wards weren't to keep people out, they were to keep them *in*.

Prison wards. Empyrean magic, too, so they were strong. With all four walls and the roof warded, the building had become indestructible. It was the one of the oldest tricks in the book, and honestly, it was a little embarrassing they hadn't seen it coming.

As for dying, Meph wasn't overly concerned. Grigori weren't full-fledged angels anymore which meant they were less powerful. They could be defeated, but it still wasn't easy. Meph was the youngest of his brothers, which made him more vulnerable to pricks like these self-righteous angel dropouts—especially because under no circumstances would he shift into demon form, even if it made him exponentially stronger.

But it wasn't himself he was worried about. It was Belial.

Bel was doing his damnedest to be a good boy. He had worked hard to find a way for the four of them to get to Earth without being caught, and now he was working even harder to make sure they stayed free, all while trying to manage his dark side.

Jacqui's asshole husband tightened the hold around her with his left arm and unsheathed a dagger from the thigh holster with his right, shifting his stance to attack position. As if he was going to battle them with his wife pinned to his side or some shit? Not cool.

"Do you know who I am?" Bel asked coolly, maintaining a casual pose. Except Meph could tell there was nothing casual about his brother right now.

Bel stood with those tree-trunk arms crossed over his chest and his legs slightly spread, all that pretty blond hair spilling over his broad shoulders.

"Oh, I know very well," the Watcher replied.

"Dan, put me *down*, damn it!" Jacqui hissed at him, still valiantly struggling in his arms. "I swear to god I'll never forgive you for this!"

"Do you not understand the consequences of pissing me off?" Bel's voice was getting deeper and louder, though it never wavered from that ice-cold level tone. The hairs on the back of Meph's neck rose. "Because you're really starting to piss me off."

"Shit," Raum said, exchanging a glance with Meph.

Even the Grigori looked a little wary. Which was dumb because what the hell had he expected when he threatened fucking Belial? You didn't go around threatening Belial unless you could back your shit up.

"Okayyy," Meph said, maneuvering his way beside him. He did his best to push his brother back from the threshold a little, but it was like trying to move a skyscraper. He gave that up and put what he hoped was a reassuring hand on Belial's bicep—which was several inches thicker than it had been a moment ago.

Bastard was growing. Not a good sign.

"Dan, is it? How do ya do. I'm Meph. We aren't looking for trouble. We have no sinister agenda and mean no harm to any humans. All we want is to go our merry way and be left to our own devices. Isn't that right, Bel, my big bro?" Meph gave Bel's huge bicep a reassuring pat.

Belial was frozen, staring at Jacqui's husband with his hands curled into boulder-sized fists.

"Bel here has been working really hard on his anger management," Meph said. "Wouldn't it be a shame to undo all that now? He's getting a little worked up with you tossing threats around. And it seems like your lovely wife there really isn't enjoying being restrained. I'm all for a little kink, but consent is key, you feel me? So why don't you put Jacqui down, and we can all take a second to chill, and we'll talk this out like— *Oomph*!"

Pain sliced through him, effectively cutting off his valiant speech.

Meph glanced down.

The motherfucker had tossed a fucking knife into his chest!

He opened his mouth to speak but choked. Blood came out. And then more pain. A shitload of pain. Because Dan had nailed him with a consecrated weapon, and he could feel it burning him up from the inside out.

Trying to keep his cool, Meph tried to speak, but he just choked again. And now the world was spinning. Cool. He looked up at Belial and saw the shock written all over his brother's face.

Actually, it felt like time had frozen, because Bel's mouth was opening really slowly. In his peripherals, Meph was aware of Raum leaping toward him, but it was like those scenes in action movies where the character ran in slow-mo to escape the blast, shouting, "*Noooooooooo*," ten octaves lower than normal.

Meph stumbled to the side. That was lame. He was going to fall on his ass with a consecrated blade in his chest, right in front of his new human friend and her douchebag husband. And that asshole had thrown the knife at him while he was trying to call a truce. So embarrassing.

He heard Jacqui screaming. Maybe she was concerned for him. That'd be nice. Eva's mom was cool, and she'd said she liked his tattoos, and no one said that. Most people gawked at him with judgment written all over their faces, not that he cared. Actually, he liked making people uncomfortable. It was one of his greatest pleasures in life.

He thought all these admittedly pointless thoughts in that little pause of slowed time, and then his respite was over, and the world went full speed ahead once more.

Meph hit the ground, blood all over him. Jacqui was still screaming. Raum landed at his side and tried to yank the knife out, except it seared his hand when he touched it.

And . . . Belial went off.

Meph wanted to tell him it was all good and not to bother losing his shit over him, but he'd already tried speaking and it hadn't worked out so well. Plus, it wasn't like Bel would listen.

Nope, his brother totally lost it. He really blew.

First, he grew. Had to be thirteen feet tall, the size of a freakin' Mack truck. He had to stoop way down to fit under the doorframe, and Raum had to drag Meph out of the way by the armpits so the two of them didn't get crushed.

Belial stretched his palms forward and pressed, putting all his strength into breaking the ward, which flashed with white light and flexed outward as he tested its power. Anyone else would have been blasted back twenty feet by magic that powerful, but not Bel.

It was a good thing he hadn't had time to cut his hair, because it would have grown back right then. The white-blond locks blew all around his head in a phantom wind. The sky darkened. Lightning crashed around them for added effect. Huge, white-feathered wings burst from Belial's back, tearing his too-tight shirt right off his body, and he levitated off the ground a few inches, pushing harder against the magic keeping him trapped.

And, of course, he burst into flames.

Raum dragged Meph further inside amidst Jacqui's continued screaming. She was probably screaming more about

Belial now than Meph and the whole knife-in-his-chest thing. Especially because Belial started launching fireballs through the ward at Dan, forcing him to duck and weave all over the place with Jacqui along for the ride. Poor lady.

Raum hunched over Meph, trying to pull out the blade in his chest, but the consecrated weapon was burning his brother's palms up good. Every time Raum got a good grip on it, his hands would start to smoke and flame until he had to yank them away.

He ripped his shirt over his head and wrapped his fist in it, but consecrated weapons were no joke. It gave him a couple seconds of extra yank time—that blade was in Meph's sternum good—but then Raum's shirt burst into white fire and became more of a hindrance than a help.

The world was kind of going black now, which sucked because Meph actually could die from this wound. He'd been looking forward to tearing shit up with his trusty bros, but instead he was going to die in a pool of his own blood because he'd tried negotiating with an angel. Stupid. Lesson learned on that front.

"Help me!" Raum was yelling. "Fucking help me, Bel!"

Aw. A tiny tear actually gathered in Meph's eye. Raum was the quiet one, always calm and collected, and he didn't like the desperate tone of his voice, especially because he knew Bel wasn't going to help. When Bel was this far gone, he lost all reason and rationale and existed purely as a force of destruction with a burning desire to kill everything.

Distantly, Meph remarked that the building was now on fire as Bel continued his Satanic tantrum, spewing hellfire at the Grigori and roaring so loudly it obliterated all else. The ward was flexing outward so far now, Bel was standing all the way outside. It looked like he might actually be able to break it, which was badass.

For once, the fire wasn't an unwelcome sight. The outside

of the building may have been rendered indestructible, but the inside wasn't, and if Bel destroyed it enough, it could collapse internally and free them.

Meph hoped his cool vulture statue would survive though. Good thing it was made of metal.

His last thought was that he wished Jacqui hadn't had to see her husband murder him because that shit was bound to be traumatizing. And then the world faded to black.

FREE FALL

ASH STARED ACROSS THE LIVING ROOM AT THE WOMAN chained to the staircase, yanking furiously at the metal handcuff at her wrist, and the truth hit him like a ton of bricks.

"He's your father?"

"Yes, and I'll kill him!" Eva was yanking at her cuffed wrist hard enough to bloody herself. "I can't believe he handcuffed me to the freaking stairs!"

"Your father . . ."

"Yes, him!" Eva screeched. "My idiotic, stubborn, pig-headed father!"

". . . is a Grigori."

Oh, hell no, this could not be happening.

"You're a Nephilim," he said aloud just to help the horror sink in a little. "That's why you have the Sight. That's why you could see through my curse. Because you have angel blood in your veins."

And no, he was *not* pleased about that, thank you very much.

In that moment, he didn't give two shits if his ass was dragged back to Hell and tortured for all eternity, or if Eva's Grigori father chopped off his head with a consecrated sword. He didn't give a shit about the fact that he'd inadvertently stumbled upon a live Nephilim, though they were supposedly extinct, and a tiny vial of their blood cost more than most humans made in their lifetime.

In that moment, he would have given anything so Eva didn't have to spend her life looking over her shoulder, distrusting everyone she met and hiding behind wards.

Eva stopped her futile struggles and froze, the truth of what she was finally washing over her. "Oh, shit."

They stared at each other.

"But . . . how? Wouldn't you have noticed? Wouldn't *I* have noticed?"

He nodded slowly. That *was* strange. How the hell hadn't he noticed? He hadn't actually tasted her blood, but he'd gotten about as close to her as he could get otherwise, and he hadn't detected anything angelic in her scent or energy, not that he was the best judge of what his crippled senses could tell him.

But still. There was no missing that. At the very least, his brothers should have sensed it. But none of them had.

"Maybe you're not," he said, hope rising. "Maybe you were adopted. Or maybe your mother got pregnant by another man."

Eva's eyes got wider, and he realized that wasn't as reassuring to her as it was to him. Then her gaze shifted to the blood streaked all over his abdomen. "Are you okay? I can't believe he stabbed you." Her voice hitched a little.

Ash looked down at himself and realized he was still in demon form—red skin, horns, wings, and all. He looked back at Eva and didn't see fear of him on her face, and something tightened in his chest at her acceptance of him. It meant something profound, but he wasn't quite sure what.

Damn it, though, he needed to learn to understand this shit fast because Eva had said he needed to tell her stuff if they were going to make their relationship work, and he wanted it to work. The alternative was unthinkable.

Still, now wasn't the time for contemplating feelings. Instead, he shifted partially, reverting to his human size and skin color. He thought this might help Eva calm down, but instead, it seemed to have the opposite effect.

"Oh my god, Ash!" She yanked on the handcuffs with renewed ferocity. He looked down at himself again, wondering what he'd done wrong, and then realized that with his skin no longer crimson, the blood from his wounds was more visible against his paler human skin.

"I'm fine," he said quickly.

Unfortunately, his curse was still lifted and that meant he could feel the blood leaking out of him, unlike the last time he'd been wounded. It hurt like a bitch. Damn it, it really hurt a lot.

For the first time ever, he almost wished for a return to his black-and-white world. But then he looked at Eva, at that rich dark skin, those brown-black curls and tantalizing silver eyes, and he quickly changed his mind. She was a masterpiece meant to be viewed in color.

"Damn it, I'll *kill* my dad for this!" She tugged again on the handcuffs.

"Eva, stop, you're going to hurt yourself."

"Argh!" She looked down at the sigil at his feet. "You're really stuck inside that thing?"

"Empyrean magic is powerful. I can't break this." He cursed. "Damn it, I'm worried about my brothers. They have no idea he's here."

As in on cue, Belial's great roar echoed through the forest.

Their gazes snapped together. "That did not sound good," Eva said.

Bel roared again.

"Fuck!" Knowing it was futile, Ash threw his weight against the mystical barriers of the sigil in some vain hope that he might magically burst through. His brothers were in trouble. At the very least, Bel needed him to talk him down before he started a goddamn forest fire.

Unfortunately for Ash, he hadn't been kidding when he said Empyrean magic was powerful. As soon as he touched the edge of the barrier, he got electrocuted like he'd touched a live wire and thrown backward.

He hit the ground, cursing the goddamn Grigori to Hell and back again.

Apparently, they couldn't catch a break, because next thing he knew, Eva was freaking out again, and Bel was roaring, and he was busy being useless, stuck in a goddamn angel trap.

And then . . . he felt something in the air.

It was some kind of electricity, but not like the sigil's kind that had knocked him on his ass. Something different. Eva was screaming his name, and strangely, her voice sounded amplified. Ethereal. Haunting.

He swept the hair off his face so he could see her, and his mouth fell open.

Eva's beautiful eyes were glowing. *Glowing.*

And oh, *will ya look at that*, she was growing too. Over six and a half feet tall all of a sudden, she stared at him with those glowing eyes and gave a harpy-like shriek of fury. And then, with one smooth jerk, she ripped the wrought-iron post she was handcuffed to clean off the banister.

There went his hopes about her not being a Nephilim.

But damn, she was hot.

She ran to him and smudged the chalk line of the sigil with a foot, and instantly, he was free and throwing his arms around her. Except she was taller than him now, which was a bit weird, so he shifted back to demon form so he could hug her properly.

She was shaking as if scared by what she'd just done. "Ash, w-what—?"

Bel's next roar was so loud it rattled the windows.

They pulled apart, and he realized there wasn't time for an explanation. He grabbed her hand, clawed fingers linking with her delicate ones, and they ran out of the house together toward the chaos.

Jacqueline Gregory was just a human. No secret, angelic bloodline, no special abilities.

And yet, a fierce determination that felt powerful had filled her to bursting. She had to help Meph.

Belial launched another stream of flame, forcing Dan to leap back, and she realized he was retreating. What his plans were, she couldn't say, but she wasn't sticking around to find out.

She took a second to take stock of her surroundings. Dan was clutching another knife from the holster at his thigh, and it looked like he was gearing up to throw it. He also had a large broadsword holstered at his left hip, but it was unreachable because he had pinned Jacqui against him on top of it. She knew this because the hilt was digging painfully into her side.

Before he had a chance to throw the blade, Jacqui acted. Twisting in his grip, she managed to spin within the circle of his arm so she faced upward, freeing her hands.

And then she punched him in the face.

She wasn't a fighter, but she'd taken a few martial arts classes in her day and knew how to throw a punch. And throw a punch she did. In fact, she threw several. She threw them as hard as she could, her fear for Meph giving her the strength to keep punching through the unbelievable pain in her knuckles.

Caught by surprise, Dan stumbled and dropped her.

Landing hard, she rolled away and then sprang up and sprinted toward the building. Not a second too soon, too, because Belial's next fireball smacked Dan square in the chest, launching him back through the air.

As she reached the building, the heat coming off Belial grew intense, the air wavering with a mirage that made everything look like it was rippling. Eyes stinging, she dropped to her knees, covered her head, and somehow managed to crawl through the doorway inside. She waited for the magic barrier to electrocute her as it was Belial, despite knowing she had passed through it before with no ill effect.

It didn't, however. Inside, everything was on fire, but there wasn't time to worry about that. Raum saw her coming and hope filled his golden eyes, replacing the despair that had been there moments before.

"Help him!" he shouted as she scrambled toward them. "I can't pull it out!"

He held up his hands and Jacqui recoiled. They'd been burned down to the bone. Nothing but blood and gore and strips of flesh remained, and his fingers had been incinerated to the first knuckle joint. If it did that much damage to him, what must it be doing to Meph?

"It's consecrated. It's burning him alive every second it touches him. *Please.*"

She didn't waste another second. Crawling to Meph's side, she wrapped her fingers around the knife hilt, half expecting her own palms to melt off. When nothing happened, she yanked. The knife barely budged. Jesus, how hard had Dan thrown the thing?

She shifted position, bracing the soles of her feet against Meph's still body. Throwing herself backward and using her body weight for added momentum, she *pulled.*

The knife finally slid free. Jacqui tumbled backward. Meph howled.

And Belial's fire extinguished at the sound of his brother's cry.

Tossing the blade away, she scrambled back to Meph and dragged him into her lap, cradling him like he was her own child, tears streaming down her face. In the doorway, Belial dropped to his knees and gripped his head like he was fighting for control, a low groan escaping him.

Looking up, she saw Dan standing outside, a look of horror plastered across his face. He wasn't holding any weapons and didn't appear to have violent intent, so she dismissed him from her thoughts for now, more concerned about the demon in her arms.

She looked up at Raum, who was cradling his horribly injured hands against his bare chest. "Is he okay?" Meph was so pale and still, and it terrified her.

Raum nodded. "We can't die from blood loss. Without the weapon in him, that's the only thing wrong with him now. He'll just be unconscious for a while."

"Are *you* okay?" His hands were horrific. "Your fingers . . ."

"They'll grow back. Thank you for saving him."

Belial scrambled over on his hands and knees, long hair falling over his face. "I'm sorry," he was muttering, "I'm sorry, I'm sorry . . ." He was still gigantic, and his massive wings dragged on the floor behind him. "Meph . . ."

"He's okay," Raum said. "Jacqui saved him."

Belial jerked his head up and Jacqui flinched. His eyes were completely obscured by dancing flames. But then he whispered, "Thank you," crawled the rest of the way to her side, and engulfed both her and the unconscious Meph in his enormous arms.

She went rigid, expecting to be crushed to death, but relaxed a moment later when she realized it was just a hug. She looked at Raum on the ground nearby, watching with those big golden eyes, and she couldn't resist beckoning him. He shuffled over, and Belial opened his humongous arms and swallowed him up too.

And that was how she found herself in a cuddle pile with three demons.

Dan stared in disbelief at the scene before him. His wife was in a group hug with a King of Hell, and he wasn't even concerned for her safety. Because only a fool would miss that Belial cared for her and the other demons, and Jacqui cared for them right back.

Just to make him feel like more of an asshole, at that moment, Eva and Asmodeus came running down the path, hand in hand. Or rather, hand in claw. The day was already so full of impossibilities, it didn't even surprise him to see that they had escaped.

As they reached Dan, standing rooted to the ground outside the studio, Eva shot him a glare full of loathing that cut to the bone. "What have you done?" Without waiting for an answer, she ran to the cuddle pile with Asmodeus by her side.

Belial opened his wings to admit them, and Eva gasped when she saw Meph. Asmodeus's head snapped up to look at Dan, and his lips peeled off his fangs in a snarl.

"He's okay," Raum said, "Jacqui got to him—"

"Oh my god, your hands!" Eva screamed.

"They'll grow back."

"B-but—"

"I'm sorry," Belial was still saying.

"It's not your fault, Bel," Raum said.

He hung his head. "I could have pulled the blade out, but I was lost to the fucking rage, and I couldn't think straight. He could have died, and it would have been my fault." As he spoke, his body returned to its original size, and his white-feathered wings shrank with him. Angelic white, because Belial was, in actuality, a fallen angel. The second most powerful angel to ever defect from Heaven.

Dan should have marveled that he was looking at the great demon in the flesh. He should have been taking the chance to kill him. But no. He was standing there feeling like the biggest jerk on the planet. All this grief and shame and heartache was his fault. Not Belial's for losing his temper. His.

And judging by the look Eva was giving him, she knew it too.

26

The Aftermath

Eva was so past being in shock that nothing could faze her anymore. So her dad was a fallen angel. *Cool, cool, cool*— Okay, she was still freaking out.

Once the numbness wore off, she knew she'd be livid. As far as she was concerned, her entire life was a lie. And so was her mom's.

"You're her father," Ash growled, glaring daggers at Dan, "which makes her a—"

"Don't say it." Dan's voice was hoarse. "Don't even think it. You have no idea the lengths I'll go to protect that secret. To protect her from being hunted and used by the likes of you."

It was like Ash didn't hear him. "*Nephilim!*" His voice was so loud, Eva cringed and slapped her palms over her ears. What was with demons and preternaturally loud shouting? "And you left her unprotected!"

She climbed to her feet and placed a hand on his back beneath the wound between his wings. His skin was burning hot and wet with blood. "I'm fine, Ash. I'm right here and I'm okay."

Ash's head whipped around, and he stared at her with those creepy black eyes. She tried not to let her wariness of his demon form show. The last thing he needed right now was to think she was afraid of him.

"He didn't protect you," he growled. "You could have been hurt."

"I did protect her!" Dan threw up his hands. "I can't believe a goddamn demon is berating me for how I raised my own daughter. I spent the first three years of her life perfecting a binding spell that trapped all her Nephilim powers and made her completely human. Even if someone tasted her blood, they would taste nothing but human. Her lifespan, human. Why do you think you never realized what she is? No one can detect her as long as she remains under the binding."

"You put a spell on our daughter and you never told me?" Jacqui asked in a hollow voice. She was staring at Dan like she'd never seen him before. Eva knew the feeling.

"I couldn't. It was for your own protection."

Ash's eyes narrowed. "Explain how she has the Sight, then."

"She didn't used to. I know that for a fact because I tested it when she was young." Dan dragged a hand down his face. "Evidently, the repression of that ability only worked to a point. I guess having a bunch of demons standing right in front of her was enough to snap her out of it."

"How does the binding break?"

"As if I'd tell you that."

"She consumed my blood," Ash said, which seemed a random thing to say.

Except Dan went white as a sheet. "No."

"Yes. She had to in order to travel through the gate to get here, since I believed she was human."

"I didn't think of that." He cursed. "Of course she did."

Eva frowned. "Why is that relevant?"

"Blood is usually the catalyst in powerful magic," Ash explained. "I didn't know you were under a protection spell, or I never would have risked giving you mine."

"Right." Her dad rolled his eyes. "More likely, you're salivating at the chance to get your hands on her. Until now, no one knew of her existence but me, and I intend to keep it that way."

Eva dragged her hands down her face. Her logical mind wasn't ready to accept that she was some freaky hybrid thing that was hunted by angels and demons alike. She'd barely come to terms with Ash being supernatural, and now she'd suddenly joined the club.

But she didn't have a choice but to accept it, did she? Not after what had happened back at the house.

What *had* happened? She'd snapped that wrought-iron banister like a twig, that was what. She had the handcuff still dangling from her wrist to prove it.

This is who you really are, the dark whisper inside of her said. Finally, it was content, and that dissociated feeling was gone. She no longer felt separate from herself, like the missing piece of the Eva puzzle had finally been put in its place.

It was such a subtle shift, she might never have noticed it if that damned feeling hadn't haunted her her entire life. But now that it was gone, she felt whole, and she couldn't regret it even if it meant she was in danger.

"Explain how to break the binding," Ash growled at Dan.

"No. As long as it's intact, her blood has no value to you."

But how could it be intact if she'd snapped the banister? She certainly hadn't done anything like that before. And why would she suddenly feel whole if nothing had changed?

"Tell me so I can protect her in the future as you failed to do," Ash said.

"You have no future. There's no way I'm letting you go knowing what she is."

"You're not touching him!" Eva snapped, beyond done with the threats. "And I want to know how the binding breaks because I deserve to have that important information about my own damn life!"

Dan's grimace was properly remorseful. When he spoke, this time, he addressed his daughter. "You're right, Eva, and I'm sorry. As you guessed, the catalyst is demon blood. But it's two-sided. Not only do you have to drink demon blood, but a demon also has to consume your blood. And the catch is, it has to be the same demon, and it has to be within a twenty-four hour period. A blood swap, going both ways. I assumed you'd be safe because what were the odds you'd go around swapping blood with people?"

Well, that explains it. Eva stared at Raum and Belial. Raum and Belial stared back.

Ash relaxed visibly. "I haven't consumed her blood. She's safe."

Dan breathed a sigh of relief.

Eva, however, made a small choking noise. "Actually . . ." She looked at Ash. "You may have had a little."

"Don't say it," her dad whispered.

"I haven't." Ash shook his head. "I would remember if I had."

"Not if you were unconscious at the time," Eva said weakly.

"What are you talking about?"

She spoke in a rush. "It was after the fight with Mist when you passed out. Bel let it slip that if you drank blood you'd heal faster, and then Raum came to burn your wound shut, and it was so awful that I convinced him to let me give you mine."

Ash pinned Raum and Bel with a furious glare. "I'll kill you both."

"It's not their fault," she said quickly. "Raum tried to talk me out of it, but I insisted."

Dan spoke in a flat voice. "You're telling me you drank his blood. And he drank yours. Within a twenty-four hour period."

She nodded.

Dan closed his eyes. "Then the binding is broken."

That definitely explains it.

"Put it back," Ash snapped. "Fix it."

"I can't."

"Why not!"

"Because it's a once-per-lifetime kind of thing. It can't be remade. I did it once, and that's it. It's a one-time deal."

"Then do a different binding."

"There is no other!"

"What does this mean?" Jacqui cut in. Her mom had been mostly silent this whole time, watching the exchange with wide eyes. She was probably in shock. Again, Eva knew the feeling. "Why is this so important?"

"Eva will spend her life being hunted," Ash said. "Angels will try to kill her simply for existing."

"Demons will try to manipulate her into thinking they care about her so they can use her as a blood source," Dan growled. "And wouldn't it be *so* convenient for Asmodeus here to have a fresh supply of Nephilim blood available to him."

"I would never use her that way."

"Oh, yeah? What happens when your money runs out, and you can't find any more blood? What happens when you have no other options?"

"Then I'd willingly give him my blood," Eva said, and everyone stared at her. "I caught a glimpse of Hell on my way here, and it was awful. Ash and his brothers escaped because they wanted a new life, and if giving them my blood could help them, I'd be happy to make that sacrifice." She looked at Ash. "Remember that talk we had about trust? This is one of those times. I'd be trusting you not to tell other demons what I am and to protect me from anyone who might come after me."

"I'll protect you regardless. But I'm not taking your blood. We'll find another binding spell." He growled at Dan. "He will fix this and make you safe again."

"I've never heard of another binding spell." Dan's expression was haunted. "And I have to kill you because of what you know. There's no alternative."

A dark fury built inside Eva. It was the whisper, she realized, only it was no longer just a whisper. It roared like a river about to launch into an unstoppable waterfall, and she didn't try to push it back. After so many years feeling hollow, she welcomed this new side of herself with open arms.

She was sick of telling Dan not to kill Asmodeus. He was hers.

"You will not touch him!"

Apparently, it was her turn to have a go at the whole super loud, preternatural shouting thing. The dark force built with heady strength, and she let it consume her. She felt powerful, limitless.

"You will not harm Asmodeus. He is mine."

Everyone stared at her with varying expressions of shock. Except Belial, who looked strangely delighted. Probably because, for once, he wasn't the one having the temper tantrum.

"He is mine!"

It felt so damned good to lay claim to the fierce demon beside her. He would make a worthy mate. He would protect her and be loyal and sate her body's needs. She would give him the same in return.

Ash pulled her into his arms, and they stared heatedly into each other's eyes. His blood soaked her clothing where their bodies pressed together, but neither of them paid it any mind.

"Eva, snap out of it!" her dad shouted from far away, but it was easy to ignore him.

"You're mine," she said again to Ash.

"And you're mine," he replied, lips curving into a smile. "And I will eviscerate anyone who touches you."

God, he was sexy when he talked like that. But her demon was injured. Reaching up, she curled her hands around those sleek black horns and pulled him down for a kiss. When their lips met, she poured a little of her potent power into him, willing it to heal his wounds. Then, she sent it out to do the same to his injured brothers.

She and Ash broke apart and stared at each other, and just like that, the dark rush felt sated, as if sensing that, with her demon's vow of protection and the knowledge she had protected him in turn, it was safe to slumber again. Giving a sleepy sigh of satisfaction, it retreated within her.

She felt herself shrinking, returning to her normal height and frame of mind. In the aftermath, she felt a little shell-shocked, but she wasn't disconnected from herself anymore, and that was all that mattered. *Never again.*

"Holy shit," someone said.

She looked at Ash, still in his impressive demon form, and took a moment to admire his horns. Had she thought them freaky before? Because she couldn't get the feeling of gripping them out of her head and wanted to do it again.

Except her parents and his brothers were right there, and that was just embarrassing.

She turned to face them with a grimace. "Um . . ."

Dan dragged a hand down his face. "I see your powers have already awoken."

"You healed me." Ash stared at his chest in amazement. His skin was unmarred, as if the wound had never existed. He could tell his back was healed too. Such a complete recovery would normally take all night or longer, especially for a wound made by a consecrated weapon.

"And me." Raum was looking at his hands. Sure enough, the gory, mangled flesh was as good as new. All his fingers had regrown.

"And Meph," Bel said. Though he was still unconscious, the wound in Meph's chest had closed over as if it had never been.

"I don't know how I . . ." Eva looked dazed, not that Ash blamed her. This was a lot for even him to take in.

"You can never use your power that way again," Dan said. "It's against the rules."

Everyone glared at him.

"Look, I get I made a mistake here, but I was only trying to protect Eva. Everything I've ever done since the day she was born was to protect Eva." Dan looked at his daughter. "Every time you use your angelic abilities, it leaves traces in the ether that could leave a trail for others trying to track you. If an angel discovers you, you will be destroyed on the spot. No trials, no questions asked. Do you understand?"

Eva nodded mutely.

"I never planned to have you, but I've never once regretted it. You've brought more light into my life than anything I've ever known. I'm sorry I lied to you, but as far as I knew, you were going to live a normal human life. I would have done anything to prevent this"—he gestured at the destruction around them—"from happening. I would have paid any price, even if it meant you stayed angry at me for the rest of your life."

"It's okay, Dad," Eva said softly. Was it okay? She didn't know. "But everything is different now." She turned to face the demons. "I propose a trade. You offer me protection and teach me how to use whatever powers I can to protect myself. In exchange, I'll give you my fancy blood and keep you hidden."

"Eva, no," Ash said.

"The fact that you're resisting proves how worthy you are." Their gazes locked. "You've made me happier than I've ever been and done your best to protect me from danger."

"Danger *I* brought into your life," he muttered, not feeling particularly heroic.

"Danger that, evidently, was part of my life all along. Honestly, I'm glad this happened. Not only because it brought me to you, but because I'd rather know who I really am than spend my life believing I'm something I'm not. My whole life, I felt this sense of disconnect, like a part of myself was missing. For the first time, I feel whole. I wouldn't trade that for all the safety in the world."

Ash hesitated, trying to come up with some excuse to talk her out of this. She didn't give him a chance, walking up and throwing her arms around his waist. He returned the embrace, holding her close though he was so much taller than her in this form.

"I just want you to be safe," he muttered.

"I know you do," she replied, face pressed against his bare skin. "And I love you for it."

"Love?"

"Yes, *love*. I love you, you silly demon."

Awe filled him. Elation, gratitude, sheer fucking joy. *She loved him.*

Since they were going for the full shock effect, he decided to throw caution to the wind and go for it. Head first, no holds barred.

"I love you too," he said, and damn if he didn't mean it.

Eva's head came back, and she stared up at him with round eyes. Raum and Belial were looking at him with similar expressions. Dan looked like a UFO full of green aliens had just landed right in front of him and made a crop circle. Jacqui, however, was smiling.

Ash didn't care what anyone else was doing. He felt free. He knew he'd spoken the truth and that he really was capable of love.

Asmodeus, Prince of Hell, was in love.

"I love you," he said again just to hear the words. To taste them on his tongue. To feel them in his fucking heart like a total sap.

"I love you too," Eva said, a tear from her gray eyes trailing down her cheek as she smiled at him.

That intense, indescribable feeling crashed over him like a tidal wave, making his head spin like he'd just taken a hit of the world's most powerful dopamine-enhancing drug. His head began to pound. His vision began to swim.

"Ash?" Now she looked concerned.

He swayed, awash in that powerful sensation, his sight darkening at the edges. "Love . . . you . . ."

"Ash!" Eva sounded panicked.

He hadn't meant to scare her, but it was a little late to backtrack. He briefly wondered if he was going to burst into flame or something since he wasn't technically supposed to be able to fall in love.

And then he passed out.

27

FARE THEE WELL, LOVE

DAN FOUND JACQUI STANDING BY THE WINDOW IN their bedroom, staring out at the darkening skies reflecting in the calm ocean. After Asmodeus had lost consciousness, there had been several seconds of undiluted panic.

Eva had screamed in a way that told Dan she hadn't been kidding when she told the damn demon she loved him, and Belial and Raum had rushed over, hovering about like they were equally concerned. Dan had found himself begrudgingly reassuring them Asmodeus was fine. He'd obviously just been overwhelmed by powerful positive emotions he wasn't used to experiencing.

Dan couldn't deny it anymore. If he'd hoped to believe that Asmodeus was lying about loving Eva, the fact that he'd passed out proved otherwise. There was no faking that kind of reaction, as much as Dan wished it weren't so. As much as he still wanted to stab the bastard.

And speaking of stabbing bastards, Mephistopheles had woken up not long after that and been all wounded puppy,

Aurora Ascher

staring at Dan with those big red eyes like he'd been betrayed by his best friend. It hadn't helped him feel any better about himself for launching the dagger in the first place, especially because Jacqui had proceeded to fuss over the guy like he was her own son.

Belial had carried Asmodeus inside and, after dropping him unceremoniously in the shower to wash off the blood, deposited him in Eva's bed to sleep off his love hangover. Then the goddamned King of Hell had cooked the rest of them a five-course haute-cuisine meal, and they'd eaten in awkward silence amidst inappropriate comments from Mephistopheles and responding insults from his brothers.

It was one of the most bizarre meals Dan had ever endured, and that said a lot, considering how old he was and some of the situations he'd found himself in over the ages.

Afterward, it was time for him to leave. He knew it was coming, knew his wife needed time and space and a break. Maybe a permanent one, though he couldn't bear to think about that yet. Or ever. But he knew he owed it to her to give her what she needed.

He also owed it to her to be honest, which meant that before he left, they needed to talk.

Which was how he found himself in their bedroom, watching her as she stood staring at that ocean view they both loved. He came up behind her, longing to touch her, to pull her into his arms, but he knew better. Instead, he sat on the edge of bed and waited.

There was so much to say. Too much. So he said nothing, knowing Jacqui would speak when she was ready.

She did, eventually, though she never turned away from the glass. "Why didn't you tell me?"

"To protect you. And Eva. I was never supposed to—" He stopped, rubbing his temples. He had to say this right, had to make sure he didn't make it worse. And yet, it seemed there

307

was no right way. "I broke the rules, Jacqui. But I hoped that if you didn't know, if I was ever caught, it would protect you. You couldn't be guilty if you didn't know."

"And what about Eva? What if she was caught?" Her voice hitched. "Belial said they would *execute* her, Dan."

"That was what the binding spell was all about. It was perfect. It even altered her lifespan. There would have been no way anyone, even her, would have ever learned what she was." He breathed a bitter, regretful laugh. "It was sheer dumb luck that she got mixed up with demons and started giving them her blood." He rubbed his eyes so hard he saw stars. "Why the hell did she do that?"

"She would have known not to if you'd just told her."

It was true. There was nothing he could say to excuse that, nothing he could say to justify that colossal mistake. He had fucked up, but his fuck-up had gone beyond just screwing up his own life. He'd put his daughter in danger, whom he loved more than anything in the world. He was pretty sure he could live until the sun exploded and he would never forgive himself for that.

"What do you mean about her lifespan?" Jacqui asked, finally turning away from the window to look at him. There was a crease in her brow, her eyes full of trepidation.

She was right to be concerned.

"She's half angel. Angels are immortal. Humans aren't. That means, she'll live indefinitely, until such a time as she chooses to cross over. Then, her soul will go to Heaven."

"Angels are immortal," Jacqui repeated, staring at him.

He nodded, knowing where this was going and dreading it with everything he was.

"Are you . . . ?"

He nodded again.

Her eyes widened. "Dan . . ." Her breaths grew shallow. So did his as he waited for her to put it together.

"How old are you?" she finally whispered in horror.

"Old."

"How old?"

"Really old."

"How old, Dan?"

He blew out a breath. "I fell thousands of years ago. Before that, I can't say. Angels don't experience time the way we do."

"Thousands . . ."

He nodded.

Her hands covered her mouth, and she sank slowly to the floor, her back against the glass. "Why . . . ?"

There were so many questions that could begin with that, and he had no idea which one she was asking in particular. "Why did I fall? Or why don't angels experience time like we do?"

But she shook her head. "Why did you choose me? Marry me? Live here with me?"

He blinked. "Because I love you."

She blinked back. They stared at each other. "But . . ."

"Jacqui, you've known me for twenty-seven years. I know our concepts of time are different, but we both know that's long enough to know someone. You know I love you, and I know you know."

"But why did you fall in love with me in the first place? I was just a girl. Twenty years old. I barely knew myself!"

He winced. "I know. It sounds bad, I know. But there was something about you that drew me. There always has been. Your light, your energy, your ability to find the good in all things . . . And I was right to fall in love with you—every day I've known you, I've only grown to love you more. But even then, despite all that, I never intended to stay, but . . ."

"But then we had Eva."

He nodded. Evangeline, his beautiful, accidental daughter. "Eva changed everything. When she was born, I took one look at her tiny face, and I knew I wasn't going anywhere. Maybe if it was just us, I might have had the courage to leave, but you and Eva together . . . I didn't stand a chance."

It was his turn to stare blankly out the window from his seat on the bed. He would move heaven and earth to protect his family. He would break any rule, take any chance, risk any repercussion if it meant they would be safe.

"You're not going to age." Jacqui breathed a bitter laugh. "I had this talk with Eva the other day. I told her that even if Ash was the perfect man, she had to consider the fact that he was immortal. I told her she could never fully commit to him because one day, someone would ask her if she was his mother, and then his grandmother, and that it would torture her. Guess it wasn't Eva who needed that advice after all."

Her eyes were haunted as she stared ahead at nothing. "At least I'll never have to worry about outliving my child. Both my husband and my daughter are going to live forever."

Damn, his heart ached. It felt like someone had punched a fist through his chest and gripped the thing in cold, clammy fingers. "I'm sorry, Jacqui."

"What were you going to do, Dan? Keep lying and hope I never noticed? I'd already begun to notice. In fact, I remember thinking recently how uncanny it was that you never seemed to age. You looked too old for me when we met, and now you're starting to look too young. My friends are always telling me how great you look for your age, asking me what your secret is. I tell them good diet and exercise." Again with that bitter laugh. "Maybe that'll fly for now, but what happens in another ten years? Another twenty?"

"I don't know." It was the god's honest truth. "I never planned for this." He stared at his palms in his lap, open to the heavens as if begging for a miracle. "I never wanted to put you in this position, but I couldn't leave. I love you and Eva too much. I couldn't make myself leave."

Jacqui hunched forward and buried her face in her hands. "How could you do this to me, Dan?"

His eyes stung with tears, and the aching in his chest was so intense, it was hard to breathe around it. He could say nothing, do nothing to make this better.

His beautiful, vibrant wife was mortal, and she was aging, and he was going to walk the earth until the day the world ended or some demon finally succeeded in killing him. It had never bothered him before, but now, he was certain he would rather die than go on without her. Honestly, he felt like he could die right now, knowing she might never forgive him for this. Not that he expected her to.

What had he been thinking all these years? That if he waited long enough, somehow, his problems would sort themselves out? That wasn't how the world worked. Problems ignored built until they gathered tsunami-like force and crashed onto the shores of carefully laid plans and destroyed them all.

Dan wanted to blame everything on Asmodeus for dragging Eva into this hidden, dangerous world, but he knew the blame fell squarely on his shoulders. A demon fresh from Hell had been more honest with his daughter than Dan had been with his wife of twenty-seven years. And there were no words he could say to make it right, nothing he could do to fix it. He could only sit there and know that he deserved every little bit of misery he was enduring now.

But Jacqui deserved none of it.

"I'm so sorry," was all he could think to say. He wanted to tell her he loved her, but he knew she knew it already. And unfortunately, in this instance, his love wasn't enough.

"I don't know what you want me to tell you," she replied in that tiny, broken voice that flayed him alive. "That I forgive you? That I can accept this, and things can go back to how they were? Because I can't, and I don't know if they can. If they ever will."

"I don't expect you to forgive me," he said, trying not to gasp at the pain in his chest. "And I know things can't go back to how they were. Honestly, I'm just grateful we had what we did for this long. Twenty-seven years isn't much when you've lived as long as I have, but it's damn well better than nothing. I'm not sorry I stayed and raised our daughter with you. I'm only sorry for the pain it's causing you now."

She lifted her head from her arms and stared at him. He stared right back. She was so familiar. The sight of her warm face with those deep, dark eyes felt like coming home. But right now, there were oceans of distance between them. Oceans he might never be able to cross.

"I need time to think," she said softly. "And even then, I'm not sure . . . I don't know if I can ever . . ." She couldn't seem to find the words to finish. He was glad. He didn't need to hear the rest of the sentence to know what she was trying to say.

All of a sudden, he couldn't take it anymore. He stood quickly. "I understand. It's for the best. It was bound to come to this anyway." He walked around the edge of the bed and headed to the door, his eyes stinging.

Hand on the doorknob, he turned back to his wife one last time, drinking in the sight of her beautiful face and knowing that even if he never saw her again, he would love her until the world ended just the same. "If you ever want to talk, I'll have my phone."

She nodded, frowning slightly, and then opened her mouth, probably to ask him where he was going to go.

He didn't give her the chance, because frankly, he wasn't sure himself. Wherever it was, he'd still be keeping an eye on both Eva and Jacqui, whether they knew it or not. Instead, he said, "I love you," and then left, closing the door behind him. He waited in the hallway in case, by some freak stroke of luck, she decided to chase after him, but she never came.

It was better this way, he told himself. Even if she'd chased after him and forgiven him on the spot, it wouldn't solve the problem that she was mortal and he was not, and there was nothing they could do to make their relationship any less impossible.

It was time to go.

He walked down the hallway to Eva's bedroom, pausing outside the door. His senses told him she was in there with Asmodeus, so he took a moment to listen because he really didn't want to interrupt anything.

Dan rubbed his face and stifled a groan. Asmodeus, Prince of Hell, was in his daughter's bedroom. That was going to take some getting used to. But the bloody demon loved her. He really, actually loved her, and Dan couldn't deny it.

Though a large part of him still wanted to impale him on his sword, another part of him accepted that having Asmodeus in Eva's life was actually for the best. Asmodeus and his "brothers" would protect her, and the protection of four demons of their caliber was no small thing.

He heard nothing from Eva's room, so he took a chance and opened the door, peeking inside. Eva and Asmodeus were sleeping. She was curled against him, and his arms and legs were wrapped around her like he was holding onto her with everything he had. His face was buried in her neck the same way Dan did to Jacqui, and he had left his big leathery wings out. The bottom one lay stretched out on the bed behind him, but the top wing curved over their bodies like a protective shield.

Eva was smiling in her sleep.

Damn it. Dan rubbed his eyes again. Nope, not even that romantic little picture made it any easier to see a demon with his arms around his daughter. But she looked happy, and that was all he'd ever wanted for her.

Tiptoeing across the room to her bedside, he bent and kissed her forehead like he'd done when she was a babe. He remembered the first time he'd ever held her. The newborn had stirred awake and then blinked up at him, so tiny in his arms, and he'd gasped at the unusual silver shade of her eyes that marked her as his forbidden daughter. He'd known right then he would never have the courage to leave.

Now, he stroked her forehead and murmured, "Sleep tight, Evangeline. I love you with all my heart."

When he straightened, Asmodeus was awake and watching him, his head lifted slightly off the pillow. Their gazes met.

"You're leaving," Asmodeus said quietly.

Dan nodded.

He expected some kind of smug reaction. The demon had won. He had turned the family against him, wooed the girl, and scored an unlimited supply of Nephilim blood. Why wouldn't he be smug? But instead, his brow furrowed, and a solemn expression crossed his noble features. He appeared almost remorseful.

Asmodeus sat up slowly, taking a moment to adjust the blankets over Eva with tender care. Then he fixed his dark blue eyes on Dan, all that long hair falling all over his bare torso. The guy was good looking, even Dan could admit. But then, of course he was. He was a demon.

"You will visit Eva often," the Prince of Hell declared as if he was still commanding his legions.

"If she wants to see me," Dan said, "I'll be there."

"Visit regardless. She'll come around. And so will Jacqui."

He wished it were so simple. But how nice of the demon to try to comfort him. God, this was weird.

"Take care of her," Dan said, looking at his sleeping daughter's face. "Make her happy or I will hunt you down and decapitate you."

Asmodeus grinned into the dark. "I will."

Maybe Dan had finally lost it, but he actually believed the guy.

"Where will you go?" Asmodeus asked.

"I don't know. Maybe I'll find some more of my kind and take up hunting again." Asmodeus cocked a brow and Dan waved a hand. "I want you four idiots guarding my daughter. As long as you don't start making a scene I'll leave you to your own devices, and I won't tell anyone where you are."

His eyes narrowed, but he nodded. "We won't be in the clear until we find the Hunter."

"That's easy. I left him trapped in a sigil in Eva's living room. I couldn't destroy him without attracting attention to myself, but you can. You're already in enough trouble as it is, and I know you've got the tools to dispatch him permanently."

Asmodeus flashed that wolfish grin again. "You know, you're not so bad, Grigori."

"I don't know whether to be insulted or complimented by your approval."

"Probably both."

A snort escaped Dan before he could remind himself that he was supposed to hate the bastard. "Tell Eva if she wants to talk, I have my phone."

"I will."

"I know I said it before, but tell her . . . Tell her I'm sorry."

"I will."

The Grigori nodded. The demon nodded back.

Damn it, he was feeling a strange kinship with the guy that was too uncomfortable. He shook his head, not ready to get all buddy-buddy with Asmodeus yet.

With one last look at his daughter, one last deep breath of the house he'd raised her in, one last moment of gratitude for the life he'd had that never should have been his to begin with, Dan concentrated his power and teleported away.

28

LOVE HANDLES

A SHAFT OF SUNLIGHT ON HER FACE WOKE EVA, AND SHE blinked, cracking her eyelids to read the display on the clock. Ten o'clock. A little later than she normally cared to sleep in, but then, last night had been pretty full-on. Honestly, it was amazing she'd woken up at all and not just died of shock.

There was a heavy arm slung over her side, a strong thigh shoved between her legs, and a leathery wing draped over her body. That last one was a bit weird, but it was all part of the package of her demon lover, and she wouldn't have changed him for the world.

My funny valentine, she thought with a smile.

With that in mind, she rolled onto her other side so she was facing him. He was still sleeping, his handsome face relaxed into a softness she'd never see otherwise. Thick lashes lay against his cheeks, the kind that would make a girl envious, and that hair . . . It was all over the place. Between their bodies, trapped by his arms, under his head, her head, and spilling all over the pillows. She loved it. It was beautiful. It was *him*.

"What are you smiling at?" he mumbled without opening his eyes.

"How do you know I'm smiling?"

He cracked one eyelid, revealing a stunning indigo iris. "I can just tell."

"I was thinking you look handsome when you sleep."

His other eye opened, lips curving up.

"But you look even better when you're awake and looking at me like that."

He rolled, coming over top of her. He moved slowly, still groggy, but there was nothing sleepy about the erection suddenly nudging between her legs. The little nightie she'd gone to bed in was conveniently bunched around her waist, and she hadn't worn underwear at all.

"I like your wings," she said, and she did. They didn't freak her out at all anymore.

He tensed. "I forgot." He started folding them back like he was going to disappear them, so she quickly reached over his shoulder to stroke the fine boney ridge of one.

"Leave them. I mean it. I like them."

He searched her face as if looking for signs of untruth, and then slowly, he unfolded them again until they were draped over the edges of the bed. She looked at that guarded expression and realized that if they were going to do this, she'd better make it very clear that she accepted him for who he was. Horrible, dark past included. Wings, horns, and red skin included.

And they *were* going to do this. She *did* accept him. She hadn't been kidding when she told him she loved him, and damn it, she was going to make sure he knew it.

She lifted the hand from his wing and placed it on his cheek. "I want to see the horns too."

His brows rose slightly, but he didn't refuse. A moment later, his horns grew out of his skull as if by magic—and she supposed it was—curving down and then swooping up to sharp points. Wow, that was going to take some getting used to.

She had a pretty good idea where to start. Reaching up, she gripped both horns and yanked him down for a kiss. "Love handles," she murmured against his lips.

"Mm?"

"You can grab me by my love handles, and I can grab you by yours."

He pulled back a little though she didn't let go of him. "You don't have horns."

She grinned. "No, love handles are the flesh on a woman's body right here." She released one horn to grab the skin above her hip. Ash's eyes darkened as he surveyed.

"I like this term." He replaced her hand with his own and gripped her tightly, hauling her against him and working his hips against hers nice and slow.

She tipped her head back with a moan, eyes falling shut. God, that felt good.

He continued his ministrations, releasing her hip to slide his fingers through her wetness to stroke her clit until her nerves were singing and she was nearly ready to come already. Just as she hovered on the edge, he slid that hand down and under her thigh, lifting her leg and hooking it over his forearm so she was spread wide for him. He positioned himself at her entrance and then pushed inside, inch by agonizing, glorious inch.

"Condom?" she managed, though it was the hardest thing she'd ever done to focus through the haze of pleasure.

"I can't get you pregnant, Eva."

Her eyes opened. Was it just her or did he look sad? Still, she wasn't in a hurry to bring any babies into the middle of all this. "Are you sure?"

He nodded. "Demons don't reproduce that way. Or at all. We're created from hellfire—long story. But I've been around a long time. I would know if it were possible."

"So you used them before because . . . ?"

"So you wouldn't know I was different."

"Well, now I know, so you don't have to hide, right?"

He nodded, but seemed wary, like he expected her to be mad.

She wasn't. "Babe, you're inside me right now, so can we talk about the logistics of demon babies another time? I'm finding it kinda hard to focus."

Her comment had the desired effect. He smirked and then got right back into the sex, working her with slow, easy thrusts while she gripped his strong shoulders.

She slid her palms down to his biceps and then back up through his silky hair to grab his horns again, which were so incredibly sexy she was going to make sure he had horns every time they made love from now on. He released her leg, so she wrapped them both around his hips and dug her heels into his delicious, tight ass, encouraging his thrusts.

"I love fucking you like this," he murmured, kissing down her neck. "Nice and slow."

"More," she moaned, tipping her head back to give him better access.

"Not yet."

She responded by digging her heels extra hard into his ass.

He responded by biting her lightly on the throat, which only increased her passion. "Open your eyes, Eva. I want you to see who's inside you."

She did as he asked and opened her eyes.

And stiffened in surprise.

He was red. And his eyes were black.

"Ash," she moaned. The sight of him like that had somehow gone from frightening to sexy as fuck, and her blood heated with desire.

Then, as she watched, he grew to his seven-foot-tall size. His shoulders were so broad, they blocked out her view of the room. He grew *everywhere*, in fact, and she gasped at the sudden stretch inside her, the tightness almost unbearable.

"Oh fuck, Ash!" She gripped his biceps desperately, the muscles rigid beneath her fingers.

He stilled his thrusts, giving her a chance to adjust to his new size, but those freaky, all-black eyes narrowed in challenge.

He was daring her to accept him, she realized. Accept all of him. Even his hands had turned to claws, though he was careful where he held her not to scratch her.

As she panted through the intensity, a sense of forbidden desire came over her. She should have been afraid to make love to a monster. He was a big, red beast and the furthest thing from human. She should have been afraid, but she wasn't.

She was really turned on and feeling like a naughty girl.

"Can you take it?" he growled. "Can you take me?"

"Fuck. *Yes.*" She slid her hands up his arms and over his shoulders, and then she buried them in his hair. "Give me everything."

"Your eyes are glowing again." His voice was reverent. "You're so beautiful."

"*Ash* . . ."

Finally, he began to move. He did a slow slide out of her and then pushed back in, finishing with a roll of his hips that made her see stars. His cock was borderline too big in this form, but she was loving the stretch. She moaned at the exquisite fullness, bordering on the edge of pain.

"Who's fucking you right now, Eva?"

"You are."

His hips rolled again. "Who am I?"

"Asmodeus."

And again. "Who am I?"

"My demon. Mine. My big, red demon with his big, red co— *Fuck*, Ash."

His next thrust sent her core clenching up, and it was his turn to moan. "You feel so good. You're squeezing me so tight."

"More, baby. I can take more."

Sharp teeth nipped at her sensitive throat. "Don't want to hurt you."

"I don't care if it hurts. More."

He gave her what she wanted, bracing his hands on either side of her and rising up to thrust deeper. From this position, she caught a full view of the beast taking her, and it was so alien, so forbidden, and yet so *right*, that it sent her flying over the edge.

She came hard, feeling the contractions of her inner muscles rippling around his thick length. Ash moaned, thrusting harder and faster until he was throwing his head back, spine arching as he fell into his own climax.

He collapsed atop her, and she wrapped her arms and legs as tightly as she could around him and held him close, loving the way he groaned softly as he came down from the orgasm's high. Loving the way his broad back expanded and retracted with his heaving breaths. Loving the way his weight crushed her into the mattress. Loving the fact that there were leathery wings draped over them the entire time they made love.

He rolled suddenly, gathering her into his arms as he turned onto his back, his wings folding beneath him. Black claws stroked a stray curl from her face as solid black eyes stared into hers.

"You are so precious," he said. "Like a treasure. *My* treasure."

She smiled. He might still be learning what love was, but he used other words he did understand to say the same thing. In a way, it was almost more meaningful because it was his own unique way of expressing himself.

"I love you too," she told him.

He blinked as if he'd forgotten the meaning of that word again. But then he said, "I love you."

They both tensed, waiting to see if he'd pass out this time. When nothing happened, Eva chuckled and Ash smiled.

"What's your middle name?" he asked.

"Ariel."

"Ariel. That's nice."

"Why?"

His expression became serious. "I love you, Evangeline Ariel Gregory." He smiled again. "How does that sound?"

Heart melting. "It sounds perfect. Music to my ears. What about you? Do you have any fancy names?"

He shrugged a muscled, red shoulder. "Asmodeus, Ashmedai, Asmodai, Asmodaios, Hashmedai, Khashmodai, Hammadai, Shamdon, Shidonai . . . and a few more that I can't remember right now."

Eva's mouth was open. "Oh my god."

"You asked."

"I think I'll stick with Ash."

"Fine by me."

"Well, Ash, Asmodeus, Ashme-doo-da-day, I love you too."

He smiled. "Music to my ears."

After a shower that turned into another sexual marathon, they headed downstairs for breakfast. Meph was back to his usual, grinning self while Raum brooded and cuddled with Thelonious, and Bel busied himself in the kitchen like yesterday had never happened.

The only clue that things were not back to normal was Jacqui.

For Eva's entire life, her parents had always been rock solid. She'd never seen them have a serious fight, and until now, it hadn't occurred to her that they *could* fight. But if there was ever a good reason to, this was surely it.

Though she tried her hardest to smile and participate in the conversations, Eva could tell her mom's heart was broken, and it broke her own heart to see it. Worse, she was leaving back to Montreal today, and her mom would be alone in the big house.

She was so angry at her dad for all the lies.

She was angry at him for being the cause of that emptiness she'd struggled with her whole life. She realized now it was a result of her Nephilim side being bound with powerful magic. If Ash hadn't come along, she probably would have gone to her grave never knowing why she'd always felt like a piece of herself was missing.

And she would have died after a human's lifespan, because the binding Dan had put on her cut her off from her immortality. He'd believed he was giving her a chance at a safe, human life, but the fact that he'd taken such a huge decision out of her hands was a betrayal.

But more than anger on her own behalf, she was angry at Dan for hurting Jacqui.

She couldn't imagine how her mom was feeling, her partner of almost thirty years suddenly revealing that he was not who she'd believed he was. That the life they'd built together was built on a lie.

If the foundation is weak, the structure will fall. Well, it had finally fallen, and Jacqui was left behind in the wreckage.

Eva was so angry at her dad she wanted to scream . . . but he was still her dad. She needed time to come to terms with everything, but she wasn't going to cut him out of her life. Immortal Grigori or not, she knew Dan would be suffering just as much as Jacqui in the coming months.

Her parents had given her so much love and support throughout her life. She wanted to be there for them now—for both of them—in whatever way she could.

"Are you sure you don't want to come back with us?" she asked her mom again. "You could stay with me. I don't have much room, but we could make it work."

Jacqui smiled, but her eyes were sad. "That's sweet, honey, but I'll be fine. I think some alone time will do me good, actually. I'll focus on my work if I get lonely. But I might decide to take you up on that so keep your couch open."

"It's always open to you, Mom."

She pulled Eva into her arms and hugged her tightly. Neither of them let go for a time. When they finally pulled apart, Jacqui gently wiped a tear from Eva's cheek.

"Don't worry about me, dear," she said softly. "I'll be okay."

"Mom . . ."

"I love you, my beautiful daughter. And I'm so proud of you."

"I love you too," Eva said hoarsely, watching as Jacqui brushed tears from her own eyes and smiled warmly.

And then it was time to go. Jacqui fussed over them and made them all promise to come visit soon. She told Belial he could cook in her kitchen whenever he wanted, and she told Meph he could come build stuff in the studio.

They headed out together to the barn, Raum carrying Thelonious, and stepped through the ruined front doors. The walls were blackened, most of the windows blown out, and the overpowering scent of burnt building materials stung the nostrils and made Eva's eyes water.

They crossed the wreckage into Dan's office where she noted the grimoire her mom had told her about was absent. They cleared a bit of floor space, and Belial borrowed chalk from the blackboard and whipped off the complicated gate sigil in record speed.

"There." He tossed the chalk back on the tray and dusted his hands off.

"That's incredible," Jacqui said, surveying the complex design with an awed expression.

He shrugged. "It's just a gate."

"You drew it so fast and so perfectly."

"He's been drawing those things since the dawn of time," Ash said. "I'd hope he'd have mastered it by now."

She chuckled. "Well, I'm still impressed."

"Wait until you see them step into it and disappear," Eva said.

"Time to go, then," Bel said. "Meph! Get your ass in here."

Meph appeared in the doorway, token devilish grin in place. "Ready?"

"I'm going to shove you in to get you back for the last time, asswipe."

Meph dodged Bel's reaching arms and darted around the outside of the circle. To everyone's surprise, he swept up Jacqui into a hug, lifting her effortlessly with those ripped, tattooed arms, and spun her around in a circle.

She laughed and smiled her first real smile since Dan had left, and Eva could have hugged the stupid demon herself for cheering her mom up.

"Bye, Jacks," Meph said, grinning. "Thanks for crying over my lifeless body."

Raum smacked him on the back of the head. "Don't be a dick."

He rubbed his head and glared at his brother. "I was being serious! No one's ever cried over me before."

Jacqui was blushing, but she said, "You're welcome. Try to stay out of trouble."

"Can't make any promises."

"I said *try.*"

Belial grabbed him and threw him into the gate, and he was gone. "Oh my—" Jacqui gasped. "You weren't kidding when you said they just disappeared! Is he okay?"

"He's fine." Then he and Raum and Thelonious said their goodbyes and stepped through the gate.

When it was just Eva and Ash remaining, Eva turned to him with a frown. "Do I have to drink your blood again?"

He shook his head. "It's still in your system from before. And actually, Nephilim can teleport. You just have to learn how."

Her eyes widened. "I can *teleport*?"

He nodded, lips curving. "You'll have to practice though. Maybe your dad can teach you."

"Good idea," Jacqui agreed. "It's important you learn how to protect yourself."

"I intend to," Eva promised. And then, after more heartfelt goodbyes and promises to visit and call, she and Ash held hands and stepped through the gate and found themselves back in Belial's bedroom in their dumpy apartment.

They didn't waste time there, but all loaded up in Eva's car and headed back to her place. She couldn't stop laughing at the sight of the four huge men trying to fit in her tiny car. She took pity on Belial and gave him the front passenger seat—there was no way she was letting any of them drive after seeing Ash behind the wheel—but he was still folded nearly in half and his head pressed into the roof. He scowled the entire drive.

When she parked in her spot behind her building, the demons jerked open the doors and sort of spilled out of the car, stretching and complaining about their aching bodies.

Chuckling, Eva looked up, seeking out her apartment window as she remembered with a sigh that it was smashed out and needed repairing. Except, as she looked, she saw nothing but smooth glass. She searched all the windows, certain she must be mixing up which apartment was hers, but none of them showed any signs of breakage.

"That's weird." She pointed up. "My window should be smashed, but it's not."

"Maybe your dad fixed it when he was here," Ash suggested.

"Maybe."

They headed inside and climbed on the elevator, where Meph proceeded to push the buttons for every single floor, earning another smack on the head from Raum. Finally, they arrived on Eva's floor—the elevator continuing its diligent journey onward—and headed down the hall to stop outside her door.

Abruptly, the mood shifted from casual to tense, that dark look of focus coming into all four demons' eyes that had freaked Eva out before. Now, she was just glad they were on her side.

"You're sure he's here?" Bel whispered.

Ash nodded. "Dan told me he trapped him in a sigil."

Bel sighed. "I don't want to do this. Mishetsu isn't bad."

"We have to. For Eva's safety."

Bel nodded and gestured for Eva to unlock the door, so she did. Ash held her back with a hand and Bel entered the apartment.

"Shit."

That didn't sound good. Heart speeding up, she filed inside behind Meph and Raum and surveyed her home. The smashed window had indeed been fixed, and the carnage from the battle was mysteriously absent. The upended pots were righted, the paintings hanging straight, the instruments put in their places. The only thing that didn't belong was the sigil drawn on the living room floor, this one even more complex than the hellgate.

It was empty.

"Motherfucker," said Meph.

"Where'd he go?"

Bel crossed the room. "The line is broken here." He pointed to the infinitesimal smudge with his shoe. "It's enough for a demon as powerful as him to escape."

Eva wandered into the kitchen. "What the hell?" There were dishes in the drainer that had already been cleaned. Dishes *she* hadn't used. She opened the fridge. There was a pot of food she hadn't cooked in it.

"I think someone's been living here."

As if summoned by her very words, the bedroom door creaked open, and a tall, gray-skinned demon stepped out, rubbing sleep from his yellow eyes and stretching his arms above his head and his wings out to the sides.

He froze when he saw them all staring at him, arms still in the air.

His arms dropped.

"What the fuck?" Meph echoed Eva's thoughts precisely.

The Hunter's black hair was mussed from sleep, hanging in thick strands onto his face and over his chest, a few sticking straight up. His long, whip-like tail waved steadily as if it had a mind of its own.

"You escaped," Bel said, stating the obvious. "Why are you still here?"

Mist looked at Eva and at Ash, and then he looked back at Belial. "I have decided to take a vaca—"

He stopped, head snapping back to Eva. Then he sniffed once, and his eyes widened.

"*Nephilim.*"

HOME IS WHERE
THE HEART IS

A BUNCH OF STUFF HAPPENED REALLY FAST.
Eva cursed, and so did Meph and Raum. Ash growled and lunged at Mist, and so did Belial. And Mist dissolved into, well, mist. They were left frantically searching around the room, until the demon reformed on the other side of the kitchen island.

"I would like to negotiate," he said calmly.

Ash wasn't hearing it; he lunged again. Again, Mist dissolved.

"What kind of negotiation?" Belial asked.

Mist reformed again, this time in front of the newly re-placed windows. They all swiveled around at the sound of his voice. "I have been watching you since the day I found Asmodeus. Actually, I've been watching her." He pointed a claw at Eva.

Ash growled and moved to attack again, but Bel stopped him with a palm on his chest. "Let's hear him out."

Ash glared at his brother. "He knows about Eva. We have to kill him."

"The odds of success are low," Mist said as if they were discussing the weather forecast and not his potential demise. "And if you try and fail, I will have no reason to continue aiding you. I will report to my mistress that you are here and in the company of a Nephilim. Or, we can negotiate and come to an agreement that benefits both parties."

The demon was blackmailing them. And with his fancy mist trick, he was right that he stood a pretty good chance of escaping if they tried to catch him. By the furious look on Ash's face, he'd come to the same conclusion.

"You say you've been aiding us?" Belial asked. "How?"

Yellow eyes blinked on an expressionless face. "I will explain once you agree to negotiate."

Bel looked at Ash, waiting for his agreement. After some more grumbling and growling, Ash finally relented with a sharp nod, moving to stand in front of Eva.

"As I said, I've been watching you."

"How'd you find me so quickly in the first place?" Ash asked.

"I am the Hunter. I hunted you." He spoke like he was mildly offended by the question. "As I explained at our previous encounter, I traced your scent here and simply waited for you to return. As I did, I observed the human, and I became . . . fascinated." He stared at Eva with those creepy eyes. "She is such a simple creature."

Eva glared at him. She was not *simple*, thank you very much.

"And then, when Asmodeus protected her, proving he had formed an attachment, my fascination increased. I gave the matter deep consideration, and finally, I concluded that I would like a human pet of my own."

Everyone stared at him.

"Uh, what?" said Meph, which pretty much summed it up.

"I wish to experience this form of attachment," Mist said, like that was a perfectly reasonable explanation. "So, when I was interrogated by the Watcher, I did not reveal your whereabouts. And after he left and I escaped the sigil, I chose to remain here and await your return to negotiate." He glanced at the window beside him. "I also called a human to repair the glass and keep out the draft."

"Wait." Bel held up a hand and then rubbed his forehead. "I'm still not clear on what you want."

"I would like to form an attachment with a human pet like Asmodeus and Eli— like Asmodeus. I want to know about this experience."

Meph burst out laughing. Even Raum couldn't hold in his chuckles.

"Excuse me," Eva snapped, stepping around Ash. "I am not a *pet*."

Mist cocked his head at her like a freaking insect, and it took all her courage not to retreat right back behind Ash's tall body. "You allow Asmodeus to care for you. He takes you with him when he goes out. He shares sex with you. I want a human for these purposes as well."

"She is not a pet," Ash said. "She chooses to be with me. We're equals."

Mist shrugged. "Whatever you choose to call it, I want to experience the same for myself."

"But Ash is breaking the rules," Bel said slowly. "You've never broken the rules before, Mishetsu."

The Hunter blinked. "I have."

"When?"

He simply stared at Belial, obviously unwilling to divulge that information.

"So that's all you want?" Bel asked when it became obvious he wasn't going to answer. "You're willing to go rogue and risk everything just because you want a girlfriend?"

"Girl . . . friend?"

Bel waved a hand. "Pet, girlfriend, whatever. The term isn't important."

"Oh my god," Eva groaned. "I can't believe I'm hearing this."

"I will not go rogue," Mist said. "I'll simply continue my mission of hunting you without any success and without stumbling upon a Nephilim, while in actuality, I will live here, and you will teach me how to secure my own human girl friend."

"You're going to lie?" Bel seemed to have a hard time wrapping his head around this.

Mist nodded.

"But your track record is infallible. You've never not succeeded. You've never bent a rule. You think they'll buy it?"

"They will buy it because of my infallible record. And eventually, before suspicion can arise, I will tire of my pet and other Earth experiences, and then I can return to hunting. That is my true calling, and my only purpose."

"And then you'll just sell us out?" Ash asked, cocking a brow.

"No. We can formulate a nondisclosure contract." Mist seemed unconcerned. "I will report my first ever failure and say that the great Belial was powerful enough to outsmart me. No one will ever learn that I actually found you within a week of your escape."

Bel grimaced. Silence reigned for a few tense moments.

Surprisingly, it was Raum who spoke first. "He just wants what we do—a chance to live a little without the rules hanging over his head. I don't see why we can't help him out."

"He could have already sold us out if he intended to," Meph pointed out.

"But the minute he gets bored, he could change his mind," Ash said. He glanced briefly at Eva. "There's more to consider than our own safety."

"We'll do a blood contract, then," Raum suggested. "We'll make it so he's incapable of betraying us or Eva even after he returns to his duty."

Ash held up a hand. "This is Eva's decision. She's the one put most at risk by this." He looked at her. "What do you think?"

She had to smile at him. She'd definitely caught the good brother. *Phew.* The rest of them were still figuring out the difference between a pet and a girlfriend, for god's sake.

Then, she looked at Mist. Not long ago, she would have taken one look at him and run screaming from the room. In fact, that was literally what had occurred.

But her eyes had been opened now. Really opened. As in, her eyelids had been peeled off with torture-clamp thingies and held forcibly wide so she couldn't blink no matter how badly she wanted to.

She'd learned that not only were demons real, but not all of them fit the mold. Some were evolving and didn't want to be evil anymore. In her mind, that meant that as a compassionate human, it was her duty to support them in those efforts.

If Mist was serious about living in the human world, then he deserved a chance. He was going to have to work on his perception of humans before she let him near any women, however.

Not to mention, Mist had the upper hand here. At any time, he could mist out the window and disappear and then tell the world what she was. It seemed to her that agreeing to his bargain and binding him in a contract was by far the safest option.

"If we do this," she told the gray-skinned demon, "we're going to have to set some ground rules."

Mist smiled and nodded, flashing two rows of sharklike teeth.

She winced. "First, you're going to need a human form like Ash and his brothers."

His smile disappeared. "I've never had a human form before."

"Well, you're going to have to get one." She looked at Ash. "Can he do that? Make himself a human form?"

"We all have one. He just hasn't used it before."

She turned back to Mist. "Well, let's see it, then."

Mist shifted on his feet. "I don't know how."

"It's easy," Meph said. "Just imagine yourself as a squishy human with stubby hands, and it'll happen."

"I'll try." Mist closed his eyes and focused. Nothing happened.

And then it did.

"It's working!" Eva whispered, caught up in the excitement despite herself.

First, he shrank about a foot, ending up several inches over six feet instead of his former giant size. Then his skin changed from ashy gray to a golden tan, darker than Ash but not as dark as her or Raum.

The swirling patterns that were barely noticeable against his dark gray skin became black tribal-like tattoos on his neck, chest and forearms. The design on his chest was circular and reminded Eva of a sigil, while the ones on his neck and forearms were like thick bands.

His messy hair stayed the same, but his body got broader and more muscular. His claws became hands. The bone structure softened in his face, leaving behind a defined jawline and high cheekbones. He opened his eyes. Beneath dark, expressive brows, the glowing yellow had darkened to a warm amber.

All in all, he was freaking gorgeous.

"Wow." Eva stared in amazement. Not at all what she had expected.

"Not bad," Meph agreed, nodding. "And nice tats."

"They're not tattoos," Bel said. "They're brands."

Something dark flashed in Mist's eyes.

Sensing this was a sensitive subject, she quickly changed it. "You forgot to disappear your tail."

Mist frowned, closing his eyes. His skin became gray once again, but his tail vanished.

"But your skin . . ."

He opened his eyes, looked at himself and growled, and she realized he still had a mouth full of shark teeth. "This is difficult." As he spoke, his eyes filled in with that glowing yellow and the reptile pupils returned.

"Well, Rome wasn't built in a day," Eva said weakly, watching as Mist shook his head and grew in height until he was back to his original form. "You'll just have to practice."

He nodded eagerly, snake eyes aglow. She couldn't help but smile back. What was wrong with her that she kept meeting scary monsters and finding them sweet?

"You are going to have to learn a lot about humans," she said. "We're not pets." She looked at the brothers and amended her words. "Honestly, you *all* need 'How to Human' lessons. Some of the stuff that comes out of your mouths . . ."

They all grinned, unashamed.

She rolled her eyes and turned back to Mist. "And lastly, you need to find somewhere else to live, because you can't stay here."

He stroked his chin with his claws. "I wonder if there are any apartments open in this building. I like it here."

"No," Eva said quickly, "That's not—"

"That's a good idea." Bel's eyes lit up. "We should all move here."

"No, really, I don't think—"

"Ash will be here more often than not, so if we live here too, we'll be close by in case of emergencies."

"Really, I'm sure you don't want—"

"And then we can hang out at Eva's place whenever we want." Raum's golden eyes were twinkling.

"It's safer for Eva if we are close at all times," Ash agreed. Eva groaned. God help her.

A few days later, Ash sat at the grand piano in Eva's living room, trying to find the perfect chord to link two others together. He was so close, yet it wasn't quite right.

It would have helped if he'd actually been focused. Instead, he was mostly watching Eva from across the room. She lay on her back on the sofa, clad only in a slinky little bathrobe, her feet straight up against the wall as she chatted to her friend Skye on the phone. Thelonious sat beside her in a patch of sunlight streaming in through the big windows, and she stroked him while she talked, wiggling her toes absentmindedly.

He smiled. Damn, he really loved her.

And what the hell was she doing with her bare legs up in the air like that? Did she not know how enticing she looked? How was he supposed to focus on anything with all that gorgeous brown skin waving around like a homing beacon, guiding him right between those curvy thighs?

Brown. He blinked, noticing the green plants, the orange sofa, the purple painting on the wall. The scent of coffee in the air.

His curse was lifted again. But how? He hadn't done anything on the piano beyond trying to mash a few chords together. The other times he'd had to play for a while before it lifted. He wondered what had happened differently this time, and then his gaze landed back on Eva, and it dawned on him.

He'd been sitting there thinking that he loved her. And love was pretty much the furthest thing from demonic as one could get. Could it really be that simple? Could he be liberated from his black-and-white, invisible existence forever just by loving her?

Eva glanced over then. Seeing him watching her, she smiled and blew a kiss without interrupting her conversation. A sense of contentment unlike anything he'd ever known filled him, and he realized that yes, it really could be that simple.

Eva said goodbye to her friend a minute later, flipping her feet down and crossing the room. When she reached him, she swung a leg over and sat in his lap, that perfect ass of hers pressed against the piano keys.

"How's Skye?" he asked, gripping her soft thighs and loving the way her flesh overfilled his hands. She smelled so fucking good too. Her flowery soap and the coconut oil she put in her hair mixed with that unique, sweet scent that was just his Eva.

"I couldn't focus on a damn thing she was saying with you looking at me like that," she replied, cocking a brow.

"I couldn't focus on a damn thing either with you waving your bare legs around like that."

Smiling, she draped her arms over his shoulders and kissed him lazily. Like they had all the time in the world together. Because they did.

His phone vibrated in his pocket. Eva leaned back and helped him pull it out, though he didn't know why he bothered because as soon as he saw who it was, he rolled his eyes and tossed it on top of the piano.

"Bel again?" Eva asked.

He nodded. "Fucker's way too excited about moving."

"I would be too if it meant leaving that crappy apartment."

"True." His gaze shifted away. He hadn't checked Bel's text because he already knew what it would say. And he still didn't have an answer for Bel because he'd been putting off the conversation.

"What?" Eva asked immediately, and he should have known better than to think he could hide from her. He didn't want to hide from her anyway.

"I have to ask you something." He forced himself to meet her gaze. "Bel found an apartment in your building that he wants to rent."

"Great."

Ash cocked a brow, and she rolled her eyes.

"I know, I know, it'll be a pain in the ass, and we'll never get any privacy, but it will be nice to have your brothers close, and you're right about the whole safety-in-numbers thing." She frowned at the expression on his face. "So what's the problem?"

"It's a four bedroom."

"Perfect, then."

"Well, not if . . . Since Mist is with them, it's not . . . We might need something bigger if . . ."

"What?"

He looked at her. "Should I tell Bel I need a room in our new place?"

Eva blinked.

Immediately, he backtracked. "I wasn't sure what you wanted, and I wanted to be clear, but there's no problem if you don't want—"

"Why would you need a room? Aren't you living here?"

It was his turn to blink. "Uh . . ."

And then it was Eva's turn to backtrack awkwardly. Wow, they made quite the pair. "I assumed you would be, but that doesn't mean you have to, and I don't want you to—"

"You want me to live here? With you?"

"Um, yeah. I thought that's what we were doing?"

He started to smile.

"Babe, your stuff is already strewn all over my apartment. I even cleared you a drawer. What was I supposed to think?"

"I dunno."

"Do you want to live with me?"

He pretended to have to think. "Hm. Live with the sexy woman sitting on my lap, or live with four obnoxious demons with no sense of boundaries or taste in music. That's tough."

She laughed and smacked his arm. "I'll take that as a yes."

"Take that as a fuck yes. I just wasn't sure you wanted me here all the time."

"Are you kidding? Getting up this morning to find you'd made coffee and were sitting at my piano wearing nothing but a towel?" She sighed dreamily. "I want every day to start that way."

"Your cat hates me," he reminded her.

"He'll get over it."

"Good." He wrapped his arms around her. "Because there's nowhere I'd rather be."

"My demon, the romantic. You're so sweet." She rubbed her nose against his. He tilted his head and turned it into a kiss.

His phone rang, and he growled at it. To his surprise, Eva reached back and snagged it off the piano "Bel? It's Eva. Ash doesn't need a room because he's living with me. And you have my blessing to move into my apartment building, not that you care, I know. But I'm warning you, you'd better never barge in here without calling first because I plan on keeping your brother *very* busy."

Eva hung up the phone and tossed it back onto the piano. "There," she said, leaning in for another kiss. "You're all mine."

"Yours," he agreed, and maybe he should have done some dominance thing where he reminded her that *she* was *his*, but he didn't. He was happy to belong to her.

So what if he'd gone soft. He didn't give a shit.

She leaned back and stroked his cheek with a grin. "My funny valentine."

Dear Reader,

THANK YOU FOR COMING ALONG ON THAT JOURNEY with me! Ash and Eva's story is special because it's inspired by my own experiences as a musician living in Montreal. (If you haven't guessed, I'm a piano player.) The Thursday-night jazz jam at Bootleg is based on a real jam I used to go to, and I loved imagining Eva and Ash onstage late at night. I know I'd stay up for that show.

The next book is the Hunter's story. Unfortunately for Mist, it's not going to be quite so easy as taking a vacation for him to find what he's looking for. He's got a battle ahead for freedom and love, but I promise it'll be worth it.

Most of the demons in the Hell Bent series are (very) loosely based on the "evil spirits" listed in the *Ars Goetia*, part of the *Lesser Key of Solomon*. (Belial, Asmodeus, Raum, Eligos, etc.) There are many interpretations of those old occult texts, and mine is certainly not meant to be anything but an expression of my overactive imagination.

Mephistopheles, however, is from the German legend of Faust, and Naiamah (more commonly spelled "Naamah") originated from Jewish scriptural texts. Mishetsumephtai's tongue twister of a name is entirely of my own invention. Don't ask me what I was thinking when I came up with that because I have no idea.

If you enjoyed this book, please leave a review. I want to know your thoughts, and leaving reviews helps authors out in so many ways. Even just a few words makes a difference, and I thank you for it.

Until we meet again . . .

Much love and happy reading,
Aurora

P.S. Follow me on social media (@aurora.ascher.author) and join my mailing list so you don't miss out on my next release.

If you're curious about Eligos and Natalie, check out the Hell Bent prequel, *My Demon Romance*. It's free and exclusive to my newsletter subscribers.

You can find links to everything on my website:

auroraascher.com

Not ready to leave the underworld yet?

Join Aurora's Underworld Patreon to unlock exclusive art and short stories featuring your favorite characters. You'll get access to illustrations by me (some NSFW!) and cute, funny, and sexy tales to relieve your book hangover.

Join a passionate community of romance lovers, and be part of the adventure!

patreon.com/auroraascher

Playlist for
ΠY FUNNY DEΠON VALENTINE

"Chia"
Bill Laurance

"Waterfall (I Adore You)"
Yebba

"C#-"
Avishai Cohen

"Waltz for J.B." (Live)
Brad Mehldau

"OCEAN"
Moses Yoofee Trio

"Dancing on the Ceiling" (Remastered)
Oscar Peterson

"My Funny Valentine"
Chet Baker

"Chameleon"
Herbie Hancock

https://spoti.fi/3WN6nu8

MY DEMON HUNTER

The hunter shall become the hunted . . .

Enslaved to an evil demon queen for millennia, Mishetsumephtai has only ever served one purpose. He is the Hunter, the one who drags the guilty back to Hell. But tasting freedom on Earth has changed him, and for the first time, Mist questions his duty. The human female, who smiles at him with no idea what a monster he is, draws him in, and he'll do anything to possess her.

. . . and the timid shall become the fierce.

Lily Donovan thought the most dangerous thing about running to the corner store at night would be the aisles of junk food. She didn't bargain on encountering chaos in the form of a man with unusual tattoos and beguiling amber eyes, stalking her through the ice cream section.

Since the death of her parents, Lily has tried to forget what she is. But denial is not an option when she's suddenly confronted with everything she's been running from.

Neither Mist nor Lily can ignore the burning magnetism between them. But Mist's reprieve from Hell was always temporary, and the punishment for disobedience will be worse than death. Yet he can't relinquish the woman whose scent calls to him like nothing he's hunted before.

Turn the page for a sneak peek of Mist's story . . .

Excerpt from
MY DEMON HUNTER

MISHETSUMEPHTAI SELECTED A PIECE OF POPCORN from the bowl with careful claws. Setting the buttery morsel upon his tongue, his head tilted as he chewed. The flavor was bland, the texture crunchy and chewy at the same time. He could tell it held little nutritional value. And yet, something had him reaching for a second piece as soon as he finished the first.

"See?" the human beside him said. "It's good, right?"

Technically, Eva was only half human, but she had only recently discovered that.

"I don't know that I care for it," Mist replied, selecting a third piece.

"And yet you keep eating it."

"I can't seem to stop myself."

Eva chuckled and then winced, shifting atop her pile of couch pillows with a hand over her abdomen. A movie played on the TV that neither of them paid much attention to. "I think that means you like it."

His eyes narrowed as he chewed his fourth piece. "I remain unconvinced."

Eva shifted again with a muffled groan. "These cramps are a bitch."

As far as Mist was concerned, she was clearly a human— angel blood or not, she still suffered from the agonies of the human female race.

"And this movie's terrible, isn't it?"

"It is difficult to grasp the appeal of watching humans that don't exist struggle with problems that aren't real." He watched the on-screen couple regard each other warily from across a crowded room. "I have observed many real humans with real problems. I don't see the need to invent new ones for entertainment."

"Maybe it's so we can dissociate from our own for a while." Eva grabbed a handful of popcorn and consumed it with relish.

"Their issues could be solved in one conversation. Why are they incapable of basic communication?"

She laughed, though it ended with another wince. "You just summarized half the romance genre in two sentences. Though to be fair, this movie is especially bad."

Mist watched her grimace as she held her abdomen. "You appear to be in pain."

She cocked a brow. "Ya think?"

"Where is your electrical blanket? Have you taken a numbing pill?"

She burst out laughing. "You crack me up, Mist."

He frowned.

"I have my blanket here, but I'm sweating already in this heat, and I don't want to be any hotter. And I already took a painkiller. But . . . there is something I want."

"What?"

She closed her eyes, and a wistful smile overtook her face. "Ice cream."

"Ice cream?"

"Chocolate ice cream. With chunks of chocolate. And swirls of chocolate. And sprinkles of chocolate."

"That sounds like a lot of chocolate."

"The more the merrier."

"Perhaps you can arrange for Asmodeus to procure this for you."

"It's Thursday night, remember? He's at Bootleg, and there's no way I'm calling him back." The jazz club Eva worked at had a weekly jam she and Asmodeus often attended. "I'm still amazed he went without me. I'm so proud of him for coming out of his shell."

Mist tilted his head as he considered this. "Asmodeus is lucky to have you."

"He is, isn't he? I'm quite a catch."

"Catch? But you told me you were with him willingly. How can that be if he had to catch you?"

"No, that's not—" She dragged a hand down her face. "It's a figure of speech. Nobody caught anybody. That's not how real relationships work. Everything is mutual and consensual."

He supposed he did recognize the expression—demons could intuitively speak all languages and adopt current speech patterns to better blend on Earth—but he was inexperienced at human interaction. For all his many millennia of hunting, he had never conversed with humans until now and had much to learn.

A month and a half had passed since the commencement of his temporary vacation and, thanks to Eva's instruction, he'd since discovered humans were not as simple as he'd always believed. For example, if he wanted a human friend—they were called "friends," not pets—it wasn't as easy as picking one out from a crowd, though he still thought it ought to be. He was a powerful, immortal being. Humans were small and weak, with short lifespans.

But Eva had told him he had to see them as equals and learn to appreciate the nuances of their differing personalities. He had to learn to tell them apart.

"I have an idea," she said, smiling mischievously. "You go."

"Go where?"

"To the dep. For ice cream."

"What is a dep?"

"Depanneur. Corner store, Quebec style. Ice cream supplier extraordinaire."

He sat upright. "You want me to go to the store?"

She nodded.

"But—" He looked down at himself.

His skin was ash gray, his fingers tipped with claws, every tooth in his mouth a razor-sharp point. His leathery wings draped off the end of the couch, and his tail curled in his lap, long and smooth like a coiled whip.

He looked nothing like a human, and, as a result, he would be invisible to them, thanks to the glamor that disguised the supernatural world from unsuspecting mortals.

Until he'd met Eva, he had never taken human form in all his long existence. He hadn't needed or wanted to. His job was much better suited to a stealthy, invisible demon than a soft human with fleshy fingertips.

But something had shifted in him since the day he'd broken the rules for the first time, and try as he might, he couldn't put it back. He was curious and restless and in search of something, though he didn't know what. He just hoped he found it before he inevitably had to return to Hell.

"There's a dep at the end of the block," Eva said. "All you have to do is go there and get the chocolatiest ice cream you can find. The only person you have to talk to is the cashier."

Mist twisted his claws together. "I would have to hold human form for the duration."

"You've been practicing and you're getting good. You're

ready for this." When he still hesitated, she added with a smirk, "I think you're scared."

His spine stiffened. "I am the Hunter. I am not scared."

"Tell that to yourself. I know you can hold on to your human form now, yet you always choose to stay behind when we go out. I thought you wanted to interact with humans."

"I do," he grumbled.

"Then challenge yourself. Go get me ice cream. Plus, hello, I have my period right now, and it's your duty as a male to bring me anything I want."

She was right, he realized. He was ready. He could do this.

He rose from the sofa and stretched his wings, stiff from sitting on them for so long. "I require a shirt." He rarely wore them. For a winged demon, they were inconvenient, to say the least.

"You can borrow one of Ash's if you don't want to go upstairs."

He was currently staying with Asmodeus's brothers in an apartment on the floor above. He slept on a mattress instead of a cold stone floor, and in the morning, sunlight entered through his very own window. Belial often prepared him human food dishes to sample, and if he chose, he could do nothing but relax for an entire day. He had never experienced such things before, but he reminded himself constantly not to become complacent.

All of this was only a temporary reprieve.

Five minutes later, he was in human form, wingless and wearing a borrowed black T-shirt, and he and Eva had rehearsed his future transaction. She'd explained several times why he had to *pay* for the ice cream instead of just taking it, and he was beginning to understand. If nothing else, he would abstain from thievery to avoid attracting attention.

"You look great," Eva said, smiling from her pillow pile. "You make a very handsome human."

Though considerably shorter than his full demonic height,

he was still taller than most humans, standing several inches over six feet. His skin was bronze, and the brands hidden on his gray skin now looked like bold tattoos.

It was the thing he disliked most about this form. As a demon, it was easy to pretend the markings weren't there. As a human, he had no choice but to be reminded of their existence every time he caught his reflection.

"Take one of my reusable bags from the basket by the door," Eva said as he readied to depart. "And my keys so I don't have to buzz you in. You can't do your mist trick to get in since you're supposed to be practicing being human, and that's cheating."

Agreeing to play mortal, Mist rode the lift down and stepped onto the sidewalk. There he paused, taking a deep inhalation of the humid summer air and double-checking that he still held on to his human form.

He ran his tongue over his teeth. *Still flat.* He checked the skin of his arm. *Still light brown.*

The darkness was illuminated by overhead lamps and light from the storefronts. Across the street, people were spilling out of a restaurant and lounging on the terrasse of a pub. Somewhere down the block, the sound of live music wafted on the hot breeze.

Someone walked past Mist, and their eyes traveled over him. They saw him. They were looking right at him and seeing nothing but a regular man. He headed down the street in the direction Eva had told him to go, confidence building with every step.

At the end of the block, right where she'd said it would be, there was a small convenience store with faded cardboard adverts in the windows for beer and ice cream. Steel bars intersected over the panes of glass, and an array of cigarette butts littered the ground outside. Overhead, a neon sign read "Dépanneur Au Coin," though the lower half of all the letters had burnt out.

It was beautiful. A shining example of current human consciousness. Paradise, compared to anything in Hell.

Taking a breath, he entered the store, all his hunter instincts fixed on locating the ice cream freezer.

Lily Donovan stared at the row of dreadful, delicious chocolate bars and questioned her life choices.

How the hell had she come to be standing in a dep at ten thirty on a Thursday night, debating which sugary monstrosity to consume alone in her apartment?

Well, she wasn't quite alone. She was babysitting her sister's grumpy cat, and she had his charming company to look forward to. *Grand. Just grand.*

After finishing university last year, Lily had searched high and low for a job in her field of environmental engineering, but it seemed like there wasn't anyone in this city who gave a damn about designing things that were environmentally friendly. Or maybe she was just terrible at job interviews.

Whatever the case, a year later, she was still making all her income selling her clothing designs online, and she was beginning to wonder why she'd bothered torturing herself with four years of university and student debt in the first place.

Stop complaining. She usually tried never to fall into the mire of self-pity, but on nights like tonight, it was hard not to. She had friends, but she'd refused all offers of socializing in favor of staying home with Grimalkin and her sewing machine.

She'd accidentally-on-purpose missed her yoga class today, only to end up at this dep perusing the chocolate bar selection.

Her sister said she was "curvy" or "thick." Lily didn't give a damn what she called it. At the end of the day, she still had to sew all her own clothes because the ones she liked in stores never came in her size. The girls in her favorite novels and movies never looked like her, and any product designed for a woman of her build was for the purpose of weight loss.

Annoyed with her spiraling thoughts, she snatched a chocolate bar off the shelf, going for the only fair-trade option this depanneur sold. She may have been sabotaging her dieting efforts, but that didn't mean she couldn't make ethical purchases whenever possible.

She grabbed two for good measure.

And then decided to get a bottle of wine while she was at it.

Heading down the aisle to the alcohol section, Lily stopped in her tracks when she saw a man at the end staring determinedly at the Ben & Jerry's freezer.

He was tall. Very tall. Taller than tall people, and she definitely wasn't one of those. And he was broad, his muscular back and shoulders stretching his black T-shirt in all the right places.

As she watched, he dragged a hand through his mop of messy black hair, the ends brushing his shoulders.

In another life, she might have been attracted to a man like that, but in this one, she was just intimidated. It was a healthy response for a woman of her size, especially one who hated exercise and had no badass self-defense skills.

Unfortunately, the wine selection was right beside him.

It was either brave proximity to the muscled giant or forgo the wine. And, okay, she was a bit of a chickenshit, but she wasn't *that* bad.

Or maybe she just really wanted wine.

Taking a deep breath, she headed down the aisle, stopping beside him. She tried to study the selection but couldn't focus on anything except the looming presence beside her. All she felt was this burning intensity that made her heart pound and her palms sweat.

Deep inside, long-buried instincts suddenly flared to life for the first time in years, warning her that she was in the presence of something dangerous. All the labels and prices blurred together into a stew of brewing panic.

Screw it, it's all wine in the end. Snatching up a random bottle, she was seconds away from escaping when the stranger spoke.

"Excuse me."

Oh, god. He wasn't talking to her, was he? No, he was probably on the phone. She hadn't seen a phone in his hand, though. Oh wait, he probably had a Bluetooth earpiece, and she just couldn't see it. She grabbed her bottle, turned—

And stopped dead.

He was looking right at her, and he'd definitely been speaking to her.

This time, she felt a glimmer of attraction shine through all the wariness. His eyes were beautiful. A warm amber, like glittering gemstones, and so bright they were mesmerizing.

His face was masculine yet elegant, his clean-shaven jaw square while his mouth was soft. His tanned skin and deep black hair made her think of deserts baking in the sun in a faraway land. Somewhat more intimidating was the thick, black tribal tattoo encircling his neck like a collar.

She just stared at him, though she knew it was embarrassing as hell.

"Excuse me," he said again.

"Y-yes?"

This was the city. People didn't make small talk with strangers in the city, and they certainly didn't converse in depanneurs.

There was an unwritten rule that deps were safe zones. No matter what weird stuff you were in the middle of doing, nobody would bother you as long as you didn't break any laws. You kept your eyes down, paid for your stuff, and got out of there unscathed.

Lily had been counting on that. She never would've braved

a trip here if she'd imagined she would be forced to converse with strange, gorgeous men.

"You are female," he stated.

Her eyes widened. Okay, that was weird. And creepy. How did she extract herself from this?

At least he hadn't spoken French. Montreal was a bilingual city, but she still hadn't learned the language in the nine years she'd lived here. She'd been too busy trying to hide her Irish accent, and her broken, disjointed French made her feel self-conscious, so she never practiced.

"Um . . ." Was he going to proposition her? Try to assault her? Oh god, why didn't she carry pepper spray? If she survived this, she would buy some first thing tomorrow. And why hadn't she spent her entire life in rigorous martial arts training? In fact, why had she thought it was a good idea to leave her house at all? She should have known better. She should have—

"Which of these flavors has more chocolate?"

He held out two cartons of Ben & Jerry's.

She stared at them, confusion overriding every other thought in her brain. "W-what?"

"I'm purchasing ice cream for a menstruating female. She demanded chocolate. But these both have the word 'chocolate' in the title, and I don't know which she would prefer."

Her eyes wandered from the ice cream back up to his striking face, which she stared at with amazement. He was completely sincere. This utterly gorgeous, tall, muscular man with neck tattoos was buying ice cream for his "menstruating" girlfriend.

Forget being afraid, she was in love.

Where can I get myself a man like that?

"Buy them both," she said. "That way she can choose one now and have more for later."

His eyes widened. "That's good advice."

She found herself smiling, her earlier fear dissipating. "Well, I'm an expert in all things chocolate."

"You enjoy it too?"

She nodded and held up her chocolate bars with a sheepish smile.

"You should buy ice cream as well."

"Oh, no, I can't. That stuff goes straight to my hips, which are big enough already, thank you."

His gaze slid down her body. "You're very small. I don't see a problem."

She wanted to melt into a puddle and ooze through the cracks in the faded linoleum. "Small in height, sure, but not in width."

He blinked, gaze returning to her face. "I don't see a problem."

She stared at his puzzled look. Did he genuinely not understand why she cared about her size?

Her gaze flicked to a faded advertisement on the wall beside them of a thin, blond model licking an ice cream cone suggestively. There were images everywhere of what the ideal female body ought to look like, even here in this crummy old dep. How could he have failed to notice any of that?

He turned from her then, opening the freezer and grabbing another carton of ice cream. She expected him to try to give it to her, but he didn't. *Guess he wants to be certain he got the right one for his girlfriend.*

Whoever this girl was, Lily hoped she appreciated what she had, because *damn.* A man who looked like that, buying a girl ice cream on her period? It sounded like something out of a romance novel. She'd bet her right boob that girlfriend was stick-thin runway material.

There was an awkward moment of shuffling as they determined who would walk down the aisle first to reach the cash register. Or maybe it was just awkward for her. Mr. Tall, Dark, and Handsome just watched her with those hypnotic eyes as he stood back and waited for her to go first.

Cheeks still flaming, she did, wishing she'd put on a longer shirt before she left the house. The tank top she wore didn't cover her butt, and she was wearing yoga tights. Yoga tights made for chicks who shouldn't wear yoga tights. God help her if he looked at her ass.

She paid for her Single Girl's Night Alone supplies—all that was missing was batteries for her vibrator—cast a farewell smile to the hot stranger, and stepped back outside. The air was humid, the temperature barely any lower than during the day. Another summer heatwave.

She made it only a few steps before she heard, "Wait!" from behind her. Glancing back, she saw the mystery man standing outside, a reusable cloth bag in one hand.

He had gone to the dep prepared with his own shopping bag. Who was this guy?

Maybe it was foolish, but she stood and waited while his long strides ate up the distance between them. "Is it safe for you to walk alone?"

She stared at him. "Um, yeah, I do it all the time. Montreal's a pretty safe city."

He frowned, tilting his head in a way that she had never seen a person do before. A reptile, maybe. But not a person. "I would like to escort you for protection."

She hesitated. Hot or not, there was no way she was letting some rando walk her home and find out where she lived.

His eyes widened suddenly. "But you should refuse because it's not wise to allow a stranger to discover your lair."

Her *lair*? She almost burst out laughing. Wow, he spoke strangely, especially because he had no trace of an accent.

"Um . . ." She didn't want to offend him, but he was bang on the money.

"You're very wise," he said, and this time she did laugh.

"I hope your girlfriend likes the ice cream."

"She is a friend that is a girl, a girl friend, but not a girl-friend." His face scrunched up. "I find this term confusing."

Another startled laugh escaped her. He really did say the weirdest stuff.

"That's really nice of you to take care of your friend," she said with a smile, utterly charmed by this strange, strange man. "Have a nice night."

"This is for you." He dug into the shopping bag and held out a carton of Ben & Jerry's.

Her heart melted faster than the ice cream in this heat. He *had* picked the extra one up for her.

"It's good to have things you enjoy. Human lives are short. It's better to leave your mark on the world by being full of contentment than full of longing."

Lily stared at him, tilting her head back to look into those beautiful, guileless eyes. Slowly, she stretched out a hand and accepted the ice cream. The flavor was "Chocolate Therapy."

"Thank you," she said softly.

"I'm glad we met this evening."

Her gaze shot back up to his. He nodded once and the turned to go.

He made it halfway down the street before she called out "Wait!"

He turned back, brows lifting in question.

"Maybe . . . I would like you to walk me home after all."

Look for MY DEMON HUNTER coming soon from Kensington Books!

About the Author

© Sergio Veranes

Aurora Ascher is a *New York Times* and *USA Today* best-selling fantasy and paranormal romance author. She loves misunderstood monsters, redeemable anti-heroes, and epic happily-ever-afters. A woman of many creative pursuits, Aurora is also a musician and visual artist. She is currently based between Montreal and British Columbia, Canada. Visit her online at auroraascher.com.